DR CHANDLER'S
SLEEPING BEAUTY

BY
MELANIE MILBURNE

HER
CHRISTMAS EVE
DIAMOND

BY
SCARLET WILSON

To Nancy
Hope you enjoy!
Love Scarlet
x

MILLS &
BOON

From as soon as **Melanie Milburne** could pick up a pen she knew she wanted to write. It was when she picked up her first Mills and Boon® at seventeen that she realised she wanted to write romance. After being distracted for a few years by meeting and marrying her own handsome hero, surgeon husband Steve, and having two boys, plus completing a Masters of Education and becoming a nationally ranked athlcte (masters swimming), she decided to write. Five submissions later she sold her first book, and is now a multi-published, award-winning, *USA TODAY* bestselling author. In 2008 she won the Australian Readers Association most popular category/series romance, and in 2011 she won the prestigious Romance Writers of Australia R*BY award.

Melanie loves to hear from her readers via her website, www.melaniemilburne.com.au, or on Facebook: http://www.facebook.com/pages/Melanie-Milburne/351594482609

Scarlet Wilson wrote her first story aged eight and has never stopped. Her family have fond memories of 'Shirley and the Magic Purse', with its army of mice all with names beginning with the letter 'M'. An avid reader, Scarlet started with every Enid Blyton book, moved on to the Chalet School series, and many years later found Mills and Boon®.

She trained and worked as a nurse and health visitor, and currently works in public health. For her, finding Medical Romances™ was a match made in heaven. She is delighted to find herself among the authors she has read for many years.

Scarlet lives on the West Coast of Scotland, with her fiancé and their two sons.

DR CHANDLER'S SLEEPING BEAUTY

BY
MELANIE MILBURNE

To Andrea Debomford, who gave me the inspiration
for the way Jake and Kitty first meet.
Thanks for your friendship. Love you. xxx

First published in Great Britain 2012
by Mills & Boon, an imprint of Harlequin (UK) Limited.
Harlequin (UK) Limited, Eton House, 18-24 Paradise Road,
Richmond, Surrey TW9 1SR

© Melanie Milburne 2012

ISBN: 978 0 263 89207 9

Harlequin (UK) policy is to use papers that are natural, renewable and recyclable products and made from wood grown in sustainable forests. The logging and manufacturing process conform to the legal environmental regulations of the country of origin.

Printed and bound in Spain
by Blackprint CPI, Barcelona

Dear Reader

While I was writing my last Medical, THE SURGEON SHE NEVER FORGOT, I had a scene where an Accident and Emergency doctor came in to talk to my hero Lewis Beck about his ill father. I found my next medical hero Jake Chandler right then and there. I just love it when characters come to me and beg me to write their story!

Jake was tall and incredibly good-looking, with dark blue eyes. I knew immediately that he was a bit of a playboy. I even knew why he was so against settling down. His backstory was like a download in my head.

All I needed now was a suitable heroine to rock Jake's world. And in no time at all newly qualified A&E doctor Kitty Cargill came along. Again it was like a download. I knew immediately Kitty would be a classic fish out of water. I also knew she would be an old-fashioned English girl from an unconventional background.

A sweetheart home girl with a broken heart meets a commitment-phobe, notoriously sexy playboy. What a perfect mix for a pulse-racing romance!

I love writing the scene where my characters meet for the first time. I have so much fun thinking of ways they can take an instant dislike to each other, or get the wrong impression, or strike passionate sparks from the first moment their eyes meet. Jake and Kitty certainly didn't let me down. Kitty makes a first impression on Jake that is nothing like the impression she hoped to make on her devilishly handsome boss!

I hope you enjoy reading about how Jake and Kitty met and fell in love, and that you laugh and cry with them along the way. I certainly did!

Warmest wishes

Melanie Milburne

Recent titles by Melanie Milburne:

SYDNEY HARBOUR HOSPITAL: LEXI'S SECRET*
THE SURGEON SHE NEVER FORGOT
THE MAN WITH THE LOCKED AWAY HEART

*Sydney Harbour Hospital

**These books are also available in eBook format
from www.millsandboon.co.uk**

CHAPTER ONE

'I CAN'T believe you talked me into wearing this,' Kitty Cargill said to her cousin as they entered the city hotel where Julie's 'Pimps and Prostitutes' fancy dress thirtieth birthday party was being held. 'I'm sure it's because I'm still suffering from jet lag and I'm not in my right mind.'

'You look awesome,' Julie said. 'I never knew you had such great legs. That PVC skirt really shows some serious thigh.'

Kitty pulled the skirt—which in her opinion was too skimpy even to qualify for the term—down over the ladder in the black fishnet tights that her cousin had insisted was an essential part of the get-up. 'Now I can see where my mother got her wacky out-there genes,' she said, cringing in embarrassment at some of the looks she was attracting as they made their way to the function room.

'Lighten up, hon,' Julie said. 'You're not going to last long in Aussieland unless you strap on a sense of humour. You're way too conservative. You Brits all act like you've been potty-trained at gunpoint.'

'Ha, ha, ha,' Kitty said. 'I'll have you know I wasn't potty-trained at all. My parents thought it was far more progressive and fundamental to my development that I sorted it all out for myself when I was good and ready.'

Julie grinned at her. 'So should I be worried about you going where you shouldn't while you're bunking down with me?'

Kitty gave her a look. 'Don't worry,' she said. 'I won't be with you much longer. I've already found a town house to rent online. The real estate agent confirmed it this afternoon. It's not far from the hospital and even closer to the beach at Bondi.'

'It sounds perfect,' Julie said. 'Have you met anyone from St Benedict's yet? Your boss in A&E or the CEO?'

'Not yet,' Kitty said. 'I'm going to introduce myself in the next day or so. I'm not due to start until next week, but I thought it'd be polite to put in an appearance—given I didn't go through the normal face-to-face interview process.'

'I still can't quite get my head around you being a fully-fledged doctor,' Julie said, giving her a playful shoulder-bump. 'Last time I saw you, when Mum and I came to London for Christmas, you were playing with dolls.'

Life was certainly a whole lot simpler then, Kitty thought wistfully as she followed her cousin into the party room, which was thumping with deafening music.

Jake Chandler was on night shift for the fourth night in a row and feeling it. Friday and Saturday nights were not his favourite times to be on duty. Far too many party-goers with too much alcohol on board and too little common sense clogged public A&E departments like his all over the country. In their noisy midst were the seriously sick and injured.

So far tonight he'd had to deal with the death of a sixteen-year-old girl in a motorcycle accident and a serious stabbing. The girl had been riding pillion on the back of her boyfriend's bike. It had been her first time on a motorbike and her second date with the boyfriend. She had been the only child of a single mother. Jake could still see the collapse of the girl's mother's face when he had told her.

The stabbing had been a drug deal turned sour. The guy had almost bled out before Jake could stem the bleeding. The guy was twenty-four years old—the same age as Jake's younger brother, Robbie. Would this be how *his* kid brother ended up? Found in some sleazy back alley, mortally wounded, stoned and senseless? How could he stop it? What more could he do? Robbie's refusal to grow up and take responsibility for himself made Jake feel he had failed.

He had let his family down.

He had let his mother down.

Jake glanced at the clock on the wall on his way back from escorting the stabbing victim to Theatre.

Five minutes to midnight.

It was about time for the drunk and disorderly to come spilling in. He just hoped Robbie wasn't one of them.

'Dr Chandler?' Jake's registrar Lei Chung approached him while he was washing his hands at one of the sterilising basins. 'I have a couple of tipsy call girls in Bay Five. One of them has a suspected broken ankle.'

Jake mentally rolled his eyes as he tugged some paper towels out to dry his hands. 'They *told* you they were call girls?' he asked.

'They didn't have to,' Lei said, rolling his eyes. 'Just wait until you see them.'

'They're entitled to the same level of care as anyone else,' Jake said, tossing the screwed-up paper in the bin before reaching for a new pair of gloves. 'Have you ordered an X-ray?'

'The radiographer will be down in ten minutes,' Lei said. 'He's seeing a patient on the orthopaedic ward. One of his hip patients had a fall.'

Jake twitched the curtain aside of Bay Five. 'Hello,' he said. 'I'm Dr Chandler.'

The girl sitting beside the one lying on the trolley shot to her feet. 'I'm so terribly sorry about this,' she said, speaking in a cut-glass London accent that didn't fool Jake for a moment. 'I don't think it's broken. I'm sure it's just a sprain. But my cousin is in so much pain I thought we should have it X-rayed. I thought it best if—'

Jake quirked one brow upwards. 'Your...cousin?'

'Her name is Julie Banning, and I'm—'

'Hello, Julie,' Jake said, turning to the girl on the trolley. 'Can you tell me what happened?'

'I was dancing with this guy and his legs got twisted with mine,' Julie said, with an Australian accent even broader than his. 'I hit the floor and twisted my ankle. I heard something snap—I swear to God I did. It hurts like freaking hell.'

'Let's have a look, shall we?' Jake said.

He examined the ankle, but found only swelling and tenderness over the lateral ligaments and no obvious fracture. He checked the patient for any other injuries, but apart from a bruise on her elbow she was all clear—which was lucky considering how much alcohol he could smell on her and her posh-sounding little sidekick.

'I'll order an X-ray just to be on the safe side,' he said. 'An orderly will be with you shortly. And go easy on the partying, OK? You could've really done some serious damage. You might not be so lucky next time.' He gave the other young woman a cursory nod and left the cubicle.

'Dr Chandler?' The young woman spoke from behind him just as he got to his office.

Jake turned to look at her. 'Yes?'

She shifted her weight from foot to foot, looking distinctly uncomfortable. He didn't know working girls *could* blush. Maybe she was new to the game. She didn't look very old. Her skin was porcelain-smooth and her eyes—in spite of the heavy eyeshadow—were clear and bright and a rather stunning shade of grey. Perhaps she was worried he was going to ask for a drug screen on her 'cousin', or a blood alcohol level.

'I wanted to say thank you for seeing my cousin so promptly,' she said. 'I was worried it might take hours and hours. She seemed in a lot of pain and I—'

'Do you realise the dangers of binge drinking?' Jake asked, frowning at her reproachfully.

Her eyes flickered. 'Pardon?'

He stripped her with his gaze. 'You smell like a brewery, the both of you.'

Her cheeks flushed bright red. 'I'm not drunk!'

He rolled his eyes in disdain. 'Yeah, that's what they all say.'

'But I'm not!' she said. 'Julie spilt her drink on the floor when she fell. I knelt down to help her and got soaked in it. I've only had half a glass of champagne the whole night.'

'How much has your cousin had to drink?' he asked.

'A bit…' She bit her bottom lip. 'A lot…quite a lot… loads, actually. It's her thirtieth birthday. I told her to slow down but she wouldn't listen.' She made a self-deprecating movement of her mouth. 'She thinks I'm too conservative.'

Jake flicked his gaze over her sinfully short PVC skirt and the black bustier top that showcased a rack that was small but no less impressive. 'I can see what she means,' he said dryly.

Her big grey eyes with their raccoon-like eyeshadow widened in affront and her small neat chin came up. 'Dr Chandler, perhaps I should take this opportunity to properly introduce myself,' she said. 'My name is Kitty Car—'

'Kitty as in Kitty Litter?' Jake put in, without holding back on his mocking smile.

Her generously plumped mouth flattened. 'No,' she said, those storm cloud eyes flashing at him resentfully. 'Kitty as in Katherine. Katherine Cargill. *Dr* Katherine Cargill, to be precise.'

Jake rocked back on his heels. So *this* was the new three-month appointment who had been recruited while he'd been away on leave. He'd been wrong about the accent. Funny, but he'd thought it way too posh to be for real. Maybe it was time to have a little fun. Let her get to know the colonial natives, so to speak. God knew he could do with a bit of a laugh after the night he'd had.

'Have things got so bad in the public health system that junior doctors have to moonlight in other less salubrious professions?' he asked.

She glared at him. 'This is not what it looks like,' she said, waving a stiff hand to encompass her attire. 'It's a *costume*.'

Jake leisurely ran his gaze over every inch of her outfit, right down her long shapely legs encased in sexy fishnets to the scarily high heels on her dainty feet. 'It's very convincing,' he said.

She frowned at him. 'Haven't you been to a fancy dress party before?'

'Yeah,' he drawled. 'I went as the Big Bad Wolf. I huffed and I puffed and brought the whole house down.'

She gave him a haughty look down the length of her nose that was right out the pages of a Jane Austen novel. 'At least you wouldn't have had to go to the trouble and expense of hiring a costume,' she said. 'You would have gone just as you are.'

Jake held her feisty little eye-lock. He felt a stirring in his groin that had nothing to do with her skimpy outfit. There was something about her imperious air and her toffee-nosed accent that made his flesh tingle from head to foot.

Was it his self-imposed dating drought that had stirred his senses so intensely? He'd made a bet with his sister at Christmas that he could give up sex for the rest of the summer. Rosie had criticised his playboy lifestyle, even going as far as saying it was setting a bad example for her young son, Nathan. If he lost the bet he would have to pay Rosie a thousand dollars towards Nathan's education fund. He had no problem with donating the money for Nathan. He would give that and more, bet or no bet. But he *did* have a problem with his kid sister thinking he had no self-control and discipline. So he'd set a new record for himself—a new personal best. He didn't like admitting it, but abstinence had been good for him. His sex life *had* become a bit boring and predictable over the last year. But he didn't want anything long-term. He was happy with his fancy-free approach to relationships. It had just been a bad year, that was all.

Besides, he *liked* his flings short and uncomplicated.

No strings.

No rings.

No promises.

Once his period of celibacy was up, Kitty Cargill, with her I'm-just-pretending-to-be-a-wild-child routine, could be just the one to kick things off for the rest of this year.

'You can take your cousin home as soon as she's had her X-ray,' Jake said. 'And I hope when I next see you in this unit you're wearing something a little more appropriate. We're supposed to be saving patients' lives here, not giving them myocardial infarcts. Understood?'

She gave him a glittering glare. 'Perfectly, Dr Chandler.'

'Grrrgghhh!' Kitty was still fuming as she unpacked her things at her new town house three days later. She cringed in embarrassment when she thought of turning up for work the following Monday. How on earth was she going to face him?

Julie, damn her, was *still* laughing about it, in spite of hobbling about on crutches and having to take time off from her job as a beautician. Her cousin thought the sprained ankle was worth it to have seen someone as prim and proper as Kitty floundering so far out of her depth.

'God, he was *so* gorgeous,' Julie had said only that

morning when Kitty had rung to check on her. 'Did you see how dark his blue eyes were? And so tall! He must have been six foot three or four, don't you think?'

'I'm trying *not* to think about him,' Kitty said. 'That was singularly the most excruciatingly embarrassing evening of my entire life.' *Well, apart from finding my best friend, Sophie, in bed with my long-term boyfriend the very weekend I thought he was going to propose to me.* 'I wonder if it's too late to ask for a transfer to another hospital...' She bit down on her lip, daunted at the thought of finding a new placement at such short notice.

'He had great hands,' Julie rabbited on. 'So strong and capable and masculine. I wonder if he's married. I don't think he was wearing a ring. But he was wearing gloves, so who knows? Maybe a little fling with your new boss will be just the trick to get that two-timing jerk Charles Wetherby out of your system once and for all.'

'Will you stop it, for pity's sake?' Kitty said. 'I don't want to talk about Dr Chandler.' *Or Charles*, she added silently, with a tight cramping pain over her heart.

But even so her mind kept rerunning the whole debacle like a DVD-player jammed on replay. Jake Chandler had accused her of being drunk and yet she was more or less a teetotaller. He'd thought she was a prostitute, and yet she was twenty-six years old and had only had one lover—her childhood sweetheart, who had turned out not to be such a sweetheart after all.

This three-month trip Down Under was part of her coping strategy.

Kitty had always considered herself a gracious and forgiving type, but staying in London while Charles got married to Sophie Hamilton was stretching the bounds of her grace and forgiveness a little too far.

Kitty had grown up with Charles. He had lived in the same village, on the same street, in a house only four doors down from hers. She had gone through infants, primary school, high school and medical school with him. They had done their residency and internship at the same hospitals. They had practically been joined at the hip. Everyone had described them as the perfect couple. They'd never argued. They'd been best friends. They'd enjoyed the same things. They'd had the same friends. They had wanted the same things—or so Kitty had thought.

For months she had been expecting a romantic proposal. She had even secretly chosen a ring to match the promise ring Charles had given her on her sixteenth birthday. She had walked into bridal shops and dreamily tried on gorgeous gowns and voluminous veils. She had bought dozens of bridal magazines, making copious notes as she flicked through them. She had even—she cringed in embarrassment even now—gone to several wedding venues to check on prices and availability.

Now Charles was gone and she was on her own.

No perfect white wedding.

No honeymoon in a luxurious and exotic location.

No happy ever after.

Kitty worked on flattening cardboard boxes for the recycling bin in the town house complex car park. She was hot and sweaty. She wondered if she would ever get used to this oppressively humid heat. Just as well she was only staying twelve weeks. London could get hot in summer, but Sydney in early February was like living in a pizza oven. She had been to the beach, but the sun—in spite of layers of sunscreen—had scorched her pale skin and given her even more freckles on her nose. Tendrils of her thick chestnut hair were sticking to her neck, even though she had piled it as high as she could in a ponytail-cum-knot on the top of her head.

She brushed her forearm across her perspiring brow and reached for the last box. The last box, however, was reluctant to be reduced to a flat layer. She stomped on it, but it flapped back up to snap at her ankles. 'Down, down, *down*, damn you to sodding hell and back,' she cursed, and she gave it one last almighty stomp by jumping on it with both feet.

'Need some help?' A deep male voice drawled from behind her.

Kitty swung around so fast she almost lost her footing. Her eyes went wide and her heart gave a flap like a sail in a fifty-knot wind. *'You!'* she gasped.

He gave a sweeping obsequious bow. 'At your service, ma'am.'

Kitty felt her skin pebble all over with irritation and embarrassment. 'I was just—' She waved her hand at the recycling bin. 'Um…recycling…'

His eyes were smiling, no—*laughing* at her. 'Looks like you need a man to do that for you,' he said.

'I do *not* need a man.' She felt the slow burn of Jake Chandler's gaze as it took in her baggy track pants and tank top, pausing for a heartstopping moment on her breasts. Her stomach felt as if it was being stirred by a long-handled spoon and her heart kept leaping and jumping as if it was being prodded by the wire of a high-voltage electric current.

She couldn't remember Charles ever looking at her like that—as if he could see right through her clothes to the flesh beneath. She couldn't remember feeling so taken aback by a man's looks before, either. She had to admit Jake Chandler had looked pretty hot in theatre scrubs on Saturday night, but dressed in dark blue jeans and a white T-shirt he looked staggeringly gorgeous. The white of the T-shirt highlighted his naturally olive-toned skin, and his perfectly formed pectoral muscles and flat, toned stomach indicated he was a man who worked hard and played harder. He was certainly every bit as tall as Julie had suggested, and because Kitty wasn't wearing four-inch heels she had to crane her neck to meet his dark sapphire-blue eyes.

'Are you the new tenant?' he asked.

'Yes, I'm renting number three,' she said, with the sort of cool composure that would have earned her an Oscar if she were an actor. But she certainly didn't feel cool around Jake Chandler. She felt blisteringly hot, and it didn't have a thing to do with the searing temperature of the summer day. There was something about his dark blue gaze that made her feel as if each time he looked at her he wasn't seeing her as she was dressed now but as she had been dressed the other night. 'Don't let me keep you,' she said, bending down to scoop up the recalcitrant cardboard.

'Here,' he said, reaching for the bundle that was almost as tall as her. 'Let me help you with that.'

Kitty felt one of his hands brush against her right breast in the exchange. It was like a strike of lightning against her flesh. It zapped right through her body, sizzling it with erotic heat and making every hair on her head rise up from her scalp. She stepped back as if she had been burnt, her face flaming, her heart going at a pace that would have made any decent cardiologist call for an immediate ECG.

But Jake Chandler seemed totally unaffected. He stuffed the cardboard into the bin and shoved it down as if it were a marshmallow with a powerful press of his muscled and deeply tanned arm. 'Do you need anything else done?' he asked. 'Furniture shifted? Boxes carried up the stairs?' His dark blue eyes glinted again. 'Costumes unpacked—that sort of thing?'

'I'm fine... Thank you,' she said, wishing she could stop blushing like a silly little schoolgirl. What was it about this man that made her feel so gauche? Was it his laughing blue eyes or his in-your-face masculinity or both? 'You've done quite enough.'

A tiny silence crept past as he continued to hold her flustered gaze with his unwavering one.

'I'm having a few people over for a barbecue this evening,' he said. 'Nothing fancy. No cucumber sandwiches or anything. Just a few steaks and snags slapped on the grill and some beers. Feel free to pop over and join us.'

Kitty thought of the frozen, calorie-controlled, most probably hideously tasteless dinner she had bought. She thought of eating it alone, just like all the other frozen meals she had mechanically consumed with tears on the side since the break-up. She hadn't seen the point in cooking for one person so she had stopped.

But then she thought of spending the evening with Jake Chandler and his coterie of like-minded beer-swilling friends. What if some of them were other staff members from St Benedict's? He was probably only inviting her so he could make fun of her in front of them.

She had met his type before: the confident, smooth-talking charmer who was the life of every party.

She would be roasted alive.

'Thank you for the invitation, but I think I'll pass,' she said.

'I hope we don't keep you awake,' he said. 'I wasn't expecting anyone to move in for another week or two. The people between your house and mine are overseas. Feel free to pop over if you change your mind or find yourself at a loose end.'

'Thank you, but no,' she said, even more crisply this time.

His dark eyes twinkled again. 'Social diary that full already, is it?' he asked.

She sent him a flinty look. 'Packed,' she said, and turned and left.

At just before midnight Kitty stuck her head under the pillow for the tenth time but it didn't make a single bit of difference. The *doof-doof* of Jake Chandler's sound system reverberated through her building. He was on the opposite side of the complex but it felt as if he was in the next room. She was surprised no one else had complained, but then she remembered the other occupants were away on a trip overseas.

She threw the pillow aside and stomped over to the window overlooking the small courtyard that separated their town houses. She could see people drinking and dancing in Jake's living room. All the lights were blaring and the appetising smell of steak and sausages and onions was still lingering in the air. The sight of all that fun going on was a cruel reminder of her aching loneliness. She hated feeling so bitter, but how could she help it? Everywhere she looked people were acting as if they had not a care in the world.

Didn't Jake Chandler have to show up for work in the morning? What was he thinking, partying on as if there was no tomorrow? So much for his sanctimonious lecture on binge drinking. What a hypocrite!

Kitty decided there was only one way to attack and that was on the front line. She ditched her nightwear and dressed in her track pants and a shapeless cotton shirt and slipped her feet into a pair of flip-flops. It wasn't sophisticated or glamorous, but at this ungodly hour she didn't give a damn.

'Wasn't that the doorbell?' asked Rosie, Jake's younger sister, her eyes brightening with hope. 'Maybe Robbie decided to come after all.'

Jake gave her shoulder a gentle squeeze. 'Don't get your hopes up, kiddo,' he said. 'You know what he's like. He probably won't even remember it's your birthday.'

'Yeah, what was I thinking?' Rosie's shoulders dropped resignedly and she made her way back to her friends.

Jake let out a quick sigh before he turned to open the door to find his cute posh little neighbour standing there. 'Hey,' he said flashing her a smile. 'You changed your mind. Do you want a beer?'

'Your music is keeping me awake,' she said, sending him an arctic look. 'I would very much appreciate it if you would turn it down.'

Jake ran his gaze over her pretty girl-next-door face with its cloud of chestnut hair that was currently looking more bird's nest than brushed. Her cheeks had two spots of bright red on them and her plump pink mouth was pushed forward in a pout. 'My kind of music not your thing, huh?' he said. He leant indolently against the doorjamb, one ankle crossed over the other, as he rubbed at the regrowth on his jaw. 'Let me guess... Classical, right?'

Her gunmetal-grey eyes flashed at him. 'I hardly see how my taste in music has anything to do with you,' she said.

'It will if you play the violin at all hours of the day and night.' He narrowed his eyes at her enquiringly. 'You don't, do you? Play the violin, I mean.'

She gave a little shuffle from foot to foot, as if the ground beneath her feet had suddenly become too hot to stand on. 'What do you have against the violin?' she asked, looking at him with an equally narrow-eyed look.

'I knew it!' he said, thumping the doorjamb with the flat of his palm in victory. 'It was either that or the viola or the cello. You don't strike me as a woodwind or brass girl. Strings are your thing.'

'And I suppose no strings is yours?' she returned, with an arch of one of her brows.

'How'd you guess?' Jake said, grinning.

Her eyes gave a disparaging little roll. 'I can recognise a player at three paces,' she said.

'We're not talking about musical instruments, are we?' he asked.

Her mouth tightened primly, reminding him of his kindergarten teacher when he'd brought a dead mouse in for Show and Tell.

'I'm not interested in what you do in your private life,' she said. 'You can play as hard and as often as you like.'

'Oh, I always play hard and often,' Jake drawled, watching in amusement as her face deepened even more in a blush as she realised her unintentional *double entendre*.

'I can see there is no point in continuing this discussion,' she said in a starchy tone. 'But let me tell you: your puerile sense of humour is not what I was expecting in an A&E director.'

Jake looked down at her uptilted heart-shaped face with its glorious crown of tousled hair. He could smell the sweet, old-fashioned but delightful white lilac scent of her shampoo. It danced around his nostrils, teasing them into an involuntary flare. He could see the tiny dusting of freckles on the aristocratic slope of her nose. He could see her currently pursed but tempting full-lipped mouth.

He felt lust hit him in his gut like a closed-fist punch coming out of nowhere.

He wanted to bend down and cover those lips and feel them soften and swell beneath his. He wanted to taste the silk of her skin, to run his hands over the gentle slope of her breasts to see if they felt as soft and gorgeous as they looked. He wanted to feel her hands on him, their softness exploring his hardness. He wanted her to come down off that high horse of hers and ride him instead.

Whoa, there. He slammed the brakes on his thoughts. He had a whole month to go before he cashed in on the bet with his sister. The shortest month, admittedly, but it could prove to be the longest—especially if Kitty Cargill kept turning up in front of him looking so hot and sexy and combative.

'I can't say you're quite what I was expecting, either,' he said.

Her brows knitted together over her eyes. 'What do you mean by that?'

Jake allowed himself a quick study of her mouth before he met her gaze. 'I had a read-through of your application,' he said. 'I was away when the acting director approved your appointment.'

Her slim throat rose and fell, the action like a small creature wriggling under a carpet. 'And?' she said.

'I noted that you'd failed the practical on your ATLs,' he said.

Her small white teeth nibbled at her bottom lip. 'Yes... I'm thinking about doing the Australian equivalent while I'm here,' she said.

'I expect every member of my team to be on top of their game,' Jake said. 'There's an EMST course I'm directing in a month's time. There might be a space left if you contact the course co-ordinator, otherwise book in to do the next available one.'

'I'll look into it,' she said.

'What made you come all the way out to Australia for three months?' he asked.

Her eyes moved slightly to the left of his. 'It seemed like a good opportunity to get to know my aunt and uncle and three cousins who live here,' she said. 'I hadn't seen them in a while. Years, actually.'

Jake nodded towards her town house. 'You bring anyone with you?' he asked. 'Boyfriend? Partner?'

A flush came over her cheeks and her eyes moved away from his. 'No.'

His eyes went to her left hand, where a pretty little

ring rested. 'Is that just for show or is there a fiancé waiting for you back in England?'

She twirled the ring on her finger with her thumb. 'I'm not engaged,' she said. 'This is a—'

'Let me guess,' Jake said, flashing her another quick grin. 'A costume?'

She gave him a gimlet glare. 'It's a promise ring,' she said. 'I got it when I was sixteen. I can't get it off.'

'You could have it cut off,' Jake said. 'Or would that be breaking the promise?'

She frowned at him. 'Is this inquisition really necessary?'

He gave a negligent shrug. 'Just making conversation,' he said. 'You sure you wouldn't like a drink? I'll get the gang to turn the music down. I might even be able to find some Vivaldi or something on the playlist on my iPod.'

'Please don't put yourself out on my behalf,' she said, sending him another one of her icy looks. 'Goodnight, Dr Chandler.'

'Goodnight, Dr Cargill,' Jake said, but she had already stalked back across the courtyard.

CHAPTER TWO

'AND this is the staff tea room,' Gwen Harold, the unit's ward clerk, informed Kitty on Monday morning. 'There's a larger doctors' room upstairs, but the lifts are so busy that by the time you get there it's almost time to get back. Dr Chandler organised this little room for us instead. Have you met him yet?'

'Um…yes,' Kitty said, trying not to blush. 'A couple of times now.'

Gwen smiled. 'He's a fabulous director,' she said. 'He's tough, but fair. And he's got a great sense of humour. I've worked with a lot of A&E directors in my time but Jake's the best by a long shot. The way I see it, we have enough drama coming through the doors without adding to it with rants and raves from the top. Jake's always cool in a crisis. Never seen him lose his temper—not even with the junior staff.'

'He sounds like the perfect boss,' Kitty said with a forced smile.

'Oh, he's got his faults,' Gwen said. 'He's quite the playboy. I don't think he's ever had a relationship last longer than a couple of months. A heartbreaker, that's what he is.' She gave Kitty a little wink. 'Don't say I didn't warn you.'

'Thanks for the warning, but my heart is quite safe,' Kitty said in a self-assured tone.

'Got someone back in England?' Gwen asked.

'No,' Kitty said. 'Not any more.'

'Never mind, dear,' Gwen said, patting Kitty on the arm. 'Plenty more fish in the sea, as they say. Let's hope you don't land yourself a shark while you're here, hey?'

'I'm keeping well away from the water,' Kitty said.

Gwen looked past Kitty and smiled. 'Ah, speak of the devil,' she said. 'Jake, I believe you've already met our new doctor—Kitty Cargill from London?'

'Sure did,' Jake said with an easy smile. 'Did she tell you she was dressed like a hooker at the time?'

Kitty threw him a furious little glare before turning to Gwen. 'I was at a fancy dress party with my cousin,' she explained. 'I thought she'd broken her ankle, and since this was the closest emergency department I brought her in here. But I dearly wish I hadn't, because it's clear that Dr Chandler thinks it's highly amusing to embarrass me about it at every available opportunity.'

'Bad Jake,' Gwen remonstrated playfully. 'Leave the poor girl alone.' The buzzer rang at the front desk. 'That's my break over. Hope you settle in well, Dr Cargill. Call me if you need anything. Bye.'

Kitty was still fuming. 'Is there anyone in the hospital you *haven't* told?' she asked. 'What about the cleaners and cooks and orderlies? Maybe you could release the CCTV footage. That would be quite hilarious, don't you think?'

'Now, why didn't I think of that?' Jake said with a gleaming smile.

Kitty reined in her temper with an effort. 'I'd like to put that embarrassing episode behind me,' she said.

'I have to work here in a professional capacity. I don't want patients and staff giggling behind my back every time I come to work.'

'You're very uptight, aren't you?'

Her brows snapped together. 'Pardon me for being a little tense, but right at this minute I'm having trouble figuring out if you are the director of this department or the ringmaster at a circus.'

The silence rang like the one left after the sudden cracking of a stock whip.

'My office,' he said. 'Ten minutes.'

Kitty saw the hint of steel in his dark blue eyes before he strode away. Her stomach gave a nervous little flutter. She hadn't been at work more than an hour. Was she going to be sacked on her very first day?

Jake Chandler's office was down at the end of the unit, next to the ultrasound room. Kitty straightened her shoulders and gave the door a tentative rap.

'Come in,' he commanded.

She stepped into the office and closed the door behind her. 'I'd like to apologise,' she said, clasping and unclasping her sweaty hands. 'I was unpardonably rude to you. I don't know what came over me. It was unprofessional of me. I'm sorry.'

He remained seated behind his desk, his dark blue eyes quietly assessing her as he clicked a ballpoint pen on and off.

Kitty chewed at her lower lip. 'I suppose you think I've got no sense of humour.'

'What I think is you're only apologising because you're afraid you're going to get fired.'

She met his diamond-hard gaze. '*Am* I going to get fired?' she asked.

He gave the pen another few clicks. 'Do you think you deserve to be dismissed?' he asked still nailing her with his gaze.

She quickly moistened her pavement-dry lips. 'It depends.'

'On what?'

'On whether you have a sense of humour.'

He held her challenging look with implacable force. 'Dr Cargill,' he said. 'I would like to make something quite clear right from the outset. I enjoy a joke with the best of them. I don't believe in making an already tense and unpredictable workplace unbearable with autocratic or tyrannical behaviour. Humour is at times a safety valve in a department where life and death walk the same tightrope, to borrow the metaphor you used earlier. But one thing I will not tolerate in any shape or form is outright impertinence—especially from a newly appointed staff member who has not yet completed a full day of work. Do I make myself clear?'

Kitty ground her teeth until her jaw ached. 'Yes, Dr Chandler.'

His bluer-than-blue eyes tussled with hers in a lock that made the silence hum with tension.

A funny fizzing sensation bubbled in her belly as his steely gaze slipped to her mouth. Her lips felt the brush of his gaze as if his lips had physically rested there. It was the strangest feeling—one she had never experienced before. She became aware of her mouth, her skin, her body and her senses in a way she never had previously.

It was disquieting.

It was unsettling.

It was threatening and yet somehow...*alluring*...

Kitty gave herself a mental slap. Jake Chandler was a playboy. She had already been warned about him. He was a heartbreaker, and the last thing she needed was another blow to her confidence by a player, not a stayer.

'May I go now?' she asked.

He gave his pen one last click before tossing it to one side and leaning back in his chair. 'What did you do all weekend?' he asked. 'I didn't see you come out of your house even once.'

'I was unpacking.' *And moping and crying and wallowing in self-pity.*

'The social committee have organised a welcome-to-the-unit thing for all new staff members on Friday night at a bar in Bondi,' he said. 'Gwen will give you the details. It'll be a chance to meet most of the permanent staff.' His lips moved in a tiniest of twitches. 'That is unless you have something or someone else already booked in your diary?'

She gave him a look. 'So far I'm free.'

'So it's a date, then.' He got to his feet and the room instantly shrank to the size of a shoebox.

Kitty tried to ignore the way his commanding presence made her feel so tiny and feminine. She had been an inch taller than Charles. She had worn ballet flats most of the time to compensate. But even in those ridiculous heels the other night Jake Chandler had towered over her.

But it wasn't just his height. Something about him made her feel super-aware and edgy.

He *exuded* raw masculinity.

He was all primal male in the prime of his life. Testosterone pumped through his body like fuel through a Formula One car on full throttle.

Her mind began to drift... How would it feel to have that firm mouth press down on hers? She had never kissed anyone but Charles. Would it feel different? *How* different? What would it feel like to have Jake Chandler's strong, capable hands explore her contours? Her belly gave a little tumble-turn as she thought of his body touching hers, moving against hers...

She blinked herself out of her disturbing little day-dream. 'I—I'd best be getting back to work,' she said. 'My shift started ten minutes ago.'

He held her gaze for a moment longer than was necessary. Had he sensed where her mind had been? she wondered. Was that why his eyes were so dark and glittering, and his mouth tilted upwards in that almost-smile?

'I'll see you out there in a couple of hours,' he said, resuming his seat and reaching for the phone on his desk. 'I have a couple of calls to make as well as a management meeting.'

'Why is the patient from Bay Three being sent for a CT?' Jake asked Lei Chung on his way back on the unit.

'Dr Cargill ordered it,' Lei said.

'But it's a straight-out case of appendicitis,' Jake said. 'What else is she hoping to find in there? The crown jewels?'

'She's certainly very thorough,' Lei said. 'You should see the blood-work she's ordered on Mrs Harper in Bay Nine. Pathology's going to be backed up for hours getting through that lot.'

Jake frowned as he made his way to the main A&E office, where he could see Kitty Cargill sitting writing up patient notes. His meeting with hospital management hadn't gone well. Patient work-up times had to go down and more beds were being cut. He had one staff member off sick and another one out on stress leave. There were times when he wondered why he had chosen A&E as a specialty. Right now dermatology was looking pretty damn good.

'Got a minute, Dr Cargill?' he asked.

She looked up from her notes. 'Is it about Mr O'Brien in Bay Four?' she asked, pushing her chair back and rising to her feet. 'I'm waiting to hear back from MRI. They think they can squeeze him in just after lunch.'

'Why are you sending him for an MRI?' Jake asked.

'He's got symptoms of acute sciatica with muscle weakness in one leg,' she said. 'He also complained of bladder frequency. He's probably got nerve compression starting to damage nerve root function, but we need to exclude a spinal tumour.'

'But if you think he's got cord compression why wouldn't you just refer him straight on to neurosurgery?' Jake asked.

Her grey eyes flickered and then hardened. 'I thought it was important to have an exact diagnosis first,' she said.

'That's not our job here. You're wasting precious time and valuable resources doing other people's jobs for them,' Jake said. 'We have a top-notch neurosurgical team at St Benedict's, headed by Lewis Beck. His registrar is more than capable of dealing with this while you get on with assessing the next patient.'

She stood very straight and stiff before him, her chin set at a haughty height. 'It takes time to do a proper work-up,' she said. 'I don't believe in taking shortcuts and handing patients over half assessed. If my diagnosis is wrong, then it's wasting the time of other services.'

'Listen—our job is to efficiently assess them, not find out their star sign,' Jake said. 'While you're busily documenting their favourite colour and what their neighbour's dog's name is, another patient is waiting in the back of an ambulance trying to get in here to one of our blocked beds.'

Her jaw worked for a moment, as if she was forcibly holding back a stinging retort. 'Will that be all, Dr Chandler?' she said.

Jake felt that stirring in his groin again. Something about Kitty Cargill with her feisty little eye-locks and her stubbornly upthrust chin made him want to back her into the nearest storeroom and steal a kiss from that tempting mouth of hers. He couldn't remember a time when he had felt such a powerful attraction to a woman. The betraying little movements and gestures of her face and body indicated she was just as acutely aware of him as he was of her. He could see it now, in the way her grey gaze kept slipping to his mouth as if she had no control over it. The tip of her tongue sneaked out and swept over her lips as if preparing them for the descent of his.

'It's not in my nature to run this department like a drill sergeant,' he said, forcing himself to focus on her eyes, not her mouth. 'I expect a lot from my team, but I don't ask anything of them I wouldn't be prepared to do myself. I realise it will take time for you to learn the ropes of how things are done here. I'm prepared to give you some leeway while you settle in. We'll assess things in a week or two.'

A little frown appeared over her eyes. 'Are you putting me on some type of probation?' she asked.

'That will be all, Dr Cargill,' Jake said, dismissing her. 'You'd better get back on the ward. There are patients to see.'

Kitty seethed all the way home from the hospital. She had mostly managed to avoid Jake during the rest of her shift. A steady stream of patients had needed attending to, but nothing major that had required her to interact with him directly.

She didn't like the thought of his wait-and-see approach to her appointment. She had got the position on merit and she expected to keep it. What right did he have to question her management of patients? She had been trained by some of London's best. How dared Jake Chandler leave her in such a horrid state of limbo? She had moved all the way across the globe to take this post. He had no right to make her feel insecure and inadequate. She was competent and hardworking. That was the one thing that had carried her through the heartache of the last few months. She might not be the biggest extrovert, or one of those effortlessly glamorous party girls, but she was damn good at her job.

Once she got back to the town house she changed into her one-piece bathing costume and some casual separates and headed straight for the beach. The sting of the sun had eased now it was early evening. The iconic arc of Bondi Beach was still heavily dotted with bodies making the most of the long, hot summer. Dozens of fit-looking surfers were out at the back of the swell, waiting for the perfect wave. Kitty couldn't help envying their agility and grace. She had never been all that confident around water. She could swim…well, maybe that was stretching it a teensy bit. She could get from one end of a very short pool to the other. The ocean was another thing entirely. She had been to the beach plenty of times, but gentle, bay-like ones—ones with shingle or pebbles, not sand as fine as sugar and a swell that was rolling in with a roar that sounded like thunder as each wave crashed against the shore.

Kitty laid out her towel on the sand, anchoring the four corners with each of her flip-flops and two shells. She carefully tucked her keys inside her hat, along with her sunglasses, before she walked down to the water's edge between the lifesaver patrol flags.

The water was warmer than she was used to and yet refreshing as she let it froth over her ankles and shins. She went in up to her knees and stood there watching as children half her height went out further, shrieking and squealing in delight as they jumped over or dived under the waves.

The lowering sun was like a warm caress on her back and shoulders, easing some of the tight golfball-sized knots that had gathered there.

'Watch me, Uncle Jake!' A young boy's voice rang out over the sound of the surf.

Kitty felt the hairs on the back of her neck stand up and the golfballs in her shoulders knock together.

How many Jakes were there *in* Sydney and *at* Bondi Beach on *this* particular evening?

She looked to her right and saw Jake Chandler—*the Jake Chandler*—standing watching as a young boy bodysurfed a small wave.

Her heart tripped.

Her belly hollowed.

Her mouth watered.

Jake was standing less than a metre away from her. He was naked from the waist up. He was wet. He was tanned. He was lean. He was muscular in all the right places.

He was gorgeous.

'Why is that lady staring at you, Uncle Jake?'

Kitty blinked herself out of her stasis, embarrassed colour shooting to her face as Jake's blue gaze turned and met hers. 'I'm not staring…' she said, and stared.

Jake's thick dark lashes were spiky with seawater. He had a lazy smile playing about his mouth. He had a day's growth of sexy stubble. His black hair was wet. His shoulders were broad, his hips narrow. His abdomen washboard-flat, his groin—

Kitty swallowed and blushed some more as she dragged her gaze back to his. 'I didn't know you were an uncle,' she said, in a paltry effort to cover her mortification.

Jake put his hand on his nephew's wiry shoulder. 'Nathan,' he said. 'I'd like you to meet a new member of my staff at the hospital. This is Dr Cargill.'

Kitty smiled at the child, who looked about nine or ten years old. 'Hi. I'm pleased to meet you, Nathan.'

'You talk funny,' Nathan said, screwing up his face.

'It's called the Queen's English, Nate,' Jake said. 'You'd do well to learn it—and some manners while you're at it.'

The boy wriggled out from under Jake's hand. 'Can I surf some more?' he asked.

'Yeah, but stay between the flags,' Jake said. He turned and looked at Kitty again. 'Sorry about that. He's a good kid but he needs a bit of polish.'

Kitty tried not to stare at those long spiky eyelashes. 'He's very like you,' she said.

His brow came up in a sardonic arc. 'You think I need a bit of a polish too, do you, Dr Cargill?'

She felt her cheeks burn as she fought to hold his gaze. 'That's not what I meant at all,' she said, with as much composure as she could muster whilst standing partially naked before him. 'I meant you're like him in looks. Your eyes, your hair—that sort of thing.'

Jake returned his gaze to the waves, where his nephew was bodysurfing with varying degrees of success. 'He's a handful,' he said. 'I try and wear him out for my sister Rosie.' He glanced at her again. 'That's whose party it was the other night. As a single mum she doesn't get to kick up her heels much.'

'Oh.' Kitty caught her bottom lip with her teeth.

'Nathan's father shot through before he was born.'

'I'm sorry...'

'She's not,' Jake said, swinging his gaze back to hers. 'She's better off without him.'

She tugged at her lip some more. 'I mean I'm sorry about complaining about the music the other night,' she said. 'It must have seemed so...so petty.'

He checked on his nephew again before turning his gaze back to her. 'You don't like being out of your depth, do you?' he asked.

'What makes you say that?'

'You're only wet up to your knees,' he said. 'We usually have to drag overseas tourists unconscious from this beach. A lot of them dive in without checking the conditions first.'

'I don't like leaping before I look,' she said.

'Can you swim?'

Kitty flashed him an affronted look. 'Of course I can swim.'

'Give me a shout if you need a hand with some stroke correction,' he said.

'No doubt breaststroke is *your* particular specialty?' she said with an arch look.

His lips curved upwards in a sexy smile, but not before his glinting eyes had dipped to the hint of her cleavage first. 'How'd you guess?' he said, and then before she could think of a return he had joined his nephew in the rushing waves.

CHAPTER THREE

KITTY went back to her towel. Resting her chin on her bent knees, she concentrated on watching the surfers further out, but her gaze kept drifting back to where Jake was coaching his nephew. He looked so magnificently male, so vital and fit and healthy. She couldn't help thinking of Charles, with his fair skin, his slight paunch and his receding hairline.

She pulled her thoughts back into line. She wasn't the shallow looks-are-everything type. She was attracted to depth of character, to strong values and dedication and ambition, to caring for others...

She chewed at her lip as she watched Jake scoop his nephew out of a particularly rough wave, holding him steady against him until Nathan got his breath back and found his feet.

He would make a wonderful father.

Kitty felt ambushed by the errant thought. What did she care what sort of father he would make? It had nothing to do with her. What right did her belly have to give a soft little flutter at the thought of him holding a tiny baby in his large masculine hands?

She got to her feet and shook the sand off her towel, frowning as she folded it into a neat square. It might be close to seven-thirty in the evening but she'd clearly had way too much sun.

'Leaving already?' Jake asked as he came towards her across the sand.

Kitty drank in the sight of him. How could anyone look *that* good after a twelve-hour day at work and an hour of kid-sitting at the beach? 'I—I have to wash my hair,' she said, flustered, putting a hand to her hair.

'You didn't even get it wet,' he said.

She ignored his comment and looked past him. 'Where's your nephew?' she asked.

'My sister collected him a few minutes ago,' he said. 'I would've introduced you to her but she was in a hurry.'

Kitty hugged her towel against her chest as if that would stop her heart from beating so erratically and so fast. His skin glistened with droplets of water, and she watched in spellbound fascination as they rolled like a row of glittering diamonds down over his muscled chest. He smelt of the sea, with a grace note of something else—perhaps a lingering trace of his citrus aftershave or shampoo.

He was standing close enough for her to feel a tiny shower of water drops land on her skin when he finger-combed his hair back off his face. She didn't understand how such a sensation could have a disturbing undercurrent of intimacy about it, but it did. Her skin shivered as if he had slowly run his long tanned fingers down the slim length of her bare arms. She moistened her lips and tried to get her brain to work.

'I have to get going...' she said, but her feet didn't move. It felt as if the sand had suddenly turned into quick-setting concrete.

'I'll go in with you if you like,' he said, nodding towards the ocean. 'Just till you get your confidence. Your first time can be a bit scary.'

Kitty's breath stalled. It was tempting. It was hot, and the water felt marvellous around her knees, but what if he *touched* her? What if those strongly muscled arms actually *held* her? 'You don't have to babysit me,' she said with icy hauteur. 'I'm perfectly able to take care of myself.'

He took the towel she was holding like a lifeline and tossed it to the sand at their feet, his dark blue eyes never once leaving hers. 'Prove it,' he said.

Kitty put her shoulders back and her chin up. 'All right,' she said, and spun around and made her way to the water. She splashed through the waves until she was in up to her waist before she turned to look at him. But he wasn't watching from the beach. He had followed her in. He was less than half a metre away. Did he think she was *that* hopeless?

She gritted her teeth.

She would show him.

'Watch out!' he said suddenly.

Kitty turned just as a bigger than normal wave smashed into her. She felt as if she had been thrown into a washing machine on a rapid wash cycle. She couldn't see. She couldn't breathe. She couldn't stand up even if she had known which way was up.

Suddenly a strong hand gripped one of her arms and hauled her upright. She blinked the briny water out of her stinging eyes and looked up at Jake's face. Her body was pressed against the rock-like wall of his by the force of the water. Every hard plane of his body was imprinted on her softer ones. Her breasts were pushed up against his chest, her belly against his washboard abdomen. One of his arms was like a band of iron behind her back; the other was holding her hand in an equally firm grip, his long fingers entwined with hers. His strong legs were slightly apart to brace against the undertow of the water, and the cradle of his pelvis against hers reminded her shockingly, alarmingly, *deliciously* of all that was different between them.

She felt a flickering between her thighs, like a thousand tiny wings beating inside a cramped space. Electricity shot through her veins, sending sparks of reaction up and down her spine, through every limb, even to the very ends of her fizzing fingertips and her curling toes.

Her eyes went to his mouth. She couldn't stop staring at the rough stubble that surrounded it. The desire to reach up and trace that sexy masculine regrowth with her fingertips was almost overwhelming. Her hands were splayed against the hard wall of his chest, and that electrifying sensation was passing from his body to hers through the sensitive pads of her fingers. She could feel the thudding of his heartbeat drumming into her palm.

She couldn't remember the last time she had been this close to a man... Well, she could, but that final goodbye hug from Charles hadn't felt anything like this.

'You're way out of your depth,' Jake said, with an unreadable expression on his face.

Kitty couldn't get her breathing to steady, but it had very little to do with the water she'd inadvertently swallowed. 'A little...perhaps...'

He braced her against him as another wave bore down on them. 'Hold on,' he said.

The crazy water swished and swirled around them

but Kitty barely noticed. She was acutely aware of his body pressed against hers, from her soft breasts to his hard chest, from her smooth slim legs to his strong hair-roughened thighs. She felt the imprint of his arousal against her belly. That starkly primal instinctive reaction of male to female sent her senses into a madcap frenzy. His body seemed to thicken and harden as each heart-stopping second passed. She felt his heartbeat pick up under her hand. It was just a hint of escalation, but it relayed a message that was older than time itself.

Their gazes locked for a moment.

The sound of the ocean and people bathing around them faded. It was like being in a vacuum where no one else existed.

It was just the two of them: a man and a woman, male and female—*alone*.

Jake's gaze slipped to her mouth, those dark blue eyes perusing it for long pulsing seconds as if memorising every tiny crease and line of her lips. 'Time to get you out of danger,' he said, blinking a couple of times. 'You don't want to get dumped unexpectedly again.'

Kitty ran her tongue over her mouth, tasting the ocean and a need so strong she felt it tingling under the surface of her lips. 'I thought it was supposed to be safe between the flags,' she said.

'It depends,' he said as he led her by the hand to shallower water.

She flicked her wet hair back over her shoulders and glanced at him as she sloshed through the lace-like foam of the shallows, trying not to notice how his fingers were so warm and strong where they were curled around hers. 'On what?'

'On whether you can handle the conditions,' he said,

releasing her hand once she was steady on her feet. 'Swimming in a pool is not the same as swimming in the ocean. Every day at the beach is different. You never know when a bigger than normal wave is going to come unless you have experience at reading the swell.'

'Maybe I'll stick to the paddling pool for the time being,' she said. 'At least there are no sharks there.'

His dark blue eyes glinted down at her. 'I think you'll be fine once you gain your confidence,' he said. 'In no time at all you'll be riding those waves like the best of them.'

Kitty had a feeling he wasn't talking just about the ocean. But she wasn't sure if he was talking about gaining confidence at work or in her private life. Was he warning her about getting involved with him? Letting her know the rules from the outset? Her instincts warned her that a relationship with him would not be a safe but boring mechanical lapping of a municipal pool. It would be diving head-first into a surging tide of deep rushing water that carried a constant threat of imminent danger.

She'd be best to stay well clear of it.

She reached for her towel and wrapped herself in it even though she wasn't in the least bit cold. In fact she felt hot, both inside and out. Her skin still tingled and fizzed where he had touched her. And those tiny wings were still beating a soft but insistent rhythm deep inside her every time his eyes met hers, with that ancient primal message of male and female attraction virtually impossible to ignore.

Like right now.

Kitty suppressed a shiver as those blue eyes—as

dark and deep as the ocean that surged and pulsed behind him—held hers.

The raw energy of his body reached out in invisible
waves to wash over her, mesmerising her, tantalising
her, consuming her. She felt the magnetic force-field of
his tall masculine frame standing in front of her.

If she took a step forward she would be able to touch
him. The temptation to do so was almost overwhelming.
She wanted to place her hands on that muscular chest,
to slide her palms over that damp hot skin, to feel those
hard planes and contours, to look up and see the answering attraction in his eyes. But somehow she scrunched
her fingers into her palms and stepped back instead.

'I have to get going…' she said, and almost tripped
over her own feet in the loose sand in her haste to es-
cape.

One of his hands shot out and steadied her, his fingers wrapping around her wrist like a steel bracelet.
'Careful,' he said.

Kitty swallowed as she glanced down at his fingers
overlapping each other on the slender bones of her wrist.
They looked so exotic and dark against the creamy pale-
ness of her skin. Her pulse hammered beneath his touch.
It felt as if a hummingbird was trapped inside her veins.
She wondered if he could feel it. Was that why he had
not let her go even though she was no longer in any
danger of tripping?

She gave him a sheepish look. 'You can let me go
now.'

He slowly unwound his fingers, his eyes still meshed
with hers. 'I guess I'll see you around,' he said.

'Yes, I expect so,' Kitty said. She waited a beat before adding, 'Thank you for the…rescue.'

He flashed a brief on-off smile. 'You're welcome.'

And without another word he ambled off to where he had left his towel further along the beach, turning every female head as he went.

Kitty slowly released a breath and only just resisted the urge to fan her face with one of her hands. 'Way too much sun, my girl,' she said under her breath and, trudging through the sand, headed home.

As soon as Jake walked into the A&E unit the next morning Gwen and a nurse and a resident who were in the office went silent, just as if someone had flicked a volume switch to mute.

'What's going on?' he asked.

'I have to check some bloods,' the resident said, and dashed out.

'Er…me too,' the nurse said, and quickly followed the resident.

Jake eyeballed Gwen. 'What gives?' he asked.

'You were seen canoodling with Dr Cargill,' Gwen said as she folded her arms across her ample chest. 'Apparently it's all over the hospital.'

Jake frowned. 'Canoodling?'

'Yes,' Gwen said in mild reproach. 'I thought you liked to keep your private life separate from your professional one—or are you making a special exception this time?'

'Canoodling?' he said again. 'What the hell is that supposed to mean?'

'You know exactly what it means,' Gwen said. 'What are you thinking, Jake? You know how awkward it gets when staff members have flings with each other. It's bad enough when they work in separate departments, but on the same unit? Everyone feels the fall-out when it's bye-bye time.'

'I am not involved with Dr Cargill,' he said. *Yet*, he tacked on silently. 'Who the hell put that rumour out there?'

'You work together,' Gwen said. 'Word has it you live in the same town house block, and now we hear you're playing together.'

He looked at her blankly. 'Playing together?'

Gwen gave him a look. 'On the beach,' she said. 'In full view of everyone.'

Jake barked out a laugh. 'I was teaching her to swim…or sort of.'

Gwen rolled her eyes. 'Well, whatever you were doing with her has been witnessed and reported. I thought you should know.'

'Thanks a bunch,' Jake said, grinning. 'Does Dr Cargill know we are now an item?'

'Not yet,' Gwen said with grim foreboding. 'But I hope I'm not around when she finds out.'

CHAPTER FOUR

KITTY was examining a patient with a mild blunt force trauma to his forehead in Cubicle Four when she overheard two junior nurses talking as they changed the linen in cubicle three.

'Talk about a fast worker,' one of them said. 'She's only been here a day or two and she's already got her hooks into him.'

'Yeah, well, she certainly got his attention by turning up in that hooker costume the other night,' the other one said. 'Do you reckon it was staged?'

'Must've been,' the other one said. 'What a slut.'

Kitty's heart slammed into her breastbone. She broke out in a sweat, her cheeks firing up and her skin prickling all over in outrage.

'Is everything all right?' the patient lying on the bed asked worriedly. 'I'm not going to die, am I?'

Kitty forced a cool professional smile to her stiff features. 'No, Mr Jenkins,' she said. 'You have a small haematoma that will take a day or two to subside. The skin isn't broken, so there's a slim to none chance of infection. You're not showing any signs of a concussion, but you need to take things easy over the next day or so. Don't drive, operate heavy machinery or consume alcohol for the next twenty-four hours.'

'Thanks, Doctor,' the man said. 'The wife will kill me if I cark it now. We've got a cruise booked for next month. We've been saving up for it for five years.'

'You'll be fine by then,' Kitty said, patting his arm before she left the cubicle.

During her lunch break Kitty went in search of Jake Chandler, but he wasn't on the floor or in either of the doctors' rooms. He was in his office. She felt every eye following her as she made her way through the unit. She had been the subject of hospital gossip before. Her break-up with Charles had done the rounds. It had been excruciating to know everyone was talking about her private life in such lurid detail. She had felt so exposed; so raw and vulnerable. She knew it would only have got worse after Charles's wedding so she had decided to take herself out of the picture. But it seemed that even on the other side of the world people with pathetically small lives thought it sport to speculate on the lives of others. She didn't have the option of running away this time. She would have to face it and deal with it.

She took a calming breath and rapped firmly on the door.

'Come in, Dr Cargill.'

Kitty's hand stilled where it rested on the doorknob. So he had been expecting her, had he? What was he playing at? Was this his idea of a joke? Did he have nothing better to do than make a laughing-stock out of her?

She pulled her shoulders back and kept her chin up, and turned the knob and entered the office, closing the door with a resounding click behind her. 'I hate to in-terrupt you when you're busy, but—'

'It's all right,' he said. 'I've ordered the invitations, and I know a really cool florist who'll do the flowers for mate's rates, not retail.'

Kitty blinked. 'Pardon?'

'The wedding,' he said indolently, swivelling his of-fice chair from side to side.

'Wedding?' She frowned until her forehead ached. 'What wedding?'

His blue eyes shone with amusement. 'Ours,' he said. 'Apparently we're engaged and expecting triplets.'

She felt her jaw drop. 'Are you out of your mind?'

He smiled a breath-stealing smile. 'Gossip,' he said. 'You only have to look at someone around here and people start planning the guest list for the wedding.'

Kitty opened and closed her mouth, totally lost for words.

'Apparently we were caught canoodling,' he said.

'Canoodling?'

He gave her a been-there-asked-that look. 'Yeah,' he said. 'I looked it up in the dictionary. It means to kiss and cuddle amorously.'

'But we didn't do any such thing!' she blurted.

He lifted one of his broad shoulders up and down in a casual shrug. 'Doesn't matter,' he said. 'It looked like it. That's enough to set the tongues wagging around here. No one believes me when I tell them I was actu-ally saving your life.'

'You weren't saving my life,' she said, sending him an affronted glare. 'I wasn't drowning.'

'And I wasn't kissing and cuddling you amorously, but there you go,' he said. 'What's done is done.'

Kitty clenched her fists by her sides. 'Then it will have to be undone,' she insisted. 'I don't want people speculating on my private life.'

'Relax,' he said. 'They'll find someone else to talk about soon enough.'

She strode over and slammed her hands on the desk in front of him, leaning forward to drive home her point. 'Relax?' she said. 'How can I relax? I heard two nurses talking about me in the next cubicle while I was with a patient. I was totally mortified. They called me a slut. They said I'd staged it the night I brought my cousin into A&E just to get your attention.'

His eyes took their merry time meeting hers, taking a sensual detour to the shadow of her cleavage, which she had inadvertently exposed to him. She quickly straightened, but it was too late. She could see the gleam of male appraisal in the depths of his dark blue gaze as it met with hers. The temperature of her skin went up to blistering hot and a hollow feeling opened up in her stomach.

'I'll have a word with them and put them straight,' he said. 'And if I hear any further gossip I'll categorically deny we have anything going on.'

'Thank you,' she said, pressing her lips together for a moment. 'I would appreciate it.'

He leaned back in his chair with a squeak of vinyl. 'Just for the record, Dr Cargill,' he said. 'Next time you come in here you'd better not close the door.'

'Pardon?'

He nodded towards the door behind her which she had clicked shut on her entry. 'You know how people's minds work,' he said. 'A man and a woman in an office together behind a closed door… Who knows what they might get up to.'

Kitty's cheeks exploded with colour. 'That might be how other people's minds work but it's certainly not the way mine operates,' she said.

A lazy smile lurked around the edges of his mouth. 'Good for you,' he said. 'Nice to know there's still some innocence in this big, bad old world of ours.'

She narrowed her eyes at him. 'You think I'm naive and inexperienced, don't you?' she asked.

He pushed back his chair and sauntered over to the office door, standing with a hand on the doorknob without turning it. 'I think, Dr Cargill,' he said, 'that you should get back to work before someone comes looking for you. We don't want any more gossip circulating about us, do we?'

Kitty snatched in a quick unsteady breath. She could smell his clean citrus and wood smell. She could see the individual pinpricks of his cleanly shaven jaw. She could see the sensual contours of his sinfully tempting mouth. She could see the flare of those ink-black pupils in the dark blue sea of his eyes. She was barely aware of sending her tongue out to moisten her lips until she saw those sapphire-blue eyes drop to her mouth to track the movement.

Something tightened in the air.

It was an invisible energy, a force Kitty could feel passing over the entire surface of her skin, disrupting the nerves inside and out, making them super-aware and super-sensitive.

She became aware of the deep thudding of her heart: a *boom, boom, boom* sensation inside her ribcage that was almost audible.

His eyes moved from her mouth to mesh with hers in a heart-stopping little lockdown that sent her senses into a tailspin. 'You know, there is an alternative to handling this situation we find ourselves in,' he said, in a deep and husky tone that sent a shower of reaction down her spine.

'Th-there is?' she said in an equally raspy voice.

His eyes went to her mouth again, resting there an infinitesimal moment before meeting her eyes once more. 'Instead of denying it we could say it's true,' he said. 'Then everyone will stop speculating about us.'

Kitty blinked. 'But...but it's not true.'

One side of his mouth tilted. 'I know, but only we would know that.'

She frowned. 'So you're saying we should *pretend* we're having a fling just to stop people gossiping about us?' she asked.

'It could work,' he said. 'It'll stop the "are they?" or "aren't they?" comments.'

Kitty made a little scoffing sound. 'But you're not my type. I would never in a million years date someone like you.'

'Same goes.'

She pursed her lips as she considered his comeback. Why wouldn't he date someone like her? What was wrong with her?

Wasn't she pretty enough?

Smart enough?

Too smart?

'I can imagine I don't quite fit the stereotype for your usual bedmate,' she said. 'A brain is not essential—only a pulse, right?'

He gave her one of his lazy smiles. 'It has to be a

strong, healthy pulse,' he said. 'Great stamina is required when sleeping with me.'

Kitty could have cooked a raw egg on both cheeks. 'I am *not* sleeping with you, Dr Chandler,' she said. 'Not in pretence or in reality.'

He opened the door for her with exaggerated gallantry. 'Then it's best if we keep our distance, don't you think?'

She put her chin up. 'That's exactly what I intend to do,' she said, and stalked out.

Jake was about to leave his office for a meeting when his mobile rang. He glanced at the caller ID on the screen and muttered a swearword under his breath before he answered it. 'You'd better have a good excuse for not showing up for Rosie's birthday,' he said to his younger brother.

'When was it her birthday?' Robbie asked.

Jake rolled his eyes. 'Why haven't you returned any of my calls or texts?'

'I ran out of credit on my phone.'

'What? Again?' Jake asked. 'I gave you heaps of credit only a fortnight ago.'

'Yeah, well, I had to make a lot of calls,' Robbie said in a surly tone.

'What a pity one of them wasn't to one of your sisters or to me,' Jake muttered.

'Get off my case, Jake, you're not my father.'

Jake pinched the bridge of his nose to clear the red mist of anger that appeared before his eyes. 'No, I'm damn well not,' he said. 'You know, I never thought I'd say this, but I'm glad Mum didn't survive that car accident. It would've broken her heart to see you stuff your life up like this. What were you thinking, Robbie? This time two years ago you were halfway through your engineering degree. Now you're living on the streets.'

'I'm not living on the streets,' Robbie said. 'I've got mates I'm hanging with.'

'You know what they say about lying down with stray dogs,' Jake said. 'Sooner or later you're going to get fleas.'

'You're just pissed because I'm out having fun and you're not,' Robbie said.

'You call getting hammered or stoned every night *fun*?' Jake said, anger and frustration making his throat tight and his voice hoarse. 'Where's the fun in getting Hep C or AIDS from a dirty needle, huh? Tell me that. Tell me what's fun about wrecking your life and everyone else's in the process.'

'I'm not using any more,' Robbie said. 'I'm clean, man.'

Jake was holding his phone so tightly he thought the screen was going to crack. How could he trust a word that Robbie said? Sometimes it felt as if someone had hijacked his little brother's body. It was Robbie on the outside, but it wasn't his kid brother on the inside. Where had that sunny faced, happy-go-lucky kid gone? Where was the boy he had coached through the turbulent years of adolescence in the absence of their deadbeat father, who hadn't even stayed around long enough to see Robbie born? Where was the pimply teenager he had taught to drive? Where was the young man who'd used to drop in to his flat at least three times a week just to hang out after lectures? Who'd talked to him late into the night of his hopes and dreams and aspirations?

Who had looked up to him not just as an older brother, but also as a mentor?

And, even more heart wrenching, would Jake ever be able to get him back?

He pinched the bridge of his nose again, taking a calming breath before he spoke. 'Tell me where you are and I'll come and get you,' he said. 'You can stay with me for a few days. We'll sort something out.'

'I don't need a place to stay,' Robbie said. 'I just need some cash.'

Jake dropped his hand from his face. 'You know what I feel about handing you money, Robbie. If you need food I'll buy it. If you need rent paid I'll pay it. But don't ask me to hand you money to pay for drink or drugs. I can't do that. I *won't* do that.'

The phone went dead.

Jake put the phone back on the desk and dragged his hand over his face. Was this nightmare ever going to end? Where had he gone wrong? He had thought it bad enough when Rosie had got herself pregnant by that jerk who had left her stranded at the age of nineteen. But that was nothing compared to this. Robbie was hellbent on self-destruction and there wasn't a thing he or anyone could do to stop it.

All the sacrifices he had made to keep his family together were *still* not enough. All the opportunities he could have taken he had gladly relinquished, just to see his siblings make their way in the world. He had curtailed many of his own plans to make sure his siblings got the care and the resources they needed. The girls were finally on their feet now. And he had been so proud that Robbie had decided to go to university— thrilled that all the hopes their mother had had for each of her children were finally coming to fruition. He had thought when Robbie was doing well in his studies that things would be smooth sailing from then on. But just when he had thought it was safe to have a life of his own, free of the responsibilities he had shouldered for so long, everything had come crashing down.

What more could he do? Did he have to spend the rest of his life worrying about his brother? Was Robbie ever going to grow out of this stage and be responsible for himself? Or was this how it was going to be for ever?

'What's this I hear about you getting it on with the new recruit in A&E?' asked Greg Hickey, one of the orthopaedic surgeons, in the doctors' room later that day.

Jake put his teaspoon down on the sink. 'Just a rumour, Greg,' he said. 'You know what this place is like. You only have to look at someone and everyone thinks you're sleeping with them.'

Greg gave him a cynical grin. 'That's because you usually are.'

Jake gave a dismissive shrug. 'She's not my type.'

'She's a London girl, isn't she?' Greg asked as he poured himself a coffee from the brew on the hotplate.

'Yeah,' Jake said, thinking of Kitty's cute little accent and the way she put her nose in the air when she wanted to make a point.

'And quite pretty, so I've been told,' Greg added.

Jake took a sip of his coffee as he thought about the heart-shaped face and the stormy grey eyes that had stared him down across his desk earlier that day. His body had leapt to attention. He had felt so tempted to come around from behind his desk and taste the temptation of her full mouth. Was it really as soft as it looked?

She wasn't the lipstick type, but she wore a shimmery lip gloss that made her lips look luscious. Would they taste of vanilla or strawberries?

Her hair had been pulled back in a tight, school-marmish knot at the back of her head. He had wanted to release it from its prim confines and let it cascade freely around her shoulders. He had wanted to run his fingers through it to see if it was as silky as it looked. He couldn't quite rid his mind of imagining her cloud of hair spread out over the pillows on his bed, her slim, creamy limbs entwined with his. Would she be a kitten or a tigress in bed? He got hard just thinking about it. He couldn't rid his mind of her fragrance, either. She had smelled of frangipanis this time, an exotic and alluring scent that had lingered in his office for hours.

'She's all right, I guess,' he said, with another casual up-and-down movement of his shoulders.

Greg chuckled as he reached for the artificial sweetener on the counter. 'You've got it bad, Jakey boy,' he said. 'I can see all the signs.'

'What d'you mean?' Jake asked, frowning. 'What signs?'

'Every time I mentioned her just then you got this goofy sort of dreamy look on your face,' Greg said, leaning back against the counter. 'I reckon you're falling for her.'

Jake gave an uncomfortable laugh. 'You're crazy. I've never fallen for anyone in my life and I'm not going to start now.'

Greg kept grinning. 'Gotta be a first time for everything, right?'

'Wrong,' Jake said, putting his mug down on the table with a little *thwack*. 'Kitty Cargill's far too conservative for me. She doesn't have a funny bone in her body. She's prim and proper and she sweats over the small stuff all the time. She doesn't smile—she glowers. Besides, she's still hankering over some guy who broke her heart back in the home country. I don't think she's here to advance her career at all. She's running away from her failed love-life. I don't need any lame ducks on my staff; God knows it's hard enough to keep everyone's morale up as it is with all these wretched cutbacks. I don't want to have to babysit someone who isn't up to the task.'

'What? You don't think she's competent?' Greg asked, frowning over the rim of his coffee cup.

Jake released a breath and rubbed at the tight muscles at the back of his neck. Maybe he'd laid it on a bit strong. It wouldn't do to sound *too* defensive. 'No, I'm not saying that. She's conscientious—a little too much so if anything. She's eager to learn and the patients like her. She'll find her feet soon enough.'

'Might be just what she needs to boost her confidence,' Greg said. 'A meaningless affair with a man she won't think twice about leaving when it's time to say goodbye.'

'I'm not putting my hand up for the job just yet,' Jake said. 'Not unless I hand over a thousand bucks to one of my sisters.'

'What do you mean?'

'I made a bet with her over Christmas dinner,' Jake said. 'No sex for three months.'

Greg's brows rose. 'So how's that working out for you?'

Jake gave him a rueful look as he shouldered open the door. 'Let's put it this way,' he said. 'I'm spending a whole lot more time at the gym.'

CHAPTER FIVE

JAKE was on his way back to his town house after a heavy session at the gym when he saw Kitty in the car park, washing a car that had seen better days. She was wearing a pair of shorts that ended at mid-thigh and a loose-fitting T-shirt. Her hair was up in a high pony-tail, swinging from side to side as she rubbed the soapy sponge over the duco of her four-cylinder vehicle. She looked young and nubile and so sexy he felt a surge of lust go through him like a rocket blast. Her small but perfect breasts were outlined behind the clingy damp-ness of her T-shirt, and every time she bent over he caught a delectable glimpse of her creamy flesh. She was humming to herself—a tune he was familiar with but couldn't quite place. She had a hose in her other hand and it was spraying water all over the concrete, running in wasteful rivulets down the storm water drain.

'I hate to take on the role of the fun police but you can't do that around here,' he said.

She jumped and turned around so quickly the high-pressure hose in her hand shot him straight in the groin with a blast of cold water.

He let out a stiff curse as he stepped out of the line of fire. 'What the hell?'

'Sorry,' she said, pointing the hose at the ground, where it sprayed water all over the concrete at her feet. 'I didn't hear you. You scared the wits out of me, coming from nowhere like that.'

He frowned in irritation as he brushed off what water he could from his sodden gym shorts. 'Will you turn off the damn hose, for God's sake?'

She gave her head a little toss that sent her ponytail swinging again. 'I'm washing my new car.'

'You can't use a hose to do that.'

'Why ever not?' she asked, looking at him defiantly. 'How else am I supposed to wash it? Lick it clean?'

Jake looked at her mouth— a habit of his just lately that he couldn't seem to break. He could think of places he would much rather have her lick with her tongue than the dusty duco of her second-hand bomb. 'We have water restrictions here,' he said. 'You can't use a hose to water the garden or wash your car during summer. You have to use a bucket. If you get caught there are hefty fines.'

'Oh…' She looked at the running hose and bit down on her lip. 'I didn't realise.'

Jake moved over to turn the hose off at the tap, asking over his shoulder. 'Where did you get the car?'

Her chin came up a fraction. 'I bought it.'

He came over and ran a hand over the dented paintwork of the front fender. 'How much did you pay for it?' he asked.

She pursed her lips for a tiny heartbeat. 'It wasn't expensive,' she said. 'I didn't want to spend a fortune because I'm only going to be using it for three months.'

'Let's hope it lasts that long,' Jake said, kicking one of the threadbare tyres with his right foot.

'I'm sure it's perfectly fine,' she said, with a little flash of her grey gaze.

'Did you take it for a test drive?'

Her eyes flickered a little, as if something behind them had come loose. 'I drove it around the block at the owner's house and then back to here,' she said. 'It ran smoothly enough.'

Jake grunted. 'Good luck on restarting it.'

Her lips went tight again. 'I'm sure it will start first go,' she said. 'It's only had one owner.'

'How many clicks on the clock?'

A little frown pulled at her brow. 'Clicks?'

'Kilometres.'

'Oh…' She nibbled at her lip again and stepped past him to peer through the driver's window. 'Forty-two thousand.'

Jake rolled his eyes. 'Make that *two hundred* and forty-two thousand—maybe even more.'

She frowned at him again. 'What do you mean?'

'That model is ten years old,' he said. 'Even a little old lady only driving to church on Sundays would've clicked up more than that. You've been sold a lemon, Dr Cargill. Someone's turned the clock back on it for sure.'

She shifted her eyes from his to the car and back again. 'I suppose you think I'm gullible,' she said with a hint of defiance.

'Have you ever bought a car before?' Jake asked.

'I…' Her slim throat rose and fell as she swallowed. 'I used to share one. I lived close to the hospital in London so I didn't really need one of my own.'

Jake gave the windscreen wipers a quick inspection. 'These need replacing,' he said, dusting his hands on his shorts. 'I can get a new set of rubbers for you from a mate of mine. He owns an auto parts shop.'

'I wouldn't want to put you or your friend to any bother,' she said, looking resentful and yet vulnerable and adorably cute all at the same time.

'It's no trouble,' Jake said. 'You'll need new tyres soon too. That rear one is practically bald.'

She worked at her bottom lip again with her teeth, looking at the car with a defeated look on her expressive heart-shaped face.

'Don't worry,' Jake said. 'I'm sure it'll get you to the hospital and back all right. But I wouldn't take it on any long journeys until you've had it checked by a mechanic. I can give you the name of one who'll take care of it for you without ripping you off.'

'Thank you...' She tucked a strand of hair behind her ear in a discomfited gesture.

'I'll get you a bucket,' he said. 'I have one in my garage.'

'Please don't bother,' she said.

'It's no bother.' Jake walked towards his garage and, fishing his remote out of his shorts pocket, activated the roller door. He ducked his head as the door was rising and grabbed the bucket next to his toolbox. 'Can't leave a job half done, now, can we?' he said as he took the bucket over to the tap and filled it.

'What are you doing?' she asked.

Jake took the sponge from her hand, watching as her eyes flared when his fingers brushed against hers. 'Stand back,' he said with a lopsided smile. 'This is no job for a lady.'

'I'm not sure what gives you the impression I'm completely rubbish at taking care of the simplest tasks,' she

said, bristling like a pedigree Persian cat in front of a
scruffy mongrel dog. 'But I'll have you know I can wash
a car all by myself.'

Jake moved past her stiff little body to soap up the
bonnet of the car. 'It won't take a minute,' he said.
'You're too short to reach the roof in any case.'

She stood back with her arms folded crossly, her
plump mouth pushed forward in a pout. 'That's why
I was using the hose,' she said, shooting him a look.

'Yeah, well, don't blame the drought on me,' Jake
said, bending over to re-soap the sponge. 'I suppose
you don't have to wash cars in England.'

'Why do you say that?' she asked.

'Doesn't it rain all the time?' he asked as he cleaned
the rooftop of the car.

'Not *all* the time,' she said, with a hint of defen-
siveness.

A little silence passed.

'Have you been to Britain?' she asked.

Jake squatted down to soap up the rim of the nearest tyre. He thought of the ticket to London he'd had to
cancel when he'd found out about Rosie's pregnancy.
He'd only planned to go for a couple of months the year
after he'd finished medical school. He'd organised for
Robbie to stay with a reliable family and the girls with
friends. He had counted the days until his first real holiday free of responsibility. But when Rosie had tearfully
confessed her predicament he had cancelled his trip and
had never got around to booking another.

'It's on my list of things to do.'

'Have you been to Europe?'

'Not yet.'

'Why not?' she asked. 'I thought a man like you would have gone far and wide to sow your wild oats.'

Jake straightened and tossed the sponge in the bucket like a basketball player landing a game-winning shot. 'It hasn't been a priority,' he said. 'Australia's plenty big enough and exciting enough for me.'

'That's rather parochial of you, don't you think?' she said.

He shrugged. 'I figure there'll be plenty of time for me to travel the world when I get other stuff out of the way.'

'What other stuff?' she asked. 'Career stuff? Surely it's in your interests career-wise to have lived and worked overseas as so many of your colleagues do?'

Jake emptied the bucket and rinsed out the sponge at the tap. 'Is that why you're here?' he asked, glancing at her over his shoulder. 'To further your career?'

Her eyes moved out of range of his. 'Of course it is.'

He picked up the bucket of rinsing water. 'Three months isn't very long,' he said as he set to work on the car again.

'It's long enough.'

'To further your career or mend a broken heart?'

The air stiffened in silence.

'I haven't got a broken heart,' she said.

Jake looked at her over the top of the car. 'Looks like it to me.'

She straightened her slumped shoulders and sent him one of her Jane Austen looks. 'And I suppose you know all the signs because you've broken so many female hearts yourself,' she said.

'I haven't broken any just lately,' he said. 'Anyway, it's not something I set out to do deliberately.'

She gave a little laugh that was not even a distant cousin to humour. 'I'm sure you don't,' she said, kicking at one of the tyres with her foot. 'My ex claimed he didn't do it on purpose, either.'

'How long were you together?' Jake asked.

She let out a long sigh before she faced him. 'For ever.'

He came back around to her side and leaned against the car. 'Want to talk about it?'

Her eyes skittered away from his. 'Not particularly.'

'I take it he found someone else?' Jake said.

Her gaze was glazed with bitterness, like a coating of shellac. 'My best friend.'

'Ouch,' he said, wincing in empathy. 'That would've hurt.'

'It did.' She bit her lip until the blood drained away. 'It does…'

Jake hardly realised he had moved away from the car and put a hand on the top of her slim shoulder until he felt the lightning strike shock of the contact run up his arm from the cup of his palm.

Her eyes met his and locked.

Electricity zapped and fired.

Desire roared through his veins like a runaway freight train. He could see the answering flare in her grey gaze. He felt the gentle shudder of her flesh beneath his hand. He stood mesmerised as the tip of her tongue snaked out and brushed over her soft lips in a single heartbeat of time that seemed immeasurable.

He lowered his head fraction by fraction, frame by frame, like a film being played in slow motion. The stop signals and flashing red lights in the rational side of his brain were overruled by the need to taste the sweet pillow of her mouth, to press against those soft contours and forget about everything but the sensual energy that flowed in a spine-tingling current between them.

He cupped his other palm against the soft satiny curve of her cheek, watching as her serious smoky grey eyes registered the contact with a dilation of her pupils.

Her lips parted slightly, her vanilla-scented breath tantalising him as he came even closer.

The dark fan of her eyelashes lowered over her eyes, but just as he was about to make contact her eyes suddenly sprang open and she stumbled backwards out of his light hold.

'I'm sorry,' she said, blushing furiously. 'I can't do this.'

Jake gave a casual *whatever* shrug and put his hands out of temptation's way in the pockets of his shorts. 'No problem,' he said.

She pressed her lips together tightly for a moment, actively avoiding his gaze. 'I don't want you to get the wrong idea about me...'

'My bad,' Jake said. 'I overstepped the line. Blame my sister Rosie.'

She cautiously met his gaze. 'Your...sister?'

'I'm trying to win a bet,' he said. 'No sex this summer. I've just about made it too. Only twenty-two days to go.'

Her cheeks turned rosy red. 'How morally upright of you,' she said. 'So come the first of March anyone is pretty much fair game?'

He gave her a glinting look. 'I do have *some* standards.'

'Oh, yes,' she said with her customary hauteur. 'A strong working pulse. I almost forgot.'

Jake smiled wryly as he picked up his bucket. 'Do you want me to run a chamois over your car to dry it off?' he asked.

'No, thank you,' she said, with schoolmarmish primness.

He tapped the bonnet with his hand. 'Give me a shout if you need a jump start in the morning,' he said. 'I have the necessary equipment.'

'I'm quite sure I won't be needing *any* of your equipment,' she said, that dainty chin going up another notch.

'Well,' Jake said, giving her a deliberately smouldering look, 'you know where it is if and when you do.'

CHAPTER SIX

KITTY was putting her things in the locker in the staff changing room the next morning when one of the nurses on duty came in.

'Hi, Dr Cargill,' the nurse said. 'I'm Cathy Oxley. I haven't been rostered on with you yet. How are you settling in?'

'Fine,' Kitty said. 'It's a bit of a steep learning curve. I'm still finding my feet.'

Cathy's brown eyes twinkled meaningfully. 'I'm sure our gorgeous boss is helping you with that after hours.'

Kitty felt her cheeks heat up. 'I'm not sure what you mean by that,' she said, closing her locker door with a little rattle. 'I'm not seeing Dr Chandler after hours.'

'Oh, sorry,' Cathy said. 'I must have got my wires crossed. I could've sworn someone said you two were dating. Mind you, it would be a first for him if you were.'

'A first?' Kitty frowned. 'In what way?'

'I don't think he's ever dated anyone on his immediate staff before,' Cathy said as she stored her bag in a locker two doors away from Kitty's. She closed and locked the locker and turned back to face Kitty. 'One of the nurses last year actually asked for a transfer to another department so he would take her out. Not that it lasted all that long. But that's Jake-break-your-heart-Chandler for you. It'll be a very special woman indeed who manages to lure him to an altar any time soon.'

Kitty turned and worked on smoothing over her tightly restrained hair in front of the mirror. 'Not all men are cut out for the responsibility of commitment and marriage,' she said. 'It's all a matter of maturity.'

'I don't think Jake would like to hear you describe him as immature,' Cathy said with a little chuckle.

'Men can be commitment-shy for all sorts of reasons, I guess. Particularly if they haven't had a great experience of commitment in their own family.'

'Jake doesn't talk about his background,' Cathy said. 'He's a bit of dark horse in that regard. I know he's got siblings. His brother's just as gorgeous in looks, apparently. A younger sister of one of the nurses on the neuro ward went out with him a couple of times.'

'Looks aren't everything,' Kitty said. 'What about character and values?'

'Our Jake's got those as well,' Cathy said. 'You just have to go searching for them. He doesn't wear his heart on his sleeve.'

'Has he even got a heart?' Kitty asked with an arch of one of her brows.

Cathy grinned as she shouldered open the locker room door. 'Last time I looked—but who knows? Maybe someone's stolen it by now.'

Kitty had barely been on the floor of the unit thirty seconds when Jake Chandler informed her there was a critical incident unfolding right outside the A&E department.

'Two teenagers have been knocked down by a car,' he said, issuing orders to the nurses on duty as he strode through. 'Cathy, Tanya, get airway and trauma kits, hard collars, IV equipment and spinal boards.'

Kitty followed Jake and Lei and four nurses out to the street outside the A&E receiving area, where the police were diverting the traffic and securing the scene from bystanders.

She felt her heart pounding behind the framework of her ribs. She was used to dealing with patients in the unit, not out on the street. She had never attended a real accident, only mock-up ones.

Two kids—a girl and a boy—in their mid-teens were lying on the road. Horns were blaring. Sirens were screaming and lights were flashing. People were screaming and shouting. The police were doing their best to control the scene, but it was nothing short of mayhem given it was smack-bang in the middle of peak hour.

'Dr Cargill,' said Jake, calmly but with unmistakable authority. 'Take Cathy and Tanya and do a primary survey on the girl and tell me what equipment you need. Lei, take Lara and Tim and get started on the boy.'

Kitty started her assessment of the girl who was unconscious. 'AVPU is P,' she said. 'I don't have an airway.'

'Get the neck stable and get her intubated,' Jake ordered.

Kitty felt a flutter of panic rush through her stomach like a rapidly shuffled deck of cards. 'I can maintain her airway without intubating her out here.'

'You need to secure the airway and get the rest of the primary survey done now,' Jake said. 'We're not moving her until she's assessed. Do you want me to intubate her?'

'No,' Kitty said, mentally crossing her fingers and her toes. 'I can manage.'

'Good,' he said. 'Get it done and then give me the primary survey.' He turned to the registrar. 'Lei, what's your assessment?'

'GCS thirteen, Dr Chandler,' Lei said. 'Airway patent, multiple fractured right ribs and a flail segment. Probably right pneumothorax. Pulse one-twenty, BP one hundred on sixty. No external bleeding.'

Kitty kept working on her patient, wishing she were half as confident as the registrar appeared to be.

She tried to focus.

To keep calm.

This was not the time to doubt her skills. She had been trained for this. She had worked on similar cases inside A&E.

Come on, she gave herself a little pep talk. *You've intubated loads of patients before. Why should this one be any different?*

'Good work, Lei,' Jake was saying. 'Is it a tension pneumothorax?'

'No tension, Dr Chandler,' Lei said. 'Fair air entry and no mediastinal shift.'

'Brilliant,' Jake said. 'Get a collar on and do a quick secondary survey. Log roll and check the spine. If that's all, pack him up onto the spinal board, get in a cannula, get him inside and continue in there.'

'Will do.'

Kitty could feel the sweat pouring down between her shoulderblades as she tried again to intubate the girl. The sun was burning down like a blowtorch on the top of her scalp. Panic was no longer fluttering in the pit of her stomach; it was flapping like a bedsheet in a hurricane-force wind.

This was not a dummy patient.

This was someone's daughter, someone's little girl, someone's sister and someone's friend. If this young girl died someone's life—many people's lives—would be shattered.

The sun burned even more fiercely and the trickle of sweat down between the straps of her bra became a torrent. Her head started to pound as if a construction site had taken up residence inside. The sunlight was so bright her vision blurred. She blinked and white flashes floated past her eyes like silverfish.

'What's the problem?' Jake asked as he came over.

'This is not the ideal environment to do an intubation,' Kitty muttered in frustration. 'It's too bright and I can't see the cords.'

'Accidents don't happen in ideal environments, Dr Cargill,' he said. 'We're not moving her until the airway and neck is secured. You stabilise her neck while I intubate.'

Kitty moved aside as Jake came around to the head of the patient and took over the laryngoscope. 'Hold the head from below,' he ordered.

She did as he directed and watched as he inserted the laryngoscope. It was genuinely a difficult task, which should have made Kitty feel less of a failure, but it was pretty obvious Jake had had extensive training and was far more experienced at resuscitating on site. Everything he did he did with cool and calm confidence. He kept his emotions in check. Not a muscle on his face showed any sign of personal distress or crisis. He was simply getting on with the job.

'Listen to the chest, Dr Cargill,' he said. 'What's the air entry?'

Kitty listened to the patient's chest. 'There's no air entry on the right and mediastinal shift to the left.'

'Get a needle in the chest,' he said. 'We can put a chest tube in inside.' He called out to the nurse. 'Kate—here. Ventilate the patient while I get the collar back on and get a drip in.'

Finally the patients were transferred inside and taken to ICU once stabilised.

'Good work, everyone,' Jake said, stripping off his gloves and tossing them in the bin.

Kitty couldn't help feeling she didn't deserve to be included in that statement. She concentrated on washing her hands at the basin, hanging her aching head down, feeling the sweat still sticky beneath her clothes.

'You too, Dr Cargill,' Jake said as he reached for some paper towels alongside her basin. 'That was a tough call.'

Kitty looked up at him. 'I was out of my depth and you know it,' she said.

'You'll get better once you do EMST,' he said. 'It's all a matter of confidence. The same skills apply inside here or outside there.'

'I was nearly roasted alive out there,' she said. 'It looked like you didn't even break a sweat.'

His dark blue gaze scanned her flushed face. 'You

look like you caught the sun,' he said. 'Your nose is a little pink.'

'Great,' she said with a rueful grimace. 'More freckles.'

'Kisses from the sun,' he said. 'Or so my mother called them when I was a kid.'

'But you don't have any freckles.'

The corner of his mouth tipped up and a glint appeared in his eyes. 'None that you can see.'

Kitty flushed to the roots of her hair but stalwartly held his gaze. 'I'll pass on the guided tour, thanks very much,' she said.

'I wasn't offering one.'

His blue eyes played tug-of-war with hers in a moment that vibrated with palpable tension.

'Sorry to interrupt, Jake,' Gwen said as she approached. 'Your brother is here to see you. He's waiting in Reception. He told me to tell you it's important.'

Jake's expression tightened, and then locked down to a blank impenetrable mask. 'Call me on my mobile if anything urgent comes in,' he said gruffly to Kitty. 'I'll be ten minutes.'

Gwen let out a sigh as Jake disappeared through the entrance to A&E. 'I wish Jake would tell me what's going on.'

Kitty frowned. 'Going on?'

'With Robbie,' Gwen said. 'I can tell Jake's worried sick about him but he won't talk about it. I guess he's used to dealing with his family on his own. God knows he's been doing it long enough.'

'What do you mean?' Kitty asked.

'Jake's mother was killed in a car accident when he was sixteen,' Gwen said. 'And that's another thing he won't talk about. I only heard about it because one of the paramedics who attended the accident worked with my husband in the fire department. A drunk driver hit Jake's mother head-on. She made it to hospital but died a few hours later.'

'That's terrible,' Kitty said. 'What about his father?'

Gwen rolled her eyes. 'That's another one of Jake's no-go areas,' she said. 'I don't think he's seen his father since he was a kid. I don't think Robbie has even met him.'

'Who looked after Jake and his siblings after their mother was killed?' Kitty asked.

'I think they stayed with his mother's parents for a bit, but it didn't last,' Gwen said. 'They'd disowned their daughter when she hooked up with Jake's father. They didn't even know the kids when they were plonked on their doorstep. Jake got his own place as soon as he could afford it and made his own way. Can't have been easy. He's done such a good job of taking care of them all, but now Robbie's got some sort of issue. God knows what it is. Jake certainly won't let on.'

Kitty looked towards the doors Jake had just gone through. She thought back to her conversation with him about why he hadn't travelled abroad. Had he stayed home in order to watch over his siblings? How had he coped financially? Had his mother left them well provided for or did he have to struggle to make ends meet? What else had he sacrificed to be there for his family?

The image of him as a protective father figure was at odds with her impression of him as a fun-loving, laid-back playboy. But then she thought of the day she'd seen him at the beach with his young nephew. No one could ask for a more devoted uncle and mentor. Strict but fair, strong but nurturing—all the things young kids and in particular boys needed to grow. Jake had apparently had no such mentor himself. Instead he had been the man of the house for most of his thirty-four years.

Kitty turned and saw Gwen looking at her speculatively. 'What were you two talking about just then, anyway?' Gwen asked. 'You looked rather cosy.'

Kitty felt a flush pass over her cheeks. 'It was just… nothing.'

Gwen gave her a motherly smile of caution. 'Tread carefully, my dear,' she said. 'He's a gorgeous man in looks and in temperament, but he doesn't play for keeps.'

'I don't know how many times I have to tell everyone I'm not interested in Jake Chandler,' Kitty said with an irritated frown.

Gwen's look was long and measuring. 'Not that you wouldn't make a lovely couple or anything,' she said. 'I can see the sparks that fly between you.'

'I'm sure you're imagining it,' Kitty said, still frowning. 'Personally, I think he can't wait until I hop on that plane back to Britain. He thinks I'm not up to the task.'

'You're handling things just fine,' Gwen said. 'Jake's not one to stroke egos unnecessarily. If he was unhappy with your work he'd soon let you know.'

Kitty gave her a grim look. 'That's exactly what I'm afraid of,' she said, and turned back to the unit.

CHAPTER SEVEN

KITTY didn't see Jake face-to-face for the rest of her shift. He had come back to the unit after a few minutes, but she had been tied up with a patient with chronic asthma whose condition hadn't been properly managed by either the patient or his doctor. By the time she'd sorted the middle-aged man out Jake had been busy with other patients.

But when she was walking along the Bondi shopping and café strip later that evening, in search of somewhere to grab some dinner, she saw him coming towards her.

He looked preoccupied. There was a frown between his brows and his jaw looked as if it had been carved from stone. He didn't even see her until she was practically under his nose.

'Dr Chandler?'

Her softly spoken greeting didn't even register, so she reached out and touched him on the bare tanned skin of his forearm with her fingertips.

'Jake?'

He jumped as if she had probed him with an electrode. 'Oh,' he said, absently rubbing at his arm. 'It's you.'

'Yes...' Kitty shifted her weight from foot to foot. 'Are you OK?'

His marble mask stayed in place. 'Sure. Why wouldn't I be?'

'I just thought you might like to…talk.'

Something moved across his gaze, leaving in its wake a layer of ice. 'About what?'

'Gwen told me you were having some trouble with your brother and I thought—'

'You thought what, Dr Cargill?' he asked with a mocking look. 'That you'd offer your sweet little shoulder for me to cry on?'

Kitty held his glacial gaze for a beat or two before giving up. 'I've obviously caught you at a bad time,' she said, stepping away from him. 'I'm sorry, I didn't mean to interfere.'

She had walked past three shopfronts before he caught up with her. He didn't touch her. He walked alongside her, shoulder to shoulder—well, not exactly shoulder to shoulder, given he was so much taller. Kitty was wearing ballet flats, which put the top of her head in line with the top of his shoulder. She felt the warmth of his body. She had to fight to keep walking in a straight line in case her body betrayed her with its traitorous, shameless desires.

'Don't let me keep you,' she said, sending him a sideways glance that made her loose hair momentarily brush against his arm. She grabbed at the wayward strands and fixed them firmly behind her ear.

'Sorry,' he said in a gruff tone. 'That was uncalled-for.'

'It's OK,' she said, only marginally mollified.

They walked a few more paces in silence. Kitty wasn't sure what to say, so said nothing. She figured if he wanted to talk to her he would. Every time she sneaked a glance at him he was frowning broodingly. His shoulders looked tight and were hunched forward slightly, as if he was carrying an invisible weight that was incredibly burdensome.

'Have you got any siblings?' he finally asked.

'No, there's just me,' Kitty said.

'Happy childhood?'

'Mostly.'

'Are your parents still married to each other?' he asked.

Kitty gave him another sideways glance, trying to ignore the way her heart kicked in her chest when she encountered the unfathomable darkness of his sapphire-blue gaze. 'My parents didn't get married in the first place,' she said. 'They met at a free love commune. They're still together, more or less. They occasionally have other partners. They have what they call an "open" relationship.'

His eyebrows lifted. 'I wouldn't have picked you as a hippy couple's kid,' he said. 'Did the stork get the wrong address or something?'

Kitty couldn't hold back a little rueful smile. 'My parents have spent a great deal of the last twenty-six years looking at each other in a kind of dumbfounded way,' she said. 'They were hoping for a free-spirited indie child much like themselves. I constantly embarrass them.'

His mouth kicked up at the corners. 'I just bet you do.'

Kitty caught a whiff of his cologne as he raised a hand to brush his hair back off his forehead. The faint hint of hard-working male was like a potent elixir to her nostrils. She even felt herself leaning closer to catch more of his alluring scent.

He met her gaze again, holding it with the dark intensity of his. 'I lost my mother when I was sixteen,' he said. 'And my father...' He paused, a frown cutting his forehead in two, and the lines and planes of his face clouding. 'My father left us before my brother was born. My two sisters can barely remember him. None of us have seen or heard of him since he left. Not even when Mum died.'

'I'm very sorry,' Kitty said. 'Life can be pretty brutal at times. You must have had a hard time of it.'

'Yeah, you could say that,' he said, stepping aside for a group of teenagers carrying bodyboards to pass between them.

'What about your sisters?' Kitty asked when he didn't offer anything else once they had resumed walking side by side. 'What do they do?'

'Jen's a hairdresser,' he said. 'She's saving up to buy her own salon. Rosie works part-time as a teacher's aide. She's studying to be a teacher.'

A small silence passed.

'And your brother?' Kitty asked.

His gaze cut to hers. 'Didn't Gwen tell you during your little heart-to-heart session? I'm sure she along with everyone else at the hospital has a theory or two on why Robbie's running amok.'

'I didn't probe her for information,' she said. 'She didn't know much in any case. She simply told me she sensed that your brother seemed to have some...issues.'

'Issues.' He gave a harsh laugh. 'That's how everyone makes excuses for any sort of bad behaviour today. They've got *issues*. Do you know what bugs me about that? It's *always* someone else's fault. It's a get out of jail free card. No one has to take responsibility for their own actions any more. There's always someone else to blame. Bad childhood or bad parenting. Or in my case practically no parenting. I hate that victim mentality that everyone adopts these days. It achieves nothing. You just have to get on with life. There's no point wishing things were different. You get what you get and you damn well have to deal with it.'

Kitty walked with him for a few more paces. 'I guess different people cope with things in different ways,' she said after a moment. 'What makes one person stronger makes another one crumble.'

'Yeah, well, I just wish my brother would snap out of this phase of his,' he said. 'I'm sick and tired of cleaning up his mess.'

'You sound just like a concerned parent,' she said. 'At least you'll have had plenty of practice when it comes to having your own kids.'

His expression became even more dark and brooding. 'No way,' he said. 'I'm not making that mistake.'

'You don't want kids?'

'Why would I want kids when I've already brought up three?' he asked.

'Helping to rear your siblings is not the same as having your own children,' Kitty said.

He gave a grunt. 'It is for me,' he said. 'I've made enough packed lunches to last me a lifetime.'

'Having children is much more than just packed lunches,' she said.

'Yeah,' he said. 'And don't I know it. The cute chubby cheeks stage is over before you know it. Then it's suddenly all about spending hours awake at night wondering where they are and who they're with and what they're doing. I'm not putting myself through that again. No way.'

'What about marriage?' she asked. 'Are you against that too?'

'I'm not against it in principle,' he said. 'I have plenty of friends who are married and it seems to work for them. I just don't think I'm cut out for it. I think I'd get bored with the same person.'

'Maybe you haven't met the right person yet.'

He shrugged indifferently. 'Maybe.'

They'd walked halfway along the next block when Jake suddenly stopped and turned to look at her. 'Have you had dinner?' he asked.

'No, I was just about to get some when I saw you.'

'Have dinner with me.'

She arched a brow at him. 'Are you asking or telling me?'

'Are you refusing or accepting?'

'I'm thinking about it.'

'What's to think about?' he asked. 'You're hungry and you need food.'

'It's not that simple…'

'Are you worried about the boyfriend back home in Britain?'

Kitty avoided his penetrating gaze. 'It has nothing to do with Charles,' she said. 'I don't want people to talk.'

'They're already talking,' he said. 'Besides, what's one casual dinner going to do?' He stopped outside a bar and grill restaurant. 'Is this OK? A friend of mine owns it. He'll squeeze us in without a booking.'

Kitty met his impossibly blue gaze with her guarded one. 'So it's not a date or anything?' she asked.

'No,' he said, giving her a glinting smile. 'I'd have to pay my sister a thousand bucks if so.'

Kitty tried not to blush but with little success. 'So an official date with you usually leads to sex, does it?'

He held the door of the restaurant open for her. 'It depends.'

'On what?'

'Chemistry. Animal attraction. Lust.'

Kitty pursed her lips disapprovingly even though her skin tingled and prickled as his gaze held hers. 'What about getting to know someone as a person first?' she asked. 'Finding common ground, similar values and interests, mutual admiration and respect?'

His gaze moved from her eyes to her mouth. Something shifted in the pit of her belly as his eyes meshed with hers once more. Their dark glittering intensity triggered a primal response she had no control over. Fluttery fairy-soft footsteps of excitement danced along the floor of her stomach at the thought of him pressing that sinfully sensual mouth against hers, having his arms go around her and crush her to his hard tall frame, feeling his arousal potent and persistent against the yielding softness of her body. She drew in a little shuddering breath, wondering if he could sense how deeply affected she was by him.

But of course, she thought.

He was a practised flirt. A charmer—a playboy who loved nothing better than indulging the flesh without the restraints of a formal relationship—a born seducer who loved and left his partners without a second thought.

Falling in love with him would be the biggest mistake of her life. She knew it and yet there was something about him that drew her inexorably to him. She felt the magnetic force of him even now. The way his gaze tethered her to him, those ocean-blue depths communicating without words the desire that crackled like an electrical current between them.

'I find out just about all I need to know about the other person with the first kiss,' he said.

'Oh, really?'

'You'd be surprised how much information that reveals.'

Kitty gave him an arch look. 'You mean other than the flavour of their toothpaste?'

He smiled that glinting smile. 'Having dinner with them is another revelation,' he said. 'Picky eaters tend to have body issues. A healthy appetite is a good sign, but someone who is keen to try different cuisines or exotic flavours gets my attention every time.'

Kitty felt heat rise up from the soles of her feet to her face. What would he think of her cardboard meals of late? 'You seem to have it down to a science,' she said.

'Hey, Jake!' A stocky blond-haired man came over with a twinkling smile on his face. 'A cosy, romantic table for two?'

Kitty gave Jake a look. 'How many times have you been here?'

'Lost count,' Jake said, and grinned at his mate. 'How're you doing, Brad? Hot in the kitchen?'

'That's why I'm out here,' Brad said, and smiling at Kitty added, 'So this is...?'

'Dr Kitty Cargill,' Jake said.

Brad's eyebrows lifted. 'Bringing work home with you, Jake?'

'It's not what you think,' Jake said.

'Sure,' Brad said with a grin. 'Follow me. I have just the table for you.'

Once Brad had left them settled with drinks, Kitty met Jake's gaze across the small intimate table that was positioned in the quietest part of the restaurant. 'Let me guess,' she said. 'At about ten p.m. or so a woman will come past the table selling roses.'

He gave her a slanting smile. 'Do you want one?'

'Certainly not!'

He reached over to top up her water glass from the frosted bottle on the table. 'So, tell me about Charles.'

Kitty watched as the bubbles from the mineral water rose in a series of vertical lines like tiny necklaces to the surface of her glass. 'There's not much to tell,' she said. 'We grew up together. I can't think of a time in my life when Charles hasn't been a part of it. We did everything together. I thought we'd continue to do everything together.' She released a little sigh and met Jake's gaze. 'I was so busy planning our future that I didn't notice what was going on in the present.'

'Do you still love him?'

Kitty looked at the bubbles again, her finger tracing the dew on the outside of the glass. 'I think there's a part of me that will always love Charles,' she said. 'I loved his family too. I liked that they were so…so normal. I felt at home with them. I blended in as if I had always been there.'

She looked up to find his dark blue gaze centred on hers. He had a way of looking at her that made her whole body break out in a shiver. She became aware of every cell of her skin, from the top of her tingling scalp, right to the very soles of her feet.

She gave herself a mental shake and reached for her

wine glass. 'What did your brother want when he came to the unit today?' she asked.

A mask slipped over his features. 'I thought we were talking about you,' he said.

'We were,' she said. 'But now it's your turn to talk about you.'

'What if I don't want to talk about me?'

'Then talk about your brother.'

He frowned as he reached for his own wine glass, but he didn't drink from it. He just sat there twirling the stem round and round between his finger and thumb. 'I hate talking about my brother,' he said. 'Talking doesn't change anything. He's a fully-grown adult and yet just lately he's been acting like a kid. He used to have a part-time job to fund his way through university, but he lost that over some run-in with the boss. He's been putting the hard word on Rosie and Jen for money and when he's really getting desperate he comes to me.'

'Where does he live?'

'In some doss house in the inner city,' he said, scraping a hand through his hair. He made a despairing sound. 'My kid brother bunks down with every other desperado on the streets. My mother is probably spinning in her grave.'

Kitty put out a hand and touched his arm. His muscles flexed then stilled under her touch.

After a long moment his eyes met hers. 'Do you know what gets me?' he asked. 'He had everything going so well. He was a straight A student. He was up for a university prize in engineering. He's so damn bright—much brighter than me. I've had to work damn hard to get where I've got. But he's thrown it all away. It's such a damn waste.'

'Is he doing drugs?' Kitty asked.

He rubbed a hand over his face. 'I don't know if he's touched the hard stuff. He says not, but how can I trust him? He probably doesn't remember from one day to the next what he's been doing.'

'What about rehab?' she asked.

His eyes hit hers. 'You think I haven't tried that?' he asked. 'I even paid up-front for a private clinic, but he didn't show up on admission day. I couldn't find him for a fortnight. The clinic had a waiting list a mile long so I couldn't get him in even when I found him.'

'Sometimes it's hard for family members to be the ones to help,' Kitty said. 'You're too close and they don't always want to listen.'

His fingers tightened around the stem of his glass. 'The sick irony is I've spent the last twenty-four years of my life being a substitute father for my sisters and brother,' he said. 'Don't get me wrong—I was glad to be able to do something. My mother wanted each of us to have better opportunities than she'd had. It was up to me to see that her vision for us as a family was fulfilled.'

'That's why you've never travelled, isn't it?' Kitty asked.

'I had a ticket booked once.' He gave her a brief glance before focussing on the contents of his glass. 'I had all my siblings sorted, or so I thought. I was going to head off to Europe for a couple of months. Kick my heels up a bit, have a life, have some fun without the pressure of responsibility.'

'What happened?'

He looked at her again, the line of his mouth grim. 'Rosie came to me late one night and told me she was pregnant. She'd known for weeks but had been too scared to tell me. She was just nineteen years old. Still a kid herself. I couldn't leave her to deal with that, even for a couple of months. I didn't want her to feel pressured into a termination. I wanted her to feel supported in whatever she decided to do. Her boyfriend was useless. And what sort of brother would I be if I just flew out of the country at a time like that?'

'From what I can tell you've been an amazing brother and uncle,' Kitty said. 'Look at the way you gave that party for her. And then you took your nephew surfing, on top of a full day at work.'

'It's not enough,' he said. 'I can't be there all the time.'

'I'm sure no one expects you to,' she said. 'You're entitled to your own life.'

His eyes came back to hers, a wry smile kicking up the corners of his mouth. 'That's one very soft shoulder you've got there, Dr Cargill,' he said.

Kitty smiled back. 'Glad to be of service.'

It was close to eleven when Jake walked Kitty to the door of her town house. A light sea breeze had come in and taken the stifling heat out of the evening, bringing with it the tang of brine from the ocean.

She stood fumbling with her keys in the lock, conscious of him standing behind her, his tall frame within touching distance of hers. She could smell the hint of lemon in his aftershave. She could even hear his breathing—steady and slow, unlike hers, which was skittering all over the place.

'Do you want me to unlock it for you?' he asked.

'No, I'm fine… Oh, damn,' she said as she dropped her keys with a loud clatter to the tiled floor.

He bent down, scooped them off the floor and

handed them to her. His fingers brushed against her open palm, sending electric shocks right up her arm. 'You don't need to be nervous, Dr Cargill,' he said.

'Nervous?' Kitty tucked a strand of hair behind her ear, her tongue sneaking out quickly to moisten her mouth. 'Why on earth would I be nervous?'

He smiled at her. It was the tiniest movement of his lips and yet it unravelled her insides like a skein of wool thrown by a spin-bowler. 'When was the last time you asked a man in for coffee?' he asked.

She tore her gaze away from his sexily slanted mouth. 'When I was in junior high,' she said. 'But it wasn't for coffee. It was for orange juice.'

'Cute.'

Kitty unlocked the door and then faced him. 'I have coffee if you'd like some,' she said, waving a hand in the vague direction of the kitchen.

His sapphire gaze glinted. 'Got any orange juice?'

'Fresh or reconstituted?'

'You can't beat fresh,' he said as he closed the door behind him with a soft click. 'It tastes completely different.'

'I can never tell the difference,' she said, with a huskiness that was nothing like her usual dulcet tones. 'But then, I guess I'm not much of an orange juice connoisseur.'

The space in the foyer seemed to shrink now that he shared it with her. The air seemed to tighten, to crackle and vibrate with an energy that made the hairs on her head push away from her scalp. The skin on her arms went up in goosebumps and her stomach pitched and tilted as he closed the distance between them with a single step.

His hooded gaze zeroed in on her mouth as he planted a hand on the wall beside her head. 'This is the part where you're supposed to ask me what the hell I think I'm doing,' he said in a gravel-rough tone.

'I am?'

'Yeah,' he said. 'But since you missed your cue maybe we can jump ahead to the next bit.'

Kitty's heart flapped like a shredded truck tyre on tarmac. 'What's the next bit?' she asked in a soft whisper.

His warm minty breath caressed her parted lips as he inched closer and closer. 'Why don't I show you?' he said, and then he sealed her mouth with his.

CHAPTER EIGHT

KITTY felt a shockwave ripple through her body when his lips made that first contact with hers. His lips moved against hers in a slow, sensual manner, tasting, teasing and tempting her into a heated response that made the base of her spine melt like butter and every hair on her head tremble with delight. His kiss was soft and experimental, a tantalising assault on her senses that made her skin tauten all over in fiery response.

He threaded his hands through her hair, his fingers splaying over her tingling scalp as he scorched the seam of her mouth with the bold stroke of his tongue.

She opened to him and the world exploded in a burst of colour and leaping flares of searing heat. His tongue tangled with hers in a sexy dance that made her heart race and her belly flip and then flop.

This was no tame boy-next-door kiss. This was a man's kiss—the kiss of a full-blooded man who wanted sex and wanted it *now*.

Kitty felt the ridge of hard male desire against her quivering belly. She felt the instinctual, primal tug of her flesh towards it. She shifted her body against his, her heart skipping a beat when she heard the deep sound of male approval come from his throat.

Her breasts were jammed up against the hard plane of his chest. She had never been so aware of them before. They swelled and strained behind the lace cage of her bra, hungry for more intimate contact.

She shivered when his hands went to her hips, holding her closer to the cradle of his pelvis. Every delicious male inch of him was imprinted on her flesh. She felt the pounding roar of his blood through his clothes. It echoed the rampant need that was surging inside her.

His mouth continued its fiery exchange with hers, his tongue calling hers into a brazen tango that mimicked the need charging through his body as well as her own.

He shifted one of his hands from her hips to the small of her back, the subtle pressure sending her senses into a crazy spin. Desire licked along her flesh like a trail of racing flames, her need as insistent as a tribal drumbeat deep inside her body.

His hand on her hip moved upwards in a slow-moving caress that stopped just below her right breast. She felt her nerves tighten in awareness. The tingling and twitching of her flesh was almost unbearable. She pressed herself against him in a silent signal of female want, a desperate plea for him to satisfy the deepest yearnings of her body.

Kitty kissed him back with brazen hunger. Her lips nibbled and nipped at his. Her tongue swirled and circled and swept against his in a sensual combat that made her spine turn to liquid. He fought back with another deep groan of approval and pulled her even closer to the rampant need of his body.

She fisted a hand in his shirt and he plunged deeper into her mouth, his strongly muscled thighs moving against hers to nudge her back against the wall. The body-to-body contact fuelled her desire to an unmanageable level. She pushed herself up on tiptoe so she could feel more of his hard heat against her feminine need. Her insides melted and pulsed with longing. Desire was like a runaway train. It was flashing past every station, siding or level crossing of caution and common sense she had erected in her brain.

Jake lifted his mouth off hers and looked down at her, his expression darkly satirical. 'Well, I guess that clears up that little detail,' he said.

Kitty blinked herself out of her sensual daze and stepped out of his hold. She tucked a strand of hair behind her ear, feeling gauche and flustered. 'I'm not sure what you mean,' she said.

His mouth kicked up in a wry smile. 'You're not the shy, uptight type after all, are you?'

Kitty pressed her lips together for a moment. 'I'm sure I don't need to tell you you're a very good kisser.'

'You pack a pretty awesome punch yourself, Dr Cargill,' he said.

She tried to act casual about it, affecting a pose of indifference that belied the turmoil she felt inside. 'Do you still want coffee?'

He reached out and passed one of his bent knuckles over the curve of her cheek in a light caress, his eyes so dark she couldn't tell where his pupils began and ended. 'You don't really think I came in here for coffee, do you?' he asked.

Kitty swept the tip of her tongue over her kiss-swollen lips, her heart skipping all over the place. 'I guess not...'

He held her gaze captive for a long heart-stopping moment. 'I want you.'

The blunt statement shocked and yet thrilled her. Charles had waited *years* before asking her to sleep with him. 'But for how long?' she asked.

'That's not a question anyone can answer specifically,' he said. 'Relationships run their course. Some last days, others weeks, others years.'

She toyed with a button on his shirt rather than meet his gaze. 'Yours don't last years, though, do they?' she said.

It seemed a long time before he answered. 'I'm not promising anything long-term, Kitty. You're only here until the end of April. It wouldn't be fair to pretend this could turn into an affair of a lifetime.'

Kitty raised her eyes to his. 'Because you don't want to fall in love.'

'You don't have to be in love with someone to have great sex,' he said. 'Aren't your parents proof of that?'

Her shoulders went down on a little sigh as she moved away. 'I'm not like my parents,' she said. 'I couldn't bear to live the way they do. I don't want to play musical beds with faceless strangers. I want security. I want love. I want marriage and babies and happy ever after.'

He gave a cynical crack of laughter. 'You want a fairytale that doesn't exist in the real world. Fifty percent of marriages end up in divorce. The other fifty live snappily ever after.'

She threw him an exasperated look. 'There's no point arguing with you. I can see you've collated enough evidence to support your cynical take on things. But there are plenty of relationships that last the distance. I see them all the time in A&E. Old couples who've spent a whole lifetime loving each other. I *want* that. I want to be with someone for my whole life—not a month here or there or a measly week or two.'

'Then I'm not your man,' he said, his expression stony, his voice even harder. 'I'm happy to have a bit of fun, but don't expect anything else from me.'

Kitty held that steely blue gaze. 'I feel sorry for men like you, Jake. You have plenty of fun now, but what about later? What about when you're old and sick and no one wants you any more?'

A muscle flexed in his jaw. 'I'll take my chances.'

'You'll end up lonely and alone,' she said. 'You'll have no shared memories of the phases of life you've journeyed through. No children to share your genes. No grandchild—'

'Look,' he said, cutting her short. 'I get what you're saying. Do you think I haven't thought through all of that? Of course I have. I just can't make promises I'm not sure I'll be able to keep.'

Kitty nailed him with a flinty look. 'You don't *want* to make promises.'

He held her gaze for a second or two before he blew out a breath on a long exhale. He tipped up her chin using two fingers, while his thumb moved back and forth over the cushion of her bottom lip. 'It wouldn't work, you know,' he said. 'You. Me. Us. You're too innocent for someone as hard-boiled as me. I'd end up walking all over you.'

'I know how to take care of myself.'

'Do you, Kitty?' he asked looking at her intently. 'Do you really?'

Her heart tripped as his gaze centred on her mouth. Heat pooled in her belly and her legs felt that betraying tremble again. 'Of course I do,' she said. 'I'm a big girl now.'

He brushed an imaginary hair away from her face. 'Even big girls can get their hearts broken.'

'So can big boys.'

He gave her a twisted smile as he reached for the door. 'Not this big boy.'

'You're not truly alive if you don't allow yourself to be open to happiness and to hurt,' she said. 'It's what makes life so rich and rewarding—the highs and the lows and all the bits in between.'

'Goodnight, Dr Cargill,' he said. 'Sweet dreams.'

Kitty blew out a breath when the door clicked shut behind him. 'Watch it, my girl,' she said in an undertone. 'Just watch it, OK?'

'Where's Kitty?' Gwen asked, looking past Jake's shoulders when he arrived at the new staff welcome drinks on Friday night. 'I thought she might be coming with you.'

Jake took one of the light beers off a tray that was being handed around by one of the interns. 'Then you thought wrong,' he said.

Gwen angled her head at him. 'What's going on with you two?'

'Nothing.' He took a sip of froth off the top of his beer.

'You had dinner with her,' Gwen said. 'Brad told me when I had lunch with my daughter at the grill yesterday.'

He shrugged. 'So?'

'Don't break her heart, Jake.'

'I have no intention of doing any such thing.'

'She's not your type.'

Jake frowned as he put his beer on the chest-high drinks stand beside him. 'That's surely up to her to decide, isn't it?'

Gwen lifted her brows. 'I'm just saying.'

'Then don't,' he said, shooting her a look.

'How is Robbie?'

He shifted his gaze, his left hand tightening to a fist inside his trouser pocket. 'I'd rather not talk about my brother right now.'

'You never want to talk about him, Jake,' Gwen said. 'You used to chat about him all the time. How well he was doing. How nice it was to have him drop by with his friends. What's going on? Is he in some sort of trouble?'

Jake glared at her. 'Leave it, Gwen, OK? I don't want everyone talking about what a crap job I've done of watching out for my brother. He's an adult. I can't control him any more.'

'No one could possibly criticise you for what you've done for your family, Jake,' she said gently.

He let out a weary breath. 'Sorry, Gwen,' he said. 'I know you mean well. It's just that things are pretty tough right now. Robbie's being so irresponsible. I don't know how to handle him any more. It's like I'm dealing with someone else entirely.'

'Jim and I had a rough trot with one of our boys a few years back,' Gwen said. 'Matt gave us a couple of years of hell but he eventually grew out of it. Maybe Robbie's just going through a similar thing.'

Jake looked at her. 'When he first started acting up I thought he was sick or something,' he said. 'It was so out of character for him to be partying hard and neglecting his studies.'

'Did he see a doctor?'

'Yeah,' he said. 'I sent him to his GP for a battery of tests.'

'All clear?'

'Apparently,' he said. 'He didn't show me the scans. He said the GP told him there was nothing wrong. It was a long shot in any case. I've met stacks of parents of wayward kids who've insisted there must be something clinically wrong. It's the first thing you think of. No one wants to think their kid or brother or sister wilfully chooses to go and stuff up their life.'

'It's a stage a lot of young people seem to go through these days,' Gwen said. 'They like to kick up their heels before they settle down. Robbie's a good lad. You've always done the right thing by him. Hopefully he'll sort himself out before too much longer.'

'Yeah,' Jake said on another sigh. 'That what I'm hoping.'

'Aren't you supposed to be at the drinks thing tonight?' Cathy Oxley asked in A&E.

Kitty leafed through the blood results she had been waiting for. 'Yes, but I got held up with a patient.'

'All work and no play,' Cathy said in a singsong voice.

Kitty's gaze narrowed in concentration as she looked at the white cell count in front of her.

'Is something wrong?' Cathy asked.

Kitty lowered the sheaf of papers. 'Lara Fletcher,' she said. 'The twenty-four-year-old in Bay Four with breathlessness and swollen ankles. She's been back and forth to her GP for months with a host of vague symptoms. Not once has he or anyone else ordered a blood test. She's been fobbed off by two other medical clinics. One of them even gave her antidepressants, telling her she was depressed.'

'You found something?' Cathy asked, looking over her shoulder.

'Aplastic anaemia,' Kitty said heavily. 'How could that have been missed for all this time?'

'Not everyone is as meticulous as you.'

'All it took was a blood test.'

'Tell that to Jake Chandler next time he bawls you out for over-testing the patients,' Cathy said with a little wink.

'I will,' Kitty said.

'I didn't realise you were working this weekend,' said Trish Wellington, one of the more senior A&E specialists, when Jake came on duty on Saturday evening.

'I'm just doing a fill-in shift for David Godfrey,' Jake said. 'He's going to his sister's wedding.'

'Well, how about that?' Trish said with a speculative smile. 'Kitty Cargill's doing a double tonight. Mike called in sick at the last minute.'

Jake slung his stethoscope around his neck. 'I hope she's not overdoing it,' he said.

Trish leaned against the wall as she toyed with her hospital lanyard. 'She's a sharp little tack, isn't she?'

Jake soaped up his hands at the basin. 'She's competent enough.'

'Pretty little thing,' Trish said. 'Gorgeous grey eyes.'

'Haven't noticed.'

Trish laughed as she pushed herself away from the wall. '*So* glad I've worked here long enough to see it.'

He frowned at her darkly. 'Long enough to see what?' he asked.

She pointed at his chest. 'To see your heart get a run for its money,' she said.

Jake rolled his eyes. 'Oh, for pity's sake.'

'Dr Chandler?'

Jake felt the hairs on his arms lift up when that posh little voice sounded behind him. He turned and looked at Kitty's heart-shaped face looking up at him. She had smudges under her grey eyes and her skin was paler than usual, making the light sprinkling of freckles on her nose stand out.

'Dr Cargill,' he said formally. 'Thanks for doing overtime.'

'That's OK,' she said.

A beat of silence ticked past.

'Was there something else?' he asked.

'I'm sorry I didn't make it to the drinks thing,' she said. 'I hope you didn't think I snubbed...everyone?'

'I was only there for a couple of minutes myself.'

'Oh...' Her expression faltered for a moment. 'Well, I got held up with a patient.'

'Taking down their family tree, were we?' he asked.

Her eyes blinked and then hardened like frost. 'No,' she said. 'I diagnosed a blood disorder that had gone undetected for several months. I lost count of how many GPs the patient had seen. Not one of them performed a blood screen on her.'

'It happens.'

She frowned at him. 'How can it happen? How can someone slip through the cracks like that?'

'GPs are pushed for time just like everyone else in the medical profession,' Jake said. 'The larger medical clinics are problematic because the patient doesn't always see the same doctor each visit. There's not much continuity.'

'Then all the more reason to check and double-check,' she said.

'Testing every patient for every disease is expensive and time-wasting,' he said. 'Diagnostic skills vary between doctors, but mostly they get it right.'

'Not in this case,' she said. 'That young woman's outcome could be severely compromised.'

'We can't save everyone, Dr Cargill,' he said. 'There will always be people who slip through the system.'

'I don't want to miss *anyone*,' she said. 'It's our job to diagnose and treat patients, not fob them off with a couple of painkillers.'

'You can't CT scan every patient who comes through the door,' Jake argued. 'Not on this campus, in any case.'

Her grey eyes challenged his. 'Are you forbidding me from conducting the tests I deem appropriate?' she asked.

'I would hope your diagnostic skills are of a standard such that you don't require exposing a patient to high levels of radiation in order to confirm your diagnosis.'

'I'd rather not leave patients' lives up to gut feeling,' she said with an insolent look.

'What do you mean by that?' he asked.

Her grey eyes flashed at him. 'You can't possibly get it right all of the time,' she said. 'It's not a matter of guesswork or intuition. We have to rely on cold, hard science.'

'The human body isn't an exact science,' he said. 'Patients don't always give a complete history. Tests can be inconclusive. We need to be able to understand anatomy and physiology in order make a correct diagnosis.'

'Will that be all, Dr Chandler?' she asked stiffly.

Jake looked at her mouth and felt a tidal wave of raw, primal need course through him. He couldn't stop thinking about that kiss. He thought of how soft her mouth was, how sweet it had tasted, how yielding it had been, how tentative and shy her tongue had been and then how brazen and uncontrollable it had become when she had let herself go. He thought of how her slim little body had pressed against his as if she had been tailored exactly to his specifications. He thought of how much he wanted to kiss her again, to move his hands over her creamy skin without the barrier of clothes. He wanted to run his hands through the chestnut silk of her hair, to breathe in its flowery fragrance.

He wanted her.

Had he ever wanted someone more? It was this wretched bet, that was what it was. It had to be. He'd been celibate too long. He wasn't cut out for the life of a monk. It wasn't that he was developing an attachment to Kitty. She wasn't staying in Australia long enough to consider anything more than a casual fling. She would probably go back when her term was over and pick up again with someone from her side of the tracks—not someone with dependent siblings, not to mention the debt and drama that came along for the ride.

If she hooked up with him it would be a package deal. How long before she would get sick of sharing him with his siblings and nephew? His career was demanding enough. Having to spread himself so thinly didn't make for ideal relationship-building conditions. He wasn't emotionally available. He didn't want to be.

He didn't want to need someone so much he couldn't function without them. He had seen it first-hand. His mother had been absolutely devastated by the desertion of his father. Jake had lain awake at night listening to her sob her heart out in the bedroom next door. It had taken her years to recover, and even then there had been a part of her that had never fully returned. She had gone from a vibrant and fully engaged mother to a person who trudged through life with resolution rather than joy.

Jake brought his gaze to Kitty's defiant one. 'That will be all, Dr Cargill,' he said. 'For now.'

CHAPTER NINE

'So how's it going with your gorgeous boss?' Julie asked when she phoned Kitty a couple of days later.

'Next question.'

Julie laughed. 'That bad, huh?'

Kitty paced the kitchen of her town house. 'He's the most maddening man I've ever met,' she said. 'I thought I was getting to know him a little bit. He's really nice when he's not playing the big bad boss. He was really supportive when we had this crazy emergency outside the hospital the other day. And he even told me about his family circumstances over dinner, and—'

'Dinner?' Julie said. 'Hey, back up a bit. You didn't tell me you had dinner with him. When was that?'

'It wasn't a date or anything,' Kitty said. 'We ran into each other and it sort of…happened.'

'What sort of happened?'

Kitty closed her mind to that kiss. 'Nothing happened,' she said. 'We just had a meal at his friend's restaurant.'

'And then?'

'And then he walked me home.'

'Did he kiss you?' Julie asked.

'What makes you think he would've kissed me?' Kitty asked.

'He's a man.'

'I'd rather not talk about it.'

'So he *did* kiss you,' Julie said. 'How was it?'

'I told you I'm not going to talk about it.'

'I bet it was completely different from Charles.'

'I'm not listening,' she said in a singsong tone.

'Are you going to see him again?' Julie asked.

'I can hardly avoid it when he works at the same hospital, can I?'

'I mean see him as in *see* him.'

Kitty thought of how distant and formal Jake had been the other night at the hospital. It had been a stark turnaround from the intimate exchange they had shared. It was as if he had regretted talking to her about his family circumstances and his brother's situation in particular. He had lowered his guard just long enough for her to glimpse some of his pain and frustration, but he had snapped the drawbridge back up as soon as he could, locking her out. He was prepared to offer her a no-strings relationship but not access to the innermost yearnings of his heart.

'Jake Chandler isn't really interested in me other than as a one-off affair,' she said. 'I haven't been around the block enough times for him. He likes his women casual and carefree.'

'You mark my words,' Julie said. 'It's the cynical ones who always fall for sweet, homespun girls like you. But anyway, why shouldn't you have a little fling with him while you're here? Isn't it time you had a bit of fun? You spent years and years with the same guy, for God's sake. For years you've acted like an old married lady. But you're single now. You can do what you want with whoever you want. This is your chance to let your hair down a bit. Live a little. Put yourself out there. You're only twenty-six. There'll be plenty of time for settling down with Mr Right later on. What have you got to lose?'

'I don't want to get hurt,' Kitty said.

'You take life way too seriously, Kitty-Kat,' Julie said. 'You always have. You're allowed to have sex without being in love with someone, you know. And you don't need a ring on your finger, either.'

Kitty looked at the promise ring that was too tight on her hand. Was it time to put the past aside and do as her cousin said?

Kitty was on her way to her first practice session with the combined hospitals doctors' orchestra she had been invited to join when her car refused to start. The engine coughed and spluttered and then died. She turned the key again, but this time there was only a clicking sound—and a faint one at that.

'I don't believe this,' she muttered. 'Why are you doing this to me now?'

A shadow blocked out the driver's side window. 'Need any help?' Jake asked.

She clenched her hands on the steering wheel and stared straight ahead. 'If you're going to say "I told you so", then please don't.'

'Wouldn't dream of it.'

She blew out a breath and threw him a frustrated glance. 'I can't get my car to start.'

'Want me to have a look?'

'Be my guest,' she said, cranking open the driver's door. She squeezed out past him, her body tingling where it brushed against his in the confined space between her car and the wall.

He sat in the driver's seat and turned on the ignition while his foot gave the throttle a couple of pumps. 'Sounds like a blockage in the fuel line.' He leaned down and popped the bonnet lever. 'I'll have a quick look under the hood.'

Kitty sucked in her tummy as he moved past her. He looked so vital and male dressed in a black T-shirt and chinos. Every muscle looked as if it had been carved to his torso by a master sculptor. He smelt like summer—a mixture of surf and sweat, sunscreen and aftershave. She wanted to run her hands down the muscular slope of his back and shoulders, to press her mouth to his and feel him shudder with need.

Maybe her cousin was right. What would be so wrong about indulging her senses for once? What harm would there be in a relationship with him, even if it was on his terms? Wasn't it time she lived a little? It wasn't as if she had to be as progressive as her parents. Even a short-term relationship could be exclusive. She wouldn't settle for anything less. It was just so tempting to explore the chemistry she shared with Jake. What if she never felt this level of excitement again? She would regret it for the rest of her life. She would spend the rest of her days wondering what she'd missed out on. She would have no memories of his possession. No images in her head of their bodies entwined in passion. Her body would never know the full extent of its sensual response in his arms.

She *wanted* to know.

'Want to give it another try?' Jake called out.

Kitty snapped out of her reverie and turned the ignition. The engine choked and spluttered and then died. 'Am I doing something wrong?' she asked.

'No,' he said, coming round to her side as he wiped his hands on a handkerchief. 'The fuel line was definitely blocked but it sounds like your battery's had it as well. I can hook it up to my charger overnight.'

'But I have to get to my practice session,' she said, frowning at him in worry. 'I've joined a local doctors' orchestra. It's our first session tonight.'

'I can give you a lift.'

Kitty gnawed at her lip. 'What if people see me getting out of your car?'

A smile lifted the edges of his mouth. 'I promise not to kiss you goodbye, OK?'

She gave him a guarded look. 'How do I know if I can trust you on that?' she asked.

His sapphire-blue gaze flicked to her mouth for a heartbeat. 'You can't,' he said, and then turned and led the way to his car.

Jake pulled up outside the church hall where the orchestra was rehearsing in the suburb of Annandale on the other side of the city. 'How long will you be?' he asked.

'You don't have to wait for me,' Kitty said. 'I'll get one of the other doctors to drop me off near a bus stop or a cab rank.'

'I don't mind waiting,' he said, putting on the handbrake. 'Even better, why don't I come in and listen?'

'It's probably not to your taste.'

He gave her a sardonic smile. 'A little too highbrow for someone like me, huh?'

She tightened her mouth. 'I didn't say that.'

'I've heard about this orchestra but I've never been

to any of their concerts,' he said. 'Maybe it's time I stretched my horizons a bit.'

'Please don't feel you have to do so on my account,' she said. 'I'm quite happy to make my own arrangements.'

He got out of the car and came around to open her door for her. 'I've got nothing better to do this evening,' he said.

Kitty tried to concentrate on the conductor's beat but her gaze kept drifting to where Jake was sitting in the stalls. He kept smiling at her in that indolent way of his, making her fingers fumble over the notes like a nervous schoolgirl at her first school concert. But about halfway through the rehearsal she noticed him glance at his phone. It must have been important because he got up and left the hall and it was at least ten or fifteen minutes before he came back.

'That's it, everyone,' the conductor said as the session drew to an end. 'Same time next week if you can make it.'

Kitty made her way to where Jake was chatting to a couple of the doctors he had introduced her to earlier. 'Thanks for waiting,' she said, once they had moved on. 'I hope you weren't too bored.'

'Not at all,' he said. 'I found it relaxing. I had no idea you could play like that.'

'I'm not that good,' she said. 'I need to do much more practice.'

'Well, from my end it certainly didn't sound as if any cats were being tortured.'

She gave him a sideways glance. 'Thanks.'

'How long have you been playing?'

'I started when I was six,' she said. 'My parents wanted me to experiment with a whole range of instruments, but I only ever wanted to play the violin. I finally wore them down.'

He gave her a crooked smile as he led the way out to the car. 'Not many kids nag their parents to learn a classical instrument,' he said. 'Isn't it normally the other way around?'

'I know,' Kitty said wryly. 'I think I'm a throwback. My parents are quite ashamed of me for being so conservative. I haven't got a single piercing or a tattoo. I don't even dye my hair.'

'Why would you want to?' he said. 'It's fine the way it is.'

'It's boring.'

He stopped, reaching out and picking up a stray lock of her hair. He coiled it around his finger. 'It's not boring,' he said. 'It's beautiful—especially when it's loose like this.'

Kitty felt the voltage of his touch all the way down the shafts of her hair to the skin of her sensitive scalp. The skin on her body tingled in sharpened awareness as he came that little bit closer.

Her breasts tightened behind her clothes.

Her breath stalled in her throat.

Her pulse rate escalated.

Her mind turned to mush.

The warm fragrant night air cast its spell of seduction around her, making her forget everything but the way his mouth had felt on hers. She felt the hard tug of attraction deep in the pit of her belly, pulling her towards his body like a magnet does a tiny iron filing.

'I should get you home,' he said as he stepped back from her.

'Yes…I've taken up far too much of your time as it is.'

Kitty was acutely aware of him sitting so close to her inside the confines of his car. Her gaze kept tracking to his tanned arm as it worked the gear shift. And his muscular thigh as it bunched and released when he pressed down on the clutch. She imagined those muscles in the throes of passion. She imagined those hands exploring her body, touching her in places that made the breath hitch in her throat. She remembered the intimate stroke of his tongue and wondered what it would feel like to have it lick and stroke her breasts or between her thighs. She had never felt comfortable enough to allow Charles to explore her so intimately. But somehow she sensed that nothing would be off-limits to Jake Chandler. He would be a masterful and exciting lover—and a demanding one. She had felt it in that disturbingly erotic kiss. Her body had responded with such fervency to the head-spinning experience of his mouth commandeering hers. It had probably been just another kiss to him, but to her it had been a revelation. It had shown her how out of control her needs could be given the right inducement.

She had never thought of herself as a particularly passionate person. She had put her lacklustre love-life with Charles down to a mixture of long-term familiarity and the exhausting demands of their careers. But in Jake Chandler's arms she had been transformed into a wild woman with even wilder needs. She thought again of what would happen if she gave in to those needs. So many young women her age enjoyed casual flings. It was part of life these days. She was becoming a bit of an anachronism with her white picket fence and pram mentality. Why couldn't she have the same freedom as other girls her age? It wasn't as if she had to fall in love with him. He was hardly likely to fall in love with her. Could she be brave enough to step out of her comfort zone and live a little?

Jake's phone rang and he answered it via the Bluetooth device on the steering wheel. 'Jake Chandler.'

'Hi, Jake, it's Tiffany. Remember me?'

'Tiffany…' He scratched his jaw. 'From the gym, right?'

The woman gave a tinkling laugh. 'That's the one,' she said. 'Are you up for a drink some time?'

Kitty rolled her eyes and looked out of the window, a fist of jealousy clutching at her insides. What a silly fool she had been to think he would wait patiently for her to make up her mind.

Of course he wouldn't wait.

He probably had a waiting list of potential lovers. She was just a temporary diversion from his usual list of candidates. Her temporary appointment at St Benedict's gave him a perfect get-out clause—a three-month affair with no strings.

'Yeah, why not?' Jake was saying. 'How about tomorrow at Brad's place? Shall we say around nine?'

'Lovely,' the woman said. 'I'll look forward to it.'

'See you then, Tiffany,' he said. *'Ciao.'*

Kitty threw him a look of disgust. 'You could have at least waited until I was out of the car before you planned your next seduction.'

'We're just meeting for a drink,' he said.

'You don't even remember who she is, do you?'

'I can picture her,' he said, frowning as if trying to recall. 'Blonde hair, long legs, nice smile.'

'Have you slept with her?'

'Not yet.'

Kitty's insides clenched again. 'What's stopping you?'

'There's the little matter of a thousand bucks, for one thing,' he said. 'I'm not going to lose a bet like that unless I'm sure it's going to be worth it.'

Did he think *she* would be worth it? Kitty wondered. Could it be possible that he found her just as exciting and tempting as she found him? It had certainly felt that way while he was kissing her. She had felt the powerful charge of his desire. His body had left an imprint on hers she could feel even now.

'And the other thing is I like to be the one who does the chasing,' he added.

'Isn't that a little old fashioned of you?'

He flashed her a quick grin as he swung his car into the car park. 'Look who's talking, Miss Nineteenth Century.'

As soon as the car drew to a halt Kitty opened the passenger door. 'Thank you for taking me,' she said stiffly. 'I hope I didn't disrupt your plans for tonight too much.'

'It was fine,' he said. 'I enjoyed myself.'

'Goodnight.'

He waved a hand. ''Night.'

CHAPTER TEN

'STUPID, stupid, *stupid*,' Kitty berated herself as she cleansed her face in her bathroom a few minutes later. 'What were you thinking?' She grabbed a bunch of tissues and savagely wiped off her cleanser. 'Miss Nineteenth Century. What a jerk!'

The doorbell sounded.

Kitty tossed the tissues in the bin and went down to open the door—to find Jake standing there with her violin case.

'You forgot something,' he said, holding the case out to her.

'Oh…' She took it from him with a sheepish look. 'Thanks.'

'I called my mate about your car,' he said. 'I told him I'd drop it off at his workshop once I get the battery charged.'

'Thank you, but I don't want to put you to any more trouble.'

'No problem,' he said.

Kitty went to close the door but he put a foot out to stop it from closing. 'Aren't you going to ask me in for a coffee or something?' he asked.

'I'm sure you've had much better offers this evening,' she said with a speaking look.

'Phone's been running hot, but I thought I'd have a quiet one tonight.'

'Good for you.' She pushed against the door again. 'Do you mind?'

His gaze ran over her teddy bear pyjamas. 'Am I keeping you out of bed?'

'Not at all,' she said. 'It's not even eleven o'clock.'

'Then let's have a nightcap,' he said. 'You owe me one for driving you all that way tonight.'

She stepped back from the door. 'You said it wasn't a problem.'

'It wasn't. But then I found your violin case. The least you could do is offer me a drink for delivering it to your door.'

She blew out a breath of resignation. 'What would you like?' she asked.

'What are you having?'

Kitty hoped he couldn't see the milk and choc-chip cookies she had laid out on the table for her supper. 'I was thinking about a glass of wine,' she said, surreptitiously blocking his view of the kitchen. 'Do you like red or white?'

'What have you got open?'

'Nothing as yet,' she said. 'I'm not a big drinker.'

'Then don't open anything on my account.'

'I have a bottle of red one of the patients gave me,' she said. 'They dropped it off the other day.'

'It's nice when they do that,' he said. 'We patch them up and move them on, but now and again someone recognises what we actually do.'

Kitty handed him a glass of the wine. 'It's one of the downsides of working in A&E,' she said. 'We only see them the once and they move on.'

'I think it's one of the good sides,' he said. 'You don't have to get too involved.'

She studied him for a moment as he took a sip of his wine. 'Your professional life has a lot in common with your private one,' she said. 'Both are full of brief encounters where no feelings get involved.'

'Works for me.'

'Don't you get tired of that sea of nameless faces coming and going in your life?'

He took another measured sip of his wine. 'Nope.'

'But it's so selfish and…and so pointless,' she said. 'How can you not feel something for the women you sleep with?'

One of his shoulders rose and fell in an offhand shrug. 'Guess I'm not built that way.'

'So it's just sex,' she said with a disparaging look. 'Nothing more than inserting Item A in Slot B.'

His mouth tilted. 'I have a little more finesse than your charming description allows,' he said. 'But then, perhaps your own experience has somewhat limited your outlook.'

Kitty felt a blush steal over her face and neck. 'I have enough experience to know that sex is not just a physical connection,' she said. 'It's a deeply emotional experience.'

'Clearly your boyfriend didn't find it so emotionally satisfying, otherwise why did he find someone else?'

She threw him an arctic glare. 'I think it might be time for you to leave.'

He held her look with a cynical glitter in his eye. 'You need to grow up, Kitty,' he said. 'You're a young, fanciful girl in a woman's body. Life isn't a fairytale. There are no handsome princes out there who'll declare undying love for you and carry you off into the sunset. There are no fairy godmothers to make everything turn out right in the end. There are no genies in bottles, no magic spells, and sure as hell there are precious few happy ever afters.'

Kitty folded her arms imperiously. 'Are you done?'

The air crackled with electric tension as dark blue eyes warred with grey.

'No,' he said, eyes glittering as he closed the distance between them in one stride. 'Not quite.'

She took a step backwards as he came towards her but the sofa was in the way. She gave a little startled gasp as his strong hands gripped her by the upper arms, pulling her to him. Her body jolted with sensual energy when it came into contact with his. It was like a dead battery being plugged into a power source. Currents of energy flowed through her, kick-starting her senses into throbbing, pulsing life. His mouth came down and blazed with furnace-hot heat against hers. As the kiss progressed in intensity raw need licked along her flesh like trails of runaway fire. Desire pooled in her belly, hot and liquid, melting her to the backbone. His tongue thrust boldly into her mouth, commanding and conquering, demanding and deliciously, dangerously male.

For a moment, a mere nanosecond, she thought about resisting. But the feel of his tongue weaving seductively around hers was her undoing. She wound her arms around his neck, leaning into his kiss, giving back, responding in an unabashed way she wouldn't have believed possible just a few days ago. Red-hot need rose in her like a hungry beast waking after a long hibernation. It roared from deep within her, great primal bellows of unmet wants that refused to be ignored and denied or suppressed any longer.

Her fingers delved deep into the thick pelt of his hair. His hard chest wall abraded her breasts as she pressed herself closer and closer. She felt the swelling ridge of his erection against her feminine mound, a tantalising reminder of his power and strength and her primitive need to yield to it.

One of his hands pressed against the small of her back and the other went to her hair, his fingers splaying against her scalp as he kissed her deeply and urgently.

Her tongue played cat and mouse with his. She brazenly teased and tantalised him with darting, flicking movements of her own. He took control back from her with another shift in position. His hand went from her hair to her breast, cupping it possessively, his palm moulding its contour with sensual expertise.

Kitty was breathless with escalating need. She hadn't realised her breasts could feel quite so sensitive. The nipples were tight, and aching for more of his touch. As if he read her mind, or indeed her body, he glided his hand up under her pyjama top and captured her naked breast. Lightning bolts of desire zapped through her body at that shamelessly intimate contact. Her nipple budded into his palm; she felt the delicious pressure and wanted more. His thumb moved over the tight nub, back and forth in a mesmerising motion that set every nerve singing.

And then, most shocking of all, he bent his head and took her nipple and its areola into his hot, moist mouth. She clung to him as the world spun, soft little whimpers coming from deep inside her throat as his tongue stroked her into mindlessness.

He moved to her other breast, taking his time over exploring it, teasing it with his teeth and tongue. A shiver scuttled over her flesh—how could her body not have known such exquisite pleasure existed? How could she not have felt such earth-shattering sensations before?

He worked his way back to her mouth, lingering over the sensitive skin of her neck until he claimed her lips once more. This kiss had an undercurrent of desperation to it. She felt his need building, a rampage of want that thundered through his blood. She felt the potent power of him surging against her body. It awoke a primal need inside her to open to him. Her body pulsed and vibrated with a longing so intense it made a mockery of anything she had experienced before. She had never felt such powerful, all-consuming desire. It took over every thought. It blocked out every resistance. It was as if he had unlocked a part of her being she hadn't known existed.

How could it be *her* hands greedily seeking his naked chest underneath his T-shirt?

How could it be *her* mouth responding to his with such reckless abandon?

How could *her* body be rubbing up against his like a shameless wanton?

Suddenly it was over.

He put her from him almost roughly. 'What the hell do you think you're doing?'

Kitty took umbrage at his attitude. 'Me?' she asked. 'You started it!'

He raked a hand through his disordered hair, his breathing still heavy and uneven. 'I know, and now I've stopped it,' he said.

She crossed her arms over her chest. 'I would have stopped it before it went too much further.'

His eyes were like a laser as they held hers. 'You were taking your merry time about it, sweetheart.'

Kitty shot him an icy glare. 'You caught me off guard. It's late and I'm tired and not thinking straight.'

His lip curled mockingly. 'Still think sex is all about emotion?'

She felt her cheeks radiate with colour. 'We didn't have sex.'

'We weren't far off it.'

'I would *never* have let you make love to me.'

He came up close again, capturing her chin between his thumb and forefinger, his eyes holding hers in a hot, tense little lockdown that sent a shudder of reaction all the way down her spine. 'I could've had you flat on your back and screaming all the way to heaven and back and you damn well know it,' he said.

Kitty felt the echo of his incendiary statement deep in the pit of her belly. She wanted to make him take those shamelessly coarse words back. God help her, she wanted those shamelessly coarse words *not* to have a grain of truth in them.

She wrenched out of his hold, rubbing at her chin as if it had been stung. 'You are a loathsome, diabolical, arrogant man,' she said through gritted teeth. 'I detest men like you. You think you can have any woman you want, any time you want, but you can't. You can't have *me*.'

His mouth still had that slant of mockery in place. 'You really shouldn't have thrown down such a delightful little gauntlet,' he said. 'Now I'll have to prove you wrong.'

She held herself stiffly: arms folded, back straight, mouth tight. 'You'd be wasting your time.'

'I don't know about that,' he said as his gaze ran over her indolently. 'It'd sure be fun trying.'

Kitty glowered at him. 'What about your bet?'

'Some rules are made to be broken,' he said. 'Anyway, everyone already thinks we're doing it. Why not do it for real?'

'I'd rather die.'

'You're afraid, aren't you?' he asked. 'You're afraid of being out of your depth in a relationship. That's why you chose a boyfriend you'd known for ages. He was safe and predictable. You could control things with him. But that's not what you need.'

'I hardly think you're the person to tell me what I need,' she tossed back. 'You barely know me.'

'I know you well enough to know that behind that starchy schoolmistress thing you've got going on is a young woman who longs to let her hair down,' he said.

Kitty gave a scathing little laugh. 'And I suppose you think you're exactly the person I should let it down with? Thanks, but no thanks.'

He strode across to the door. 'Let me know if you change your mind,' he said. 'You know where to find me.'

CHAPTER ELEVEN

'WHAT'S wrong with this place?' Julie asked outside Brad's bar and grill the following evening, when they were scouting for somewhere to have dinner.

'I'm not going in *there*,' Kitty said, turning up her nose.

'What's wrong with it? It looks nice, and they have live music.'

'It's a pick-up joint,' Kitty said. 'Let's go somewhere more sophisticated.'

'But I'm thirty and I'm single,' Julie wailed. 'I *need* a pick-up joint.'

'Well, *I* don't.'

'You're single too,' Julie said. 'Or has that changed since we last spoke?'

'I hate men,' Kitty said, scowling. 'They're so shallow and selfish.'

'I know, but that's part of the attraction,' Julie said. 'We're so giving and selfless. It's that whole opposites attract thing. Hey, isn't that your boss?'

Kitty put her head down. 'Keep moving,' she said. 'We'll find another place further along.'

'God, he's even hotter than I remembered,' Julie said. 'Maybe he'll join us. Why don't you invite him?'

'He already has plans,' Kitty said, tugging at Julie's arm. *'Come on.'*

Julie shrugged off Kitty's hand. 'I'm going to thank him for checking me out,' she said. 'I should've thought to drop in a bottle of wine or something. I bet he would've appreciated that.'

'He wouldn't have remembered who you were,' Kitty muttered.

'Hi,' Julie said as she blocked Jake from moving any further along the footpath. 'I'm Kitty's cousin. You saw me in A&E a few days ago.'

'How could I forget?' Jake said with a smile. 'How's the ankle?'

'I'm off the crutches, as you can see,' Julie said. 'How is Kitty shaping up?'

'She's proving to be quite an asset to the team,' he said. 'We wonder now how we managed without her.'

Kitty glowered at him. 'We mustn't keep you,' she said. 'Come on, Julie. Dr Chandler has an important date.'

'She cancelled,' Jake said.

'How dreadfully disappointing for you,' Kitty said.

'You win some, you lose some,' he said with a dismissive shrug. 'Plenty more fish in the sea.'

'So you're putting your line out again this evening?' Kitty asked with a pert look. 'Good luck with that.'

He smiled a lazy smile. 'What about you?' he asked. 'A hot night on the town?'

'I wish,' Julie said, rolling her eyes. 'Why don't you join us?'

'I'm sure Dr Chandler has much better things to do than keep us company,' Kitty said.

'I'd love to join you, but I'm meeting someone,' he said.

Kitty curled her lip. 'That was quick.'

'Yeah,' he said. 'Nothing like the right bait. Works like a charm.'

Kitty looped her arm through her cousin's. 'Don't let us keep you.'

'What was all that about?' Julie asked when they had walked on a bit.

'What do you mean?'

'You were spitting chips at each other,' Julie said. 'I could've cut the air with a knife.'

'That man has a revolving door on his bedroom,' Kitty said in disgust. 'He's the biggest playboy imaginable. He had the gall to set up one of his shallow hook-ups while I was sitting right beside him in the car.'

'What were you doing beside him in his car?'

'It's a long story.'

'Tell me.'

'He took me to my orchestra rehearsal,' she said. 'My car broke down.'

'That was nice of him.'

'He only did it to rub my nose in it.'

'What do you mean?' Julie asked.

'He gave me a lecture about buying secondhand cars,' Kitty said. 'Honestly, you'd think I'd committed a crime. And that was on top of the dressing down he gave me about water restrictions. How was I to know you're not supposed to use a hose to wash your car?'

'I should've told you about that—sorry.'

'It's not *your* fault.'

'It's not his fault, either.'

'Yes, it is,' Kitty said. 'He just loves to lord it over

me. He doesn't like the way I pay attention to detail at work. But I don't have his depth of experience or confidence. I can't just waltz in and diagnose everyone just like that. I need to feel my way.'

'I'm sure he's only trying to help you,' Julie said. 'He seemed quite positive about your being a part of the team when I asked him.'

'He doesn't think I'm up to the task,' Kitty said. 'He thinks I'm scared of being out of my depth.'

'But you are,' Julie said. 'It's what I was telling you the other day. You're a classic control freak. Sooner or later you're going to have to realise you can't control everything in life. Anyway, how boring would that be?'

'I'm perfectly happy with my life the way it is,' Kitty said.

'I wish I could say the same,' Julie said wistfully. 'I wonder if I'll ever meet someone who wants the same things I do.'

Kitty squeezed her cousin's hand. 'That's the fairytale, isn't it? We have to believe, otherwise what hope is there?'

Jake checked his watch yet again. It wasn't the first time his brother had stood him up. He had been left waiting on numerous occasions, but he could never bring himself to leave until he was absolutely sure Robbie wasn't going to show. He always gave him a chance to redeem himself. The psychologists would probably call it enabling behaviour, but what else could he do? Robbie was his flesh and blood. He hated to think of him out on the streets, desperate for food or shelter. He had to do what he could to protect him.

'Got a dollar, mate?' A voice spoke from a bundle of rags on the sidewalk.

Jake fished in his pocket for some money. 'Why are you on the streets?' he asked, dropping the coins in the tin.

'Got nowhere else to go,' the man said, quickly pocketing the money.

'What about shelters?'

'Cost money.'

'What about your family?'

'Don't have no family.'

'Everyone has family,' Jake said.

'Not me,' the guy said. 'You?'

'Yeah,' Jake said. 'They drive me nuts.'

'That's what families do.'

Jake took out his wallet and peeled off a few notes. 'Here,' he said, handing them to him. 'Find yourself a hotel or something. Don't blow it on drugs or drink.'

Kitty padded out to her kitchen early the following morning for a glass of water before her shower. She pulled up the blind on the kitchen window and saw Jake in his own kitchen on the opposite side of the courtyard. He was standing in front of his open refrigerator—and he was naked.

Her eyes drank in the sight of him, all bronzed and buffed, every muscle toned and taut with good health and vigour. He looked as if he had just stepped off a marble plinth in a museum. Not a gram of fat on him anywhere, just strong lean planes of hard male flesh.

She gave a little gulp.

He closed the fridge and turned and saw her staring at him. A slow smile spread over his features. He raised the carton of juice he was holding in a salute and mouthed, *Good morning*.

Kitty pulled the blind back down with more haste than efficiency. She clutched the edge of the sink, breathing hard. What must he think of her, gawping at him like that? Had he done it on purpose? Did he make a habit of wandering around naked in full view of the neighbours? So what if she was the only neighbour residing here just now—he had no right to flaunt himself like that!

Then she remembered his hot little hook-up. He probably had *her* there, still lying languorously in his bed after a bed-wrecking night of sex.

She stomped off to the shower, but as the water flowed over her in stinging little needles she thought of him having a shower next door, no doubt sharing it with his lover. Was he soaping up her breasts? Was he kissing her neck and décolletage?

'Grrrrggh.' Kitty reached for a towel and scrubbed herself dry. 'I hate that man!'

Kitty was on her way to her car to drive to work when she remembered Jake had arranged to deliver it to his mate's workshop. Just as she was about to call a cab on her mobile, he appeared from round the corner.

'Want a lift?' he asked.

Kitty couldn't control her fiery blush. 'Please don't put yourself out any further,' she said. 'I can easily call a cab.'

'At this time of the morning?' he said. 'It's bedlam out there. I just fought my way through it with your heap of rust. Only just made it too. I think the radiator's about to go on it as well.'

'I'm sorry you've had such a trying start to the morning,' she said.

His dark blue eyes glinted. 'My morning started out just fine.'

Kitty opened the passenger door and bundled herself inside, cheeks still burning hot. Did he have to embarrass her even further?

'How did your night on the town go?' he asked once he was behind the wheel.

She threw him a flinty look. 'It was probably excruciatingly tedious compared to yours.'

'I don't know about that,' he said, checking for traffic as he pulled into the street. 'I've had better.'

Kitty glanced at him but his expression was unfathomable. 'Are you going to see her again?' she asked.

'Who?'

'Your hot date last night.'

He changed lanes before he answered. 'Maybe. It depends.'

'On what?'

He glanced at her wryly. 'Why the sudden interest? Are you thinking of joining the queue?'

'Don't be daft,' she scoffed.

His mouth slanted in a smile. 'Frightened you might get trampled in the rush?'

Kitty pressed her lips together and refused to say another word until he pulled into the hospital car park. 'Thank you for the lift,' she said.

'I'd offer to run you home again, but I have another commitment straight after work,' he said.

'I'll make my own arrangements,' she said.

'Here's my mate's card,' he said, reaching for a business card from one of the dashboard compartments.

'You can give him a call to find out when your car will be ready.'

Kitty felt the brush of his fingers as he handed her the card and her belly gave a little flutter. 'Thanks...'

His eyes meshed with hers, dark and intense and *knowing*.

Could he feel the sexual energy she could feel? Did it make his skin ache to feel her touch? Did his lips tingle at the memory of hers moving against them? Did his blood roar through his veins at the thought of holding her in his arms, moulding her to him, *making love* to her?

'I like how you had your hair this morning,' he said.

Kitty put a hand up to her neat chignon. 'My...hair?'

'First thing,' he said. 'It was down and all tousled. That just-out-of-bed look really suits you.'

'You caught me by surprise.'

He gave her an indolent smile. 'Ditto.'

'I'm going to work,' she said, swinging her bag over her shoulder. 'I'll see you inside.'

CHAPTER TWELVE

'WAS that Jake Chandler's car I saw you getting out of this morning?' Cathy Oxley asked in the locker room.

Kitty put her bag in the locker and closed the door. 'He gave me a lift to work as my car is being repaired.'

'What is going on with you two?' Cathy asked, 'One of the doctors from Paediatrics said Jake took you to an orchestra rehearsal. Are you or aren't you an item?'

'Nothing's going on,' Kitty said. 'Dr Chandler kindly offered to take me to the rehearsal at short notice when my car refused to start. He also kindly offered to deliver my car to his friend's workshop.'

'Why would he do that if he wasn't interested in you?'

'He was just being neighbourly.'

'Some people have all the luck,' Cathy said. 'All my neighbour does is complain about my cat or my kids.'

'I'm not Dr Chandler's type,' Kitty said. 'Apparently I don't let my hair down enough.'

'Did he say that to you?'

Kitty compressed her lips. 'Amongst other things.'

Cathy grinned. 'I think he likes you. I've seen the way he looks at you. He sure as hell doesn't look at anyone else like that.'

'He has a different lover every night,' Kitty said,

scowling furiously. 'He probably doesn't have time to look at them before he shoves them out the door again.'

'You know it's the hardened playboys who always fall for the old-fashioned girls in the long run,' Cathy said. 'I've seen it many a time.'

'You won't be seeing it this time,' Kitty said as they walked out of the locker room together. 'I've never met a more irritating, beastly, odious man.'

'Er...' Cathy gave a grimace. 'I've got to go. See you.'

Kitty turned around to see Jake Chandler standing there with an inscrutable look on his face.

'Haven't you got better things to do than discuss me with the nursing staff?' he asked.

She stood her ground. 'I'm trying to put out the rumours that are circulating about us,' she said. 'I thought if everyone knew how much I hated you it would stop them speculating.'

'Hate is a strong word, Dr Cargill.'

She refused to be intimidated by his steely gaze. 'I know,' she said. 'But it's appropriate in this case.'

'I have a feeling you don't hate me as much as you'd like to,' he said. 'I threaten you. That's what you hate, isn't it, Kitty? I make you feel things you don't want to feel. You don't want to feel desire, do you? It frightens the hell out of you.'

Kitty glowered at him. 'I don't feel any such thing.'

'Sure you do, sweetheart,' he drawled. 'You want me. You want me real bad.'

'You're mistaken,' she said, her heart racing, her breath catching.

He captured her wrist in his strong fingers, his thumb finding her pounding pulse. 'This is what I do to you, isn't it?' he asked. 'It's the same thing you do to me.'

Kitty swallowed again, her stomach plummeting when she saw the naked desire in his gaze. She felt the sensual pull of his body, and the heat and fire of his touch set off every nerve screaming for more.

She *was* frightened by how he made her feel. Frightened and yet exhilarated.

'Dr Chandler?' One of the residents approached from further down the corridor.

Jake dropped Kitty's wrist and turned around. 'Yes?'

The resident looked from Kitty to Jake. 'I'm sorry to interrupt…'

'You're not interrupting anything,' Jake said, dropping his hand by his side.

'There's a patient just come in who keeps asking for you,' the intern said. 'He says he's your brother.'

Jake went to Bay Two, where Robbie was lying groaning on the trolley. It angered him to see his younger brother so wasted at this time of the day. His skin looked grey and pasty and his hair looked as if it hadn't been washed in a week. His clothes were little more than filthy rags and his shoes had holes in them. How had his kid brother got to this? What choices had he made that had sent him on this crazy, senseless trajectory? Why couldn't he just turn his life around? Did he have no self-control or self-respect? Didn't he want things to be different? How could he expect to live a full life when he was abusing his health so wilfully?

'Isn't it a bit early for a hangover?' he said as he twitched the curtain closed. 'Or is this one left over from last night?'

Robbie clutched at his head. 'Don't talk so loud.'

'You know, if you're here for a hand-out there are much better ways to do it.' Jake said. 'I told you I'd pay for rent and food. You don't have to use emotional blackmail.'

'I'm sick, damn it,' Robbie said.

'Yeah, well, I would be too if I was on the same liquid diet you're on,' Jake said. 'When was the last time you had a proper meal?'

'I don't know…couple of days ago, I think.'

'Perhaps I should assess him?' Kitty said. 'I'm not family. I can be a bit more objective.'

Jake fought with himself. He was used to handling his family issues on his own. He didn't want the train wreck of his brother's issues to intersect with his professional life. It wasn't only that it was embarrassing. He felt so damned helpless. He was used to sorting out other people's problems. His life was devoted to saving other people's sons and daughters, brothers and sisters, mothers and fathers, and yet he couldn't do a thing to put his kid brother's life back on track.

'Go for it,' he said. 'You won't find anything but a chip on his shoulder.'

Kitty stepped forward. 'Hello, Robbie.'

'Don't listen to him,' Robbie said. 'I *am* sick. I know I am.'

'What have you been doing to yourself?' Kitty asked as she examined him. 'Can you open both eyes for me? Yes, that's right. Sorry the light is so bright.'

'My head is killing me.'

'Have you had a recent fall?' she asked.

'I've had a few falls lately,' Robbie said.

'Excessive amounts of alcohol will do that,' Jake put in sardonically.

Kitty gave him a quelling look before turning back to his brother. 'How many falls?' she asked.

Robbie frowned. 'I can't remember...two, maybe three in the last twenty-four hours.'

'Did you know you were falling, or did it happen so fast you had no warning?' Kitty asked, examining his pupils again.

'I just found myself on the ground with no idea how I got there,' Robbie said.

'Do you take any medication?' Kitty asked. 'Prescription or otherwise?'

'Not for a while,' Robbie said. 'I used to smoke dope. I stopped a few months back.'

'Nothing else?'

'No,' Robbie said. 'I have the odd drink but I'm trying to cut back a bit. I don't like how it makes me feel any more.'

'So it feels different when you drink now from how it felt before?' Kitty asked.

'It just takes more to get him drunk than it did before,' Jake muttered.

Kitty threw him another gnarly look. 'Do you mind?' she asked.

'He's my brother.'

Her eyes flashed grey lightning. 'He's *my* patient.'

Jake twitched aside the curtains. 'I'll leave you to him,' he said. 'I have better things to do with my time than try and help people who won't even lift a finger to help themselves.'

Kitty put a hand on Robbie's shoulder. 'Sorry about that,' she said.

Robbie put a hand over his closed eyes.

Kitty sat on the edge of the bed trolley. 'Do you want to talk about it?'

He shook his head, and then grimaced as if the movement had caused him pain. 'Not much point, is there? Nothing's going to change. I've stuffed everything up.'

'It's not too late to turn things around.'

He turned his head on the pillow and cranked open one bloodshot eye. 'You think?'

She covered his thin hand with hers. 'Jake's concerned about you.'

He gave a grunt as he laid his head back down and closed his eyes. 'Jake needs to get a life.'

'Maybe he can't do that until he feels you're on the right track,' Kitty said.

A muscle ticked in Robbie's jaw, which reminded Kitty of Jake so much she felt a little ache settle around her heart.

'I'm not doing this on purpose,' he said.

'Sometimes it's hard to see that from the outside,' Kitty said. 'The effort you put in might not seem like much effort at all from Jake's perspective.'

Robbie put his wrist across his forehead and closed his eyes. 'I don't know why I'm like this,' he said. 'I just can't seem to get my life sorted out.'

'There are people who can help you with that,' she said. 'Psychologists, counsellors, even a life coach can help you put steps in place to get back on your feet.'

'I'm not going to a shrink,' Robbie said, dropping his arm back down on the bed. 'They just put you on drugs and bomb you out.'

'Not always,' Kitty said. 'If there's a mental health issue that needs to be addressed, then certainly one way of managing it is drug therapy, but there are other options.'

'I'm not a nut case,' Robbie said scowling at her.

'Then let's see if there is something else going on, shall we?' Kitty said. 'I'm going to run a couple of tests

to check your blood count and thyroid and kidney function to start with. Have you had any recent tests done?
Blood? Scans? That sort of thing?'

He looked away. 'Jake ordered some tests a while
back,' he mumbled.

'Are the results with your GP, or did Jake deal with
it directly?' Kitty asked.

'He doesn't usually treat me or my sisters,' Robbie
said. 'He'll write the occasional script but he prefers us
to have our own GP.'

'Did anything come up?'

Robbie looked sheepish. 'I only had a blood test
done. When Jake asked me about the scan he ordered I
told him it'd been clear.'

Kitty wondered why Robbie's GP hadn't formally
written to Jake to inform him of the results, as per
the usual protocol. But on questioning Robbie further
she found out that he had been attending a large and
busy medical clinic and had not seen the same practi-
tioner twice. Perhaps Jake had been satisfied another
colleague was taking over the care of his brother and
had left it at that.

Kitty took blood from Robbie's arm and popped the
vials in the appropriate bags ready for pathology. She
turned back to look at him and frowned when she no
ticed one of his eyes was twitching.

'How long have you had that twitch?' she asked.

He blinked a couple of times. 'Couple of days…
maybe more.'

Kitty examined both his pupils again. Now the left
one was slightly more dilated. 'Those falls you said you
had,' she said. 'Did you hit your head at all?'

'Not that I can remember,' he said. 'I haven't got a
bump, or anything, just the mother of all headaches.'

'I think I'll order a scan to be on the safe side,' she said. 'Then we'll take it from there.'

Jake came out of Cubicle Eight after seeing a patient with a gall bladder attack as Kitty came past. 'How's my brother doing?' he asked. 'Have you convinced him to check in to rehab?'

She stood before him, her expression sombre. 'I'm sending him for a CT scan.'

'You're wasting your time,' he said. 'I sent him for one a few months back. Nothing showed up.'

'He didn't have it done,' she said. 'There's no scan in the system. I checked. I even rang the clinic to talk to his GP. But he's not been seen by the same GP twice in the last couple of years.'

He frowned. 'He told me his GP gave him the all-clear. Why would he lie to me about that?'

'I don't know,' she said. 'I guess he didn't think the scan was warranted. You know what young guys are like. They think they're bulletproof.'

Jake exhaled a breath in self-recrimination. 'I should've followed it up. I should have called the clinic myself.' He shoved his hand through his hair. 'What was so hard about telling me he didn't get it done, for God's sake?'

'You're his brother, Jake, not his doctor,' she said. 'Anyway, I thought I'd better scan him just to be on the safe side. He's got slightly irregular pupils.'

'He's probably stoned, that's why.'

'I don't think he's stoned or drunk.'

Jake curled his lip. 'Would you even recognise stoned and drunk if you saw it?'

Her grey eyes narrowed. 'What is that supposed to mean?'

'Maybe the circles you mix in do it with a little more class than my brother does,' he said. 'But I can tell you when someone is off his face and I don't need a bloody CT scan to confirm it. Every time I've seen Robbie lately he's been hungover.'

'You're letting your personal issues cloud your clinical judgement,' she said. 'That's why you should never treat your own family. You can miss things.'

'Let me tell you what I've *missed*, Dr Cargill,' Jake said through clenched teeth as fury and frustration threatened his ironclad control. 'I've *missed* having my kid brother around. In his place I've got some weird wacko who changes mood at the blink of an eye. I *miss* the way he used to come and talk to me about stuff. He looked up to me. I liked that I was his go-to person. It meant I was doing an all right job in my mother's place. I *miss* having a normal life, without spending hours worrying myself sick over what my brother's getting up, to or who else's brother or sister he's dragging into whatever sleazy little hellhole he chooses to live in. That's what I *miss*.'

The air rang with the echo of his harshly delivered words.

Her rounded grey eyes blinked at him a couple of times. 'It must be a nightmare for you,' she said.

Jake let out a ragged sigh and shoved his hand through his hair again. 'Sorry for shouting,' he said gruffly. 'None of this is your fault.'

'I'll let you know as soon as I get the results,' she said.

'Yeah,' he said with another weary sigh. 'You do that.'

CHAPTER THIRTEEN

'ARE you sure?' Kitty asked the radiographer on duty a couple of hours later.

'Yes,' Peter Craven said. 'It's a meningioma.'

Kitty looked at the scans illuminated on the wall. 'How long do you think it's been there?' she asked.

'Quite some time, by the look of it.' He pointed to the wraparound features of the benign tumour. 'See how it's taken over the frontal lobe here and here?'

Kitty chewed at her lip. 'So that would account for some of the symptoms...'

'Personality change, moodiness, focal paralysis, hearing loss,' Peter said. He pushed back his chair. 'You'd better get Lewis Beck to have a look at it. He'd be the best neurosurgeon on staff to handle this sort of growth. Have you told Jake?'

'Not yet.'

'Want me to do it?'

Kitty shook her head. 'No, I'll tell him.'

Kitty found Jake in the A&E office writing up some patient notes. 'Jake?' she said. 'Can I have a word with you?'

He looked up from the notes, every muscle on his

face slowly coming to a standstill as he read her grave expression. 'What's going on?' he asked.

'Robbie has a meningioma,' she said. 'It looks like he's had it a while—maybe several years.'

His dark blue eyes flickered with shock, his throat moving up and down as he swallowed. 'Are you sure?' he asked.

'Peter Craven just confirmed it,' she said.

The pen he'd been using fell out of his grasp and rolled across the desk. 'So…' he said. 'It wasn't a hangover.'

'No.'

He gave her an agonised look. 'I thought he was just being a rebellious kid. For all these months—the last two years—I've been at him to sort himself out, but it wasn't his fault.'

'Anyone would have assumed the same,' Kitty said. 'You weren't to know.'

He shook his head as if he couldn't quite believe it. 'If only I'd chased him up about that scan,' he said. 'Two years ago he started acting a bit weird. Do you think…?'

She nodded. 'Peter Craven thinks it must have only started causing symptoms fairly recently. It would have been easy to put them down to other things initially.'

'Have you told Robbie yet?' he asked.

'Not yet,' she said. 'I thought you might like to do it with me after you've seen the scans. He might cope better hearing it from you.'

He met her gaze with his hollowed one. 'You'd better show me the scans.'

Jake looked at the scans of his brother's brain and felt a tsunami of remorse and regret smash into him. Every word of criticism and correction came back to haunt him. Robbie had been sick for two years, maybe even longer. Even though he had done his best to rule out other causes, a part of him had too quickly assumed Robbie was running amok like so many of his peers. How much precious time had been wasted? Why hadn't he physically taken him for the scan? He should have followed his brother through every step to make sure every base had been covered.

It was *his* fault Robbie had been sick for so long.

The truth stuck like a coat hanger in his throat.

He had done a lousy job of looking after his brother. *He had failed.*

Kitty put a hand on his arm. 'It's not your fault, Jake,' she said, as if she had been reading his mind. 'His symptoms were mostly vague and intermittent up until now.'

'Of course it's my fault,' he said. 'How can it *not* be my fault?'

'It's always tricky diagnosing your own family,' she said. 'We can't even do a good job of diagnosing ourselves. We can't get the clinical objectivity.'

Jake pushed a hand through his hair. 'I should've picked this up.'

'How could you?' she asked. 'You're not his doctor.'

'I'm his brother, for God's sake,' he said. 'I should've seen the signs.'

'It's easy to see the signs in hindsight,' she said. 'But who's to know if some of his behaviour was simply like any other young guy kicking back against authority? You can't know for sure.'

He dragged a hand over his face. 'How am I going to make it up to him?'

'By being there for him now,' she said. 'That's all you can do. It's all he will want you to do.'

He expelled a long breath. 'I owe you an apology.'

'It's fine.'

'It's not fine,' he said. 'You're a damn good doctor, Kitty. I shouldn't have criticised you the way I did.'

'I still have a lot to learn,' she said. 'I think I do rely on testing too much. I don't have the confidence to trust my clinical judgement just yet.'

'It paid off this time,' he said. 'I dread to think how long Robbie would have gone on untreated if it hadn't been for you.'

'I'm sure you would have sorted it out eventually.'

Jake wasn't so sure about that. How long would it have taken him to see past his own prejudice? He didn't like to think of how long Robbie had suffered. And the fight wasn't even over—not by a long shot. The biggest battle lay ahead. Would his kid brother survive such complex surgery?

'Have you heard how Jake's brother's getting on?' Cathy asked at the end of the day in the locker room.

'He's got an appointment to see Lewis Beck tomorrow,' Kitty said. 'I guess he'll operate as soon as there's room on one of his lists.'

'How's Jake handling it?'

'It's been a terrible shock,' Kitty said. 'He blames himself.'

'Understandable, given the circumstances,' Cathy said.

Kitty chewed at her lip. 'I know, but it's not as if he could have done any different. Robbie admitted himself that he was struggling to cope. I automatically assumed he was depressed. If I hadn't noticed his other symptoms I might have sent him home with an appointment to see a counsellor, which he probably wouldn't have kept. He would have slipped through the cracks again.'

'Gwen was telling me how tough Jake has it with his family,' Cathy said.

'Yes...'

'Kind of makes you wonder if he's not quite as selfish and shallow as you first thought.'

'Yes,' Kitty said. 'There's certainly more to Jake Chandler than meets the eye.' She thought of how Robbie told her he'd been supposed to meet Jake last night but Robbie had decided against going at the last minute. Jake had probably spent hours looking for him out on the streets, as he had apparently done many times before.

'Well, I'm off home,' Cathy said. 'Do you need a lift? I can make a detour. It's not too far out of my way.'

'No, it's all right,' Kitty said. 'I want to check in on Robbie now he's been admitted to the ward. I'll make my way home after that.'

When Kitty got to Robbie's room Jake was sitting beside the bed looking even more haggard than he had earlier. He stood up as she came in.

'He's just drifted off to sleep,' he said. 'My sisters have been in to see him.'

'How is he?' she asked.

'A bit overwhelmed by it all,' he said, running a hand through his hair. 'We all are.'

'Is there anything I can do?' Kitty asked.

'No, we're fine,' he said. 'The girls would like to meet you some time. They want to thank you.'

'It was a lucky pick-up. I might have missed it on another day.'

'Don't be so humble,' he said. 'You taught me a valuable lesson. I've always prided myself on seeing the big picture. But I can see how attention to detail is just as important in some circumstances.'

'I guess it's all a matter of balance,' Kitty said. 'It would be foolish to waste time on a detailed history if a patient was bleeding internally.'

'Do you need a lift home?' he asked.

'I can catch a cab,' she said. 'I just wanted to make sure Robbie was settled in.'

'I'm heading off now, so I'll take you,' he said.

It was a mostly silent trip home. Kitty could tell Jake was still coming to terms with his brother's condition. She could only imagine how annoyed and frustrated he would be feeling with himself. Most men didn't like being in the wrong, but she suspected it would hit Jake harder than most. His family depended on him to look out for them. He had taken on that role from a young age. He had made sacrifices that she could only guess at in order to do the right thing by his family.

'Are you doing anything for dinner?' he suddenly asked.

Kitty glanced at him. 'Not really...'

'My place in an hour?'

She pulled at her lip with her teeth. 'I'm not sure...'

'Just dinner, OK?'

'Can I bring something?' she asked.

He gave her a smile that was worn about the edges. 'Just yourself.'

Kitty pulled yet another outfit out of her wardrobe. Everything was either too conservative or too casual.

She had never felt so ill-prepared for a date. Not that it *was* a date.

It was just dinner.

At his place.

Just the two of them.

Alone.

Her stomach gave a nervous flutter. She didn't trust herself alone with Jake Chandler. He was too attractive, too masculine, and way too tempting. Her self-control completely disappeared when he touched her. Even worse was that she *wanted* him to touch her. She wanted him to make her forget about her principles and her neat and orderly plans for the future. She wanted him to make her feel something other than the lukewarm emotions she had settled for in the past. He made her feel vibrantly alive in every cell of her being. He made her heart race and her pulse pound. He made her body ache with longing—an intense ache she could feel every time he so much as looked at her with those dark blue eyes of his. Those eyes saw what she tried so hard to hide. He saw the need she shied away from. He saw the hunger. He saw how he made her feel.

Kitty took a steadying breath and tapped on his door. She heard Jake's firm tread and then the door opened. Her heart tripped and her breath caught somewhere in the middle of her chest. He had shaved, but his hair was still damp from his shower and it looked as if he had recently combed it with his fingers. He was wearing jeans and a black cotton casual shirt; the sleeves were rolled up halfway along his forearms, revealing his strong wrists. She smelt of the sharp citrus scent of sun-warmed lemons.

'Hi...' she said, thrusting a bottle of wine at his mid-section. 'I'm not sure if it's any good. I'm not really an expert or anything.'

'I'm sure it'll be fine,' he said. 'Come in.'

'I hope you haven't gone to too much trouble,' she said.

'No trouble at all,' he said, closing the door. 'You look nice. You smell nice too.'

Kitty wished she didn't blush so easily. She was so damned transparent. No wonder his eyes were always glinting at her. 'How long have you lived here?' she asked to fill in the silence.

'Four years,' he said, leading the way to the kitchen. 'I've thought about moving a few times but haven't got around to it yet.'

'Because of Robbie?'

He glanced at her before he reached for two wine glasses. 'Not just Robbie,' he said. 'My sisters have needed a bit of support over the years. I've put a lot of stuff on hold. But I figure they would've done the same in my place.'

'You've been a wonderful brother, Jake.'

He made a self-deprecating sound as he poured the wine. 'Yeah, haven't I just?'

'I mean it,' she said. 'You have to stop blaming yourself about Robbie's condition. You know the stats. People can have a meningioma for decades without symptoms.'

He passed her a glass of wine. 'I should've ruled out everything else first before I started criticising him,' he said. 'I should've insisted on seeing the scans for my-self. How could I have been so easily fobbed off? I'll tell you why,' he said, before she could answer. 'I *wanted* to believe he was acting irresponsibly. Why? Because I *resented* his freedom to do so. Here was I, giving up years of my life to make sure he and the girls got the best chance in life, and I *resented* that he didn't have to make a single sacrifice.'

Kitty reached out and touched him on the arm. 'I know how you must feel.'

'How can you possibly know?' he asked with an embittered expression. 'You're an only child. You've never had to watch out for anyone but yourself. How can you *possibly* know?'

Kitty shifted her gaze from his hardened one. She put her glass down and slipped off the stool she had perched on. 'Maybe I should leave you to wallow in your guilt,' she said. 'It's obvious I'm not much help to you.'

He stopped her at the door with a hand on her wrist. 'No,' he said, blowing out a long breath. 'Don't go. I'm sorry. Forgive me?'

She looked into his eyes and felt her heart give a stumble. 'This is a difficult time for you…I don't want to make things worse.'

'You're not making worse,' he said, absently stroking her wrist with his thumb. 'I want you here. I wouldn't have asked you if I didn't.'

Kitty felt herself drowning in the deep blue sea of his eyes. Her skin was tingling where he was stroking it. Her desire for him was unfurling inside her like the petals of an exotic flower. Her pulse quickened and her breath caught as his eyes slipped to her mouth. 'I'm not used to doing this…' she said.

'It's just dinner, Kitty.'

She moistened her lips. 'Is it?'

His eyes locked on hers. 'Do you want it to be something else?'

'I'm not sure...'

He brushed her cheek with an idle finger. 'I'm not going to deny that I want to make love to you,' he said. 'But whether I do or not is entirely up to you.'

Kitty looked at his mouth again. Was it possible to want a man so much you didn't care about anything else but the physical sensation of being in his arms? What did emotions have to do with it anyway? It was a physical need. Their bodies were designed for pleasure. The chemistry she felt with him was surely enough for now.

'The work thing...' she said, frowning. 'I hate the thought of everyone talking.'

'We can keep this out of the corridors and locker rooms,' he said. 'This is between us. It's no one else's business.'

She looked into his eyes. 'I don't want to be a one-night stand.'

'You won't be.'

'I don't want to fall in love with you, either.'

'Wise girl.'

'I mean it, Jake,' she said, putting her hands on his chest. 'I want to keep things uncomplicated.'

'No promises,' he said as he drew her closer. 'No strings.'

Kitty felt his body thicken against her. It was all she could do to stop from tearing his clothes from his body. She wanted to explore him with her hands and mouth. Ever since she had seen him naked this morning she had secretly fantasised about touching him, stroking him, holding him.

'I want you,' she said, in a voice she barely recognised as her own: it was husky, breathy, womanly.

'There's something I have to do first,' he said.

'What's that?'

'This,' he said, reaching behind her head to release the clasp that confined her hair so it tumbled freely around her shoulders.

And then his head came down slowly, ever so slowly, until his mouth stole her breath away in a kiss that branded her finally as his.

CHAPTER FOURTEEN

KITTY felt the red-hot urgency that coursed through him as his mouth ravaged hers. It whipped along her nerve-endings like an electric current, making her vibrate with longing within seconds. She clawed at him with wild hands, desperate to feel his skin against hers, to taste the salt of his flesh, to explore the contours of his body, to have him at her mercy.

She got under his shirt and stroked his chest with her hands, but it wasn't enough.

She wanted to feel *him*.

She worked at his trouser fastening, finally releasing it to claim her prize. He was powerfully aroused, hard and thick, swollen with the need she could feel hammering through his blood.

His mouth ground against hers, hungry and insatiable. Her skin shivered all over in delight as he roughly tugged at her clothes. His mouth captured her breast, sucking on it, releasing it to stroke it with her tongue, and then sucking on it again. He did the same to her other breast, making her cry out loud with the spine-tingling pleasure of it.

He went back to her mouth, walking her backwards out of the room. A stool fell over, a picture on the wall got dislodged, a lamp on a table in the hallway almost fell to the floor, but still he didn't lift his mouth off hers.

Kitty felt a mattress underneath her back and then his body coming down over her. She clung to him, kissing him back with heated fervour as he was kissing her.

Somehow she wriggled out of her clothes, while he dispensed with his in between passionate kisses and caresses that made her gasp and cry out loud.

'Now,' she panted as he came back over her, pinning her with his weight.

'Not yet,' he said, moving down her body with his hot mouth. 'I have things to do.'

Kitty snatched in a breath as he kissed and stroked his way down to her belly button. She dug her fingers into his hair as he went lower. This was new territory for her. She didn't know if she could do this. It was too intimate.

'Relax,' he said. 'You're too tense.'

'I can't.'

'Yes, you can,' he said. 'Let your thighs go. That's it. Trust me. I won't rush you. Take all the time you need.'

She closed her eyes and let herself go with the sensations as he explored her with soft strokes of his tongue. The tension built and built. All her nerves seemed to be gathered at one point, hovering there for some final trigger to catapult her over the edge.

At last she was there.

She soared over the precipice, free falling into a whirling sea of powerful sensations that drove every thought out of her head. She was suspended, floating, drifting in a world she hadn't visited before, an erotic world of delights and delicious feelings of satiation.

'Oh, God…' She put a hand over her eyes, suddenly shy at how undone she had become.

Jake came back over her, tugging her hand away from her face. 'Hey,' he said. 'Don't hide from me.'

'I can't believe you just did that,' she said. 'I can't believe *I* just did that.'

'You haven't done that before?'

'I've never felt comfortable about it,' she confessed.

He brushed her hair back off her face. 'Every couple has their comfort zones,' he said. 'What's right for one will not always be right for another.'

'I can imagine there's not much you haven't been comfortable with,' Kitty said.

He gave a could-mean-anything smile. 'I have my boundaries.'

She ran her hands over his chest, slowly tiptoeing her fingers below his navel. 'I guess I'll have to figure out what they are, won't I?'

'I can hardly wait,' he said, and covered her mouth with his.

Kitty hadn't thought it possible to feel the same level of desire so soon, but within moments she was writhing beneath him, aching for the completion she craved. She felt him hard against her, close but not close enough. She caressed him, delighting in the way he responded with a deep groan as she moved over the blunt tip of him. She felt the ooze of his pre-ejaculating fluid—that primal response of his body that left her in no doubt of how much he wanted her.

He reached past her for a condom in one of the bed-side drawers. She pushed aside the thought of all the other women he had done this with before. She had gone into this with her eyes wide open. She had known she wasn't the first. She knew she wouldn't be the last.

'What's wrong?' he asked.

Kitty painted on a carefree smile. 'Nothing.'

He captured her chin, his eyes holding hers. 'We don't have to do this if you're not ready,' he said.

'I am ready,' she said. 'It's just I can't help thinking of how many times you've done this. Do you say and do the same thing each and every time?'

He frowned. 'This is about us, Kitty. It's not about anyone else. What we experience together is unique.'

'If you close your eyes I could be just anyone.'

'You're not just anyone,' he said. 'You're you. You taste different. You feel different. You smell different. You *are* different.'

She circled one of his flat nipples with her finger. 'I want you to always remember this,' she said. 'You know…long after I've gone back to England.' She looked into his eyes. 'Will you promise me that?'

He took her hand and kissed her fingertips. 'I thought we agreed on no promises.'

'Just this one.'

He held her gaze for a heartbeat. 'I promise.'

She traced his top lip with her fingertip. 'You're a lot nicer on closer inspection, Jake Chandler,' she said. 'I think I might not detest you quite so much after all.'

He gave her a cautionary look. 'You're not falling in love with me, are you?'

'Not a chance,' she said, and pulled his head down until his mouth met hers.

Jake lay awake in the early hours of the morning, not sure what was wrong until he realised Kitty was still

lying in the bed beside him. He had a rule he stuck to
rigorously. No sleepovers. It made the boundaries blur
too much. He didn't care for the morning-after routine.
Women had a tendency to see things differently in the
cold hard light of morning. In spite of everything they
said to the contrary they *always* wanted more than he
was prepared to give. Before he knew it there would
be a toothbrush left in his bathroom or a few items of
clothes left in his wardrobe.

It was simpler to avoid the issue.

No one got hurt that way.

Last night he had acted on primal instincts alone. He
had wanted to connect with Kitty physically, to feel the
movement of her body around him, to remind himself
of the rhythms of life. He had wanted to block out the
mental anguish of his guilt. But those few precious moments of oblivion had done much more than release him
from his torment. His body had recognised something
in her that spoke to him much more than just physically. It had been like hearing a language he'd thought
he had forgotten. The caress of her mouth and hands
hadn't felt like just another sexual partner delivering
pleasure. Her hands and mouth had felt worshipful, rev-
erent almost. Her tentative touch and her passionate re-
sponses had awoken in him a desire to feel more than
sexual satisfaction.

He looked at her in the silvery light of the moon. She
was lying on her side, the cotton sheet draped over her
slim form, showing every delightful contour from her
neat bottom and thighs to her creamy breasts. Her hair
was like a fluffy cloud around her head. He couldn't
help reaching out and running his fingers through it,
tethering himself to her via those silky strands. She

gave a little murmur and nestled closer into the pillow, her lips curved in a small but blissful smile.

He leaned down and pressed a soft kiss to the satiny skin of her shoulder. She smelt of fresh flowers, but he also picked up a faint trace of his own masculine scent clinging to her skin that made something shift deep inside his stomach, like a gear slipping from its cogs.

She opened her eyes and smiled at him shyly. 'What time is it?'

Jake brushed a strand of hair off her forehead while he mentally shoved that gear back into line. 'Time you were tucked up in your own bed,' he said.

A flicker of hurt passed through her gaze. 'You want me to leave?' she asked.

'We both have to work in the morning,' he said, getting up from the bed and reaching for his boxer shorts and stepping into them. He went over to the window and stared sightlessly at the view. 'It's going to be a big day for Robbie. I want to be there for him.'

Jake heard the soft padding of her footsteps over the carpet, and then he felt her arms gently encircle his waist from behind. He put one of his hands over her linked ones, his body already aching to have her again. He felt her cheek rest against his back, her soft breath like a caress over his skin.

After a few moments he turned around and cradled her face in his hands, his eyes holding hers. 'You really should go home while you've got the chance,' he said.

She held his look with those soft grey eyes of hers. 'Maybe I'm not ready to be sent off home like a child who's overstayed her welcome.'

He stroked the cushion of her bottom lip with one of his thumbs. 'Maybe I don't want company right now,' he said, while his body betrayed him shamelessly where it was surging against the softness of hers.

She gave him a coy smile. 'Maybe you're lying.'

He brought his mouth down just above hers. 'Maybe you're right,' he said, and covered her lips with his.

Kitty slipped out of Jake's bed while he was still sleeping, just as dawn was breaking. She carried her shoes and was almost at the front door when he came out of the bedroom with just a towel draped around his hips.

'You should've woken me,' he said, rubbing a hand over his stubbly jaw.

'I wasn't sure what the protocol was,' Kitty said, dropping her shoes to place her feet in them.

He frowned and let his hand fall by his side. 'Are you angry with me?'

She shrugged. 'Why would I be angry? You told me the rules. No strings. No promises.'

There was a taut little silence.

'I liked having you stay last night,' he said. 'I liked it a lot.'

Kitty searched his gaze for a moment. 'I liked it too.'

He came over to where she was standing. Her body was within a mere hair's breadth of his. She could feel the sensual energy transmitting from his body to hers. Her insides seemed to shift inside her in an effort to bridge that tiny distance.

'I'd like to see you after work,' he said. 'Let's have dinner. I'll book somewhere on the waterfront in Rushcutters Bay.'

Kitty was conscious of the emotionally charged day ahead for him. 'What if I cook dinner for you at my place?' she suggested.

He gave her a ghost of a smile. 'The way to a man's heart?'

'I think it would take a lot more than my meagre culinary ability to break through *that* stronghold,' she said lightly.

His eyes studied hers for a heartbeat or two. 'I've never spent the whole night with anyone before,' he said.

Kitty raised her brows. 'One of your rules?'

'Sort of,' he said. 'I don't usually sleep well with someone else in the room, let alone the bed.'

'I hope I didn't snore.'

His mouth tilted in another smile. 'No, you were very quiet,' he said. 'I hardly knew you were there.'

'Such scintillating company,' Kitty said. 'I'll have to lift my game.'

His gaze waltzed with hers in a sensual two-step, each step incrementally tightening the tension that simmered between them. 'Have you got time for breakfast?' he asked.

'I've sort of got in the habit of skipping it.'

'It's the most important meal of the day.'

'So I've heard.'

He circled her waist with his arms and brought her flush against his body. 'You don't know what you're missing,' he said.

A tremor shuddered through her body. 'As of last night, I think I do,' she said. 'But I really need to shower and get ready for work. I have this boss who might fire me if I turn up late.'

'I'm sure if you just smiled at him he'd melt.'

Kitty smiled at him and watched as his dark blue eyes softened. 'Great tip—thanks,' she said. 'I'll keep it in mind.'

He pressed a brush-like kiss to her mouth. 'I'll meet you in the car park in half an hour,' he said. 'I'll drive you to my mate the mechanic's to pick up your car.'

'I can catch a cab,' Kitty said.

He trailed a finger down her cheek. 'Half an hour,' he said. 'Don't be late.'

It was close to lunchtime before Kitty saw Jake on the unit. He was walking past just as she was coming out of Bay Three, where she had finished assessing an elderly patient with a broken wrist. She almost ran into him, but he steadied her with his hands.

'Sorry,' he said. 'I wasn't looking where I was going.'

Kitty looked at the shadow of worry in his eyes. 'Is everything all right?' she asked.

He dropped his hands from her arms. 'Lewis Beck wants to operate today,' he said. 'He shuffled his cases around to fit Robbie in this afternoon. It's all happening so fast. This time yesterday I thought my brother was just a layabout jerk. Now I'm facing the prospect of losing him.'

Kitty touched him on the arm. 'Robbie's in very good hands, Jake,' she said.

'I can't tell you how many times I've tried to allay patients and their relatives' fears over surgical procedures,' he said. 'But it's so different when it's your own relative. Robbie's my kid brother. He's only twenty-four. He's got his whole life ahead of him. What if something goes wrong?'

'Nothing will go wrong, Jake,' Kitty said. 'He's young and otherwise healthy. You have to stay positive for his sake as well as your own.'

He scraped a hand through his hair. 'I know, I know.'

He dropped his hand and gave her a brief thin-lipped smile. 'Thanks.'

'No problem.'

He glanced at his watch. 'I'd better get back to see Robbie before they take him down to Theatre,' he said. 'Any problems here?'

'No, everything's fine,' Kitty said. 'Lei's a great registrar. We've got things covered.'

'Good,' he said. 'I'll be back as soon as I can.'

Jake waited until the anaesthetist had done his presurgical assessment before he entered Robbie's room. 'How are you feeling?' he asked.

'Nervous,' Robbie said. 'I'm not sure I like the thought of my head being cut open.'

'The scar will be a great talking point,' Jake said.

'I'll look like a skinhead until my hair grows back.'

'Robbie,' Jake began, 'there's something I need to say—'

'It's cool, Jake,' Robbie said. 'I was a jerk not to get the scan done. Jen and Rosie chewed my ears off about it earlier this morning. They said it's made it so much harder on you. That you feel guilty. That you feel it's your fault or something. But it's not. I'm an adult. I should've got myself checked out.'

Jake grasped his brother's hand. 'I'm sorry for not being there for you. I can't believe how badly I handled things.'

'You've managed things just fine,' Robbie said. 'You always do. You're there for all of us, all the time. I've been thinking about it…you know, while I've been lying here doing nothing. You stepped up to the plate when

Mum died. No one asked you if you wanted to. You just did it.'

'I wanted to do it.'

'Yeah, but it's not been easy, has it?' Robbie said. 'You've made a lot of sacrifices for us. When Rosie got pregnant, for instance. You were really looking forward to that trip. I know you were. If things had been different you could've worked overseas for a couple of years. But you didn't get the chance. You gave it up for us.'

Jake shrugged it off. 'I'll head overseas some time.'

'That English doctor seems nice,' Robbie said. 'What's the story with you two?'

Jake smiled. 'She's a sweetheart, isn't she?'

Robbie's brows lifted. 'Does Rosie know about this?'

'You know about that stupid bet, huh?'

'Rosie told me,' Robbie said, and punched him playfully on the upper arm. 'Looks like you'd better pay up.'

'It is that obvious?' Jake asked.

Robbie gave his eyes a little roll. 'You were always going to lose, Jake.'

'Yeah, well, I was going great guns until Kitty Cargill came along,' Jake said.

Robbie grinned. 'That's what I meant.'

CHAPTER FIFTEEN

BEFORE Kitty left work she spoke to Jake, who informed her Robbie's surgery had gone well and that he was now in recovery. Jake planned to wait until he was moved to the high dependency unit before he came home to have dinner with her.

Kitty was making a mango, rocket and feta cheese salad when her mobile started to ring. She picked it up without checking the caller ID. 'Hello?'

'Kitty, it's me—Sophie… Please don't hang up.'

Kitty drew in a little breath. 'I'm kind of busy right now,' she said. 'I have someone coming for dinner in a few minutes.'

'I won't hold you up…it's just that I really miss you,' Sophie said. 'I never thought it would be like this… You know, you so far away when I'm about to get married.'

Well, if you hadn't pinched my future husband maybe I'd be there right by your side as your maid of honour, as we'd always planned since we were seven years old, she thought.

'Sophie, this isn't a good time,' she said.

'I'm sorry,' Sophie said with a sob in her voice. 'I didn't want to hurt you like this. Charles and I fought it for so long.'

'How long?' Kitty asked.

'Remember that trip we all took to the Cotswolds a couple of years ago?'

'Yes,' Kitty said, seething with resentment as she thought of how she had got held up at the hospital and Charles had gone ahead with Sophie. She had come down later with their other friends, Tom and Claire and Finn. 'How convenient it must have been for you both to spend the first night down there without anyone else to interrupt your little love tryst.'

'It wasn't like that, Kitty,' Sophie said. 'We didn't do anything. We just talked. I was going out with Finn, as you know, but things weren't really working out. Charles was so supportive. He told me I shouldn't be wasting Finn's time if I wasn't truly in love with him.'

'What a pity he didn't take his own advice,' Kitty put in.

Sophie sighed. 'He loved you, Kitty. He still loves you. But not the way a man should love the woman he's going to marry and spend the rest of his life with.'

'He could have told me rather than have me find out the way I did,' Kitty said.

'I'm so sorry about that,' Sophie said. 'It just happened. You have to believe that. Our feelings got the better of us. We'd planned to tell you that night. It was a horrible way for you to find out. I was so ashamed. I couldn't believe I'd lost control like that. It started with a kiss and then suddenly we were in bed and... Well, you know the rest.'

Kitty pressed her lips together, her thoughts going to the kiss that had been her sensual undoing with Jake. Did she have the right to judge Sophie when she had been guilty of the very same loss of control?

Of course she had the right.

It was *totally* different.

Neither she nor Jake had betrayed anyone else in indulging their passion for each other. It was all very well for Sophie to apologise, but it didn't change the fact that her two best friends in the whole world had betrayed her in the most despicable, hurtful way.

'Look, Sophie, I really have to go,' she said. 'I appreciate the phone call, but I think it's best if we all get on with our lives and leave it at that.'

'Remember when we were little girls?' Sophie said. 'Remember when we promised each other we'd be each other's maid of honour?'

'We're not little girls any more,' Kitty said. 'Now, if you don't mind, I—'

'I won't feel married if you're not there,' Sophie said. 'It won't be the same without you. We'll be one down on the wedding party. I'm not going to ask anyone to take your place. The photos are going to look rubbish.'

'I'm sure Claire or Harriet will do a perfectly fine job of being your bridesmaid and maid of honour,' Kitty said.

'I don't want Claire or Harriet,' Sophie said. 'I want *you*. We promised, remember?'

Kitty looked at the promise ring that was creating a ridge in the flesh of her finger. 'Not all promises can be kept,' she said, and ended the call.

Jake knocked on Kitty's door and listened as her footsteps approached. The door opened and he smiled at her. 'Sorry I'm late,' he said, handing her a bottle of champagne.

'How's Robbie?' she asked.

'Awake and flirting with the nurses in HDU,' he said. 'The operation went well. Lewis Beck is confident he'll be out of hospital within a week.'

'I'm so glad,' Kitty said. 'You must be feeling very relieved.'

'Yeah,' Jake said, following her to the kitchen. 'Hey, what's cooking? It smells delicious.'

'Nothing fancy,' she said.

'No cucumber sandwiches?'

She gave him a half-hearted smile before she went in search of glasses. 'No.'

'Here, let me get those for you,' he said as she tried to reach the cupboard above her head.

'I don't think there are any champagne glasses in there,' she said.

'Nothing wrong with drinking champagne out of a wine glass,' Jake said. 'Especially tonight, when we're celebrating.'

She gave him another slightly distracted smile as she tucked a little strand of hair behind her ear. 'Of course.'

Jake put the glasses on the bench beside the champagne and put his hands about her waist, bringing her a little closer. 'What's up?' he asked.

She looked at his shirtfront. 'Nothing.'

'Hey, remember that I've got two sisters,' Jake said. 'I know enough about women to know that "nothing" means "something", and it's usually something big. So spill it. Tell me what's worrying you.'

She slowly raised her grey eyes to his. 'My ex-best friend called a few minutes ago,' she said.

'The one who hooked up with your ex?'

A resentful glitter sparked in her eyes. 'She wants me to be her maid of honour at their wedding,' she said.

'Can you believe that? As if I'd stand at the altar and smile for the cameras while she promises to love the man I thought I was going to marry! Everyone would be staring at me, pitying me—or, worse, laughing at me.'

Jake frowned in empathy. 'I can understand how tough a gig it would be for you, but wouldn't it be better to tough it out? Show them you're over it? No one will laugh at you. They'll be pleased you've moved on with your life.'

She chewed at her lip for a moment. 'I'm not ready to pretend everything's OK,' she said. 'Why should I let them have a perfect day when they've ruined everything for me?'

'Aren't you being a little bit selfish about this?' he asked.

Her frown was quick and deep. 'Selfish?' she said. 'What do you mean?'

'It's selfish to want them to suffer for your misery,' he said. 'You need to let it go, Kitty. You being angry and resentful won't stop them loving each other. Charles has made his choice. So it wasn't you? Move on. Be the bigger person. Show them how mature and grown-up you are about it all.'

Her frown relaxed a little but her mouth was still pushed forward in a little pout. 'They're the ones who are being selfish,' she said. 'They've wrecked my life.'

'Have they?' Jake asked, pulling her closer. 'Have they really?'

Her eyes meshed with his.

Jake brushed his thumb over her bottom lip. 'We wouldn't be together now if it hadn't been for them,' he said. 'You wouldn't have come all this way and turned my world upside down, not to mention make me lose a cool one thousand bucks.'

Her mouth twitched with a ghost of a smile. 'Was it worth it?' she asked.

Jake put a hand in the curve of her back to draw her even closer as he lowered his mouth to hers. 'Best thousand bucks I've ever spent,' he said, and kissed her.

Kitty leaned into Jake's kiss, her body responding to the hot hard heat of him surging against her in arrant maleness. She felt her stomach flip in excitement as his tongue boldly commanded entry to her mouth. She opened to him, whimpering in delight. Her breasts started to ache with the need to feel his touch. She rubbed against him with wanton abandon, her lower body pulsing with the need to feel his possession. She felt the honeyed slickness between her thighs.

He slipped her top off one of her shoulders and worked his way with his mouth over her sensitive skin, over her collarbone, against her neck, to just below her ear. She felt her flesh rise in tiny goosebumps as his teeth tugged at her earlobe. She rose on tiptoe to subject him to the same sensual assault. She delighted in the deep groan he gave when she tugged his shirt out of his trousers. She ran her hands over his chest, over his pectoral muscles and the taut ridges of his toned abdomen. She boldly unfastened his trousers and sought him with her hand. He groaned again as she stroked him. He was so hard and heavy she could feel the throb of his blood against her fingers.

Her insides clamped with lust. It was a consuming force that would allow no other outcome but satiation. She trailed her mouth down over his chest, down, down,

down, breathing in the pure male scent of him, teasing him with her teeth and her tongue.

He put his hands on her shoulders to halt her, but she continued determinedly on her erotic journey of discovery. She wanted to pleasure him, to have him at the mercy of his need for her. She wanted to prove how exciting she could be as a lover—not just to him, but also to herself. She wanted to taste him. To feel him shudder with release.

He fisted a hand in her hair, groaning again as she took him in her mouth after he'd quickly put on a condom. She felt him brace himself; his thighs rock-hard and slightly apart. She continued on her mission, relishing his response. She felt the exact moment he climaxed. It was so intensely intimate to receive him in such a way.

'Oh, God,' he said shakily. 'This is the most amazing dinner party I've ever been to.'

Kitty smiled as she straightened. 'That's just for starters,' she said. 'Just wait until you see what I've got for dessert.'

His eyes glinted as he backed her against the kitchen bench. 'That must mean that the main course is up to me,' he said.

Kitty shivered when his hands pulled her top over her head. He tossed it to the floor at their feet and then went to her skirt. He slid the zip down at the back and stroked his hands over her bottom. Her bra and knickers soon joined her skirt and top. She was standing there stark naked, but for some reason she didn't feel embarrassed. Instead she felt powerfully feminine. The way his gaze devoured her made her skin tingle and her spine melt. She could see the passionate intention in those dark blue depths and it made every hair on her head tingle at the roots.

He spun her around so her back was to him. Her breath hitched in her throat as she felt him nudging between her quivering thighs. She clutched at the countertop to steady herself, every nerve screaming for his first thrust. She gasped when he surged into her, her body accepting him with slick moist heat. He drove to the hilt; his movements slow at first, but then gradually building to a pace that carried her at breathtaking speed to the summit of human pleasure.

She sobbed as her body shuddered and shook with aftershocks, the spasms of her body triggering his final plunge into paradise. She felt him move against her as he emptied himself; his groans of ecstasy making her feel more like a woman than she had ever felt before.

Jake turned her around to face him. 'You're amazing,' he said, stroking his hands up and down her upper arms.

Kitty tried to play it cool and casual and looked at him from beneath her lowered lashes in a coquettish manner. 'I bet you say that to all the girls.'

A small frown pulled at his brow. 'Actually, I don't,' he said. 'There's sex and there's sex—or so I've always thought. But sex with you is something completely different.'

Kitty wanted to believe him. It had certainly felt that way to her. What she had experienced with him was so far from her experience with her ex that it was as if she were in a different body.

But she knew the rules of being involved with Jake. This was not for the long term. She would be going back to Britain before too long. He would continue with his playboy no-strings lifestyle.

They would probably never see or hear from each other again.

She pushed aside the ache that thought caused and gave him a bright smile. 'Why don't you open the champagne while I get dressed?'

His eyes ran over her like a hot blue-tipped flame. 'I've got an even better idea,' he said. 'Why don't you stay just the way you are?'

'I can't eat dinner with no clothes on,' she said, giving him a shocked look. 'What on earth would the neighbours think?'

He gave her a wolfish smile as he reached for her. 'I can't speak for the others, but personally I have no problem with it.'

Kitty shivered in delight as he bent his head to her neck. 'What about dinner?' she asked. 'Aren't you hungry yet?'

'Starving,' he said as he swooped down and captured her mouth.

CHAPTER SIXTEEN

'TODAY'S the big day,' Kitty said to Robbie when she visited him on her tea break a few days later. 'I hear you're going home.'

'Yeah,' Robbie said. 'I can't wait to get out of here.'

'Has it been that bad?'

'Not really, but I'm sick of being a patient,' he said. 'Jake and the girls keep fussing over me like I'm going to have some sort of relapse.'

'That's because they love you,' Kitty said. 'You're lucky you have siblings who are always looking out for you.'

'I know, but I want to get on with my life,' he said. 'I want to re-enrol at university. If I get my skates on I won't be too far behind.'

'Are you sure you're not rushing things?' Kitty asked. 'You've been through a big operation. You still need time to heal. It's only been a week. A three-hour anaesthetic knocks most people around a bit.'

'I'll be fine,' he said. 'I feel great. I know I look like something from a horror movie, but I feel good.'

Kitty smiled. 'Are you going to stay with Jake for a few days? He said he'd offered to look after you.'

Robbie gave a shrug. 'For a day or two maybe... I

kind of figure Jake needs his own space. I can always stay with Jen or Rosie after that.'

'I'm sure he would be happy to look after you,' Kitty said. 'He's already planned to take a few days off. We talked about it last night.'

Robbie looked at her. 'You're good for him, Kitty,' he said. 'He's happier than I've ever seen him before.'

'I'm sure that has much more to do with you getting better than anything to do with me,' she said.

Robbie frowned. 'You love him, though, don't you?'

Kitty was momentarily caught off guard. She tried not to think about her feelings for Jake. She pushed those thoughts aside every time they surfaced. She had spent a lot of time with him over the last few days. The hospital network was buzzing about their affair, but she had weathered it much better than she had expected. She had even met his sisters on a couple of occasions and had felt totally at ease. It was hard not to, given that the girls and Robbie were so lovely and friendly. Just like the siblings she'd always wished she'd had.

She hadn't wanted to admit to herself how much she enjoyed being with Jake. She had accepted the affair for what it was: a brief interlude that was part of her master plan to put her heartbreak over Charles and Sophie behind her. But somehow as each day passed she found it harder and harder to recall Charles's features, let alone his kisses.

All she could think of was Jake.

Her body felt him for hours after they'd made love. It was like carrying a part of him with her wherever she went.

She didn't want it to end.

She didn't want *them* to end.

'I'm heading back to Britain for Easter,' she said, adopting a carefree tone. 'I've really enjoyed being here, though. I've learned heaps.'

Robbie looked at her with studied concentration. 'Maybe Jake will come and visit you over there some time,' he said. 'He's always wanted to travel. He pretends he doesn't but really he does. He's given up everything for the girls and me. I wish he'd just live his own life for a change. He deserves to be happy.'

'I guess he's been taking care of you all for so long he doesn't know any other way to be happy,' she said. 'You'll have to show him you're perfectly capable of looking after yourselves.' She gave his hand a little squeeze. 'I'd better get going. A&E is probably stacked to the ceiling with patients by now.'

Robbie lifted his fingers off the bed in a farewell wave. 'See you around.'

Jake came home from work ten days later to see Robbie had packed his things and placed them by the front door. 'What's going on?' he said.

'It's time I got my own place,' Robbie said. 'I'm crowding you.'

'You're not crowding me,' Jake said, tossing his jacket over the back of the sofa. 'We've talked about this already. You can stay as long as you want. There's plenty of room.'

'But what about you and Kitty?' Robbie asked. 'You've only been over to her place a couple of times, and when she comes over here I can tell she feels she's in the way.'

'Kitty understands how things are right now,' Jake said. 'My priority is to get you back on your feet.'

'But it's not fair to her or to you,' Robbie said. 'She'll be going back before you know it, and you've hardly had any time together.'

Jake hated being reminded of Kitty's return to Britain. It was like a nagging toothache that he could mostly ignore if no one brought his attention to it. But even the staff at the hospital had taken it upon themselves to remind him of it lately. He had tried to play down his involvement with her, and Kitty too had been very tight-lipped, but it was hard to pretend he didn't enjoy having her in his life both at work and in private. Those precious few private moments he'd snatched with her over the last couple of weeks had taken on a special meaning.

'What's brought this on?' he asked.

Robbie shrugged. 'I just thought it was time to get out of your hair.'

'But I don't understand,' Jake said, frowning. 'What's the point of paying rent you can ill afford right now? It doesn't make sense when there's a room going begging here.'

'Kitty thinks it's best if I start to take more responsibility for myself,' Robbie said. 'And the girls too. We all rely on you too much. It's time we stood on our own feet.'

Jake felt his spine stiffen and his brows snapped together. 'Did *she* suggest you move out?' he asked.

'Not in so many words...'

'How many words?' Jake growled. 'For God's sake, Robbie, you've just had major surgery. You can't go back to living a normal life as if nothing's happened. Kitty shouldn't have put such a damn-fool crazy idea in your head. She has no right to get involved in what's none of her damn business.'

Robbie looked worried. 'You're not going to get mad at her, are you?' he asked.

'Get mad?' Jake asked clenching his jaw. 'I *am* mad. I'm furious with her.'

'You can't stop me from moving out,' Robbie said. 'Anyway, I think she's right. You take on too much, Jake. You've been a substitute parent for so long you don't know how to be a brother any more.'

Jake felt a strange ache in the middle of his chest. How long since he *had* been simply a brother? It seemed like decades.

It was decades.

'Where are you going to stay?' he asked, glancing at Robbie's bag.

'A mate of mine's got a place in Glebe,' Robbie said. 'It'll be close to uni. I'll be able to walk since I'm not allowed to drive just yet.'

'I'm not happy about this,' Jake said with a concerned frown, his gut churning with the pain of letting go. Was this some sort of crazy empty nest syndrome he was feeling? How was he supposed to stop worrying? How could he trust that Robbie would be all right? 'It's still early days. You shouldn't be taking any risks at this stage.'

'I'm fine, Jake,' Robbie said, reaching for his bag. 'I want to get my life back. You need to get yours back as well.'

'My life is fine just the way it is,' Jake said. *Or at least it was until a little English rose came along and poked her uptilted nose where it doesn't belong.*

Robbie put out his hand. 'Thanks for everything.'

Jake pushed Robbie's hand out of the way and gathered him in a big brother hug. 'Take care of yourself, Robbie,' he said gruffly.

Kitty had not long got back from orchestra rehearsal when she saw Jake stalking across the courtyard to her town house. She had tried to give him as much space as he and Robbie needed, but it had been so hard to keep away. Each time he looked at her she felt a thousand delicious sensations wash over her. At work they had been nothing but professional, but still when he locked gazes with her she felt the electric current of their connection pass through her entire body.

She opened the door before he pressed the doorbell. 'I was going to call you,' she said, smiling brightly. 'I made some pancakes earlier. I thought you and Robbie might like some for supper.'

His expression was as dark as thunder. 'Robbie's gone.'

'Gone?'

'Don't play the innocent with me,' he said, frowning at her savagely. 'You know damn well he's packed up and left. You were the one who bloody suggested it.'

Kitty felt a little rattle of unease move down her spine. She had never seen Jake so angry. She could feel the menacing waves of it crackling through the air towards her. She refused to be intimidated, however.

'Robbie is an adult,' she said. 'You can't keep him and your sisters chained to your side in case something goes wrong in their lives. You can't always be there to pick up the pieces. How are they ever going to learn to take care of themselves if all they ever have to do is call you and you fix things for them?'

His frown was a deep V between his brows. 'What the hell would *you* know about what it takes to be a family?' he asked. 'You with your crackpot parents who haven't even got the guts to commit to each other full-time.'

Kitty lifted one of her brows. 'Isn't that a little bit rich, coming from you?'

'What do you mean by that?'

She rolled her eyes in disdain. 'Jake, you're the biggest commitment-phobe I've ever met—and the biggest hypocrite. You criticise my parents and yet they've always been there for me, even if they haven't always been there for each other. You have no right to pass judgement. You don't even know what commitment is. You just like control.'

'If you're not happy with how things are between us then all you have to do is say so,' he said, still with that frown carving deep into his forehead, his dark blue eyes as hard as black ice. 'I told you what I could offer. I didn't lie to you. I made no promises. You came into this with your eyes wide open.'

Kitty should have backed away from the topic, but some inner demon demanded she push him regardless of the fall-out. She was tired of pretending she was OK with their arrangement. She wanted more. She wanted him to love her the way she had come to love him.

How could she *not* love him? She hadn't stood a chance right from the start. He had rocked her world the first time he had looked at her and smiled that dazzlingly sexy smile. What she had felt for Charles was nothing compared to what she felt for Jake. She was ashamed she had thought herself in love with her ex. It horrified her to think she would have married him and settled for such an insipid relationship. If what Sophie felt for Charles was even half of what she felt for Jake it was no wonder she had fallen into his arms the way she had. But, as much as she loved him, she didn't want to short-change herself in putting up with a relationship that was so out of balance. She would be a fool to think that in a few weeks there would be a tender, heart-warming airport scene where he would beg her to stay with him and marry him and have his babies.

No, he would probably wave her goodbye and then on his way home call up one of his 'friends with benefits'.

'I'm not as happy as I could be,' she said. 'And neither are you.'

He gave a harsh laugh. 'You think you know me so well, do you? Well, let me tell you I'm fine with my life right the way it is.'

'I think you want more out of life, but you're frightened of needing someone the way others need you,' she said. 'You've ruled out love because you don't want to be left like your mother was left, like *you* were left. You never got a chance to say goodbye to your father, did you? He just upped and left. You won't let that happen again. No one is going to tear your heart out again. No one. That's why it's always you who ends your relationships. You always get in first.'

A muscle moved like a hammer beneath the skin at the corner of his mouth. 'So,' he said, nailing her with his gaze, 'are you going to relieve me of the responsibility of calling it quits? Feel free. You'd be doing me a favour. This relationship has just about run its course.'

Kitty held his glittering gaze as pain at his cruel rejection moved through her body like a devastating poison. Her very bones ached with its toxicity. She had

thought finding Sophie in Charles's arms had been cru-
cifying, but it was nothing compared to this. How could
he stand there and talk of their time together as if it
meant absolutely nothing to him? Was she no more
important than any other of his shallow hook-ups? She
had foolishly thought she would win his heart. The last
couple of weeks had given her hope that he was developing feelings for her. But she could see now his heart
was never going to be available.

'It's over, Jake,' she said. 'I'm sorry but I can't be
with you on your terms. I need more.'

'Still hankering after the boyfriend at home?' he said
with a curl of his lip. 'I notice you're still wearing the
ring. He's not going to come back to you. The sooner
you accept that the better.'

She curled her fingers into her palm. 'I don't want
him to come back to me,' she said. 'I wouldn't take him
back. I know now what I want. I know what I need. I'm
not going to settle for second best.'

He held her gaze for a tense moment. A battle seemed
to be going on behind his stone-like mask. She could see
the micro-expressions on his face: a flicker of a pulse,
the twitch of a muscle, the hardening of his eyes, and
the hairpin-thinness of his lips.

'I guess that's it, then,' he said. 'I'll let you get on
with your evening. I'll see you at work.'

Kitty's shoulders went down when the door clicked
shut behind him. The sound seemed so much more than
a lock slipping into place.

It was heartbreakingly, gut-wrenchingly *final*.

CHAPTER SEVENTEEN

KITTY wasn't sure how she did it, but she got through the next couple of weeks with a courage she'd had no idea she possessed. She went to work and faced the speculation of the staff about her relationship with Jake with a poise she wouldn't have believed possible even a few weeks ago.

If Jake was upset by the termination of their brief affair he showed little sign of it. He was nothing but professional at work, although perhaps a little brusque on occasion, but Kitty kept her cool and continued to get through each day without letting him see how torn up she was. She had a particularly bad moment when she heard a rumour that he was interested in one of the nurses on the urology ward. But she never saw him bring anyone back to his place. He seemed to be working longer than normal hours, but then management had been putting a lot of pressure on keeping waiting times in A&E down.

As the date of Charles and Sophie's wedding approached, the ache Kitty had been so used to feeling about them gradually faded to a tiny pang for her fractured friendship rather than the stinging betrayal she had felt previously.

There was a bitter irony that it was Jake who had made her see the error of her ways. He had helped her to see how running away and feeling sorry for herself was not going to do anything but make her even more miserable, and how Charles's and Sophie's happiness would not be ruined by her dog-in-the-manger attitude.

He had called *her* selfish and immature, and yet what was *he* being?

She bit her lip to stop the tears from falling, as they were wont to do when she let her thoughts drift to him in unguarded moments.

She missed *everything* about him: his touch, his smell, his lazy smile and smouldering looks. She missed the closeness she had felt with him over the last few weeks.

Was she destined to be unhappy in love? Was there something horribly wrong with her that no man would love her the way she needed to be loved?

The trouble was she didn't want any other man but Jake. How could she ever be with anyone else after all she had experienced with him? Her body *ached* for him. If she so much as caught a glimpse of him at work her flesh would contract and pulse with such intense longing it took her breath away.

Kitty looked at the pretty wedding invitation that had come in the post weeks ago. She picked it up and tapped it against her lips as she looked at the calendar on the fridge. She was rostered off for five days, which would give her just enough time to fly home and attend the service without compromising her commitment to the hospital.

She would support Charles and Sophie in their love for each other. She would be happy for them. She would celebrate with them—for she knew how precious it was to find a love that surpassed all others.

As Kitty was packing her bag the evening before her flight she looked down at her promise ring. She must have lost weight in the last few days, for she could now turn it around on her finger. She went to the bathroom and soaped up her finger. It took an almighty effort, and her knuckle was probably going to be bruised and swollen as a result, but she finally got the ring off. She went back to the bedroom and slipped it inside the velvet lining of her jewellery case and gently closed the lid.

'What do you mean she's gone back to London?' Jake said to Gwen when he arrived at work on Wednesday morning. 'Why didn't she tell me she was leaving before her time was up?'

'Cool down, Jake,' Gwen said. 'She's coming back. She's only gone for a friend's wedding. She's rostered off for almost a week.'

Jake clenched his jaw. 'She should've told me she was leaving the country.'

'Why should she, Jake?' Gwen said. 'She's just another staff member. None of us have to tell you what we do in our private life. She could fly to Timbuktu on her days off and you couldn't do a thing about it.'

'I bet she doesn't come back,' he said, scowling at her furiously. 'She'll get over there and want to stay. You see if I'm not right.'

'And that would be a problem why, exactly?' Gwen asked with a raised-brow look.

Jake glowered at her. 'I'll be in my office if anyone wants me,' he said, and strode off down the corridor.

He sat brooding for an hour over paperwork. His concentration was shot. He couldn't believe Kitty had left the country without telling him. He'd only seen her the night before. Not that she had seen him. He had felt a bit like a MI5 spy or a sicko stalker, hiding behind the curtain in his kitchen, but how else was he to indulge his need to see her without her noticing his hangdog look?

It was pathetic, that was what it was. He was turning out like some sort of lovesick fool.

He was over her.

It was time to move on. Start dating again. Have some fun.

He reached for his phone and scrolled through his contacts. There were at least seven women he could call for a drink. Tasha from Urology had cornered him in the cafeteria a week or so ago and he still hadn't got back to her. Maybe it was time to get back out there. He looked at Tasha's number. His finger hovered over the call button for a moment, but instead of pressing it he pressed delete.

He put his phone down on the desk but it rang almost immediately. He snatched it up and barked, 'Yes?'

'Whoa, no need to bite my head off,' said Rosie. 'Have I caught you at a bad time?'

He leaned back in his chair with a sigh. 'No,' he said. 'I'm just trawling through some paperwork that was meant to be done yesterday.'

'You don't sound happy,' Rosie said. 'Are you OK?'

'I'm fine.'

'You don't sound fine. You sound grumpy.'

'Yeah, well, I have a lot on my mind right now.'

'This is about Kitty, isn't it?' Rosie asked. 'Why did you guys call it quits? I thought she was perfect for you.

To tell you the truth, Jake, she's the first girl you've dated that Jen and I have really liked. She'd make a fabulous sister-in-law. She's not a bimbo, for one thing. And don't forget she saved Robbie's life.'

'She's the one who broke it off,' he said, almost snapping the pen he'd picked up.

'So get back with her,' Rosie said. 'Tell her you want a second chance. Tell her you love her.'

He tossed the pen to one side. 'I'm not in love with her.'

Rosie laughed. 'Yeah, and I haven't got stretch marks. Come on, Jake. When have you been this smitten?'

'Smitten?' He recoiled at the term. 'I am *not* smitten.'

'You coughed up a thousand bucks for her,' Rosie said. 'You're smitten all right.'

Jake felt like throwing his phone at the wall. 'Did you have a reason for calling other than to rub my nose in the fact that I've been dumped?'

'I was hoping you could take Nathan for a couple of days,' Rosie said. 'You mentioned the other day at Robbie's that you've got this weekend off. It'll take your mind off things. I've got the chance to go to a health spa with a girlfriend. Should be fun.'

Jake drew in a breath and slowly exhaled. 'I was kind of hoping to have some time to myself this weekend.'

'You've been spending too much time by yourself lately,' Rosie said. 'Come on, Jake, it'll do you good to spend some quality time with Nathan. You've got nothing better to do, have you?'

Jake drummed his fingers on the desk for a moment. He could think of at least a hundred things he could do that would get him off the hook with his sister, but not one of them seemed important enough to justify spoiling her plans in order to indulge herself with a bit of R&R. The trouble was he was *always* putting other people's needs and wants before his own.

And Kitty's.

Yeah, that's right, you great big bozo, he thought in self-recrimination. *Isn't it time you thought of what she wants and needs?*

Kitty was being brave enough to travel all that way to support her friends, to put her bitterness aside. Who would support her? Who would hand her tissue after tissue during the soppy bits of the service?

Who would tell her he loved her and couldn't bear to spend another day without her in his life?

Jake shoved back his chair and stood up. 'Actually, I do have something on,' he said. 'I'm flying to London for the weekend.'

'You're *what*?' Rosie gasped. 'Did you say London? London as in England? London as in Buckingham Palace and Big Ben and the Queen and Harrods?'

'Yep.'

'Are you out of your cotton-picking mind? Rosie asked. 'Who on earth flies to London for a *weekend*?'

Jake felt a smile spread over his face. 'A man head over heels in love does,' he said, and hung up the phone.

'You look beautiful,' Kitty said as she adjusted Sophie's veil outside the church. 'I'm so happy for you.'

Sophie gripped Kitty's hands in both of hers. 'I'm so glad you came,' she said with tears in her eyes. 'It means so much to Charles and me. We could never be happy together unless we felt you were happy for us.'

'I *am* happy for you,' Kitty said. 'I'm sorry for being

such a cow about things. I can't believe I was so child-ish. You two belong together. Anyone can see that.'

Sophie beamed. 'Here's our cue,' she said as the organ started to play. 'Shall we get this show on the road?'

'Let's do it.' Kitty smiled even though a part of her ached that Jake wasn't here to see how brave she was being. She missed him more now there were so many miles between them.

But then he had always been far away—if not physi-cally then emotionally.

Jake's flight was late landing, and then there was a delay coming through Customs. He had to wait ages for a taxi, and to top it all off there was an accident a kilometre or so from the church where the wedding was taking place. He had sourced that information via Gwen, who had let slip that Kitty's best friend was being married in her home village just outside of London.

The service was well under way by the time he trudged through the snow, having paid off the taxi driver who had had no choice but to stick it out until the tow trucks cleared everything away.

It was *freezing*.

How did anyone survive this climate? His face felt as if it was being burned with the cold. The sun was like a rheumy eye behind moody clouds. Why would anyone get married on a day like this? Why not wait until spring or summer, when there was at least the faint possibility of the sun breaking through the mattress-thick clouds?

Jake slipped in the back of the church and watched the proceedings. Kitty was standing holding the bride's bouquet. She looked amazing. She was wearing a blue

V-neck satin dream of a tea dress that clung to her slim body like a glove. Her hair was in an up style that high-lighted her elegant cheekbones. Her make-up was un-derstated, but she still outshone the bride.

Quite frankly, he couldn't see what the groom was thinking in choosing the bride over Kitty. The bride looked OK—well, more than OK if you had a thing for straight raven hair and strong features. Kitty, on the other hand looked delicate and dainty. She had a smile on her face that he could only hope was genuine.

A flood of doubts suddenly assailed him. What if she sent him packing? What if he made a complete fool of himself before all these toffee-nosed guests?

He started to picture it in his head. A top-notch se-curity team would frogmarch him to the door, shoving him out into the cold…

But then Kitty shifted slightly and locked gazes with him. He saw the shock in her eyes. They opened wide, along with her mouth, but then, as if she suddenly re-membered she had a role to play as maid of honour, she turned back to the proceedings and fixed a neutral smile on her face.

Jake glanced at the ushers either side of him at the back of the church. So far so good. He wasn't identi-fied as an interloper—yet.

The bride and groom kissed and then moved to the vestry to sign the register. Kitty went with the rest of the bridal party. Jake's insides clenched when he saw the best man slide his arm around her waist in a pro-prietorial manner.

He wanted to punch the guy's lights out.

The bride and groom were announced and began to make their journey back down the aisle. Jake waited patiently as Kitty went past. She sent him a sideways glance that made his heart race. Was that a smile he could see playing about her lips? Was it for the cameras or for him?

He had to wait twenty minutes or so to find out. Finally he cornered her in between photos. 'Hi,' he said. 'Nice day for a wedding.'

'You think?' Kitty said with a wary look.

'Personally I'd opt for a summer day at the beach, with a celebrant in bare feet,' he said. 'Just a few close friends and family. And a barbecue in the park to follow—a few beers, loads of cheap champagne.'

She angled her head at him. 'No cucumber sandwiches?'

He grinned at her. 'Maybe a couple, if that's what you want.'

Her neat brows met over her eyes. 'Are you...?' She shook her head as if she was hallucinating. 'God, I knew I shouldn't have had that champagne with Sophie while we were getting our hair done. It's gone straight to my head.'

'I love you,' Jake said. 'I want to marry you.'

Kitty blinked. 'I am never going to let alcohol pass my lips again. *Ever.*' She made to move past him. 'Excuse me. I have to join the others for the official photos. They're waiting for me.'

'Hey,' Jake said, snaring her arm to bring her back to face him. 'I've just travelled close to seventeen thousand kilometres to ask you to marry me. The least you could do is give me a straight yes or no.'

Kitty ran her tongue over her lips. 'Is this a joke?' she asked. 'Are you doing this to make fun of me or something?'

He barked out a wry laugh. 'You think I'd joke about something like this? I left everything to get over here to be with you. I'll probably lose my job when the CEO finds out I've left the country. I just wanted to see you face-to-face. I've never asked someone to marry me before. I didn't want to do it over the phone or with a text or on Skype. Telling someone you love them is a big deal—or at least it is in my book.'

Kitty felt a tremor of sheer joy judder through her body. 'You love me?'

His sapphire-blue gaze softened. 'How could I *not* love you?' he asked, grasping her by the hands. 'I want to spend the rest of my life with you. Marry me, Kitty. Have babies with me. I'll be a great dad. I've had loads of practice. I'm not sure what sort of husband I'll make. I haven't had a great role model. But I know I love you so much that I can't bear the thought of spending another day of my life without you in it.'

Kitty was reeling from shock, surprise and happiness. 'But I thought you never wanted to get married,' she said. 'You said you didn't want to be tied down. That you were sick of being responsible for everyone.'

'Loving someone is all about responsibility,' Jake said. 'As soon as you love someone you become responsible for them and they become responsible for you. I've been watching out for my family for so long that I didn't realise I was part of the problem. My sisters and brother are so used to me being there for them that they've forgotten how to be there for each other. With me stepping away for these few days Rosie has turned to Jen for help. Robbie has chipped in as well.'

Kitty looked at him in wonder, still not sure if she was imagining him standing before her in person. 'I can't believe you came all this way,' she said. 'I keep thinking you're going to melt away in a puff of smoke or something.'

'*Smoke?*' He looked at her incredulously. 'Are you joking? I'm more likely to be frozen to the spot. How on earth do you live like this? It's perishingly cold out here, and there you are with bare arms and shoulders. Do you want my jacket?' He quickly shrugged himself out of it and draped it around her shoulders.

She smiled as she breathed in his scent and body warmth. 'I just want you,' she said.

He cupped her face in his hands and pressed a lingering kiss to her mouth. 'God, I've missed you *so* much,' he said, once he had raised his mouth off hers. 'You *are* coming back, aren't you? You still have six weeks to fulfil your term.'

Her eyes danced as they held his. 'So I'm not on probation any more, Dr Chandler?' she asked.

He tugged her up close, his eyes glinting down at her. 'You never were,' he said and captured her mouth beneath his.

* * * * *

HER
CHRISTMAS EVE
DIAMOND

BY
SCARLET WILSON

MILLS & BOON®

First published in Great Britain 2012
by Mills & Boon, an imprint of Harlequin (UK) Limited.
Harlequin (UK) Limited, Eton House, 18-24 Paradise Road,
Richmond, Surrey TW9 1SR

© Scarlet Wilson 2012

ISBN: 978 0 263 89207 9

Harlequin (UK) policy is to use papers that are natural, renewable
and recyclable products and made from wood grown in sustainable
forests. The logging and manufacturing process conform to the
legal environmental regulations of the country of origin.

Printed and bound in Spain
by Blackprint CPI, Barcelona

Dear Reader

Christmas is my absolute favourite time of year. I spend every Christmas Eve praying for some snow to fall and hoping we'll get a white Christmas. I love putting up my Christmas tree, wrapping presents, watching Christmas films, and most of all I love to see Christmas-themed books on the shelves—so much so I begged my editor to let me write one!

Cassidy Rae is a bit like me. She counts the number of Christmas trees in the house windows on the way to work and thrives on the Christmas spirit. But Brad Donovan doesn't share her enthusiasm. Christmas is a painful time of year for him, reminding him of what has slipped out of his grasp. He's just managing to keep his head above water and is looking for a distraction—anything to keep his mind off Christmas. So what happens when the Christmas fairy meets the Grinch? Read on and see.

What I *can* guarantee you is that there will be snowflakes on Christmas Eve!

Merry Christmas!

Scarlet Wilson

PS I love hearing from readers. Come and visit my website: www.scarlet-wilson.com

DEDICATION

This book is dedicated to the children
I've watched grow up over the years
from excitable toddlers into responsible adults.

Carissa Hyndman, Jordan Dickson, Dillon Glencross
and Carly Glencross. Life is what you make it—
reach for the stars!

And to my new editor Carly Byrne.
Thanks for all your support and encouragement.
Writing can be tricky business and you make it all
so much easier—I think we make a good team!

PROLOGUE

30 September

CASSIDY raised her hand and knocked on the dilapidated door. Behind her Lucy giggled nervously. 'Are you sure this is the right address?'

Cassidy turned to stare at her. 'You arranged this. How should I know?' She glanced at the crumpled piece of paper in her hand. 'This is definitely number seventeen.' She leaned backwards, looking at the 1960s curtains hanging in the secondary glazed double windows that rattled every time a bus went past. 'Maybe nobody's home?' she said hopefully.

This had to be the worst idea she'd ever had. No. Correction. It hadn't been her idea. In a moment of weakness she'd just agreed to come along with her colleagues to see what all the fuss was about.

'Where did you find this one, Lucy?'

Lucy had spent the past year whisking her friends off to as many different fortune-tellers as possible. By all accounts, some were good, some were bad and some were just downright scary. Cassidy had always managed to wriggle out of it—until now.

'This is the one my cousin Fran came to. She said she was fab.'

Cassidy raised her eyebrows. 'Cousin Fran who went on the reality TV show and then spent the next week hiding in the cupboard?'

Lucy nodded. 'Oh, great,' sighed Cass.

'I wonder if she'll tell me how many children I'll have,' murmured Lynn dreamily. She stuck her pointed elbow into Cassidy's ribs. 'She told Lizzie King she'd have twins and she's due any day now.'

'I just want to know if Frank is ever going to propose,' sighed Tamsin. 'If she doesn't see it in the future then I'm dumping him. Five years is long enough.'

Cassidy screwed up her nose and shook her head. 'You can't dump Frank because of something a fortune-teller says.'

But Tamsin had that expression on her face—the one that said, *Don't mess with me.* 'Watch me.'

There was a shuffle behind the door then a creak and the door swung open. 'Hello, ladies, come on in.'

Cassidy blinked. The smell of cats hit her in the face like a steamroller.

She allowed the stampede behind her to thunder inside then took a deep breath of clean outside air, before pulling the door closed behind her. A mangy-looking cat wound its way around her legs. 'Shoo!' she hissed.

'Come on, Cassidy!'

She plastered a smile on her face and joined her colleagues in smelly-cat-woman's front room. The peeling noise beneath the soles of her feet told her that the carpet was sticky. She dreaded to think what with.

Her three friends were crowded onto the brown sofa. Another cat was crawling across the back of the sofa behind their heads. Cassidy's eyes started to stream and she resisted the temptation to start rubbing them. Once she started, she couldn't stop. Cat allergies did that to you.

'So who wants to go first?'

Cassidy glanced at her watch. How had she got roped into this?

'You go first, Cass,' said Lucy, who turned to smelly-cat woman. 'You'll have to do a good job, Belinda. Our Cassidy's a non-believer.'

The small, rotund woman eyed Cassidy up and down. Her brow was as wrinkled as her clothes. 'This way, dear,' she muttered, wandering down the hallway to another room.

Cassidy swallowed nervously. Maybe it would be easier to get this over and done with. Then at least she could wait outside in the car for the others.

The room was full of clutter. And cats.

As Belinda settled herself at one side of the table and shuffled some cards, Cassidy eyed the squashed easy chair on the other side. A huge marmalade cat was sitting in pride of place, blinking at her, daring her to move him.

Her gorgeous turquoise-blue velvet pea coat would attract cat hairs like teenage girls to a Bieber concert. She should just kiss it goodbye now.

'Move, Lightning!' Belinda kicked the chair and the cat gave her a hard stare before stretching on his legs and jumping from the seat, settling at her feet.

Cassidy couldn't hide the smile from her face. It had to be the most inappropriately named cat—ever.

Belinda fixed her eyes on her. How could such a soft, round woman have such a steely glare? Her eyes weren't even blinking. She was staring so hard Cass thought she would bore a hole through her skull.

She looked around her. Books everywhere. Piles of magazines. Shelves and shelves of ornaments, all looking as though they could do with a good dust. Another allergy to set off. One, two, no, three…no, there was another one hiding in the corner. Four cats in the room. All looking at her as if she shouldn't be there. Maybe they knew something that she didn't.

'So, what do we do?' she asked quickly.

Belinda's face had appeared kindly, homely when she'd answered the door. But in here, when it was just the two of them, she looked like a cold and shrewd businesswoman. Cassidy wondered if she could read the thoughts currently in her head. That would account for the light-sabre stare.

Belinda shuffled the cards again. 'We can do whatever you prefer.' She spread the cards face down on the table. 'I can read your cards.' She reached over and grabbed hold of Cassidy's hand. 'I can read your palm. Or…' she glanced around the room '…I can channel some spirits and see what they've got to say.'

The thought sent a chill down Cassidy's spine. She wasn't sure she believed any of this. But she certainly didn't want to take the risk of channelling any unwanted spirits.

The TV special she'd watched the other day had claimed that all of this was based on reading people. Seeing the tiny, almost imperceptible reactions they had to certain words, certain gestures. Cassidy had come here tonight determined not to move a muscle, not even to blink. But her cat allergy seemed to have got the better of her, and her eyes were a red, blinking, streaming mess. So much for not moving.

She didn't like the look of the cards either. Knowing her luck, she'd turn over the death card—or the equivalent of the Joker.

'Let's just do the palm, please.' It seemed the simplest option. How much could anyone get from some lines on a palm?

Belinda leaned across the table, taking Cassidy's slim hand and wrist and encapsulating them in her pudgy fingers. There was something quite soothing about it. She wasn't examining Cassidy's palm—just holding her hand. Stroking her fingers across the back of her hand for a few silent minutes, then turning her hand over and touching the inside of her palm.

A large smile grew across her face.

The suspense was killing her. Cassidy didn't like long silences. 'What is it?'

Belinda released her hand. 'You're quite the little misery guts, aren't you?'

'What?' Cassidy was stunned. The last she'd heard, these people were only supposed to tell you good things. And certainly not assassinate your character.

Belinda nodded. 'On the surface you're quite the joker with your friends at work. On the other hand, you always see the glass half-empty. Very self-deprecating. All signs of insecurity.' She took a deep breath. 'But very particular at work. Your attention to detail makes you hard to work with. Some of your colleagues just don't know how to take you. And as for men...'

'What?' Right now, men were the last thing on her mind. And the word 'insecurity' had hit a nerve she didn't want to acknowledge. It was bad enough having parents who jet-setted around the world, without having a fiancé who'd upped and left. The last thing she wanted was some random stranger pointing it out to her.

'You're a clever girl, but sometimes you can't see what's right at the end of your nose.' She shook her head. 'You've got some very fixed ideas, and you're not very good at the art of compromise. Just as well Christmas is coming up.'

Cassidy was mad now. 'What's that got to do with anything? Christmas is still three months away.'

Belinda folded her arms across her chest, a smug expression on her face. 'You're going to be a Christmas bride.'

'What?'

The woman had clearly lost her cat-brained mind.

'How on earth can I be a Christmas bride? It's October tomorrow, and I don't have a boyfriend. And there's nobody I'm even remotely interested in.'

Belinda tapped the side of her nose, giving her shoulders an annoying little shrug. 'I only see the future. I don't tell you how you're going to get there.' She leaned over and touched the inside of Cassidy's palm. 'I can see you as a Christmas bride, along with a very handsome groom—not from around these parts either. Lucky you.'

Cassidy shook her head firmly. It had taken her months to get over her broken engagement to her Spanish fiancé—and it had not been an experience she wanted to repeat. 'You're absolutely wrong. There's no way I'm going to be a Christmas bride. And particularly not with a groom from elsewhere. I've had it with foreign men. The next man I hook up with will be a true fellow Scot, through and through.'

Belinda gave her *the look*. The look that said, *You've no idea what you're talking about*.

'That's us, then.'

Cassidy was aghast. Twenty quid for that? 'That's it?'

Belinda nodded and waved her hand. 'Send the next one in.'

Cassidy hesitated for a second, steeling herself to argue with the woman. But then the fat orange cat brushed against her legs and leapt up onto the chair beside her, determined to shed its thousands of orange cat hairs over her velvet coat. She jumped up. At least she was over and done with. She could wait outside in the car. It was almost worth the twenty quid for that alone.

She walked along the corridor, mumbling to herself, attempting to brush a big wad of clumped cat hair from her coat.

'Are you done already? What did she tell you?'

Cassidy rolled her eyes. 'It's not even worth repeating.' She jerked her head down the corridor. 'Go on, Tamsin. Go and find out when you're getting your proposal.'

Tamsin still had that determined look on her face. She stood up and straightened her pristine black mac—no orange cat hairs for her. 'You mean *if* I'm getting my proposal.' She swept down the corridor and banged the door closed behind her.

Lucy raised her eyebrows. 'Heaven help Belinda if she doesn't tell Tam what she wants to hear.' She turned back to Cassidy. 'Come on, then, spill. What did she say?'

Cassidy blew out a long, slow breath through pursed lips. She was annoyed at being called a 'misery guts.'

And she was beyond irritated at being called insecure. 'I'm apparently going to be a Christmas bride.'

'*What?*' Lucy's and Lynn's voices were in perfect tandem with their matching shocked expressions.

'Just as well Tamsin didn't hear that,' Lucy muttered.

'Oh, it gets worse. Apparently my groom is from foreign climes.' She rolled her eyes again. 'As if.'

But Lucy's and Lynn's expressions had changed, smiles creeping across their faces as their eyes met.

'Told you.'

'No way.'

Cassidy watched in bewilderment as they high-fived each other in the dingy sitting room.

'What's with you two? You know the whole thing's ridiculous. As if *I'm* going to date another foreign doctor.'

Lynn folded her arms across her chest. 'Stranger things have happened.' She had a weird look on her face. As if she knew something that Cassidy didn't.

Lucy adopted the same pose, shoulder to shoulder with Lynn. Almost as if they were ganging up on her.

Her gaze narrowed. 'I'm willing to place a bet that Belinda could be right.'

Cassidy couldn't believe what was happening. The crazy-cat-woman's disease was obviously contagious. A little seed planted in her brain. She could use this to her advantage. 'What's it worth?'

Lucy frowned. 'What do you mean?'

Cassidy smiled. 'I'll take that bet. But what's it worth?'

'Night shift Christmas Eve. Oh.' The words were out before Lucy had had time to think about them. She had her hand across her mouth. It was the most hated shift on the planet. Every year they had to draw straws to see who would take it.

'You're on.' Cassidy held out her hand towards Lucy, who nodded and shook it firmly. She had no chance of losing this bet. No chance at all.

CHAPTER ONE

1 October

CASSIDY pulled the navy-blue tunic over her head. These new-style NHS uniforms were supposed to be made from a revolutionary lightweight fabric, designed for comfort and ease of fit. The reality was they were freezing and not designed for Scottish winters in a draughty old hospital. She pulled a cardigan from her locker and headed for the stairs. Maybe running up three flights would take the chill out of her bones.

Two minutes later she arrived in the medical ward. She took a deep breath. There it was. The hospital smell. Some people hated it and shuddered walking through the very doors of the hospital. But Cassidy loved it—it was like a big security blanket, and she'd missed it. It was just before seven and the lights were still dimmed. Ruby, the night nurse, gave her a smile. 'Nice to see you back, Cassidy. How was the secondment?'

Cassidy nodded, wrapping her cardigan further around her torso. Her temperature was still barely above freezing. 'It was fine, but three months was long enough. The new community warfarin clinic is set up—all the teething problems ironed out. To be honest, though, I'm glad to be back. I missed this place.'

And she had. But at the time the three-month secondment had been perfect for her. It had given her the chance to sort out all the hassles with her gran, work regular hours and get her settled into the new nursing home—the second in a year. Her eyes swept over the whiteboard on the wall, displaying all the patient names, room numbers and named nurses. 'No beds?' She raised her eyebrows.

'Actually, we've got one. But A and E just phoned to say they're sending us an elderly lady with a chest infection, so I've put her name up on the board already. She should be up in the next ten minutes.'

Cassidy gave a nod as the rest of the day-shift staff appeared, gathering around the nurses' station for the handover report. She waited patiently, listening to the rundown of the thirty patients currently in her general medical ward, before assigning the patients to the nurses on duty and accepting the keys for the medicine and drugs cabinets.

She heard the ominous trundle of a trolley behind her. 'I'll admit this patient,' she told her staff. 'It'll get me back into the swing of things.'

She looked up as Bill, one of the porters, arrived, pulling the trolley with the elderly woman lying on top. A doctor was walking alongside them, carrying some notes and chatting to the elderly lady as they wheeled her into one of the side rooms. He gave her a smile— one that could have launched a thousand toothpaste campaigns. 'This is Mrs Elizabeth Kelly. She's eighty-four and has a history of chronic obstructive pulmonary disease. She's had a chest infection for the last seven days that hasn't responded to oral antibiotics. Her oxygen saturation is down at eighty-two and she's tachycardic. The doctor on call wanted her admitted for IV antibiotics.'

For a moment the strong Australian accent threw her—she hadn't been expecting it. Though goodness knows why not. Her hospital in the middle of Glasgow attracted staff from all over the world. His crumpled blue scrubs and even more crumpled white coat looked as though he'd slept in them—and judging by his blond hair, sticking up in every direction but the right one, he probably had.

She didn't recognise him, which meant he must be one of the new doctors who had started while she was away on secondment. And he was too handsome by far. And that cheeky twinkle in his eye was already annoying her.

After three months away, some things appeared to have changed around the hospital. It was usually one of the A and E nurses who accompanied the patient up to the ward.

Cassidy pumped up the bed and removed the headboard, pulling the patslide from the wall and sliding the patient over into the bed. The doctor helped her put the headboard back on and adjusted the backrest, rearranging the pillows so Mrs Kelly could sit upright. Cassidy attached the monitoring equipment and changed the oxygen supply over to the wall. The doctor was still standing looking at her.

For a second she almost thought he was peering at her breasts, but as she followed his gaze downwards she realised her name and designation was stitched on the front of her new tunics.

She held out her hand towards him. 'Cassidy Rae. Sister of the medical receiving unit. Though from the way you're staring at my breasts, I take it you've gathered that.'

His warm hand caught her cold one, his eyes twinkling. 'Pleased to meet you, Dragon Lady. I hope your heart isn't as cold as your hands.'

She pulled her hand away from his. 'What did you call me?'

'Dragon Lady.' He looked unashamed by the remark. 'Your reputation precedes you. I've been looking forward to meeting you, although from what I hear it's usually you who does the name-calling.'

She folded her arms across her chest, trying to stop the edges of her mouth turning upwards. 'I've no idea what you're talking about.' She picked up the patient clothing bag and bent down, starting to unpack Mrs Kelly's belongings into the cabinet next to her bed.

'I heard you called the last lot Needy, Greedy and Seedy.'

She jumped. She could feel his warm breath on her neck. He'd bent forward and whispered in her ear.

'Who told you that?' she asked incredulously. She glanced at her watch. Ten past seven on her first morning back, and already some smart-alec doc was trying to get the better of her.

'Oh, give me a minute.' The mystery doctor ducked out of the room.

It was true. She had nicknamed the last three registrars—all for obvious reasons. One had spent every waking minute eating, the other hadn't seen a patient without someone holding his hand, and as for the last one, he'd spent his year sleazing over all the female staff. And while the nursing staff knew the nicknames she'd given them, she'd no idea who'd told one of the new docs. She'd need to investigate that later.

She stood up and adjusted Mrs Kelly's venturi mask, taking a note of her thin frame and pale, papery skin. Another frail, elderly patient, just like her gran. She altered the alarms on the monitor—at their present setting they would sound every few minutes. With a history of COPD, Mrs Kelly had lower than normal oxygen levels.

'How are you feeling?' She picked up the tympanic thermometer and placed it in Mrs Kelly's ear, pressing the button to read her temperature then recording her observations in the chart. Mrs Kelly shook her pale head.

She sat down at the side of the bed. 'I need to take some details from you, Mrs Kelly. But how about I get you something to eat and drink first? I imagine you were stuck down in A and E for hours. Would you like some tea? Some toast?'

'Your wish is my command.' The steaming cup of tea and plate of buttered toast thudded down on the bedside table. 'See, Mrs Kelly? I make good on my promises.' He shook his head at Cassidy. 'There was *nothing* to eat down in A and E and I promised I'd get her some tea once we got up here.'

'Thank you, son,' Mrs Kelly said, shifting her mask and lifting the cup to her lips, 'My throat is so dry.'

He nodded slowly. Oxygen therapy frequently made patients' mouths dry and it was important to keep them hydrated.

Cassidy stared at him. Things had changed. She couldn't remember the last time she'd seen a doctor make a patient a cup of tea. It was almost unheard of.

She smiled at him. 'Makes me almost wish we could keep you,' she said quietly. 'You've obviously been well trained.'

His blue eyes glinted. 'And what makes you think you can't keep me?'

'I imagine A and E will have a whole load of patients waiting for you. Why did you come up here anyway? Was it to steal our chocolates?' She nodded towards the nursing station. The medical receiving unit was never short of chocolates, and it wasn't unknown for the doctors from other departments to sneak past and steal some.

He shook his head, the smile still stuck on his face. He held out his hand towards her. 'I forgot to introduce myself earlier. I'm one of yours—though I dread to think what nickname you'll give me. Brad Donovan, medical registrar.'

Cassidy felt herself jerk backwards in surprise. He looked too young to be a medical registrar. Maybe it was the scruffy hair? Or the Australian tan? Or maybe it was that earring glinting in his ear, along with the super-white teeth? He didn't look like any registrar she'd ever met before.

Something twisted inside her gut. No, that wasn't quite true. Bobby. For a tiny second he reminded her of Bobby. But Bobby's hair had been dark, not blond, and he'd worn it in a similar scruffy style and had the same glistening white teeth. She pushed all thoughts away. She hadn't thought about him in months. Where had that come from?

She focused her mind. This was a work colleague—albeit a cheeky one. She shook his hand firmly. 'Well,

Dr Donovan, if you're one of mine then maybe I should tell you the rules in my ward.'

His eyebrows rose, an amused expression on his face. 'You really are the Dragon Lady, aren't you?'

She ignored him. 'When you finally manage to put some clothes on, no silly ties. In fact, no ties at all and no long sleeves. They're an infection-control hazard.' She ran her eyes up and down his crumpled scrubs, 'Though from the look of you, that doesn't seem to be a problem. Always use the gel outside the patients' rooms before you touch them. And pay attention to what my nurses tell you—they spend most of their day with the patients and will generally know the patients ten times better than you will.'

His blue eyes fixed on hers. Quite unnerving for this time in the morning. His gaze was straight and didn't falter. The guy was completely unfazed by her. He seemed confident, self-assured. She would have to wait and see if his clinical competence matched his demeanour.

'I have been working here for the last two months without your rulebook. I'm sure your staff will give me a good report.' She resisted the temptation to reply. Of course her staff would give him a good report. He was like a poster boy for Surfers' Central. She could put money on it that he'd spent the last two months charming her staff with his lazy accent, straight white teeth and twinkling eyes. He handed her Mrs Kelly's case notes and prescription chart.

'I've written Mrs Kelly up for some IV antibiotics, some oral steroids and some bronchodilators. She had her arterial blood gases done in A and E and I'll check them again in a few hours. I'd like her on four-hourly obs in the meantime.' He glanced at the oxygen supply, currently running at four litres. 'Make sure she stays on the twenty-eight per cent venturi mask. One of the students in A and E didn't understand the complications of COPD and put her on ten litres of straight oxygen.'

Cassidy's mouth fell open. 'Please tell me you're joking.'

He shook his head. The effects could have been devastating. 'Her intentions were good. Mrs Kelly's lips were blue from lack of oxygen when she was admitted. The student just did what seemed natural. Luckily one of the other staff spotted her mistake quickly.'

Cassidy looked over at the frail, elderly lady on the bed, her oxygen mask currently dangling around her neck as she munched the toast from the plate in front of her. The blue tinge had obviously disappeared from her lips, but even eating the toast was adding to her breathlessness. She turned back to face Brad. 'Any relatives?'

He shook his head. 'Her husband died a few years ago and her daughter emigrated to my neck of the woods ten years before that.' He pointed to a phone number in the records. 'Do you want me to phone her, or do you want to do that?'

Cassidy felt a little pang. This poor woman must be lonely. She'd lost her husband, and her daughter lived thousands of miles away. Who did she speak to every day? One of the last elderly patients admitted to her ward had disclosed that often he went for days without a single person to speak to. Loneliness could be a terrible burden.

The doctor passed in front of her vision again, trying to catch her attention, and she pushed the uncomfortable thoughts from her head. This one was definitely too good to be true. Bringing up a patient, making tea and toast, and offering to phone relatives?

Her internal radar started to ping. She turned to Mrs Kelly. 'I'll let you finish your tea and come back in a few minutes.

'What are you up to?' She headed out the door towards the nursing station.

He fell into step beside her. 'What do you mean?'

She paused in the corridor, looking him up and down. 'You're too good to be true. Which means alarm bells are ringing in my head. What's with the nice-boy act?'

She pulled up the laptop from the nurses' station and started to input some of Mrs Kelly's details.

'Who says it's an act?'

Her eyes swept down the corridor. The case-note trolley had been pulled to the end of the corridor. Two other doctors in white coats were standing, talking over some notes. She looked at her watch—not even eight o'clock. 'And who are they?'

Brad smiled. 'That's the other registrars. Luca is from Italy, and Franco is from Hungary. They must have wanted to get a head start on the ward round.' He gave her a brazen wink. 'I guess they heard the Dragon Lady was on duty today.'

She shook her head in bewilderment. 'I go on secondment for three months, come back and I've got the poster boy for Surfers' Paradise making tea and toast for patients and two other registrars in the ward before eight a.m. Am I still dreaming? Have I woken up yet?'

'Why?' As quick as a flash he'd moved around beside her. 'Am I the kind of guy you dream about?'

'Get lost, flyboy.' She pushed Mrs Kelly's case notes back into his hands. 'You've got a patient's daughter in

Australia to go and phone. Make yourself useful while I go and find out what kind of support system she has at home.'

He paused for a second, his eyes narrowing. 'She's not even heated up the bed yet and you're planning on throwing her back out?'

Cassidy frowned. 'It's the basic principle of the receiving unit. Our first duty is to find out what systems are in place for our patients. Believe it or not, most of them don't like staying here. And if we plan ahead it means there's less chance of a delayed discharge. Sometimes it can take a few days to set up support systems to get someone home again.' She raised her hand to the whiteboard with patient names. 'In theory, we're planning for their discharge as soon as they enter A and E.'

The look on his face softened. 'In that case, I'll let you off.' He nodded towards his fellow doctors. 'Maybe they got the same alarm call that I did. Beware the Dragon!' He headed towards the doctors' office to make his call.

Dragon Lady was much more interesting than he'd been led to believe. He'd expected a sixty-year-old, grey-haired schoolmarm. Instead he'd got a young woman with a slim, curvy figure, chestnut curls and deep brown eyes. And she was feisty. He liked that.

Cassidy Rae could be fun. There it was, that strange, almost unfamiliar feeling. That first glimmer of interest in a woman. That tiny little thought that something could spark between them given half a chance. It had been so long since he'd felt it that he almost didn't know what to do about it.

He'd been here a few months, and while his colleagues were friendly, they weren't his 'friends'. And he didn't want to hang around with the female junior doctors currently batting their eyelids at him. Experience had taught him it was more trouble than it was worth.

Distraction. The word echoed around his head again as he leaned against the cold concrete wall.

Exactly what he needed. Something to keep his mind from other things—like another Christmas Day currently looming on the horizon with a huge black stormcloud hovering over it. He'd even tried to juggle the schedules so he could be working on Christmas Day. But no such luck. His Italian colleague had beat him to it, and right now he couldn't bear the thought of an empty Christmas Day in strange surroundings with no real friends or family.

Another Christmas spent wondering where his little girl was, if she was enjoying her joint birthday and Christmas Day celebrations. Wondering if she even remembered he existed.

He had no idea what she'd been told about him. The fact he'd spent the last eighteen months trying to track down his daughter at great time and expense killed him—especially in the run-up to her birthday. Everyone else around him was always full of festive spirit and fun, and no matter how hard he tried not to be the local misery guts, something inside him just felt dead.

Christmas was about families and children. And the one thing he wanted to do was sit his little girl on his knee and get her the biggest birthday and Christmas present in the world. If only he knew where she was…

There was that fist again, hovering around his stomach, tightly clenched. Every time he thought of his daughter, Melody, the visions of her mother, Alison, a junior doctor he'd worked with, appeared in his head. Alison, the woman who only liked things her way or no way at all. No negotiation. No compromise.

More importantly, no communication.

The woman who'd left a bitter taste in his mouth for the last eighteen months. Blighting every other relationship he'd tried to have. The woman who'd wrangled over every custody arrangement, telling him he was impinging on her life. Then one day that had been it. Nothing. He'd gone to pick up two-year-old Melody as planned and had turned up at an empty house. No forwarding address. Nothing.

The colleagues at the hospital where Alison had worked said she'd thought about going to America—apparently she'd fallen head over heels in love with some American doctor. But no one knew where. And he'd spent the last few years getting his solicitor to chase false leads halfway around the world. It had taken over his whole world. Every second of every day had revolved around finding his daughter. Until he'd finally cracked and some good friends had sat him down firmly and spoken to him.

It had only been in the last few months, since moving to Scotland, that he'd finally started to feel like himself again. His laid-back manner had returned, and he'd finally started to relax and be comfortable in his own skin again.

While he would still do everything in his power to find his daughter, he had to realise his limitations. He had to accept the fact he hadn't done anything wrong and he still deserved to live a life.

And while the gaggle of nurses and female junior

doctors didn't appeal to him, Cassidy Rae did. She was a different kettle of fish altogether. A fierce, sassy woman who could help him make some sparks fly. A smile crept over his face. Now there was just the small matter of the duty room to break to her. How would she react to that?

Cassidy went back to Mrs Kelly and finished her admission paperwork, rechecked her obs and helped her wash and change into a clean nightdress. By the time she'd finished, Mrs Kelly was clearly out of breath again. Even the slightest exertion seemed to fatigue her.

Cassidy hung the IV antibiotics from the drip stand and connected up the IV. 'These will take half an hour to go through. The doctor has changed the type of antibiotic that you're on so hopefully they'll be more effective than the ones you were taking at home.'

Mrs Kelly nodded. 'Thanks, love. He's a nice one, isn't he?' There was a little pause. 'And he's single. Told me so himself.'

'Who?' Cassidy had started to tidy up around about her, putting away the toilet bag and basin.

'That handsome young doctor. Reminds of that guy on TV. You know, the one from the soap opera.'

Cassidy shook her head. 'I don't watch soap operas. And anyway...' she bundled up the used towels and sheets to put in the laundry trolley '...I'm looking for a handsome Scotsman. Not someone from the other side of the world.'

She walked over to the window. The old hospital building was several storeys high, on the edge of the city. The grey clouds were hanging low this morning and some drizzly rain was falling outside, but she could still see some greenery in the distance.

'Why on earth would anyone want to leave all this behind?' she joked.

Mrs Kelly raised her eyebrows. 'Why indeed?'

Cassidy spent the rest of the morning finding her feet again in the ward. The hospital computer system had been updated, causing her to lose half her patients at the touch of a button. And the automated pharmacy delivery seemed to be on the blink again. Some poor patients' medicines would be lost in a pod stuck in a tube somewhere.

Lucy appeared from the ward next door, clutching a cup of tea, and tapped her on the shoulder. 'How does it feel to be back?'

Cassidy gave her friend a smile. 'It's good.' She picked up the off-duty book. 'I just need to get my head around the rosters again.' Her eyes fell on the sticky notes inside the book and she rolled her eyes. 'Oh, great. Seven members of staff want the same weekend off.'

Lucy laughed. 'That's nothing. One of our girls got married last weekend and I had to rope in two staff from the next ward to cover the night shift. Got time for a tea break?'

She shook her head and pointed down the corridor. 'The consultant's just about to arrive for the ward round.'

Lucy crossed her arms across her chest as she followed Cassidy's gaze to the three registrars at the bottom of the corridor. 'So what do you make of our new docs?'

Cassidy never even lifted her head. 'Funky, Chunky and Hunky?'

Lucy spluttered tea all down the front of her uniform. She looked at her watch. 'Less than two hours and you've got nicknames for them already?'

Cassidy lifted her eyebrows. 'It wasn't hard. Although Luca is drop-dead gorgeous, he's more interested in his own reflection than any of the patients. And Franco has finished off two rolls with sausages and half a box of chocolates in the last half hour.'

'So none of them have caught your eye, then?'

Cassidy turned her head at the tone in her friend's voice. She looked at her suspiciously. 'Why? What are you up to?'

Lucy's gaze was still fixed down the corridor. 'Nothing. I just wondered what you thought of them.' She started to shake her behind as she wiggled past, singing along about single ladies.

Cassidy looked back down the corridor. Her eyes were drawn in one direction. Brad's appearance hadn't improved. He was still wearing his crumpled scrubs and coat. His hair was still untamed and she could see a shadow around his jaw.

But he had spent nearly half an hour talking to Mrs Kelly's daughter and then another half hour talking Mrs Kelly through her treatment for the next few days. Then trying to persuade her that once she was fit and well, she might want to take up her daughter's offer of a visit to Australia.

Most doctors she worked with weren't that interested in their patients' holistic care. Their radar seemed to switch off as soon as they'd made a clinical diagnosis.

There was the sound of raucous laughter at the end of the corridor, and Cassidy looked up to see Brad almost bent double, talking to one of the male physios.

She shook her head and scoured the ward, looking for one of the student nurses. 'Karen?'

The student scuttled over. 'Yes, Sister?'

'Do you know how to assess a patient for the risk of pressure ulcers?'

The student nodded quickly as Cassidy handed her a plastic card with the Waterlow scale on it. 'I want you to do Mrs Kelly's assessment then come back and we'll go over it together.'

Karen nodded and hurried off down the corridor. Cassidy watched for a second. With her paper-thin skin, poor nutrition and lack of circulating oxygen, Mrs Kelly was at real risk of developing pressure sores on her body. For Cassidy, the teaching element was one of the reasons she did this job. She wanted all the students who came through her ward to understand the importance of considering all aspects of their patients' care.

There was a thud beside her. Brad was in the chair next to her, his head leaning on one hand, staring at her again with those blue eyes. He couldn't wipe the smile from his face. 'So, which one am I?'

Cassidy blew a wayward chestnut curl out of her face. 'What are you talking about now?'

He moved closer. 'Hunky, Chunky or Funky? Which one am I?' He put his hands together and pleaded in front of her. 'Please tell me I'm Hunky.'

'How on earth did you…?' Her eyes looked down the corridor to where Pete, the physio, was in conversation with one of the other doctors. He must have overheard her. 'Oh, forget it.'

She wrinkled her nose at him, leaning forward wickedly so nobody could hear. 'No way are you Hunky. That's reserved for the Italian god named Luca.' Her eyes fell on Luca, standing talking to one of her nurses. She whispered in Brad's ear, 'Have you noticed how he keeps checking out his own reflection in those highly polished Italian shoes of his?'

Brad's shoulders started to shake.

She prodded him on the shoulder. 'No. With that excuse of a haircut and that strange earring, you're definitely Funky.' She pointed at his ear. 'What is that anyway?'

Her head came forward, her nose just a few inches off his ear as she studied the twisted bit of gold in his ear. 'Is it a squashed kangaroo? Or a surfboard?'

'Neither.' He grinned at her, turning his head so their noses nearly touched. 'Believe it or not, it used to be a boomerang. My mum bought it for me when I was a teenager and I won a competition.' He touched it with his finger. 'It's a little bent out of shape now.'

Her face was serious and he could smell her perfume—or her shampoo. She smelled of strawberries. A summer smell, even though it was the middle of winter in Glasgow. He was almost tempted to reach out and touch her chestnut curls, resting just above her collarbone. But she was staring at him with those big chocolate-brown eyes. And he didn't want to move.

If this was the Dragon Lady of the medical receiving unit, he wondered if he could be her St George and try to tame her. No. That was the English patron saint and he was in Scotland. He'd learned quickly not to muddle things up around here. The Scots he'd met were wildly patriotic.

Her face broke into a smile again. Interesting. She hadn't pulled back, even though they were just inches from each other. She didn't seem intimidated by his closeness. In any other circumstances he could have leaned forward and given her a kiss. A perfect example of the sort of distraction he needed.

'Come to think of it, though…' She glanced up and down his crumpled clothes. How could she ever have thought he reminded her of Bobby? Bobby wouldn't have been seen dead in crumpled clothes. He'd always been immaculate—Brad was an entirely different kettle of fish. 'If you keep coming into my ward dressed like that, I'll have to change your name from Funky to Skunky.'

Brad automatically sat backwards in his chair, lowering his chin and sniffing. 'Why, do I smell? I was on call last night and I haven't been in the shower yet.' He started to pull at his scrub top.

She loved it. The expression of worry on his face. The way she could so easily wind him up. And the fact he had a good demeanour with the patients and staff. This guy might even be a little fun to have around. Even if he was from the other side of the world.

She shook her head. 'Stop panicking, Brad. You don't smell.' She rested her head on her hands for a second, fixing him with her eyes. Mornings on the medical receiving unit were always chaotic. Patients to be moved to other wards, new admissions and usually a huge battery of tests to be arranged. Sometimes it was nice just to take a few seconds of calm, before chaos erupted all around you.

He reached over and touched her hand, resting on top of the off-duty book. The invisible electric jolt that shot up her arm was instantaneous.

'I could help you with those. The last place I worked in Australia had a computer system for duty rosters.

You just put in the names, your shift patterns and the requests. It worked like a charm.'

Her eyes hadn't left where his hand was still touching hers. It was definitely lingering there. She'd just met this guy.

'You're going to be a pest, aren't you?' Her voice was low. For some reason she couldn't stop staring at him. It didn't help that he was easy on the eye. And that scraggy hair was kind of growing on her.

He leaned forward again. 'Is that going to be a problem?' His eyes were saying a thousand different words from his mouth. Something was in the air between them. She could practically feel the air around her crackle. This was ridiculous. She felt like a swooning teenager.

'My gran had a name for people like you.'

He moved even closer. 'And what was that?' He tilted his head to one side. 'Handsome? Clever? Smart?'

She shook her head and stood up, straightening her tunic. 'Oh, no. It was much more fitting. My gran would have called you a "wee scunner".'

His brow wrinkled. 'What on earth does that mean?'

'Just like I told you. A nuisance. A pest. But it's a much more accurate description.' She headed towards the duty room, with the off-duty book in her hand. She had to get away from him. Her brain had taken leave of her senses. She should have taken Lucy up on that offer of tea.

Brad caught her elbow. 'Actually, Cassidy, about your duty room…'

He stopped as she pushed the door open and automatically stepped inside, her foot catching on something.

'Wh-h-a-a-t?'

CHAPTER TWO

CASSIDY stared up at the white ceiling of her duty room, the wind knocked clean out of her. Something was sticking into her ribcage and she squirmed, causing an array of perilously perched cardboard boxes to topple over her head. She squealed again, batting her hands in front of her face.

A strong pair of arms grabbed her wrists and yanked her upwards, standing her on the only visible bit of carpet in the room—right at the doorway.

Brad was squirming. 'Sorry about that, Cassidy. I was trying to warn you but...'

He stopped in mid-sentence. She looked mad. She looked *really* mad. Her chestnut curls were in complete disarray, falling over her face and hiding her angry eyes. 'What is all this rubbish?' she snapped.

Brad cleared his throat. 'Well, actually, it's not "rubbish", as you put it. It's mine.' He bent over and started pushing some files back into an overturned box. They were the last thing he wanted anyone to see.

Her face was growing redder by the second. She looked down at her empty hand—obviously wondering where the off-duty book she'd been holding had got to. She bent forward to look among the upturned boxes then straightened up, shaking her head in disgust.

She planted her hands on her hips. 'You'd better have a good explanation for this. No wonder you were giving me the treatment.'

'What treatment?'

She waved her hand in dismissal. 'You know. The smiles. The whispers. The big blue eyes.' She looked at him mockingly. 'You must take me for a right sap.'

All of a sudden Brad understood the Dragon Lady label. When she was mad, she was *mad*. Heaven help the doctor who messed up on her watch.

He leaned against the doorjamb. 'I wasn't giving you the *treatment*, as you put it, Cassidy. I was trying to connect with the sister of the ward I work in. We're going to have to work closely together, and I'd like it if we were friends.'

Her face softened ever so slightly. She looked at the towering piles of boxes obliterating her duty room. 'And all this?'

He shot her a smile. 'Yes, well, there's a story about all that.'

She ran her fingers through her hair, obviously attempting to re-tame it. He almost wished he could do it for her. 'Please don't tell me you've moved in.'

He laughed. 'No. It's not that desperate. I got caught short last night and was flung out of my flat, so I had to bring all my stuff here rather than leave it all sitting in the street.'

She narrowed her eyes. 'What do you mean, you got caught short? That sounds suspiciously like you were having a party at five in the morning and the landlord threw you out.'

Brad nodded slowly. 'Let's just say I broke one of the rules of my tenancy.'

'Which one?'

'Now, that would be telling.' He pulled a set of keys from his pocket with a brown tag attached. 'But help is at hand. I've got a new flat I can move into tonight—if I can find it.'

'What do you mean—if you can find it?' Cassidy bent over and read the squiggly writing on the tag.

Brad shrugged his shoulders. 'Dowangate Lane. I'm not entirely sure where it is. One of the porters put me onto it at short notice. I needed somewhere that was furnished and was available at short notice. He says its only five minutes away from here, but I don't recognise the street name.'

Cassidy gave him a suspicious look. 'I don't suppose anyone told you that I live near there.'

'Really? No, I'd no idea. Can you give me some directions?'

Cassidy sighed. 'Sure. Go out the front of the hospital, take a left, walk a few hundred yards down the road, take a right, go halfway down the street and go down the nearby close. Dowangate Lane runs diagonally off it. But the street name fell off years ago.'

Cassidy had a far-away look in her eyes and was gesturing with her arms. Her voice got quicker and quicker as she spoke, her Scottish accent getting thicker by the second.

'I have no idea what you just said.'

Cassidy stared at him—hard. 'It would probably be easier if I just showed you.'

'Really? Would you?'

'If it means you'll get all this rubbish out of my duty room, it will be worth it.'

'Gee, thanks.'

'Do you want my help or not?'

He bent forward and caught her gesturing arms. 'I would love your help, Cassidy Rae. How does six o'clock sound?' There it was again—that strawberry scent from her hair. That could become addictive.

She stopped talking. He could feel the little goose-bumps on her bare arms. Was she cold? Or was it something else?

Whatever it was, he was feeling it, too. Not some wild, throw-her-against-the-wall attraction, although he wouldn't mind doing that. It was weird. Some kind of connection.

Maybe he wasn't the only person looking for a Christmastime distraction.

She was staring at him with those big brown eyes again. Only a few seconds must have passed but it felt like minutes.

He could almost hear her thought processes. As if she was wondering what was happening between them, too.

'Six o'clock will be fine,' she said finally, as she lowered her eyes and brushed past him.

Brad hung his white coat up behind the door and pulled his shirt over his head. He paused midway. What was he going to do with it?

Cass stuck her head around the door. 'Are you ready yet?' Her eyes caught the tanned, taut abdomen and the words stuck in her throat. She felt the colour rush into her cheeks. 'Oops, sorry.' She pulled back from the door.

All of a sudden she felt like a teenager again. And trust him to have a set of to-die-for abs. Typical. There was no way she was ever taking her clothes off in front of Mr Ripped Body.

Where had that come from? Why on earth would she ever take her clothes off in front of him? That was it. She was clearly losing her marbles.

Almost automatically, she sucked in her stomach and looked downwards. Her pink jumper hid a multitude of sins, so why on earth was she bothering?

Brad's hand rested on the edge of the door as he stuck his head back round. 'Don't be so silly, Cassidy. You're a nurse. It's not like you haven't seen it all before. Come back in. I'll be ready in a second.'

She swallowed the huge lump at the back of her throat. His shoulder was still bare. He was obviously used to stripping off in front of women and was completely uninhibited.

So why did that thought rankle her?

She took a deep breath and stepped back into the room, trying to avert her eyes without being obvious. The last thing she wanted was for him to think she was embarrassed. With an attitude like his, she'd never live it down.

He was rummaging in a black holdall. Now she could see the muscles across his back. No love handles for him. He yanked a pale blue T-shirt from the bag and pulled it over his head, turning round and tugging it down over his washboard stomach.

'Ready. Can we go?'

Cassidy had a strange expression on her face. Brad automatically looked down. Did he have a huge ketchup stain on his T-shirt? Not that he could see. Her cheeks were slightly flushed, matching the soft pink jumper she was wearing. A jumper that hugged the shape of her breasts very nicely. Pink was a good colour on her. It brought out the warm tones in her face and hair that had sometimes been lost in the navy-blue tunic she'd been wearing earlier. Her hair was pulled back from her face in a short ponytail, with a few wayward curls escaping. She was obviously serious about helping him move. No fancy coats and stiletto heels for her. Which was just as well as there were around fifty boxes to lug over to his new flat.

'Will you manage to carry some of these boxes down to my car?'

'I'll do better than that.' She opened the door to reveal one of the porters' trolleys for transporting boxes of equipment around the hospital. The huge metal cage could probably take half of his boxes in one run.

'Genius. You might be even more useful than I thought.'

'See, I'm not just a pretty face,' she shot back, to his cheeky remark. 'You do realise this is going to cost you, don't you?' She pulled the cage towards the duty room, letting him stand in the doorway and toss out boxes that she piled up methodically.

'How much?' As he tossed one of the boxes, the cardboard flaps sprang open, spilling his boxers and socks all over the floor.

Cassidy couldn't resist. The colours of every imagination caught her eyes and she lifted up a pair with Elmo from *Sesame Street* emblazoned on the front. 'Yours?' she asked, allowing them to dangle from one finger.

He grabbed them. 'Stop it.' He started ramming them

back into the box, before raising his eyebrows at her. 'I'll decide when you get to see my underwear.'

When. Not if. The thought catapulted through her brain as she tried to keep her mind on the job at hand. The boxes weren't neatly packed or taped shut. And the way he kept throwing them at her was ruining her precision stacking in the metal cage.

'Slow down,' she muttered. 'The more you irritate me, the more my price goes up. You're currently hovering around a large pizza or a sweet-and-sour chicken. Keep going like this and you'll owe me a beer as well.'

The cheeky grin appeared at her shoulder in an instant. 'You think I won't buy you a beer?' He stared at the neatly stacked boxes. 'Uh-oh. I sense a little obsessive behaviour. One of your staff warned me about wrecking the neatly packed boxes of gloves in the treatment room. I can see why.'

'Nothing wrong with being neat and tidy.' Cassidy straightened the last box. 'Okay, I think that's enough for now. We can take the rest downstairs on the second trip.'

Something flashed in front of his eyes. Something wicked. 'You think so?'

He waited while she nodded, then as quick as a flash he shoved her in the cage, clicking the door behind her and pushing the cage down the corridor.

Cassidy let out a squeal. For the second time today she was surrounded by piles of toppling boxes. 'Let me out!' She got to her knees in the cage as he stopped in front of the lifts and pushed the 'down' button.

His shoulders were shaking with laughter as he pulled a key from his pocket for the 'Supplies Only' lift and opened the door. 'What can I say? You bring out the wicked side in me. I couldn't resist wrecking your neat display.'

He pulled the cage into the lift and sprang the lock free, holding out his hands to steady her step. The lift started with a judder, and as she was in midstep—it sent her straight into his arms. 'Ow-w!

The lift was small. Even smaller with the large storage cage and two people crammed inside. And as Brad had pressed the ground-floor button as he'd pulled the cage inside, they were now trapped at the back of the lift together.

She was pressed against him. He could feel the ample swell of her breasts against his chest, her soft pink jumper tickling his skin. His hands had fallen naturally to her waist, one finger touching a little bit of soft flesh. Had she noticed?

Her curls were under his nose, but there was no way he was moving his hands to scratch the itch. She lifted her head, capturing him with her big brown eyes again.

This was crazy. This was madness.

This was someone he'd just met today. It didn't matter that he felt a pull towards her. It didn't matter that she'd offered to help him. It didn't matter that for some strange reason he liked to be close to her. It didn't matter that his eyes were currently fixed on her plump lips. He knew nothing about her.

Her reputation had preceded her. According to her colleagues she was a great nurse and a huge advocate for her patients, but her attention to detail and rulebook for the ward had become notorious.

More importantly, she knew nothing about him. She had no idea about his history, his family, his little girl out there in the world somewhere. She had no idea how the whole thing had come close to breaking him. And for some reason he didn't want to tell her.

He wanted this to be separate. A flirtation. A distraction. Something playful. With no consequences. Even if it only lasted a few weeks.

At least that would get him past Christmas.

'You can let me go now.' Her voice was quiet, her hands resting on his upper arms sending warm waves through his bare skin.

But for a second they just stood there. Unmoving.

The door pinged open and they turned their heads. His hands fell from her waist. She turned and automatically pushed the cage through the lift doors, and he fell into step next to her.

The tone and mood were broken.

'Are you sure you don't mind helping me with this? You could always just draw me a map.'

She stuck her elbow in his ribs. 'Stop trying to get out of buying me dinner. What number did you say the flat was? If I find out I've got to carry all these boxes up four flights of stairs I *won't* be happy.'

They crossed the car park and reached his car. She blinked. A Mini. For a guy that was over six feet tall.

'This is your car?'

'Do you like it?' He opened the front passenger door, moved the seat forward and started throwing boxes in the back. 'It's bigger than you think.'

'Why on earth didn't you just leave some stuff in the car?'

Brad shrugged. 'Luca borrowed my car last night after he helped me move my stuff. I think he had a date.' And some of his boxes were far too personal to be left unguarded in a car.

Cassidy shook her head and opened the boot, trying to cram as many of the boxes in there as possible. She was left with two of the larger ones still sitting on the ground.

She watched as he put the passenger seat back into place and shrugged her shoulders. 'I can just put these two on my lap. It's only a five-minute drive. It'll be fine.'

Brad pulled a face. 'You might need to put something else on your lap instead.'

She felt her stomach turn over. What now?

'Why do I get the distinct impression that nothing is straightforward with you?'

He grabbed her hand and pulled her towards the porter's lodge at the hospital gate, leaving the two boxes next to his unlocked car. 'Come on.'

'Where on earth are we going?'

'I've got something else to pick up.'

He pushed open the door to the lodge. Usually used for deliveries and collections, occasionally used by the porters who were trying to duck out of sight for five minutes, it was an old-fashioned solid stone building. The front door squeaked loudly. 'Frank? Are you there?'

Frank Wallace appeared. All twenty-five stone of him, carrying a pile of white-and-black fur in his hands. 'There you are, Dr Donovan. He's been as good as gold. Not a bit of bother. Bring him back any time.'

Frank handed over the bundle of black and white, and it took a few seconds for Cassidy to realise the shaggy bundle was a dog with a bright red collar and lead.

Brad bent down and placed the dog on the floor at their feet. It seemed to spring to life, the head coming up sharply and a little tail wagging furiously. Bright black eyes and a pink panting tongue.

'Cassidy, meet Bert. *This* is the reason I lost my tenancy.'

Cassidy watched in amazement. Bert seemed delighted to see him, jumping his paws up onto Brad's shoulders and licking at his hands furiously. His gruff little barks reverberated around the stone cottage.

He was a scruffy little mutt—with no obvious lineage or pedigree. A mongrel, by the look of him.

'Why on earth would you have a dog?' she asked incredulously. 'You live in Australia. You can't possibly have brought him with you.' Dogs she could deal with. It was cats that caused her allergies. She'd often thought about getting a pet for company—a friendly face to come home to. But long shifts weren't conducive to having a pet. She knelt on the floor next to Brad, holding her hand out cautiously while Bert took a few seconds to sniff her, before licking her with the same enthusiasm he'd shown Brad.

'I found him. A few weeks ago, in the street outside my flat. He looked emaciated and was crouched in a doorway. There was no way I could leave him alone.' *And to be honest, I needed him as much as he needed me.* Brad let the scruffy dog lick his hands. Melody would love this little dog.

'So what did you do?'

'I took him to the emergency vet, who checked him over, gave me some instructions, then I took him home.'

'And *this* is why you got flung out your flat?' There was an instant feeling of relief. He hadn't been thrown out for non-payment of rent, wild parties or dubious women. He'd been thrown out because of a dog. She glanced at his face as he continued to talk to Bert. The mutual admiration was obvious.

The rat. He must have known that a dog would have scored him brownie points. No wonder he'd kept it quiet earlier. She would have taken him for a soft touch.

She started to laugh. 'Bert? You called your dog Bert?'

He shrugged his shoulders. 'What's wrong with Bert? It's a perfectly good name.'

'What's wrong with Rocky or Buster or Duke?'

He waved his hand at her. 'Look at him. Does he look like Rocky, Buster or Duke?'

He waited a few seconds, and Bert obligingly tipped his head to one side, as if he enjoyed the admiration.

Brad was decisive. 'No way. He's a Bert. No doubt about it.'

Cassidy couldn't stop the laugh that had built up in her chest. Bert wasn't a big dog and his white hair with black patches had definitely seen better days. But his soft eyes and panting tongue were cute. And Brad was right. He looked like a Bert—it suited him. She bent down and started rubbing his ears.

'See—you like him. Everyone should. He's a good dog. Not been a bit of bother since I found him.'

'So how come you got flung out the flat? And what about the new one? I take it they're happy for you to have a dog?'

Brad pulled a face. 'One of my neighbours reported me for having a dog. And the landlord was swift and ruthless, even though you honestly wouldn't have known he was there. And it was Frank, the porter, who put me onto the new flat. So I'm sorted. They're happy for me to have a dog.'

Cassidy held out her arms to pick up the dog. 'I take it this is what I'm supposed to have on my lap in the car?'

Brad nodded. 'Thank goodness you like dogs. This could have all turned ugly.'

She shook her head, still rubbing Bert's ears. 'I'm sure it will be fine. But let's go. It's getting late and I'm starving.'

They headed back to the car and drove down the road past Glasgow University and into the west end of Glasgow. Lots of the younger hospital staff stayed in the flats around here. It wasn't really designed for kids and families, but for younger folks it was perfect, with the shops, restaurants and nightlife right at their fingertips.

'So what do you like best about staying around here?'

Cassidy glanced around about her as they drove along Byres Road. She pointed to the top of the road. 'If you go up there onto Western Road and cross the road, you get to Glasgow's Botanic Gardens. Peace, perfect peace.'

Brad looked at her in surprise. 'Really? That's a bit unusual for someone your age.'

'Why would you think that? Is it only pensioners and kids that can visit?' She gestured her thumb over her shoulder. 'Or if you go back that way, my other favourite is the Kelvingrove Art Gallery and Museum— as long as the school trips aren't there! There's even a little secret church just around the corner with an ancient cemetery—perfect for quiet book reading in the summer. Gorgeous at Christmastime.'

Brad stared at her. 'You're a dark horse, aren't you? I never figured you for a museum type.'

She shrugged her shoulders. 'It's the peace and quiet

really. The ward can be pretty hectic. Some days when I come out I'm just looking for somewhere to chill. I can be just as happy curled up with a good book or in the dark at the cinema.'

'You go to the cinema alone?'

She nodded. 'All the time. I love sci-fi. My friends all love romcoms. So I do some with my friends and some on my own.' She pointed her arm in front of them. 'Turn left here, then turn right and slow down.'

The car pulled to a halt at the side of the road next to some bollards. Cassidy looked downwards. Bert had fallen asleep in her lap. 'Looks like it's been a big day for the little guy.'

Brad jumped out of and around the car and opened the passenger door. He picked up the sleeping dog. 'Let's go up and have a look at the flat before I start to unpack the boxes.'

'You haven't seen it yet?'

He shook his head. 'How could I? I was on call last night and just had to take whatever I could get. I told you I'd no idea where this place was.'

Cassidy smiled. 'So you did. Silly me. Now, give me the key and we'll see what you've got.'

They climbed up the stairs in the old-style tenement building, onto the first floor, where number five was in front of them. Cassidy looked around. 'Well, this is better than some flats I've seen around here.' She ran her hand along the wall. 'The walls have been painted, the floors are clean, and…' she pointed to the door across the hallway '…your neighbour has some plants outside his flat. This place must be okay.'

She turned the key in the lock and pushed open the

door. Silently praying that she wouldn't be hit with the smell of cats, mould or dead bodies.

Brad flicked the light switch next to the door and stepped inside. He was trying to stop his gut from twisting. Getting a flat that accepted dogs at short notice—and five minutes away from the hospital—seemed almost too good to be true. There had to be a catch somewhere.

The catch was obvious. Cassidy burst into fits of laughter.

'No way! It's like stepping back in time. Have we just transported into the 1960s?' She turned to face him. 'That happened once in an old *Star Trek* episode. I think we're just reliving it.'

Brad was frozen. The wallpaper could set off a whole array of seizures. He couldn't even make out the individual colours, the purples and oranges all seemed to merge into one. As for the shag-pile brown carpet…

Cassidy was having the time of her life. She dashed through one of the open doors and let out a shriek. 'Avacado! It's avocado. You have an avocado bathroom! Does that colour even exist any more?' Seconds later he heard the sounds of running water before she appeared again, tears flowing down her cheeks. 'I love this place. You have to have a 1960s-style party.'

She ducked into another room then swept past him into the kitchen, while Brad tried to keep his breathing under control. Could he really live in this?

He set down the dog basket on the floor and placed the sleeping Bert inside. His quiet, peaceful dog would probably turn into a possessed, rabid monster in this place.

He sagged down onto the purple sofa that clashed

hideously with the brown shag-pile carpet. No wonder this place had been available at a moment's notice.

He could hear banging and clattering from next door—Cassidy had obviously found the kitchen. He cringed. What colour was avocado anyway? He was too scared to look.

Cassidy reappeared, one of her hands dripping wet, both perched at her waist. 'Kitchen's not too bad.' She swept her eyes around the room again, the smile automatically reappearing on her face. She walked over and sat down on the sofa next to Brad, giving his knee a friendly tap. 'Well, it has to be said, this place is spotlessly clean. And the shower's working.' She lifted her nose and sniffed the air. 'And it smells as if the carpets have just been cleaned. See—it's not so bad.'

Not so bad. She had to be joking.

And she was. He could see her shoulders start to shake again. She lifted her hands to cover her face, obviously trying to block out the laughter. His stomach fell even further.

'What is it?'

He could tell she was trying not to meet his gaze. 'Go on. What else have you discovered in this psychedelic temple of doom?' He threw up his hands.

Cassidy stood up and grabbed his hand, pulling him towards her. For a second he was confused. What was she doing? Sure, this had crossed his mind, but what did she have in mind?

She pulled him towards the other room he hadn't looked at yet—the bedroom. Surely not? He felt a rush of blood to the head and rush of something else to the groin. This couldn't be happening.

She pushed open the door to the room, turning and

giving him another smile. But the glint in her eyes was something else entirely. This was no moment of seduction. This was comedy, through and through.

He stepped inside the bedroom.

Pink. Everywhere and everything. Pink.

Rose-covered walls. A shiny, *satin* bedspread. Pink lampshades giving off a strange rose-coloured hue around the room. Pink carpet. Dark teak furniture and dressing table. He almost expected to see an eighty-year-old woman perched under the covers, staring at them.

Cassidy's laughter was building by the second. She couldn't contain herself. She spun round, her hands on his chest. 'Well, what do you think? How's this for a playboy palace?'

His reaction was instantaneous. He grabbed her around the waist and pulled her with him, toppling onto the bed, the satin bedspread sliding them along. He couldn't help it. It was too much for him and for the next few minutes they laughed so hard his belly was aching.

They lay there for a few seconds after the laughter finally subsided. Brad's eyes were fixed on the ceiling, staring at yet another rose-coloured light shade.

He turned his head to face Cassidy's. 'So, tell me truthfully. Do you think this flat will affect my pulling power?'

Cassidy straightened her face, the laughter still apparent in her eyes. She wondered how to answer the question. Something squeezed deep inside her. She didn't want Brad to have pulling power. She didn't want Brad to even consider pulling. What on earth was wrong with her? She'd only met this guy today. Her naughty streak came out. 'Put it this way. This is the first time

I've lain on a bed with a man, panting like this, and still been fully dressed.'

His eyebrows arched and he flipped round onto his side to face her. 'Well, Sister Rae, that almost sounds like a challenge. And I like a challenge.'

Cassidy attempted to change position, the satin bed-spread confounding her and causing her to slide to the floor with a heavy thud.

Brad stuck his head over the edge of the bed. 'Cass, are you okay?'

She held up her hand towards him and shook her head. 'Just feed me.'

Fifty boxes later and another trip back to the hospital, they both sagged on the sofa. Brad pulled a bunch of take-away menus from a plastic bag. 'I'd take you out for dinner but I don't think either of us could face sitting across a table right now.'

Cassidy nodded. She flicked through the menus, picking up her favourite. 'This pizza place is just around the corner and it's great. They don't take long to deliver. Will we go for this?'

'What's your favourite?'

'Thin crust. Hawaiian.'

'Pineapple—on a pizza? Sacrilege. Woman, what's wrong with you?'

She rolled her eyes. 'Don't tell me—you're a meat-feast, thick-crust man?'

He sat back, looking surprised. 'How did you know?'

'Because you're the same as ninety per cent of the other males on the planet. Let's just order two.' She picked up the phone, giving it a second glance. 'Wow, my parents had one of these in the seventies.' She listened for a dial tone. 'Never mind, it works.' She dialled the number and placed the order.

'So, what do you think of your new home? Will you still be talking to Frank in the morning?'

Brad sighed. 'I think I should be grateful, no matter how bad the décor is. I needed a furnished flat close by—it's not like I had any furniture to bring with me—so this will be fine.' He took another look around. 'You're right—it's clean. That's the most important thing.' Then he pointed to Bert in the corner. 'And if he's happy, I'm happy.' The wicked glint appeared in his eyes again. 'I can always buy a new bedspread—one that keeps the ladies on, instead of sliding them off.'

There it was again. That little twisting feeling in her gut whenever he cracked a joke about other women. For the first time in a lifetime she was feeling cave-woman primal urges. She wanted to shout, *Don't you dare!* But that would only reveal her to be a mad, crazy person, instead of the consummate professional she wanted him to think she was.

He rummaged around in a plastic bag at his feet. 'I'm afraid I can't offer you any fancy wine to drink. I've got orange or blackcurrant cordial.' He pulled the bottles from the bag. 'And I've got glasses in one of those boxes over there.'

Cassidy reached over and opened the box, grabbing two glasses and setting them on the table. 'So what's your story? What are you doing in Scotland?' *And why hasn't some woman snapped you up already?*

'You mean, what's a nice guy like me doing in a place like this?' He gestured at the psychedelic walls.

She shrugged. 'I just wondered why you'd left Australia. Do you have family there? A girlfriend?'

She couldn't help it. She really, really wanted to know. She'd wanted to ask if he had a wife or children, but that had seemed a bit too forward. He wasn't wearing a wedding ring, and he hadn't mentioned any significant other. And he'd been flirting with her. Definitely flirting with her. And for the first time in ages she felt like responding.

'I fancied a change. It seemed like a good opportunity to expand my experience. Scottish winters are notorious for medical admissions, particularly around old mining communities.' He paused for a second and then added, 'And, no, there's no wife.' He prayed she hadn't noticed the hesitation. He couldn't say the words 'no children'. He wouldn't lie about his daughter. But he just didn't want to go there right now. Not with someone he barely knew.

Cassidy nodded, sending silent prayers upwards for his last words, but fixed her expression, 'There's around two and half thousand extra deaths every winter. They can't directly link them to the cold. Only a few are from hypothermia, most are from pneumonia, heart disease or stroke. And last year was the worst. They estimated nine pensioners died every hour related to the effects of the cold. Fuel payments are through the roof right now. People just can't afford to heat their homes. Some of the cases we had last year broke my heart.'

Brad was watching her carefully. Her eyes were looking off into the distance—as if she didn't want him to notice the sheen across her eyes when she spoke. He wondered if she knew how she looked. Her soft curls shining in the dim flat light, most of them escaping from the ponytail band at the nape of her neck. It was clear this was a subject close to her heart—she knew her stuff, but as a sister on a medical receiving unit he would have expected her to.

What he hadn't expected was to see the compassion in her eyes. Her reputation was as an excellent clinician, with high standards and a strict rulebook for the staff on her ward. But this was a whole other side to her. A side he happened to like. A side he wanted to know more about.

'So, what's the story with you, then?'

She narrowed her eyes, as if startled he'd turned the question round on her. 'What do you mean?'

'What age are you, Cassidy? Twenty-seven? Twenty-eight?' He pointed to her left hand. 'Where's your other half? Here you are, on a Monday night at…' he looked at his watch '…nearly nine o'clock, helping an orphaned colleague move into his new flat. Don't you have someone to go to home to?'

Cassidy shifted uncomfortably. She didn't like being put on the spot. She didn't like the fact that in a few moments he'd stripped her bare. Nearly thirty, single and no one to go home to. Hardly an ad for Mrs Wonderful.

'I'm twenty-nine, and I was engaged a few years ago, but we split up and I'm happy on my own.' It sounded so simple when she put it like that. Leaving out the part about her not wanting to get out of bed for a month after Bobby had left. Or drinking herself into oblivion the month after that.

His eyebrows rose, his attention obviously grabbed. 'So, who was he?'

'My fiancé? He was a Spanish registrar I worked with.'

'Did you break up with him?'

The million-dollar question. The one that made you

look sad and pathetic if you said no. Had she broken up with him? Or had Bobby just told her he was returning to Spain, with no real thought to how she would feel about it? And no real distress when she'd told him she wouldn't go with him.

Looking back she wondered if he'd always known she wouldn't go. And if being with her in Scotland had just been convenient for him—a distraction even.

She took a deep breath. 'What's with the questions, nosy parker? He wanted to go home to Spain. I wanted to stay in Scotland. End of story. We broke up. He's back working in Madrid now.' She made it sound so simple. She didn't tell him how much she hated coming home to an empty house and having nobody to share her day with. She didn't say how whenever she set her single place at the table she felt a little sad. She didn't tell him how much she hated buying convenience meals for one.

'Bet he's sorry he didn't stay.'

Cassidy's face broke into a rueful smile and she shook her head. 'Oh, I don't think so. He went home, had a whirlwind romance and a few months later married that year's Miss Spain. They've got a little son now.'

She didn't want to reveal how hurt she'd been by her rapid replacement.

He moved a little closer to her. 'Didn't that make you mad? He left and played happy families with someone else?'

Cassidy shook her head determinedly. She'd had a long time to think about all this. 'No. Not really. I could have been but we obviously weren't right for each other. When we got engaged he said he would stay in Scotland, but over time he changed his mind. His heart was in Spain.'

Her eyes fell downwards for a few seconds as she drew in a sharp breath, 'And I'd made it clear I didn't want to move away. I'm a Scottish girl through and through. I don't want to move.'

Brad placed his hand on her shoulder. 'But that seems a bit off. Spain's only a few hours away on a plane. What's the big deal?'

Cassidy looked cross. He made it all sound so simple. 'I like it here. I like it where I live. I don't want to move to...' she lifted her fingers in the air '...*sunnier climes*. I want to stay here...' she pointed her finger to the floor '...in Scotland, the country that I love. And I have priorities here—responsibilities—that I couldn't take care of in another country.' She folded her arms across her chest.

'So I made myself a rule. My next other half will be a big, handsome fellow Scot. Someone who wants to stay where I do. Not someone from the other side of the planet.'

The words hung between them. Almost as if she was drawing a line in the sand. Brad paused for a second, trying to stop himself from saying what he really thought. Should he say straight away that he would never stay in Scotland either? That he wanted his life to be wherever his daughter was—and he was prepared to up sticks and go at a moment's notice?

No. He couldn't. That would instantly kill this flirtation stone dead. And that's all this would ever be—a mild flirtation. Why on earth would what she'd just said bother him? He was merely looking for a distraction—nothing more. Something to take his mind off another Christmas without his daughter.

'Just because someone is from Scotland it doesn't

mean they'll want to stay here. There have been lots of famous Scots explorers—David Livingstone, for example.' He moved forward, leaning in next to her. 'Anyway, that's a pretty big statement, Cassidy. You're ruling out ninety-nine per cent of the population of the world in your search for Mr Right. Hardly seems fair to the rest of us.' He shot her a cheeky grin. 'Some people might even call that a bit of prejudice.'

'Yeah, well, at least if I think about it this way, it saves any problems later on. I don't want to meet someone, hook up with them and fall in love, only to have my heart broken when they tell me their life's on the other side of the planet from me.' *Been there. Done that.* 'Why set myself up for a fall like that?'

'Why indeed?' He'd moved right next to her, his blue eyes fixed on hers. She was right. Cassidy wanted to stay in Scotland. Brad wanted to go wherever in the world his little girl was. A little girl he hadn't even told her about. Anything between them would be an absolute disaster. But somehow he couldn't stop the words forming on his lips.

'But what happens if your heart rules your head?' Because try as he may to think of her as a distraction, the attraction between them was real. And it had been a long time since he'd felt like this.

She could see every tiny line on his face from hours in the Australian sun, every laughter line around the corners of his eyes. His hand was still resting on her arm, and it was making her tingle. Everything about this was wrong.

She'd just spelled out all the reasons why this was so wrong. He was from Australia. The other side of the planet. He was the worst possible option for her. So why, in the space of a day, was he already getting under her skin? Why did she want to lean forward towards his lips? Why did she want to feel the muscles of his chest under the palms of her hands? He was so close right now she could feel his warm breath on her neck. It was sending shivers down her spine.

She didn't want this to be happening. She didn't want to be attracted to a man there was no future with. So why couldn't she stop this? Why couldn't she just pull away?

Ding-dong.

Both jumped backwards, startled by the noise of the bell ringing loudly. Even Bert awoke from his slumber and started barking.

Cassidy was still fixed by his eyes, the shiver continuing down her spine. A feeling of awakening. 'Pizza,' she whispered. 'It must be the pizza.'

'Saved by the bell,' murmured Brad as he stood up to answer the door. At the last second he turned back to her. A tiny little part of him was feeling guilty— guilty about the attraction between them, guilty about not mentioning his daughter, and completely irritated by her disregard for most of the men in the world.

Her mobile sounded, and Cassidy fumbled in her bag. 'Excuse me,' she murmured, glancing at the number on the screen.

She stepped outside as he was paying for the pizzas and pressed the phone to her ear. 'Hi, it's Cassidy Rae. Is something wrong with my grandmother?'

'Hi, Cassidy. It's Staff Nurse Hughes here. Sorry to call, but your gran's really agitated tonight.'

Cassidy sighed. 'What do you need me to do?' This was happening more and more. Her good-natured, placid gran was being taken over by Alzheimer's disease, at times becoming confused and agitated, leading to outbursts of aggression that were totally at odds with her normal nature. The one thing that seemed to calm her down was hearing Cassidy's voice—whether over the phone or in person.

'Can you talk to her for a few minutes? I'll hold the phone next to her.'

'Of course I will.' She took a deep breath. 'Hi, Gran, it's Cassidy. How are you feeling?' Her words didn't matter. It was the sound and tone of her voice that was important. So she kept talking, telling her gran about her day and her plans for the week.

And leaving out the thoughts about the new doctor that were currently dancing around in her brain.

Brad sat waiting patiently. What was she doing? Who was she talking to outside in that low, calm voice? And why couldn't she have taken the call in here?

More importantly, what was *he* doing?

Getting involved with someone he worked with hadn't worked out too great for him the last time. He'd had a few casual dates in the last year with work colleagues, but nothing serious. He really didn't want to go down that road again.

So what on earth was wrong with him? His attraction to this woman had totally knocked him sideways. Alison had been nothing like this. A few weeks together had proved they weren't compatible. And the pregnancy had taken them both by surprise. And although his thoughts had constantly been with his daughter, this was the first time that a woman had started to invade his mind.

His brain wasn't working properly, but his libido was firing on multiple cylinders. Which one would win the battle?

CHAPTER THREE

11 October

CASSIDY's fingers hammered on the keyboard, responding to yet another bureaucratic email.

'What's up, girl?' As if by magic, Brad was leaning across the desk towards her. 'You've got that ugly frown on your face again. That usually spells trouble for the rest of us.'

Cassidy smiled. For the last ten days, every time she'd turned around he'd been at her elbow. His mood was generally laid-back and carefree, though a couple of times she'd thought he was going to steer a conversation toward something more serious. She turned the computer monitor towards him. 'Look at this. According to "customer care" principles, we've got to answer the ward phone on the third ring.'

'Since when did our patients become "customers"?'

'Oh, don't get me started. I just replied, pointing out that patients are our first priority on the medical unit and I won't be leaving a patient's bedside to answer the phone in three rings.'

'Are you still short-staffed?' Brad looked around the

ward, noting the figures on the ward and trying to work out if everyone was there.

Cassidy pointed to the board. 'There were seven staff sick last week, but they should all be back on duty either today or tomorrow.' Her frown reappeared. 'Why, what are you about to tell me?'

Brad walked around to her side of the desk and wheeled her chair towards him. 'I was going to invite you to breakfast. It's Saturday morning, the ward's pretty quiet, so it seemed like a good time.' He pulled a face. 'Plus, those five empty beds you've got are about to be filled. I've got five patients coming into A and E via the GP on-call service who will all need to be admitted.'

Cassidy stood up. 'So what's this, the calm before the storm?'

'Something like that. Come on.' He stuck his elbow out towards her. 'You'll probably not get time for lunch later.'

Cassidy handed over the keys to one of her staff nurses and headed down to the canteen with Brad.

There was something nice about this. The easy way they'd fallen into a friendship. She'd mentioned her front door was jamming and he'd appeared around at her flat to fix it. Then they'd walked to the Botanic Gardens a few times on days off and taken Bert out in the evenings. Even though they were tiptoeing around the edges of friendship, there was still that simmering 'something' underneath.

'I see you actually managed to put some clothes on today.' She ran her eyes up and down his lean frame, taking in his trousers and casual polo shirt. 'I was beginning to wonder if you actually owned any clothes.'

They'd reached the canteen and Brad picked up a tray. 'It's a deliberate ploy. If I live my life in scrubs then the hospital does my laundry for me. And I haven't got my washing machine yet.'

Cassidy nodded. 'Ah...the truth comes out.' She walked over to the hot food and lifted a plate. 'Why didn't you just say? You could have used my washing machine.'

'You'd do my washing for me?'

Cassidy shuddered. 'No. I said you could *use* my washing machine. I didn't say *I* would do it for you. Anyway, that's one of my rules.'

He watched as she selected a roll, put something inside and picked up a sachet of ketchup.

'What do you mean—one of your rules?'

She lifted a mug and pressed the button for tea. 'I have rules. Rules for the ward, rules for life, rules for men and rules for Christmas.'

He raised his eyebrows. 'Okay, now you've intrigued me. Either that, or you're a total crank—which is a distinct possibility.' He picked up his coffee. 'So, I'm interested. I know about the rules for the ward but tell me about these rules for men.'

She handed over her money to the cashier and sat down at a nearby table. 'They're simple. No overseas men.'

'Yeah, yeah. I've heard that one. And I'm not impressed. What else?'

'No washing. No ironing. No picking up after them. I'm not their mother. Do it a few times and they start to expect it. I get annoyed, then I start picturing them as Jabba the Hut, the fat, lazy monster from *Star Wars*, and yadda, yadda, yadda.' She waved her hand in the air.

'I was right. You *are* a crank.' He prodded her roll. 'And what is that? Everyone around here seems to eat it and I've no idea what it is.'

'It's slice.'

'Slice? A slice of what?'

'No. That's what it's called—slice. It's square sausage. A Scottish delicacy.'

'That's not a sausage. That looks nothing like a sausage.'

'Well, it is. Want to try a bit?' She held up her roll towards him.

He shook his head. 'That doesn't look too healthy. Apart from the pizza the first night I met you, you seem to spend your life eating salads or apples. I've never even seen you eat the sweets on the ward.'

'But this is different. This is Saturday morning. This is the bad-girl breakfast.' She had a twinkle in her eye as she said it.

Brad moved closer, his eggs abandoned. 'Should I keep a note of this for future reference?'

There it was again—that weird little hum that seemed to hang in the air between them. Making the rest of the room fall silent and fade away into the background. Making the seconds that they held each other's gaze seem like for ever.

But he kind of liked that. He kind of liked the fact that she didn't seem to be able to pull her gaze away any more than he could. He kind of liked the fact that once he was in the vicinity of Cassidy, his brain didn't seem to be able to focus on anything else. And from right here he could study the different shades of brown in her eyes—some chocolate, some caramel, some that matched her chestnut hair perfectly.

Whoa! Since when had he, Brad Donovan, ever thought about the different shades of colour in a woman's eyes? Not once. Not ever. Until now. Where had his brain found the words 'chocolate', 'caramel' and 'chestnut'?

'Maybe you should.' The words startled him. There it was again, something in the air. The way at times her voice seemed deeper, huskier, as if she was having the same sort of thoughts that he was.

But what did she think about all this? Was he merely a distraction? After all, she didn't want a man from the other side of the world; she wanted a Scotsman. And he clearly wasn't that. So why was she even flirting with him?

But now her eyes were cast downwards, breaking his train of thought. There was a slight flush in her cheeks. Was she embarrassed? Cassidy didn't seem the bashful type. Maybe she was having the same trouble he was—trying to make sense of the thoughts that seemed to appear as soon as they were together.

He didn't like silence between them. It seemed awkward, unnatural for two people who seemed to fit so well together.

He picked up his fork and started eating his eggs. 'So, tell me about the Christmas rules?'

Cassidy sat back in her chair, a huge smile appearing on her face in an instant. Her eyes went up towards the ceiling. 'Ah, Christmas, best time of year. I love it, absolutely love it.' She counted on her fingers. 'There are lots of rules for Christmas. You need to have a proper advent calendar, not the rubbish chocolate kind. You need the old-fashioned kind with little doors that open to pictures of mistletoe and holly, sleighs, presents and reindeer. Then your Christmas tree needs to go up on the first of December.' She pointed her finger at him. 'Not on the twelfth or Christmas Eve, like some people do. You need to get into the spirit of things.'

'Should I be writing all this down?'

'Don't be sarcastic. Then there's the presents. You don't put them under the tree. That's a disaster. You bring them out on Christmas Eve.'

Brad was starting to laugh now. The enthusiasm in her face was brimming over, but she was deadly serious. 'Cassidy, do you still believe in Santa Claus?'

She sighed. 'Don't tell me you're a Christmas Grinch. There's no room for them in my ward.'

The Christmas Grinch. Actually, for the last few years, it would have been the perfect name for him. It was hard to get into the spirit of Christmas when you didn't know where your little girl was. Whether she was safe. Whether she was well. Whether she was happy. Cassidy did look literally like a child at Christmas. This was obviously her thing.

He tried to push the other thoughts from his mind. He was trying to be positive. This year he wasn't going to fall into the black hole he'd found himself in last year, dragged down by the parts of his life he couldn't control.

'Any other Christmas rules you need to tell me?'

'Well, there's all the fun stuff. Like trying to spot the first Christmas tree someone puts up in their window. I usually like to try and count them as I walk home from work every day. Then trying to guess who has got your name for the secret Santa at work. And the shops—I love the shops at Christmas. The big department store on Buchanan Street has the most gorgeous tree and decorations. They'll be up in a few weeks. You have to go and see them. And there will be ice skating in George Square. We have to go to that!'

'But it's still only October. We haven't had Hallowe'en yet.' Brad took a deep breath. He had an odd feeling in the pit of his stomach.

'We celebrate Christmas in Australia, too, you know. It might be a little different, but it's every bit as good as it sounds here. Where I live in Perth, everyone has Christmas lights on their houses. We have a huge Christmas tree in Forrest Place that gets turned on every November. Okay—maybe the temperature is around forty degrees and we might spend part of the day on the beach. But it's still a fabulous time. I'm gutted I won't be there this year.'

He was pushing his Christmas memories aside, and curiosity was curling at the bottom of his stomach. Little pieces of the puzzle that was Cassidy Rae were clicking into place. 'Have you ever celebrated Christmas anywhere else?'

Cassidy shook her head fiercely. 'I couldn't for a minute imagine being anywhere other than here at Christmas. Sometimes it even snows on Christmas Eve and Christmas Day. Then it's really magical.'

Brad frowned. 'Didn't you even celebrate Christmas in Spain with your fiancé?'

Cassidy looked at him as if he had horns on his head. 'Absolutely not.'

He folded his arms across his chest. 'Surely it doesn't matter where you celebrate Christmas—it's about who you celebrate with. It's the people, Cass, not the place.' He willed his voice not to break as he said the words. She would have no idea how much all this hurt him.

Cassidy was still shaking her head, and Brad had the distinct feeling he'd just tiptoed around the heart of the matter. She didn't want to move. She didn't want to leave. She wouldn't even consider moving anywhere else.

In some circumstances it might seem fine, patriotic even. But it irritated Brad more than he wanted to admit. How could Cass be so closed-minded? Was this really why she wouldn't even consider a relationship with him? Not that he'd asked her. But every day they were growing closer and closer.

Why hadn't he told her about Melody yet? The most important person in his life and he hadn't even mentioned her existence. He'd heard from his lawyer yesterday. Still no news. Still no sign. America was a big place. They were searching every state to see if Alison had registered as a doctor, though by now she could be married and working under a different name. If that was the case, they might never find her. And that thought made him feel physically sick.

His brain was almost trying to be rational now. Trying to figure out why Alison hadn't contacted him.

He was a good father—committed to Melody and her upbringing. He'd wanted a say in everything and that had kind of spooked Alison, who liked to be in control. And if she'd really met someone and fallen in love, he could almost figure out why she'd done things this way.

If she'd told him she wanted to move to the US, there would have been a huge custody battle. But to steal his daughter away and let eighteen months pass with no contact? That, he couldn't understand—no matter what.

He almost wanted to shout at Cassidy, *It's the people, Cass—always the people.* He couldn't care less where he was in this world, as long as he was near his daughter.

His mind flickered back to the four tightly packed boxes stuffed in the bottom of the wardrobe in his bedroom. Eighteen months of his life, with a private investigator in Australia and one in the US. Eighteen months when almost all his salary had gone on paying their fees and jumping out of his skin every time the phone rang.

No one could keep living like that. Not even him. It destroyed your physical and mental health. So he'd tried to take a step back, get some normality back into his life. He was still looking for his daughter and still had a private investigator in the US. But now he didn't require a daily update—an email once a week was enough. And the PI was under strict instructions to phone only in an emergency.

He looked at the woman across the table. He still couldn't get to the bottom of Cassidy Rae. She'd received another one of those phone calls the other day and had ducked out the ward, talking in a low, calm voice.

What on earth was going on?

Cassidy stared across the table. Maybe she'd gone a little overboard with the Christmas stuff. She always seemed to get carried away when the subject came up. It looked as if a shadow had passed across Brad's eyes. Something strange. Something she didn't recognise. Was it disappointment? She drew her breath in, leaving a tight feeling in her chest. She didn't like this.

But she didn't know him that well yet. She didn't feel as if she could share that it was just her and her gran left. And she wanted to hold on to what little family she had left. Of course Christmas was about people—even if they didn't know you were there.

She reached across the table and touched his hand. Every single time she touched him it felt like this. A tingle. Hairs standing on end. Delicious feelings creeping down her spine. The warmth of his hand was spreading through her.

He looked up and gave her a rueful smile, a little sad maybe but still a smile.

'Let's talk about something else. Like Hallowe'en. We usually have a party for the staff on the ward. I had it in my flat last year, but I think yours would be the perfect venue this time.'

Brad's smile widened. He looked relieved by the change of subject. 'I guess a Hallowe'en party wouldn't be out of the question in the House of Horrors.'

'It's not a House of Horrors. Why don't we just tell people we've got a theme for the year? It could be Hallowe'en-slash-fancy-dress, 1960s-style?'

He nodded slowly. 'I suppose we could do that. Are you going to help me with the planning?'

'Of course.' Cassidy stood up and picked up her plate and mug, 'Come on, it's time to go back upstairs. We can talk about it as we go.'

He watched her retreating back and curvy behind. One thing was crystal clear. This woman was going to drive him crazy.

30 October

Brad opened the door as yet another party reveller arrived. Bert had retreated to his basket, now in Brad's pink bedroom, in sheer horror at the number of people in the small flat. It seemed that inviting the 'medical receiving unit' to a party also included anyone who worked there, used to work there or had once thought about working there.

It also included anyone who'd ever passed through or seen the sign for the unit.

'Love the outfit!' one of the junior doctors shouted at Brad. He looked down. Cassidy had persuaded him to go all out, and his outfit certainly reflected that. The room was filled with kipper ties, psychedelic swirls, paisley patterns, and mini-skirts and beehives. For the men, stick-on beards seemed to be the most popular choice, with lots of them now sticking to arms, foreheads and chests.

Brad pushed through the crowd to the kitchen, finding an empty glass and getting some water. It was freezing outside, but inside the flat he almost felt as if he were back in Perth. He'd turned the cast-iron radiators off, but the place was still steaming, even with the windows prised open to let the cold air circulate.

He felt someone press at his back. 'Sorry, it's a bit of a squash in here.' He recognised the voice instantly.

'Where have you been? Wow!' Cassidy had helped him carry all the food and drink for the party up to the flat. Then she'd disappeared to get changed. His eyes took in her short red *Star Trek* dress, complete with black knee-high boots and gold communicator pinned to her chest. She pressed the button. *'How many to beam aboard?'*

'You didn't tell me we were doing TV. Not fair. How come you get to look smart and sexy and I get to look like some flea-bitten wino?'

She laughed and moved forward. 'I'm still in the

sixties. The first episode of *Star Trek* was screened in 1966. I'm in perfect time.'

Someone pressed past her and she struggled to keep her glass of wine straight, moving so close to Brad that their entire bodies were touching. Her eyes tilted upwards towards him. 'I kind of like your too-tight shirt and shaggy wig. It suits you in a funny way.'

'Well, that outfit definitely suits you. But I feel as if you've fitted me up. I bet you had that sexy fancy-dress outfit stashed somewhere and were just looking for an excuse to give it an outing.' His broad chest could feel her warm curves pushing against him.

'You think I look sexy?' Her voice was low again and husky. Her words only heard by him. Someone else pushed past and she moved even closer in the tiny kitchen. *'How many to beam aboard?'*

They jumped. Startled by the noise. Brad grabbed her hand and pulled her through the door, past the people in the sitting room dancing to Tom Jones and the Beatles, and into the pink bedroom, pushing the door closed behind them.

Cassidy let out a little gasp. The pink shiny bedspread was gone, replaced by a plain cotton cream cover and pillowcases. But the dark pink lampshades hadn't been replaced, leaving a pink glow around the room. 'Too many people falling off your bed?'

He pulled the wig from his head, revealing his hair sticking up in all directions. 'Now, why would you think that?' There was a smile on his face as he stepped closer, pushing her against the door. His eyes were fixed on hers. His hand ran up her body, from the top of her boot, touching the bare skin on her legs, past the edge of her dress to her waist.

'Why would something like that even occur to you,
Cass? Why would it even enter your mind? Because
you keep telling me that we're friends. Just friends.
You don't want anything more—not with someone like
me, someone from Australia.' *Or someone with a missing child.*

Cassidy's heart was thudding against the inside of
her chest. From the second he'd closed the door behind
them she'd been picturing this in her head. No. Not true.
From the first day that she'd met him she'd been picturing this in her head. It had taken her two glasses of wine
to have the courage to come back to his flat tonight.

The tension had built in the last few weeks. Every
lingering glance. Every fleeting touch sending sparks
fluttering between them. It didn't matter how much her
brain kept telling her he was the wrong fit. Her body
didn't know that. And it craved his touch.

This wasn't meant to be serious. Serious had been
the last thing on her mind—particularly with a man
from overseas. But even though she tried to push the
thoughts aside, Brad was rapidly becoming more than
just a friend. She loved the sexual undercurrent between
them, and the truth was she wanted to act on it. Now.

She leaned forward, just a little. Just enough to push
her breasts even closer to him. If he looked down, all
he would be able to see now was cleavage. *'How many
to beam aboard?'* The noise startled both of them, but
Brad only pulled her closer. She reached up and pulled
the communicator badge from her dress, tossing it onto
the bed behind them. 'I hate it when the costume takes
away from the main event.'

She could see the surprise in his eyes. He'd expected

a fight. He'd expected her to give him a reason why he shouldn't be having the same thoughts she was.

She smiled, her hand reaching out and resting on his waist. 'Sometimes my body sends me different messages from my brain.'

Brad lifted a finger, running it down the side of her cheek. The lightest touch. Her response was immediate. Her face turned towards his hand, and his fingers caught the back of her head, intertwining with her hair. She leaned back into his touch, letting out a little sigh. Her eyes were closed, and she could feel his stubble scraping her chin, his warm breath near her ear. 'And which message are you listening to?' he whispered as his other hand slid under her dress.

'Which one do you think?'

She caught his head in her hands and pulled his lips towards hers. This was what she'd been waiting for.

His lips touched hers hungrily, parting quickly, his tongue pushing against hers. She wrapped her arms around his neck.

This was it. Stars were going off in her head. If he didn't keep doing this she would explode. Because everything about this felt right. And it was just a kiss—right? Where was the harm in that?

'I've waited a whole month to kiss you,' he whispered in her ear.

'Then I've only got one thing to say— don't stop.'

CHAPTER FOUR

2 November

'WHAT are you doing here?'

It was three o'clock in the morning, and the voice should have startled her, but it didn't; it washed over her like warm treacle.

She turned her head in the darkened room where she was checking a patient's obs, an automatic smile appearing on her face. 'I got called in at eleven o'clock. Two of the night-shift staff had to go home sick, and it was too late to call in any agency staff.' She wrinkled her nose. 'Sickness bug again. What are you doing here? I thought Franco was on call.'

Brad rolled his tired eyes. 'Snap. Sickness bug, Franco phoned me half an hour ago with his head stuck down a toilet.'

Cassidy nodded. 'Figures. This bug seems to hit people really quickly. Loads of the staff are down with it. Let's just hope we manage to avoid it.' She finished recording the obs in the patients chart and started walking towards the door. Brad's arm rested lightly on her waist, and although she wanted to welcome the feel of his touch, it just didn't seem right.

'No touching at work,' she whispered.

His eyes swept up and down the dimly lit corridor. 'Even when there's no one about? Where's the fun in that?' His eyes were twinkling again, and it was doing untold damage to her flip-flopping stomach. She stopped walking and leaned against the wall.

'It's like this, Dr Donovan.' She moved her arm in a circular motion. 'I'm the master of all you can survey right now, and it wouldn't do to be caught in a compromising position with one of the doctors. That would give the hospital gossips enough ammunition for the rest of the year.' She looked down the corridor again, straightening herself up, her breasts brushing against his chest.

'I may well be the only nurse on duty in this ward right now, but I've got a reputation to maintain.' She tapped her finger on his chest. 'No matter how much men of a dubious nature try to waylay me.'

Brad kept his hands lightly resting on her waist. 'Hmm, I'm liking three o'clock in the morning, Cassidy Rae. It sounds as if there might be a bit of a bad girl in there.' He had that look in his eye again—the one he'd had when he'd finally stopped kissing her a few nights ago. The one that suggested a thousand other things they could be doing if they weren't in the wrong place at the wrong time. 'We really need to improve our timing.'

He was grinning at her now. The tiny hairs on her arms were starting to stand on end. This man was infectious. Much more dangerous than any sickness bug currently sweeping the ward.

She could feel the pressure rising in her chest. How easy would it be right now for them to kiss? And how much did she want to? But it went against all her principles for conduct and professional behaviour. So why did they currently feel as if they were flying out the window?

No matter how she tried to prevent it, this man had got totally under her skin. She was falling for him hook, line and sinker. No matter how much her brain told her not to.

She tried to break the tension between them. 'What do you want, anyway? I didn't page you. Shouldn't you be in bed?' The irony of the words hit her as soon as they left her mouth, her cheeks automatically flushing. Brad and bed. Two words that should never be together in a sentence. The images had haunted her dreams for the last few nights. And she had a very *active* imagination.

His fingers tugged her just a little closer so he could whisper in her ear. 'Bed is exactly where I'm planning on being. But not here. And not alone.'

Cassidy felt her blush intensify. Was she going to deny what had been on her mind? She wasn't normally shy around men. But something about Brad was different. Something was making her cautious.

And she wasn't sure what it was. She couldn't quite put her finger on it yet. But as long as she had the slightest inclination what it was, she didn't want to lose her heart to this guy. No matter how irresistible he was.

'I've got two patients coming up. Two young guys who've—what is it you call it here?—been out on the lash?'

Cassidy laughed and nodded at his phrasing. He really was trying to embrace the Scottish words and phrases around him. She raised her eyebrows, 'Or you could call them *blootered*.'

Brad shook his head. 'I think you all deliberately

wait until I'm around and start using all these words to confuse me.' He looked out the window into the night at the pouring rain. 'One of the other nurses down in A and E called the two young guys *drookit* and *mauchit*. I have no idea what she was talking about.'

Cassidy laughed even harder. 'Look outside, that will give you a clue. *Drookit* is absolutely soaking. *Mauchit* means really dirty. I take it the guys were found lying on the street?'

Brad nodded. 'I'm getting the hang of this, though. It's...' he lifted his fingers in the air '...going like a fair down there.'

She laughed. 'See—you're learning. Bet you hadn't heard that expression before you came to Scotland.' Her brow wrinkled. 'Hang on, where is it going like a fair? In A and E?'

'The short-stay ward is full already. That's why you're getting these two. They'll need Glasgow coma scale obs done. Are you okay with that?'

Cassidy smiled. 'Of course I am. We're used to getting some minor head injuries on the ward on a Saturday night.' She walked over to the filing cabinet and pulled out the printed sheets, attaching them to two clipboards for the bottom of the beds. She turned to face him. 'You know a group of doctors at one of the local hospitals invented this over thirty years ago.' She waved the chart at him. 'Now it's used the whole world over. One of the doctors is still there. He's a professor now.'

Brad raised his eyebrows. 'Aren't you just the little fund of information at three in the morning?' He looked around again. 'Haven't you got some help? I'm not happy about you being here alone with two drunks.

There's no telling how they'll react when they finally come round.'

Cassidy pointed to a figure coming down the corridor. 'Claire, the nursing auxiliary, is on duty with me. She was just away for a break. And if I need help from another staff nurse, I can call through to next door.'

She turned her head as she heard the lift doors opening and the first of the trolleys being pulled towards the ward. 'Here they come.' She scooted into the nearby six-bedded ward and pulled the curtains around one of the beds.

Five minutes later a very young, very drunk man was positioned in the bed, wearing a pair of hospital-issue granddad pyjamas. Cassidy wrinkled her nose at the vapours emanating from him. 'Phew! He smells like a brewery. I could get anaesthetised by these fumes.' She spent a few moments checking his blood pressure and pulse, checking his limb movements and trying to elicit a verbal and motor response from him. Finally she drew her pen torch from her pocket and checked his pupil reactions.

She shook her head as she marked the observations on the chart. 'At least his pupils are equal and reactive. He's reacting to pain, but apart from that he's completely out of it.' She checked the notes from A and E. 'Any idea of a next of kin?'

Brad shook his head. 'Neither of the guys had wallets on them. This one had a student card in his pocket but that was it.'

He raised his head as the rattle of the second trolley sounded simultaneously to his pager going off. He glanced downwards at the number. 'It's A and E again. Are you sure you're okay?'

Claire had joined her at the side of the bed. 'We'll be fine, but just remember, there are no beds left up here.'

Brad nodded. 'I'll try to come back up later,' he said as he walked down the corridor towards the lift.

Cassidy spent the next hour doing neurological observations on the two patients every fifteen minutes. Both of them started to respond a little better, even if it was belligerently. It was four o'clock in the morning now—that horrible time of night for the night shift where the need to sleep seemed to smack them straight in the head. Her eyes were beginning to droop even as she walked the length of the corridor to check on her patients. Sitting down right now would be lethal—she had to keep on the move to stay awake.

A monitor started pinging in one of the nearby rooms. 'I'll get it,' she shouted to Claire. 'The leads have probably detached again.'

She walked into the room of Mr Fletcher, a man in his sixties admitted with angina. Every time he'd turned over in his sleep tonight, one of the leads attached to his chest had moved out of place.

Cassidy flicked on the light, ready to silence the alarms on the monitor. But Mr Fletcher's leads were intact. His skin was white and drawn, his lips blue and his body rigid on the bed. The monitor showed a rapid, flickering electrical line. Ventricular fibrillation. His heart wasn't beating properly at all. Even though the monitor told her what she needed to know, she took a few seconds to check for a pulse and listen for breathing.

'Claire!' She pulled the red alarm on the wall, setting off the cardiac-arrest procedure as she released the brake on the bottom of the bed and pulled the bed out from the wall. She removed the headrest from the top of the bed and pulled out the pillows. Claire appeared at her side, pulling the cardiac-arrest trolley behind her. 'I've put out the call.' She was breathing heavily.

Cassidy took a deep breath. Brad was the senior doctor carrying the arrest page tonight. If he was still down in A and E, it would take him at least five minutes to get up here. Glasgow City Hospital was an old, sprawling building, with bits added on over time. It hadn't been designed with emergencies in mind, like some of the modern, newly built hospitals were. The anaesthetist would probably take five minutes to get here, too.

It didn't matter what the monitor said. Cassidy took a few seconds to do the old-fashioned assessment of the patient. Airway. Breathing. Circulation. No pulse. No breathing.

'Start bagging,' she instructed Claire, pointing her to the head of the bed and handing her an airway as she connected up the oxygen supply to the ambu-bag. She turned the dial on the defibrillator, slapping the pads on Mr Fletcher's chest and giving it a few seconds to pick up and confirm his rhythm.

'Stand clear,' she shouted to Claire, waiting a few seconds to check she'd stood back then looking downwards to make sure she wasn't touching the collapsed metal side rails. She pressed the button and Mr Fletcher's back arched upwards as the jolt went through his body.

Her adrenaline had kicked in now. She didn't feel sleepy or tired any more. She was wide awake and on alert, watching the monitor closely for a few seconds to see if the shock had made any impact on his heart rhythm. Nothing. Still VF.

The sound of feet thudded down the corridor as Brad appeared, closely followed by one of the anaesthetists. Brad's eyes widened as he realised who the patient was. 'VF,' she said as they entered the room. 'I've shocked him once at one hundred and twenty joules.' Even though she had only been back on the ward for a month, she was on autopilot.

'What happened?' asked Brad. 'He was pain free earlier and we had him scheduled for an angiogram tomorrow.'

'Alarm sounded and I found him like this,' she said. 'He hadn't complained of chest pain at all.' She raised her knee on the bed and positioned her hands, starting the chest compressions. The anaesthetist took over from Claire and within a few seconds inserted an endotracheal tube. Cassidy continued the cycles of compressions as Brad pulled the pre-loaded syringes from the crash cart. After five cycles she stopped and their heads turned to the monitor again to check the rhythm.

'I'm giving him some epinephrine,' Brad said as he squirted it into the cannula in the back of Mr Fletcher's hand. 'Let's shock him again.' He lifted the defibrillator paddles. 'Stand clear, everyone. Shocking at two hundred joules.'

Everyone stood back as Mr Fletcher's body arched again. Cassidy went to resume the compressions. They continued for the next ten minutes with cycles of compressions, drugs and shocking. Cassidy's arms were starting to ache. It was amazing how quickly the strain of doing cardiac massage told on shoulders and arms.

'Stop!' shouted Brad. 'We've got a rhythm.' He

waited a few seconds as he watched the green line on the monitor. 'Sinus bradycardia.'

He raised his eyes from the bed. 'Cassidy, go and tell Coronary Care we're transferring a patient to them.'

She ran next door to the coronary care unit, and one of their staff members came back through with her, propping the doors open for easy transfer. They wheeled the bed through to the unit and hooked Mr Fletcher up to the monitors in the specially designed rooms. In a matter of a few moments, he was safely installed next door.

Cassidy nodded at Brad as she left him there to continue Mr Fletcher's care. Claire gathered up his belongings and took them next door while Cassidy quickly transferred him on the computer system.

She took a deep breath and heaved a sigh of relief. The adrenaline was still flooding through her system, her arms ached and her back was sore.

Claire appeared with a cup of steaming tea, which she put on the desk in front of her. 'Okay, Cassidy? I nearly jumped out of my skin when that alarm sounded. He'd been fine all night.'

Cassidy nodded. 'I hate it when that happens. Thank goodness he was attached to a cardiac monitor. I dread to think what would have happened if he hadn't been.'

A loud groan sounded from the room opposite the nurses' station. Cassidy stood back up. 'No rest for the wicked. That will be one of our head-injury patients.'

Sure enough, one of the young men was starting to come round. Cassidy started checking his obs again, pulling her pen torch from her pocket to make sure his pupils were equal and reactive. His score had gradually started to improve as he could obey simple instructions and respond—albeit grudgingly. Hangovers didn't seem to agree with him.

She moved on to the patient next door, who still appeared to be sleeping it off. As she leaned over to check his pupils, his hand reached up and grabbed her tunic. 'Get me some water,' he growled, his breath reeking of alcohol and his eyes bloodshot.

Cassidy reacted instantly, pushing him backwards with her hands to get out of his grasp. 'Don't you dare put a hand on me,' she snarled.

'Cass.' The voice was instant, sounding behind her as Brad sidestepped around her, filling the gap between her and the patient.

The sunny surfer boy with cheerful demeanour was lost. 'Don't you dare touch my staff.' He was furious, leaning over the patient.

The drunken young man slumped back against the pillows, all energy expended. 'I need some water,' he mumbled.

Brad grabbed hold of Cassidy's hand and pulled her beyond the curtains. He ran his fingers through his hair. 'He still requires neuro obs, doesn't he?'

Cassidy nodded. 'That's the first time he's woken up. His neuro obs are scheduled to continue for the next few hours.'

Brad marched over to the phone and spoke for a few moments before putting it back down. 'I don't want you or Claire going in there on your own. Not while there's a chance he's still under the influence of alcohol and might behave inappropriately. Somebody from Security will be up in a few minutes and will stay for the rest of the shift.'

He walked into the kitchen and picked up a plastic

jug and cup, running the tap to fill them with water. 'I'll take him these. You sit down.'

Cassidy didn't like anyone telling her what to do, especially in her ward. But for some reason she was quite glad that Brad had been around. It wasn't the first time a patient had manhandled her—and she was quite sure it wouldn't be the last. But there was something about it happening in the dead of night, when there weren't many other people around, that unsettled her.

And as much as she wanted to fly the flag for independence and being able to handle everything on her own, she was quite glad one of the security staff was coming up to the ward.

Brad appeared a moment later, walking behind her and putting his hands on her taut neck and shoulders. He automatically started kneading them with his warm hands. 'You okay, Cass?'

For a second she was still tense, wondering what Claire might think if she saw him touching her, but then relaxing at his touch. Her insides felt as tight as a coiled spring. What with the cardiac massage and the reaction of her patient, this was exactly what she needed. She leaned backwards a little into his touch.

'Right there,' she murmured as he hit a nerve. 'How's Mr Fletcher doing?'

Brad's voice was calm and soothing. 'He's in the right place. The staff in Coronary Care can monitor him more easily, his bradycardia stabilised with a little atropine and his blood pressure is good. We've contacted his family, and he'll be first on the list in the morning. He'll probably need a stent put in place to clear his blocked artery.'

'That's good. Mmm...keep going.'

'Your muscles are like coiled springs. Is this because of what just happened?'

She could hear the agitation in his voice.

'I hate people who react like that. How dare they when all we're trying to do is help them? He could have died out there, lying on the street with a head injury, getting battered by the elements. It makes my blood boil. If I hadn't come in when I did...' His voice tailed off then he leaned forward and wrapped his arms around her neck—just for a second—brushing a light kiss on her cheek.

It was the briefest of contacts before he straightened up, reaching for the cup of tea Claire had made a few minutes earlier and setting it down on the desk in front of her. 'Drink this.' He folded his arms and sat down in the chair next to her, perching on the edge. 'I need to go back to Coronary Care. What are you doing on Sunday? Want to grab some lunch?'

Cassidy hesitated, her stomach plunging. She had plans on Sunday. Ones she wasn't sure about including Brad in. After all, he was just a fleeting moment in her life, a 'passing fancy', her gran would have said. She wasn't ready to introduce him to her family yet. Especially in her current circumstances.

But the hesitation wasn't lost on Brad. 'What's up? Meeting your other boyfriend?' he quipped.

Her head shook automatically. 'No, no.' Then a smile appeared. 'What do you mean, my *other boyfriend*? I wasn't aware I had a boyfriend right now.' Why did those words set her heart aflutter? This wasn't what she wanted. Not with a man from thousands of miles away. Not with someone who would leave in less than a year. So why couldn't she wipe the smile off her face?

He could see the smile. *Distraction*. Was that all that Cass was? What about how'd he had felt a few minutes ago when that drunk had touched her? The guy was lucky there hadn't been a baseball bat around. Cass was getting under his skin. In more ways than one. And it was time. Time to tell her about Melody.

It would be fine. He'd tell her on Sunday. She would understand. She would get it. He had other priorities. He wanted to find his daughter, and that could take him anywhere in the world. Cassidy would be fine about it. She didn't want a serious relationship with an Australian. She obviously didn't mind the flirtation and distraction. Maybe she wouldn't even mind a little more. Something more inevitable between them.

This wasn't anything serious—she would know that. But he just didn't want anyone else near her right now.

Brad stood back up. 'Well, you do. So there.' He planted another kiss firmly on her cheek. 'And whatever you're doing on Sunday, plan on me doing it with you.' And with those words he strode down the corridor, whistling.

7 November

'We seem to be making a habit of this.' Brad smiled at Cassidy, his mouth half-hidden by the scarf wrapped around his neck, as she turned the key in the lock of the little terraced house in the East End of Glasgow.

His leather-gloved hand was at her waist and his body huddled against hers. It was freezing cold and the pavements already glistening with frost. Cassidy pushed the door open and stepped inside. 'I'm afraid it's not much warmer inside. Gran hasn't lived here for over a year, and I have the heating on a timer at minimum to stop the pipes from freezing.'

Brad pushed the door shut behind him, closing out the biting wind. 'I can't believe how quickly the temperature's dropped in the last few days. I've had to buy a coat, a hat and a scarf.'

Cassidy stepped right in front of him, her chestnut curls tickling his nose. 'And very nice you look, too.'

He leaned forward and kissed the tip of her nose, before rubbing his gloved hands together. 'So what happens now?'

She led him into the main room of the house and pointed at some dark teak furniture. 'The van should be here any time. It's taking the chest of drawers and sideboard in here, the wardrobe in Gran's bedroom and the refrigerator from the kitchen. The furniture goes to someone from the local homeless unit who's just been rehoused.'

'I take it there's no chance your gran will ever come home.'

Cassidy shook her head fiercely, and he could see a sheen cross her eyes. 'No. She fell and broke her arm last year. It was quite a bad break—she needed a pin inserted. She's already suffered from Alzheimer's for the past few years. I'd helped with some adaptations to her home and memory aids, but I guess I didn't really understand how bad she was.'

Cassidy lifted her hands. 'Here, in her own environment, she seemed to be coping, but once she broke her arm and ended up in hospital…' Her voice trailed off and Brad wrapped his arm around her shoulders.

'So where is she now? Was there no one else to help her? Where are your mum and dad?'

'She's in a nursing home just a few miles away. And it's the second one. The first?' She shuddered, 'Don't even ask. That's why I agreed to the secondment. It meant I could spend a bit more time helping her get settled this time. Her mobility is good, but her memory is a different story—some days she doesn't even know who I am. Other days she thinks I'm my mother. I can't remember the last time she knew I was Cassidy. And now she's started to get aggressive sometimes. It's just not her at all. The only thing that helps is hearing my voice.'

The tears started to spill down her cheeks. 'I know I'm a nurse and everything but I just hate it.' Brad pulled his hand from his glove and wiped away her tears with his fingers.

He nodded slowly. So that's what the telephone calls had been about. No wonder she'd wanted some privacy to take them. 'So where's your mum and dad? Can't they help with your gran?'

Cassidy rolled her eyes. 'My mum and dad are the total opposite of me. Sometimes I feel as if I'm the parent and they're the children in this relationship. Last I heard, they were in Malaysia. They're engineers, dealing with water-pumping stations and pipelines. They basically work all over the world and hardly spend any time back here.'

His brow furrowed. He was starting to understand Cassidy a little better. Her firm stance about staying in Scotland was obviously tied into feeling responsible for her gran. 'So you don't get much support?'

She shook her head.

'Is there anything I can do to help?'

Cassidy looked around her. The pain was written all

over her face. 'Everything in this house reminds me of Gran. I packed up her clothes last month and took them to the Age Concern shop.' She walked over to a cardboard box in the corner of the room, filled with ornaments wrapped in paper, crinkling the tissue paper between her fingers. 'This all seems so final.'

The knock at the door was sharp, startling them both. Ten minutes later almost all the heavy furniture had been loaded onto the van by two burly volunteers. 'The last thing is in here.' Cassidy led them into the bedroom and pointed at the wardrobe. She stood back as the two men tilted the wardrobe on its side to get it through the narrow door. There was a clunk and a strange sliding noise.

Brad jumped forward. 'What was that? You emptied the wardrobe, didn't you, Cassidy?'

She nodded. 'I thought I had.'

He pulled open the uptilted wardrobe door and lifted up a black plastic-wrapped package that had fallen to the floor. 'You must have missed this.'

Cassidy stepped towards him and peered inside the wardrobe. 'I can't imagine how. I emptied out all the clothes last month. I was sure I got everything.' She turned the bulky package over in her hands. 'I don't know how I managed to miss this.' She gave the men a nod, and they continued out the door towards the van.

Brad thanked the men and walked back through to the bedroom. Cassidy was sitting on the bed, pulling at the plastic wrapper. There was a tiny flash of red and she gave a little gasp.

'Wow! I would never have expected this.' She shook out the tightly wrapped red wool coat and another little bundle fell to the floor. Cassidy swung the coat in front of the mirror. The coat was 1940s-style, the colour much brighter than she would have expected, with black buttons and a nipped-in waist.

'This coat is gorgeous. But I can't *ever* remember Gran wearing it. I don't even think I've seen a picture of her in it. Why on earth would she have it wrapped up at the back of her wardrobe? It looks brand new.'

Brad knelt on the floor and picked up the other package wrapped in brown paper. 'This was in there, too. Maybe you should have a look at them?'

Cassidy nodded and then gave a little shiver.

'Let's go to the coffee shop at the bottom of the road. It's too cold in here. We'll take the coat with us,' he said.

She headed through to the kitchen and pulled a plastic bag from under the sink, carefully folding the red coat and putting it inside. 'This coat feels gorgeous.' She held the edge of it up again, looking in the mirror at the door. 'And I love the colour.'

'Why don't you wear it?' Brad could see her pupils dilate, just for a second, as if she was considering the idea.

She shook her head. 'No. No, I can't. I don't know anything about it. I don't even know if it belonged to Gran.'

'Well, I think it would look perfect on you, with your dark hair and brown eyes. Red's a good colour for you. Did you inherit your colouring from your gran?'

Cassidy still had her fingers on the coat, touching it with a look of wistfulness in her eyes. 'I think so. I've only ever seen a few photos of her when she was a young girl. She was much more glamorous than me.'

Brad opened the front door as the biting wind whirled around them. He grabbed her hand. 'I've got a better idea. Why don't we get a coffee to go and just head back to my flat? It's freezing.'

Cassidy nodded as she pulled the door closed behind them and checked it was secure. They hurried over to the car and reached his flat ten minutes later, with coffee and cakes from the shop round the corner from him.

Although it was only four o'clock, the light had faded quickly and the street was already dark. 'Look!' screamed Cass. 'It's the first one!'

Brad dived to rescue the toppling coffee cups from her grasp. 'What is it?' His head flicked from side to side. 'What on earth are you talking about?'

'There!' Her eyes were lit up and her smile reached from ear to ear. He followed Cassidy's outstretched finger pointing to a flat positioned across the street above one of the shops. There, proudly displayed in the window, was a slightly bent, brightly lit-up Christmas tree.

'You have got to be joking. It's only the seventh of November. Why on earth would someone have their Christmas tree up?'

He couldn't believe the expression of absolute glee on her face. She looked like a child that had spotted Santa. 'Isn't it gorgeous?'

And there it was. That horrible twisting feeling inside his stomach. The one he was absolutely determined to avoid this year. That same empty feeling that he felt every year when he spent the whole of the Christmas season thinking about what he'd lost, what had slipped through his fingers.

He felt the wind biting at his cheek. Almost like a cold slap. Just what he needed. This year was going to be different. He'd done everything he possibly could. It was time to try and get rid of this horrible empty feeling. He'd spent last Christmas in Australia, the one before that in the US, following up some useless leads as to Alison and Melody's whereabouts.

This year would be different. That was part of the reason he'd come to Scotland. A country that had no bad memories for him. A chance to think of something new.

Cassidy's big brown eyes blinked at him in the orange lamplight. She'd pulled a hat over her curls and it suited her perfectly. 'I really want to put my tree up,' she murmured. 'But it's just too early.' She looked down at the bustling street. 'Only some of the shops have their decorations up. I wish they all had.'

This was it. This was where it started. 'Christmas means different things to different people, Cass. Not everyone loves Christmas, you know?'

He saw her flinch and pull back, confusion in her eyes. There was hesitation in her voice. 'What do you mean? Is something wrong? Did something happen to you at Christmas?'

He hesitated. How could he tell her what was currently circulating in his mind? He wasn't even sure he could put it into coherent words. Melody hadn't disappeared at Christmas, but everything about the season and the time of year just seemed to amplify the feelings, make them stronger. Most importantly, it made the yearning to see his daughter almost consume him. He blinked. She was standing in the dimmed light, her big brown eyes staring up at him with a whole host of questions.

He should tell her about Melody, he really should. But now wasn't the time or the place. A shiver crept down his spine as the cold Scottish winter crept through his clothes. A busy street filled with early festive shoppers wasn't the place to talk about his missing daughter.

And no matter how this woman was currently sending electric pulses along his skin, he wasn't entirely sure what he wanted to share. He wasn't sure he was ready.

'Brad?' Her voice cut through his thoughts, jerking him back to the passing traffic and darkened night.

He bent forward and kissed the tip of her nose, sliding his arm around her shoulders. 'Don't be silly, Cass. Nothing happened to me at Christmas.' He shrugged his shoulders as he pulled her towards him, guiding her down the street towards his flat. 'I'm just mindful that lots of the people we see in the hospital over Christmas don't have the happy stories to share that you do.'

She bit her lip, cradling the coffee cups and cakes in her arms as she matched his steps along the busy street. 'I know that. I didn't just materialise onto the medical unit from a planet far away. I've worked there a long time.'

But her words seemed lost as his steps lengthened and he pushed open the door to the close ahead of them.

Cassidy took off her bright blue parka and put it on the sofa. She'd seen something in his eyes. Almost as if a shadow had passed over them, and it had made her stomach coil. Was there something he wasn't telling her?

She pulled the coffee cups from their holder and opened the bag with the carrot cake inside. This was exactly what she needed right now. The sofa sagged next to her as Brad sat down. He was still rubbing his hands together.

'I can't believe how cold it is out there.'

She smiled at him. 'Get used to it—this is only the

start. Last year it was minus twelve on Christmas Day. My next-door neighbour is a gas engineer and his phone was ringing constantly with people's boilers breaking down.' She picked up the cup and inhaled deeply. 'Mmm. Skinny caramel latte. My favourite in the world. I haven't had one of these in ages.' She took a tiny sip then reached for the moist carrot cake.

'So I take it the fact you have a *skinny* caramel latte counteracts the effects of the carrot cake?'

She winked at him. 'Exactly.' She raised her eyes skywards. 'Finally, a man on my wavelength. They cancel each other out. And it's a skinny caramel latte with sugar-free syrup. Which means I can enjoy this all the more.' She licked the frosting from the carrot cake off the tips of her fingers.

'With this…' she nibbled a bit from the corner. '…a girl could think she was in heaven.'

'I can think of lots of other ways to put a girl in heaven,' the voice next to her mumbled.

Cassidy froze. Her second sip of coffee was currently stuck in her throat. You couldn't get much more innuendo than that. Should she respond? Or pretend she hadn't heard?

There was no denying the attraction between them. But did she really want to act on it? After a month in his company, what did she really know about Brad Donovan? She could give testimony to his medical skills and his patient care. He was amenable, well mannered and supportive to the staff.

But what did she really know about him? Only little snippets of information that he'd told her in passing. Stories about home in Australia, living in Perth and his training as a doctor. Passing remarks about childhood friends. He'd told her he had no wife or girlfriend.

So what else was it? What had made that dark shadow pass in front of his eyes? Why had he hesitated before answering the question? Or had she just imagined it all? Maybe there was nothing wrong, maybe something had caught his eye at the other side of the road, momentarily distracting him and stopping him from answering the question.

In the meantime, she could still feel that underlying buzz between them. Whenever he was near, she had visions of that night in his flat, pressed up against the wall in her sci-fi costume, wishing things could go further than they had.

Every time he touched her at work, even the merest brush of a hand was enough to set off the currents between them. It didn't matter that her head told her this wasn't sensible—he came from the other side of the world and would likely return there; her body was telling her something entirely different. Her imagination was telling her a whole host of other things...

He gave her a nudge, passing her the package he'd wedged under his jacket.

She stared down at the still-wrapped parcel in her hands, turning the brown paper package over and over.

'Are you going to open it?'

She picked at the tape in one corner. It was old, the stickiness long vanished, and it literally fell apart in her hands, revealing some white envelopes underneath. She pulled them out. Only they weren't white, they had yellowed with age, all with US postal stamps.

Her eyes lifted to meet his. Brad leaned forward, touching the pile of envelopes and spreading them out across the table. 'There must be at least twenty of them,' he said quietly. His fingers stopped at something. There, among the envelopes, was something else. A photograph. Brad slid the envelope that was covering it away and Cassidy let out a little gasp.

She leaned forward and picked up the black-and-white print. 'It's my gran!' she gasped. His head met hers as they stared at the photograph of a beautiful young woman with a smile that spread from ear to ear, wearing a beautiful coat with a nipped-in waist. Her head was turned to the side and her eyes were sparkling as she looked at the man standing next to her in a US army uniform.

Cassidy was stunned. There were a million thoughts that crowded into her mind. A million conclusions that she could jump to. But one thing stood out above all the rest. 'I've never seen her look so happy,' she whispered. 'Gran never looked like that.'

She turned to face Brad. 'I don't mean she was miserable—she was fine.' She pointed at the photograph. 'But I can't ever remember her looking like *that*.'

She didn't want to say anything else. She didn't know what to think. She'd just glimpsed a moment from the past, and it almost seemed sacred. The coat and letters had been hidden a long time ago by a woman who obviously hadn't wanted to throw them away but hadn't wanted them to be found. In a way, it almost felt like a betrayal.

She ran her finger over the photograph. 'I don't think I can even ask Gran about this. She's too far gone. I can't even remember the last time that she recognised me.'

Brad's arm wrapped around her shoulder. She could feel his breath at her neck. What would he be thinking?

The same kind of thing that she was? That her gran had lost her heart to some US soldier?

She didn't want to think like that. It seemed almost judgemental. And it seemed wrong that Brad's first glimpse into her family was revealing something she hadn't known herself.

And she couldn't pretend that it didn't hurt a little. It had been just her and Gran for the last ten years but she'd never told Cassidy anything about this. She'd been a modern woman, liberal-minded and easy to talk to. Why had she kept this to herself?

His voice was quiet and steady as he whispered in her ear. 'Don't even think about asking her about it, Cass.' He lifted the photograph from her hand and sat it back down on the table. 'Take it as it is. A happy memory from your gran's life. She's beautiful in that picture. You can see the happiness in her eyes. Why shouldn't she have had a time like that?' His finger ran down the side of her cheek. 'She looks a lot like you.'

Cassidy turned to face him. His mouth was only inches from hers and she subconsciously licked her lips. This was it. The moment she'd been waiting for.

It had taken him so long to kiss her again after the party. She didn't want to wait any longer. She didn't want to imagine any longer. She wanted to feel.

Her hands slid up around his neck as she pulled him closer. His mouth was on hers instantly, just the way she'd imagined. He pushed her backwards on the sofa, his hands on either side of her head as he kissed her, gently at first, before working his way down her neck, pushing her shirt open.

His body was warm, heating hers instantly. She could feel his whole length above her, and her hands moved from around his neck, down his back and towards his hips, pulling him closer to her.

This time there was no one else in the flat. This time they wouldn't need to stop. This time they could do what they wanted.

She pushed aside the rational side of her brain that was clamouring to be heard. She could worry about all that later. Her body was responding to him with an intensity she'd never experienced before. She'd already had a glimpse of the washboard abs when he'd changed in the doctors' office. Now she didn't just want to look—she wanted to touch, to feel, to taste.

He lifted his head, pushing himself back a little. His voice was little above a groan. 'Cass?'

The question only hung in the air for a fraction of a second. She didn't want to think about this. Right now she didn't care that he was from Australia and would probably go back there. Right now all she cared about was that he was here, *now*, with *her*.

A slow smile appeared on his face. 'Wanna stay over?'

He had no idea how sexy he was right now. His clear blue eyes were hooded with desire. She could feel his heart thudding against his chest. All for her.

She pressed herself against him again. 'I thought you'd never ask.'

He pulled her to her feet and led her towards his bedroom door, undoing the buttons on her shirt as they went. Her legs were on autopilot and she couldn't wipe the smile from her face.

He pressed her against the wall. 'I seem to remember being in this position with you before, Cassidy Rae.' His voice was deep, throaty, turning her on even more.

'I was playing hard to get,' she whispered in his ear. 'Did it work?'

He turned her around and pushed her onto the bed. 'Oh, yes.' He crawled towards her, poising himself above her. Her shirt was open now, leaving her breasts exposed in their black satin push-up bra. He bit at the edge with his teeth. 'Now, this doesn't look like ordinary underwear.' His fingers dug around her hips, sliding down the back of her jeans and finding the edge of her matching black g-string. 'Did you have something in mind when you got dressed this morning, Cass?' His low, sexy laugh sent shivers of delight down her spine.

It wasn't her normal underwear. But she could hardly even remember getting dressed this morning. Had she done this subconsciously, hoping she would end up in this position?

'Let's just say I'm a girl of many secrets.' She pulled his T-shirt over his head, revealing his pecs and tanned abdomen. If she hadn't been so turned on, she might have pulled in her stomach and worried about him seeing her curves. But from the look on his face, he liked what he was seeing. 'I have lots of gorgeous sets of underwear. If you're lucky, I'll let you see the red set,' she moaned as he started to kiss her neck, 'or the blue set...' Her hands were dipping lower on his body, to the front of his jeans where she could feel him throbbing against her. 'Or, if you're really lucky, I'll let you see the green set.'

He let out a groan. 'I can guarantee I'll love the underwear—no matter what colour. But what I love most is what's underneath. He traced his fingers down her throat as she arched her back in response. Then slid his hand underneath her, unfastening her bra strap and leaving her breasts exposed. 'Now, what can I do with these?' he murmured.

Cass pushed herself upwards, her breasts towards his mouth. 'You can start by getting rid of the rest of these clothes,' she commanded as she undid the buttons on his jeans, before wriggling out of her own. She waited as he discarded his jeans and underwear, before pushing him down on the bed and setting her legs astride him.

'I like this,' he murmured. 'A woman who likes to be in charge.'

'Oh, I'm always in charge,' she breathed in his ear as she ran her hands down his chest. 'And anyway, I'm examining your skin. You're way too tanned.' Her hands stopped at his nipples, brushing around them onto the fine hair on his chest. 'I feel it's my duty to check you for any areas of concern.' She lifted her hips and rubbed against him again.

He groaned. 'Anywhere in particular you'd like to start?'

She smiled and leaned over him again, her hardened nipples brushing against the skin on his chest. She swayed against him. 'I'll need to think about that.'

Brad let out a primal roar. He grabbed her and flipped her around on the bed so he was poised above her. 'Enough teasing. You're going to be the death of me.'

His fingers reached down and dispensed with her g-string. She could feel the heat rise inside her. She was aching for him. He touched her and she gasped, tilting her hips upwards to him. 'Oh…this is going to be so good.'

'You bet it is,' he whispered in her ear, the stubble on his jaw scraping her shoulder.

'Mmm… Where else am I going to feel that?'

'Wherever you like.'

He moved for a second, reaching into the nearby drawer, and she heard the rustle of a condom wrapper being opened. Ten seconds later he was above her again. 'Are you ready?' he whispered.

'Oh, yes…' She opened her legs further and gasped as he plunged inside her.

He stopped, just for a second. 'Okay?'

She took a deep breath, while the full sensation surrounded her. Then she pulled his hips even closer, taking him deeper inside. 'Don't you dare stop,' she groaned. 'I've got you just where I want you.'

'Ditto.' He smiled again as he moved slowly, building momentum between them as he trailed a line of kisses down the side of her face and throat.

And there it was—the fever that had been building between them for weeks. All the looks and lingering glances. All the brief touches. All the electricity buzzing around them like fireflies. The first kiss, with its strained finish. All building to this crescendo, where nothing and no one could get between them.

Cassidy could feel her skin start to tingle. Nothing else was more important than this. Nothing else had ever felt as good as this. Nothing else had ever felt this *right*. This was perfect.

She let herself go, throwing her head back and crying out his name, as she felt him stiffen at the same time.

She felt her body turn to jelly, the air whooshing out from her lungs. Brad was still above her, his whole body weight now resting on her, his heart thudding against her chest.

She let out a laugh. Sweat slicked them together as

she gave him a playful push. 'Move, mister, I can hardly breathe.'

He pushed himself up and sagged down beside her. 'Wow.'

Cassidy was breathing heavily, her eyes staring up at the ceiling and fixing on the still-pink light shade above her. She turned to the sandy-blond head on the pillow beside her, a smile creeping across her face. 'Yeah, wow,' she murmured.

CHAPTER FIVE

8 November

THE early-morning Scottish light crept across the room. Even on the greyest days the sun's rays sneaked through the clouds and scattered this room with light. Drad's brain was fuzzy. Something was different. Something had changed.

Then he felt a movement beside him, and the memories of the night before crowded into his brain. Cassidy. Wow.

Then something else hit him, charging from the dark recesses of his brain, and he stifled the groan in his throat. Melody. He hadn't told her about Melody.

He turned around in the bed, resting his hand on his arm, staring at the sleeping figure beside him. Her chestnut curls spilled across the pillow that she had wedged half under her arm as she slept on her side, facing him.

She looked beautiful. Her fair skin was smooth and unlined. Cassidy. His distraction. The woman he'd lusted after for the last month.

But his stomach clenched. He was cringing. Things in his brain just didn't add up. If Cassidy was only a distraction, why should he tell her about Melody? There should be no need.

But he knew better than that. No matter how many times he tried to use the word 'distraction' for Cassidy, she was much more than that.

In the last few weeks she had crept under his skin. Hearing her voice brought a smile to his face. Knowing she was working the same shift made his whole day seem brighter. And spending time with her outside work made the days speed past. He knew her habits—she liked to take her shoes off at the door, she sat on the left-hand side of the sofa, she only watched the news on one TV channel. His mood had lifted just by being around her.

His thoughts were always with his daughter but they didn't consume every spare second of every day.

She made him happy. Cassidy made him happy. And he was about to jeopardise all that. He knew he should have told her about Melody. He'd meant to but just hadn't found the appropriate time.

And now, after he'd slept with her, it seemed like a dirty secret. He almost wished he'd put a photo in the doctors' office in the ward as soon as he'd started there. But the truth was that office was used by lots of doctors and it wasn't appropriate to put a family picture in there. And he just hadn't been ready to answer any difficult questions about his daughter.

But now? He sagged back against the pillows. It looked as though he was hiding something. It looked as though he deliberately hadn't trusted Cassidy enough to tell her about Melody. How awkward was this conversation going to be?

He turned his head sideways to look at her again, to look at that perfect face before he ruined everything. A tiny part of him hoped that she wouldn't be annoyed at all. Maybe she would shrug her shoulders and tell him that it was fine?

Who was he kidding? How would he feel if the shoe was on the other foot? If Cassidy had a child she hadn't told him about? The thought was unimaginable. He could feel himself automatically shaking his head at the idea.

Things would be perfect if he could just freeze this moment in time. Keep everything just the way it was right now. Or, even better, just the way they'd been last night. That thought sent a smile across his face. If only...

A frown appeared on Cassidy's brow then her eyelids flickered open. Those big brown eyes that pulled him in every time. A smile appeared on her face instantly. 'Morning,' she whispered.

Relief flooded through him. She hadn't woken up and panicked. She seemed happy and comfortable around him. She obviously had no regrets about the night before. Not yet, anyway.

'Morning,' he whispered back. He couldn't help it. He was immediately drawn to her. He wanted to touch her, taste her skin again. He dropped a kiss on the tip of her nose.

A glint appeared in her eyes. Memories of last night? 'Wow,' she whispered again, her soft breath on his face.

Brad couldn't hide the smile. Her memories were obviously as good as his. If only every morning could be like this.

Her hand crept around his neck, and as much as he wanted to pull her closer and forget about everything else, he just couldn't. He had to get this over and done with.

He shifted backwards in the bed. 'How about I make you some breakfast?' His legs hit the floor before she had a chance to answer, and he pulled his underwear and jeans on rapidly. 'What would you like? Toast? Eggs? Bacon?'

Cassidy looked confused. She pushed herself upwards in the bed and adjusted the pillows behind her. 'I'll have whatever you're making,' she said quietly.

'Great. Give me five minutes and I'll give you a shout. Feel free to take a shower and freshen up.' He leaned forwards and planted another kiss on her forehead before disappearing out of the door.

Cassidy sat for a few minutes, taking deep breaths. What just happened? They'd had a fabulous night, and he'd asked her to stay over. And for a few seconds this morning when she'd woken up, everything had seemed fine. So what had made him jump out of bed like a scalded cat?

She flung back the duvet and swung her legs out of bed, wincing at the cold air in the room. There was a navy-blue dressing gown hanging up behind the bedroom door, and she wrapped it around herself, then headed to the bathroom.

She flicked the switch for the shower, grabbing an elastic band that was sitting on top of the bathroom cabinet and twisting her hair back from her face as she sat at the edge of the bath for a few moments, trying to fathom what was going on.

Was Brad regretting their night together? The thought almost made her belly ache. She couldn't imagine anything worse. Maybe he was only interested in the thrill of the chase and once that was over...

No. No, it couldn't be that. She'd got to know him over the last few weeks, and he didn't seem to be like that at all. Maybe he just felt awkward because it was the first time they'd woken up together?

Yes, that could be it. Her eyes fell to the sink. Brad had obviously been in here first as he'd left her a new toothbrush and toothpaste and a huge white soft towel. She stuck her hand under the shower. It had heated up perfectly, so she stepped into the steaming water.

There was almost a tremor on her skin. Her insides were coiling, to the point of almost feeling pain. She couldn't bear the thought of Brad wanting to walk away after their night together. And it wasn't about the humiliation or about being used. Although those things would be bad enough.

It would be the fact he didn't feel the same connection that she did. The fact that his thoughts didn't wander to her about a million times a day—the way hers did to him. It would be the fact he didn't feel the constant zing between them. Those were the things she couldn't bear.

She could still smell him on her skin and almost regretted having to wash it away, but the blue shower gel with its ocean scent reminded her of him again. She rubbed it into her body even harder, then a few minutes later stepped out of the shower and dried herself rapidly. It only took a few moments to realise she'd nothing to wear, so she padded back through to the bedroom and rummaged in a few of his drawers.

'Cassidy! Breakfast!'

The smell was drifting through the house. Eggs, bacon and tea. Perfect.

'Hey.'

She was standing in the doorway dressed in a pair of his grey jogging trousers and an oversized pale blue T-shirt. His clothes had never looked so sexy. Her hair was ruffled, some little strands around her neck still wet from the shower.

He pulled out a chair for her. 'Have a seat.' All Brad could think about right now was getting this over with. He had to come clean. Easier said than done.

He put the plates on the table and poured the tea while Cassidy watched him carefully. She wasn't stupid. She knew something was going on.

She took a sip of her tea, chasing her eggs around the plate with her fork. Watching. Waiting.

Brad pressed his lips together. He reached across the table and took her hand. 'Cass, there's something I need to tell you.'

He could see the tiny flare of panic in her eyes that she was trying to control. She set her tea back down on the table. Her voice was steady. 'So, what is it you want to tell me "the morning after the night before", Brad?'

He winced. There was no getting around this. Cassidy didn't even know what 'it' was—but the implication was there. If this was something important, he should have told her before he'd taken this relationship to the next level.

'I have a daughter.' The words were blurted out before he had a chance to think about it any longer.

'What?' The shocked expression on her face was very real. This was the last thing she'd expected to hear.

Brad took a deep breath. 'I have a daughter, Melody. She's nearly four.' His heart was beating against his chest, the words clambering to his mouth—he just couldn't speak quickly enough right now. 'I haven't seen in her over two years. Her mother, Alison, disappeared with her. We had a...' he flung his hands in the air '...sort of informal custody arrangement. Alison was a doctor as well, and we looked after Melody between us.'

Cassidy's face looked set in stone. 'She was your wife? Your girlfriend? The one you told me you didn't have?' Her tone said it all.

Brad spoke firmly. 'She wasn't my wife and she wasn't my girlfriend, well, not after a few months. We had a very short-lived fling that resulted in Melody. We'd broken up by the time Alison discovered she was pregnant, and neither of us were interested in getting back together.'

He leaned back in the chair, wishing he could tell the whole story in the blink of an eye. Everything about this was painful to him. Every time he spoke about things, he thought about the mistakes he had made and what he could have done differently.

Anything that could have affected the eventual outcome.

Cassidy hadn't moved. Her face was expressionless and her breakfast lay untouched in front of her.

'I don't really know what happened, Cass. I went to pick up Melody as arranged one day, and they were gone.' He flicked his hand in the air. 'Just like that.

Vanished. I was frantic. I went to Alison's work and found out she'd resigned and no one knew where she'd gone. Some of her colleagues said she'd met a doctor from the US and been head over heels in love. They thought she might have gone to the US with him.' He shook his head as a wave of desperation swept over him. It was the same every time he spoke about this.

'I hired a lawyer and two private investigators and tried to track her down. I've been trying to track her down for the last two years—with no success. I haven't seen or heard from her in two years. Right now, I have no idea how my little girl is, where she is or if she even remembers me.' His eyes were fixed on the window, staring out into space.

Cassidy felt numb. 'You have a daughter,' she said.

He nodded, it appeared, almost unconsciously.

'You have a daughter you "forgot" to tell me about?' She couldn't help it—she raised her hands in the air and made the sign of quotation marks.

She could feel rage and anger bubbling beneath the surface, ready to erupt at any moment. She hadn't imagined anything the other night. It hadn't been all in her head. It had been right before her eyes—or it should have been.

Brad looked in pain. He may have been gazing outside, but the look in his eyes was haunted. A father who had lost his child. She couldn't begin to imagine the pain that would cause. But right now she couldn't contain her anger.

'Why didn't you mention this before?'

He sighed. A huge sigh, as if the weight of the world was on his shoulders. His gaze went to his hands that were clenched in his lap. 'I know, I know, I should have. But it just never felt like the right time.'

'How about as soon as you met me?'

His brow wrinkled. 'Oh, yeah. Right. Pleased to meet you, I'm Brad Donovan. I've got a missing daughter, Melody, that I've been searching for the last two years. And before you ask—no—I've no idea why her mother disappeared with her. No—I didn't do anything wrong or mistreat my child. Yes—I've spent an absolute fortune trying to find her and I've been on two wild-goose chases to the US.' He waved his hand in frustration. 'Is that how you wanted me to tell you?'

Cassidy took a deep breath. She wanted to yell. She wanted to scream. She could see how damaged he was by all this. But she couldn't see past how hurt she felt. Hadn't he trusted her enough to tell her? He trusted her enough to sleep with her—but not to tell her about his daughter? It seemed unreal.

She looked around, her eyes scanning the walls. 'So where are they?'

His brow furrowed. 'Where are what?'

She threw her hands up in frustration. 'The photos of your daughter. I've never seen a single one. Where do you keep them?'

He grimaced and stood up. She could hear him walking through to the living room and opening a drawer. He walked through and sat a wooden framed photograph down on the table.

Cassidy felt her heart jump into her mouth as she stared at the image in front of her. The gorgeous toddler with blonde ringlets and Brad's eyes was as pretty as a picture. She felt her lip tremble and she lifted her eyes to meet his. 'You put these away when you knew I would be here?'

He nodded. 'I planned to tell you.' He hesitated, having the good grace to look shamefaced. 'I just hadn't got around to it.'

'Why didn't you tell me when I first asked you about your family? When I asked you if you had a wife or a girlfriend? When I told you about my ex-fiancé and his new Miss Spain wife? How about telling me then? Correct me if I'm wrong, but wasn't that your ideal opportunity?'

She folded her arms across her chest. It didn't matter that she'd tried to play down how hurt she'd been over her breakup with her fiancé. The fact was she'd *told* him about it—albeit in sparing detail. There was no way he was getting away with this. She didn't care about the wonderful night before. She didn't care how many times he'd taken her to heaven and back.

This was about trust. This was about honesty. This was about the things you *should* tell someone before you slept with them.

Brad shook his head. 'You make it all sound so simple, Cass.'

She cringed. The exact thought she'd had when he'd asked her about Bobby. 'It is.'

'No. It's not.' His voice was determined. 'Okay, so you may have asked me about a wife or girlfriend—and I didn't have either, so I didn't tell you any lies. And I'd only just met you then, Cass. I don't want everyone to know my business, and this isn't the easiest thing to talk about. People talk. People make judgements.' He pressed his fingers against his temples.

'When Alison and Melody vanished at first, people were suspicious about me in Australia. People, colleagues even, wondered if I'd done something to them. It was only after the Australian police confirmed they'd left on an international flight that people stopped assuming I'd done something awful.'

Cassidy felt her heart constrict. It was something she hadn't even considered. It hadn't even entered her mind that someone would think like that about Brad. How could friends or colleagues have done that?

Her head was instantly filled with stories in the media, and after only a few seconds she realised it was true. As soon as anyone went missing, suspicion was generally directed at those around them. What on earth would that feel like?

She could only imagine the worst. The frustration of not knowing where your child was. Continually shouting but not being heard. It must have been excruciating.

He leaned his elbows on the table. His fingers moved in small circles at the side of his head. 'It didn't stop there either.' He lifted his head and stared at Cassidy. 'Once people realised I hadn't done something unmentionable to them, they started to say that Alison must have done a runner with Melody to get away from me. As if I'd done something to my child.'

The words hung in the air. Too hideous for thoughts even to form.

'Oh, Brad,' she breathed. Now she understood. Now she understood the pain in his eyes. 'That's awful.'

'You bet it is.'

A lump stuck in her throat. She was angry. She was hurt. And she had no idea what this could mean for them. But right now she had to show some compassion. She stood up, the chair scraping along the kitchen floor, and walked around to the other side of the table.

Brad looked as if he was in shock. As if he was wondering what she might do next.

She might never have had a child stolen from her, but she knew what it was like to be left.

Her parents had done it. Bobby had done it.

But she was calm and lifted his hands from the table, sitting down on his knee and wrapping her hands around his neck, hugging him closely. She could feel his tense muscles beneath her fingers, and she rubbed her hand across his back, waiting for a few moments until he relaxed and the pent-up strain had started to abate.

After a few minutes she leaned back, watching him carefully.

'I'm not happy, Brad. I can't believe you didn't tell me something as important as this.'

She felt him take a deep breath. Right now his blue eyes were almost a window into his soul. She could see his regret. She could see his pain. And although hers could only pale in comparison, she wondered if he could see hers.

'I didn't mean things to turn out like this. This wasn't in my plans.'

In an instant she could almost feel his withdrawal. The hackles rose at the back of her neck. 'What do you mean?'

His hands touched her waist. 'This. Us. I didn't realise things would get so serious.'

'What did you expect? You've practically spent the last five weeks by my side. Every time I turn around, you're right there next to me. If you didn't want us to be more than friends, you should have stayed away.'

She hated how she sounded. She hated the tone of her voice, but she just couldn't help it.

The muscles on his shoulders tensed again and he blew some hair from his forehead, obviously in exasperation. What on earth was he thinking? She had a hollow feeling in her stomach. After the wonderful night before, did he want to walk away?

Everything about this was confusing. She didn't even know how she felt about the fact he had a daughter—she hadn't had time to process those thoughts. Why was she even considering any of this? Her head had always told her this relationship was a bad idea. She wanted someone who would stay in Scotland with her, and the sinking feeling in her stomach told her Brad could obviously never do that.

But her body and soul told her something else entirely. Brad was the first man in a long time that she'd been attracted to—that she'd even been interested in. She loved spending time in his company. She loved his normally easygoing manner. She loved the fact she could depend on him at work—his clinical skills and judgement were excellent.

But most of all she loved the way she felt around him. Even yesterday, in her grandmother's house, doing a task that should have made her feel sad and depressed, there had been so much comfort from having Brad around.

And as for how her body reacted to him...that was something else entirely.

Brad reached up and touched her hair, winding his fingers through one of her curls. Her head tilted instantly—an automatic response—towards the palm of his hand. His eyes were closed. 'How could I stay away from this, Cass?'

He pulled her head down and touched a gentle kiss to her lips. 'You're like a drug to me, Cassidy Rae. Apart from Melody, you're the first thing I think about when I get up in the morning and the last thing I think about when I fall asleep at night.' His eyes opened and she could tell instantly he meant every word.

This was no gentle let-down. This was no attempt to look for an excuse to end their relationship. He was every bit as confused as she was.

She pulled back. This was too much. She was getting in too deep. She pushed herself upwards, her legs trembling as she walked around to the other side of the table and pushed her untouched plate of food away.

'I can't think when you do that. I can't think straight when you touch me. It's too distracting.'

Brad let out a short laugh, shaking his head.

'What? What is it?'

'That word, Cass—distraction. That's what I thought about you at first.'

Cassidy frowned. A distraction. Hardly a flattering description. But he reached across the table and touched her hand again.

'You have no idea how I was feeling when I got here. I'd just had the year from hell in Australia. I'd been to the US twice, chasing false leads trying to find Melody. None of them worked. I'd spent a fortune and still had no idea about my daughter. Last Christmas…' He raised his eyes to the ceiling.

'Let's just say it was the worst ever. Then a few of my friends sat me down and had a conversation with me that was hard for all us. They told me I should never give up looking for Melody, but I had to accept I had a life of my own to live. And they came prepared—they had an armful of job ads for all over the world. I'd let my career slide. I'd been consumed by doing everything I could to find my daughter. The job I'd always loved had become a noose around my neck. I didn't make any mistakes but I'd lost the enthusiasm and passion for the job.

'My friends knew the career paths I'd been interested in before, and they convinced me it was the right time for a break—a change of scenery and a time for new horizons.'

He gave her a rueful smile. 'I didn't come to Scotland with the intention of meeting anyone. I came to Scotland to experience the infamous Scottish winter and the ream of medical admissions that always follow. I planned to just immerse myself in work. To try and give myself a break from constantly checking my emails and phoning the private investigator in the US.'

Cassidy didn't know what to think. A distraction. That's what he'd just called her. She couldn't stop herself from fixating on it. And it gave her the strangest sensation—a feeling of panic.

Maybe this was it. Maybe she should grab her clothes—wherever they were—and get out of here. She needed time to think. She needed a chance to get her head around what he'd just told her. Right now she was suffering from information overload.

Her gaze drifted out the kitchen and onto the coffee table in the living room. She hated that word. It made her feel worthless. As if he didn't value her. The way Bobby had made her feel when he'd left. He'd never used that word, but that's the way she'd felt—as if he'd used her as a distraction, as if he hadn't valued her enough to stay. The same way her parents had made her feel. As if she wasn't worth coming home for.

The only person who hadn't made her feel like that had been Gran. Solid. Dependable. Warm and loving. But even that had changed now. Her gran was a mere shadow of her former self. And what about those letters? She really needed to sit down and decide what she wanted to do with them.

'Cass?'

She was startled. Brad's forehead was wrinkled. He'd still been talking to her, and she'd been lost in her own thoughts. 'What?' she answered quickly.

'You didn't hear me, did you?'

She shook her head. 'You've given me a lot to think about. Maybe I should leave? Maybe you don't need any more distractions.' Her mind could only focus on one thing and she stood up again, ready to leave.

But he was quicker than her, and it took him less than a second to have her in his arms. His face was just above hers. His stubbled jaw, tanned skin and blue eyes definitely distracted *her*.

'I said it was nice to meet someone who enjoyed Christmas so much. Last year is something I don't want to repeat. I was hoping you would help try to get me into the spirit.'

She blinked. He was using her weak spot. Her Christmas rush. And he was doing it with that lazy smile on his face and his fingers winding under her T-shirt.

She sighed. 'This isn't all just going to be okay. I'm going to need some time—to see how I feel.' Then the sticking point came to the forefront of her brain. 'And are you still just using me as a distraction?'

His head moved slowly from side to side. 'I'm not using you as anything. I just want to be around you, Cass. I have no idea where this is going to go. I have no idea what's going to happen between us. But I'd like to find out. What do you say?'

There it was. That feeling. For five weeks he'd made her feel special. Made her feel wanted and important— as if she were the centre of his life. She wanted to say a hundred things. She wanted to sit him down and ask more questions. But his fingers were trailing up her side…

'I need some time to think about all this, Brad. You certainly know how to spring something on a girl.'

He pulled back a little. 'I know, and I'm sorry. I should have told you about Melody.'

Right now she didn't know what to do. She'd learned more about Brad in the last fifteen minutes than she had in the last five weeks. He was hurt, he was damaged. She had seen that in his eyes. And for the last five weeks he'd come to work every day and been a conscientious and proficient doctor. Could she have done the same?

Who did he really have here as a friend? Who was there for him to talk to, to share with, apart from her?

More importantly, did she really want to walk away right now?

It would be the sensible thing to do. She was already feeling hurt, and walking away now could save her from any more heartache in the future. But she'd still need to work with him, she'd still see him at work every single day. How would she cope then? And how would she feel if she saw him with anyone else?

The thought sent a chill down her spine. She didn't want to see him with anyone else. In her head he was already *hers*. And even if this didn't go anywhere, why shouldn't she enjoy what they had right now? She certainly wouldn't mind a repeat of last night. The sooner, the better.

Her hands wound around his neck. 'How about we try to create some new Christmas memories—some nice ones—ones that you could only experience here with me in Scotland?'

He nodded his head slowly. 'That sounds like a plan. What do I have to do in return?'

A thousand suggestions sprang to mind—most of them X-rated. She couldn't stand the pain she'd seen in his eyes earlier. But this definitely wasn't what she'd signed up for. She had to think about herself. She didn't want to end up hurt and alone. She didn't want to end up without Brad.

'I'm sure I'll think of something,' she murmured as she took him by the hand and led him back to the bedroom.

CHAPTER SIX

15 November

CASSIDY hurried up the stairs. Her cardigan was useless this morning, and her new-style uniform wasn't keeping out the freezing temperatures. She touched one of the old-fashioned radiators positioned nearby the hallway. Barely lukewarm. That was the trouble in old stone buildings with antiquated heating systems; the temperature barely rose to anything resembling normal.

The true Scottish winter had hit with a blast over the last few days. This morning, on the way to work Cassidy had slipped and skidded twice on the glistening pavements. She dreaded to think what A and E had been like last night.

Brad had been on call, so she hadn't seen him. He'd phoned her once, around midnight, to say he was expecting a few admissions and to chat for a few minutes. But things had felt a little strained—just as they had for the last week. She still couldn't get her head around all this. Not least the part he hadn't told her he had a daughter.

But the thing she was struggling with most was how much she actually liked him. It didn't matter her head had told her he was ultimately unsuitable. For the last few weeks she'd spent every minute with him. And no matter how confused she was, one emotion topped the rest. She was happy.

Brad made her happy. Spending time with him made her happy. Talking to him every day made her happy. Working with him made her happy. Cuddling up on the sofa with him made her happy. Kissing made her *very* happy, and anything else…

Her heart sank as she saw the bright lights and bustling figures at the end of the corridor. It wasn't even seven o'clock in the morning and her normally darkened ward was going like a fair.

She strode into the ward, glancing at the board. Jackie, one of her nurses, came out of the treatment room, holding a medicine cup with pills and clutching an electronic chart.

'What's going on, Jackie?' She could see instantly that the normally cool and reliable member of staff looked frazzled. Jackie had worked nights here for over twenty years—it took a lot to frazzle her.

Jackie looked pale and tired, and she had two cardigans wrapped around her. 'What do you think?' She pointed at the board. 'I'll give you a full report in a few minutes, but we've had six admissions in the last few hours and we need to clear some beds—there are another four in A and E waiting to come up.'

Cassidy nodded quickly. 'What kind of admissions?'

Jackie pointed at the window to the still-dark view outside. 'All elderly, all undernourished, two with hypothermia and the other four all with ailments affected by the cold. Just what we always see this time of year.'

The stream of elderly, vulnerable patients reminded Cassidy of her gran.

'You rang?' Lucy appeared at Cassidy's side.

'I heard you needed to transfer four patients to my ward. Thought it would be easier if I just came along, got the report and then transferred them along myself.'

Cassidy nodded. 'Perfect.' She walked over to Jackie and took the medicine cup and electronic chart from her hands. 'Introduce me to this patient and I'll take over from you, then you can hand over to Lucy before we do the report this morning.'

Jackie nodded happily. 'That's great. If we get these patients transferred, I'll give you a proper handover before the beds get filled again.' She shrugged her shoulders. 'Brad's around here somewhere. I saw him a few moments ago. He hasn't stopped all night and...' she smiled '...our normally tanned doctor is looking distinctly pale this morning.' She winked at Cass. 'I hope he hasn't been having too many late nights.'

Cassidy froze. The words sank in quickly. She didn't think that anyone knew about Brad and herself. But she should have known better. Word always spread quickly in a hospital like this.

She tried to regain her composure and pretend she hadn't heard the comment—best not to make a big deal of these things and hope the gossip would disperse quickly.

Half an hour later, with the report given and Jackie quickly leaving to go home, Cassidy gave a sigh and went to make a cup of tea. The breakfast trolley had just rolled onto the ward. The auxiliary nurses and domestics were helping the patients, and her two staff nurses had started the morning drug round.

Lucy appeared at her side. 'Make one for me, too, please. I've just taken the last patient round to my ward.'

Cassidy nodded and put two tea bags into mugs. She could kill for a skinny caramel latte right now.

Lucy nudged her. 'So, spill. What's happening with you and Dr Wonderful? I haven't seen you for over a week.'

Cassidy bit the inside of her lip. There was no point beating around the bush. Lucy would only pester her until she told anyway. She poured the boiling water into the cups.

Lucy nudged her again. 'Come on. Is the prediction going to come true? Are you going to be a Christmas bride?'

Cassidy dropped her teaspoon into the sink. 'What? Are you mad?' She'd forgotten all about smelly-cat woman and her mad predictions.

'What's wrong? I thought things were going swimmingly between you and surf boy. Come on, you must have done the dirty deed by now—surely?'

Cassidy felt the instant flush as the heat spilled into her cheeks. It was just a pity her body didn't know how to tell lies.

'I knew it! Well—tell all. Is he wonderful?'

She took a deep breath. 'Do you want me to answer everything at once?'

'I just want you to say something. Anything. What's wrong, Cass?'

'Well, in that case…' She counted off on her fingers. 'No, I definitely won't be a Christmas bride—and I'd forgotten all about that rubbish. Yes, I've done the dirty deed. Yes, it was wonderful—or it was until the next day when he told me he had a daughter.'

'A daughter? Brad has a daughter?'

Cassidy nodded slowly.

'Why hasn't he ever mentioned her? What's the big secret?'

Cassidy picked up her tea and leaned back against the sink. 'The big secret is he doesn't know where she is. Her mother vanished with her two years ago. Apparently she fell in love with some doctor from the US and didn't tell Brad anything about it. He thinks she didn't want to get into a custody battle with him, so basically she did a moonlight flit.'

Lucy looked stunned and shook her head slowly. 'Wow, he's a dark horse, isn't he? I would never have guessed.'

Cassidy sighed again. 'Neither would I.'

There was silence for a few seconds. Lucy touched her arm. 'Whoa, you've got it bad, girl, haven't you?'

Cassidy closed her eyes. 'You could say that.'

Lucy stepped in front of her, clutching her steaming cup of tea with one hand and wagging her finger with the other. 'What happened to Cassidy Rae and *"I'm never going to fall in love with another foreign doctor"*? Where did she go? And what's the big deal about Brad having a daughter? She's lost. The US is a big place, and chances are she might never be found.'

'Cassidy Rae met Brad Donovan. That's what happened. And as for his daughter, I've no idea what will happen. But one thing is for sure—ultimately he won't stay in Scotland with me.'

Lucy leaned forward and gave her a hug. 'Cassidy, you might be making a whole lot of something out of nothing.'

Cassidy stopped for a few moments. Maybe Lucy

was right. He hadn't managed to find Melody so far—and that was with a private investigator working for him. Maybe he would never find her? Maybe she could just forget about Melody and start to focus on them again?

But she still had an uneasy feeling in her stomach. Brad wouldn't stay in Scotland—whether he found his daughter or not. Why on earth was she pursuing a relationship with a man who wasn't right for her?

She shook her head. 'A daughter isn't nothing, Lucy. It's a whole big something. What happens if we get serious, and then he gets a call to say his daughter has been found? I'll be left high and dry while he jets off somewhere to find his lost child. It's hardly the ideal setup for a lasting relationship.'

Lucy took a sip of her tea, watching Cassidy carefully. 'That's the first time I've ever heard you say anything like that.'

'Like what?'

'The whole words—"lasting relationship". I never even heard you say that about Mr Spain. You must really like our Dr Donovan.'

'I guess I do.' There. She'd said the words out loud. And to someone other than herself. It almost felt like a confession.

A little smile appeared at the corner of Lucy's mouth. 'That's what Lynn and I were talking about at Belinda the fortune-teller's house. We'd already pegged Brad for you and thought you'd make a nice couple.'

Cassidy stared at her as memories of that night and their knowing nods sprang up in her brain. 'You've got to be joking.'

Lucy shook her head, looking quite pleased with

herself. 'No. We thought you'd be a good fit together. And we were right.'

Cassidy put down her mug and started to fiddle with her hair clip. 'Well, you can't exactly say that now, can you?'

'Yes, I can. I still think you're a good fit.' She folded her arms across her chest. 'So what's been the outcome of Brad's big disclosure? Did you run screaming from the room? Have a tantrum? Go off in a huff?'

Cassidy lowered her head. 'That's just it. There's not really been an outcome. I'm still seeing him and we've talked about it a few times—but we've really only skirted around the edges.' She shrugged her shoulders. 'I've no idea what the big outcome will be.' She shook her head, 'I don't think he knows either.'

Lucy's brow puckered. She nipped Cassidy's arm. 'Who are you, and what have you done with the real Cassidy Rae? The one that always knows precisely what she, and everyone around about her, is doing?'

'Don't, Lucy. Don't remind me how much of an idiot I'm being.'

Lucy's face broke into a smile as she tipped the rest of her tea down the sink and rinsed her cup. 'I don't think you're being an idiot, Cass. For the first time in your life I think you are head over heels in love.' And with that comment she walked out the ward, leaving a shocked Cass still standing at the sink.

The rest of Cassidy's shift was bedlam. Every patient that was admitted was elderly and suffering from effects of the cold. It broke her heart.

'Is this the last one?' she asked as Brad appeared next to another patient being wheeled onto the ward.

He shook his head and ran his hand through his rumpled hair. 'Nope. I've just been paged by the doctor on-call service. They're sending another one in. Ten patients in the last twenty-four hours, all suffering from some effects of cold.' He shook his head in disbelief. 'You don't see this often in Australia. I think I've only ever looked after one case of hypothermia before. Today has been a huge learning curve.'

'Why so many?'

'The temperature apparently dropped to minus twenty last night. Some of these patients only get so-cial-care services during the week—so some of them weren't discovered until this morning. The sad thing is, only two had heating systems that weren't working. The rest were just too scared to put them on because of the huge rise in their heating bills.'

Cassidy waited as they moved their patient over into the hospital bed. He was very frail, hardly any muscle tone at all, his skin hanging in folds around his thin frame. She bundled the covers around him. 'Go and see if you can find any spare duvets or blankets,' she asked one of the nursing auxiliaries.

Brad handed over his chart. 'Frank Johnson is eighty, lives alone and has a past history of COPD and heart disease. You can see he's underweight. He hasn't been eating, and when he was admitted his temperature was thirty-four degrees centigrade. He'd got so confused he'd actually started taking his clothes off, as he thought he was overheating. He was barely conscious when the social-care staff found him this morning.'

Cassidy nodded. It wasn't the first time she'd heard this. She looked at the IV fluids currently connected—often the patients admitted with hypothermia were also dehydrated. 'What's the plan for him?'

Brad pointed to the chart. 'He's been in A and E for a few hours, and his temperature is gradually climbing. It's thirty-six now, still below normal, but he's certainly less confused. Try and get some more fluids and some food into him. I want four-hourly obs and refer him to Social Services and Dietetics. We've got to try and get him some better assistance.' He waved his hand around the ward.

'In fact, those rules apply to just about everyone that's been admitted in the last twenty-four hours.' He looked down at his own bare arms, where his hairs were practically standing on end. 'It doesn't help that this place is freezing, too. What's going on?'

Cassidy gave him a weary smile. 'Old hospital, old heating system. This place is always like this in winter.'

'Tomorrow I'm going to bring in a sleeping bag and walk about in it. Do you think they'll get the hint and try to sort this place out?'

She laughed. 'That would be a sight to see. But good luck. Look at all the staff on the ward—all wearing two cardigans over their uniforms. I hate long sleeves—it's an infection-control hazard. But the temperature in this place is ridiculous. I can hardly tell them to take them off.'

'If you come into my office, I can think of an alternative way to heat you up.'

Cassidy's cheeks instantly flushed and she looked around to check no one had heard his comment. 'Brad!'

He gave her a wicked smile. 'We both know cold temperatures can cause confusion, and it wouldn't do for the doctors and nurses to be confused. I'm just trying to keep us at the top of our game.'

She titled her head to one side. 'Dr Donovan, if the

cold is getting to you, I'll even go so far as to make you a cup of coffee. That should heat you up.'

'And if I'd prefer something else?'

'Then you'll just have to wait.' She folded her arms across her chest. It was almost time for the shift change—time to go home. And Brad must be due to finish as he'd been on call the night before. He looked knackered. As if he could keel over at any moment. But he could still manage to give her that sexy smile and those come-to-bed eyes. And no matter how much she told herself she should walk away, she just couldn't.

'I have something for you.'

'What?'

He pulled something from the pocket of his pale blue scrubs. A pair of rumpled tickets. Cassidy recognised the insignia on them instantly. Her mouth fell open. 'The skating rink! You remembered.'

'Of course I remembered. You said you wanted to go skating the night the ice rink opened in George Square so I bought us some tickets.'

She stared at the tickets. There it was again. Just when everything in her head was giving her lots of reasons to end this relationship. Just when she hadn't been alone with him for a few days and felt as though she was starting to shake him out her system—he did something like this.

Something thoughtful. Something kind. Something that would matter only to her. He'd even managed to plan ahead—a trait distinctly lacking in most men she knew.

'So are we going to capture the spirit of Christmas?' he whispered in her ear.

One look from those big blue eyes and he was in-

stantly back in her system. Like a double-shot espresso.
'You bet ya!' She smiled at him.

20 November

'I don't think we need an ice rink. These pavements
are bad enough,' Brad grumbled as he grabbed hold
of Cassidy's waist to stop her skidding one more time.

She slid her hand, encased in a red leather glove, into
his. 'Don't be such a grump. And look at this place, it's
buzzing! Isn't it great?'

Brad looked around. He had to admit Glasgow did
the whole Christmas-decoration thing well. There were
gold and red Christmas lights strung along the length
of Buchanan Street, twinkling against the dark night
sky, trying to keep the late-night shoppers in the mood
for Christmas. The street was thronged with hundreds
of people, all wrapped against the bitter-cold weather,
their warm breath visible in the cold night air.

But even though the lights were impressive, he
couldn't take his eyes off Cassidy. She seemed to have
a coat for every colour of the rainbow. And in the last
few days he had seen them all.

But it was her grandmother's red wool coat that
suited her most, even though it probably wouldn't with-
stand the freezing temperatures of tonight.

This evening Cassidy had layered up with two cardigans beneath the slim-fitting coat. She had accesso-
rised with a black hat and scarf and red leather gloves,
with a pair of thick black boots on her feet. But even
in all those clothes it was her eyes that sparkled most.

As they turned the corner into George Square, the
lights were even brighter.

An international Christmas market filled the edges of the square, immediately swamping them in a delicious array of smells. The ice rink took up the middle of the square, with a huge Christmas tree—still to be lit—at one end and an observation wheel at the other. Around the edges were an old-fashioned helter-skelter, a café/bar and a merry-go-round. Families were everywhere, children chattering with excitement about the lights being switched on.

For a second Brad felt something twisting around his heart. He wished more than anything that Melody could be here with him now. He'd never experienced Christmas in a cold climate, and he'd love it if his daughter could see this with him. He'd even seen an ad posted on the hospital notice-board the other day about a Santa's grotto with real, live reindeer down on the Ayrshire coast. If only he could take Melody to see something like that. The thought instantly clouded his head with difficult memories and yearnings.

He watched as a father lifted his daughter up onto one of the huge white horses with red reins on the merry-go-round. As the music started and the ride slowly began to move, he could see the father standing next to the horse, holding his daughter safely in place as her face glowed with excitement.

'Brad?'

He turned abruptly. Cassidy was watching him with her all-seeing, all-knowing brown eyes. She gave his arm a little tug. 'Are you okay?'

She followed his eyes to the merry-go-round, the question hesitating on her lips.

This wasn't the time to be melancholy. This was the time to be positive and thankful that he could create new memories with someone who tugged at his heart-strings. He reached out and grabbed her leather-gloved hand. 'Have I told you how beautiful you look tonight in your grandmother's coat? That red suits you perfectly.'

He pulled her forward for a kiss, ducking underneath the black furred hat that was currently containing her wayward curls. 'Do you remember those little girls who used to be on top of the chocolate boxes at Christmas? That's just what you look like.'

'Welcome, everyone.' The compère's voice echoed around the square and they turned to face him.

'Who is he?' Brad whispered.

'Some reality TV star,' she whispered back, 'but I've no idea which one.'

The guy was swamped in the biggest coat Brad had even seen. He obviously wasn't from around these parts. 'We're here in Glasgow tonight to light up our Christmas tree.'

There was a cheer around about them.

'Can anyone guess what colour the tree lights will be this year?'

He waited as the crowd shouted out around him. 'Let's count down and see. Altogether now, ten, nine, eight...'

Cassidy started to join in, shouting down the numbers with rest of the crowd. 'Come on, you.' She nudged him.

Brad smiled and started chanting with people around them. 'Five, four, three, two, *one*!'

There was a gasp as the tree lit up instantly with a whole host of red lights, like winter berries on the tree. A few seconds later they were joined by some tiny silver twinkling stars. A round of applause went up then, and

only a few seconds later, Brad noticed Cassidy blink
as a cheer erupted all around them. People were holding their hands out and laughing as the first smattering
of snow appeared in tiny flakes around them. It only
took a few seconds for some to land in the curls of her
hair and on her cheeks. She gave a big smile, looking
upwards to the dark sky. 'Nothing like a little dusting
of snow for the occasion.'

Brad pulled his hand out of his thermal glove and
held it out like the people around them. 'First time I've
been snowed on,' he said, watching as the tiny flakes
melted instantly as they touched his hand. 'This is fabulous.'

Cassidy sighed. 'Wait until the morning. If the snow
lies on the roads and streets, it will be even more treach-
erous than before. In my experience snow generally
means we'll be more busy at work.'

Brad grabbed her waist again. 'Work? Let's not talk
about work. Let's go and have some fun.'

They walked around some of the nearby market
stalls. Cassidy sampled some sautéed potatoes with onions and bacon then moved on to the next stall to try
their vast array of chocolates. 'What's your favourite?'
Brad asked. 'I'll buy you some.'

Cassidy's nose wrinkled and she glanced over her
shoulder. 'Actually, I'm a tat collector. I'd prefer another
ornament for my Christmas tree.'

He gave her a surprised look. 'A tree ornament instead of chocolate? I would never have guessed. Well,
let's see what they've got.'

She was like a child in the proverbial sweetie shop as
she oohed and aahed over tiny green sequin trees, little
white angels and traditional wooden crafted Santa Claus

ornaments. A few moments later Cassidy had selected a Russian doll for her tree with red and gold zigzags adorning its tiny wooden frame. 'This is perfect,' she said. 'I've never seen anything like this before.'

Brad smiled and handed over some money, but not before picking up a second one for Melody. She would have loved this stall, too.

They walked over to the nearby booth to collect their skates and spent a few minutes sitting at the side, lacing them up. Cassidy stood up, wobbling around as she tried to gain her balance. Brad appeared at her side, equally unsteady. 'Are we ready for this?' He held out his hand towards her.

They stepped onto the ice together. It was busy, families skating and wobbling with interlinked hands as they tried to find their way around the ice. Brad took a few moments to get his balance—he'd only ever skated a few times in his life but had always managed to stay upright. Cassidy, however, took him completely by surprise.

She let go of his hand and within seconds was gliding over the ice as if it was something she did every day. Her paces were long and even as she bobbed and weaved through the crowd of people on the ice. She spun round, her red coat swinging out around her. Brad held on to the side rail for a few more seconds.

'Come on, Dr Donovan, show us what you're made of!' she shouted from the middle of the rink.

She looked gorgeous. Her cheeks were flushed with colour, and the red coat with its nipped-in waist highlighted her figure perfectly. The perfect Christmas picture.

Her words were like a challenge. And no matter how unsteady he was on the ice, Brad wasn't one to ignore a challenge. He pushed himself off as best he could towards her, nearly taking out a few children in the process. He reached her in a few seconds with only a few unsteady steps and wrapped his arms around her in the middle of the rink. 'You're a scammer, Cassidy Rae. You didn't say you knew how to ice skate.'

'You didn't ask.' Her eyes were twinkling as she pushed off and spun around him again, skating backwards for a few seconds before ending in an Olympic-style twirl.

'Show-off,' he growled. 'Where on earth did you learn how to do that?'

She started skating backwards around him. 'In Australia you surf—in Scotland you skate!' She reversed into him, allowing him to collapse his arms around her waist. 'That's not strictly true,' she said. 'I skated for around five years but, to be honest, as a young girl I was a bit flighty. I tried ballet, majorettes, country dancing and horse riding before I started skating.'

His head rested on her shoulder, his nose touching her pink flushed cheek. 'I like the sound of a flighty Cassidy Rae. She sounds like fun.'

Cassidy pushed off and turned to face him again, tilting her head to one side. 'Are you trying to say I'm not fun now, Dr Donovan?'

'Oh, you're lots of fun, Ms Rae.' He tried to take a grab at her, but his unsteady gait sent him wobbling across the ice. 'Help!'

She skated alongside him and slotted her hand into his. 'Let's just take things easy. We'll just skate around in a simple circle like the rest of the people are doing.' She pointed at some kids teetering past them. 'See? Anyone can do it.'

Brad groaned and tried to push more firmly on the ice. It was easier while Cassidy was gripping his hand, and he gained confidence as they circled round and round the rink. By the time the old-fashioned klaxon sounded, signalling the end of their session, Brad felt as though he could finally stand upright with some confidence.

'Is that an hour already? I can't believe it. I was finally starting to get the hang of this.'

'We can come back again,' said Cassidy with a smile as she skated around him again. The rink was starting to empty as people crowded toward the small exit. He watched for a few seconds as Cassidy took advantage of the now-empty ice and did a few twirls. A squeal stopped her in her tracks.

Brad pushed through the throng, reaching a little girl who was being pulled up by her father and clutching her hand to her chest. Her face was pale and Brad could see a few drips of crimson blood on the ice at her feet.

'Let me have a look at her,' he said, lifting her up in his strong arms. 'I'm a doctor.' He turned his head towards Cassidy, who had appeared at his back. 'Can you ask the booth if they have a first-aid kit?'

The crowd parted easily, concerned by the cries of a child, and he walked unsteadily to the adjacent wooden bench at the side of the rink. He positioned the child underneath the nearest light and held her hand tightly for a few seconds.

'What's your name?' he asked the pale-faced, trembling little girl.

'Victoria,' she whispered. Brad smiled. It was clear she was trying very hard not to cry. Her father had his arms wrapped around her shoulders.

'She just fell over as we were waiting to get off the ice. Someone must have caught her hand with their skate.'

Cassidy appeared with the first-aid kit and opened it quickly, pulling out some gloves, antiseptic wipes, sterile dressings and elastic bandages.

Brad got off the bench and lowered himself near the ground, his face parallel with Victoria's. 'I'm just going to have a little look at your hand—just for a second. Is that okay?'

She nodded but clutched her hand even closer to her chest.

He pulled off his gloves and held his hand at the side of her face. 'Can you feel how cold my fingers are?' He touched her cheek and she flinched a little, before smiling and nodding.

He picked up the gloves. 'I'm going to put these really funky blue gloves on before I have a little look. I might want to put a special bandage on your hand—is that okay?'

Victoria nodded, still looking tearful, but held her hand out tremulously to Brad.

Brad worked swiftly. He cleared her hand from her anorak sleeve and had a quick glance at the cut before stemming the flow of blood with a sterile pad. 'I'm going to give this a quick clean and bandage it up for you.' He nodded at Cassidy as she ripped open the antiseptic wipes for him.

'Ouch!' squealed Victoria, as the wipe lightly touched her skin.

'All done,' said Brad almost simultaneously. He took one more look now that the blood was clear, then applied another sterile non-adherent pad and elastic bandage to put a little pressure on the wound. He looked at Cassidy. 'Which hospital is nearest to here?'

'The Royal Infirmary,' she answered. 'Less than five minutes in a taxi.'

Brad gave the anxious father a smile. 'I'm afraid she's going to need some stitches and the wound cleaned properly. The pad shouldn't stick to her skin and the elastic bandage gives a little pressure to stem the flow of blood before you get to the hospital. But it's not a long-term solution. Are you able to take her up to the A and E unit?'

The father nodded. He pulled a phone from his pocket and started pressing buttons. 'I have a friend who's a taxi driver in the city centre. He'll come and get us.'

Brad leaned forward and whispered in Victoria's ear. 'You're a very brave girl. And do you know what brave girls get?' He reached into his pocket and pulled out his little Russian doll. It was almost identical to the one he'd just bought for Cassidy, but this one had silver and pink zigzags and a long silver string to hang it from the tree.

'This is a special Christmas-tree decoration—just for you.'

Victoria's eyes lit up, his distraction technique working like a charm. Cassidy's felt a lump at the back of her throat that she tried to swallow. He must have bought an extra ornament when he'd paid for hers earlier. And it didn't take much imagination to know who he'd bought it for.

There it was.

Right in front of her, glowing like a beacon. All the reasons why Brad shouldn't be without his daughter. She gathered up the remnants of the first-aid kit, stuffing them back inside, and disappeared back to the booth.

She couldn't watch that. She couldn't watch him interact with a child in such an easy and relaxed manner. It showed what she already knew deep down but hadn't wanted to admit.

Brad was good with kids. No, Brad was *great* with kids. He knew just when to act and what to say. He deserved to have kids. He deserved to be with his daughter. He deserved to know where she was and play a part in her life.

And even though he hadn't said much around her over the last few days, it was clear that Melody was in the forefront of his mind.

She felt ashamed. Ashamed of the words she'd uttered and the thoughts she'd had while she'd been talking to Lucy. Thoughts that he might be willing to forget about his daughter and just have a life with her. What kind of person was she?

She'd seen the haunted look in his eyes earlier when he'd been watching the father and daughter on the merry-go-round. But she hadn't been able to say the words—to ask him if he was hurting and what she could do to help.

She looked over at him now, and he gave her a wave as he walked with Victoria and her father to a black cab parked at the side of the square. Her hand lifted automatically in response, but it was the expression on his face that was killing her.

She'd never seen Brad look so comfortable and so at ease.

She knew what he needed more than anything. He needed to find his daughter.

CHAPTER SEVEN

29 November

'Hi, Cassidy, nice to see you.'

'Hi, Grace, how's Gran today?'

The nurse walked around the desk and joined Cassidy. 'She's in here today,' she said as she walked into a large sitting room looking out over well-tended gardens. 'She's been really confused these last few days, but unusually quiet, too.'

'Is she eating okay?'

Grace nodded. 'She's eating well. She seems quite focused when she gets her meals. But as soon as she's finished, she's off wandering.' She walked over and touched Cassidy's gran on her shoulder. 'Tillie, your granddaughter is here to see you again.'

Cassidy's heart fell as her gran barely even looked up, her eyes still fixed on the garden. She gave Grace a half-hearted smile. 'Thank you, Grace.'

'No problem. Give me a shout if you need anything.'

Cassidy sat down in the chair opposite her gran. Her heart was fluttering in her chest. She was wearing her gran's red wool coat and she wondered if she would notice. She pulled off her leather gloves and reached over and took her gran's hand.

'Hi, Gran.' She brushed a kiss on her cheek.

Tillie looked at her only for a second, her confusion immediately evident. She didn't recognise Cassidy.

Cassidy took a deep breath. It had been like this for the last few months. The little spells of recognition and memory were becoming fewer and fewer. She'd had some episodes where she'd mistaken Cassidy for her mother, but it had been over a year since she'd recognised Cassidy for herself.

This was the part that broke her heart. Her gran had always been her confidante, her go-to person. The person who gave her the best advice in the world—something she badly needed right now.

She opened her bag and stared at the pile of envelopes inside. They'd revealed more than she wanted to know. But it was the photograph that haunted her most. Her gran had always been warm and caring towards her. But she couldn't remember ever seeing her gran like she was in that photograph—her eyes filled with adoration for the man standing by her side. Her whole face glowing with happiness. Had she really known her gran at all?

'I've been at the house, Gran. Everything's fine.' Her fingers caught the edge of the collar of her coat and she bit her lip nervously. 'I found this beautiful coat in the one of the cupboards. It was wrapped up with some letters.' She pulled the bundle from her bag, But Tillie's eyes were still fixed on the garden. Cassidy swallowed, trying to get rid of the lump in her throat.

The garden was covered in frost and a light dusting of snow, but the beds in front of the window brimmed with life. They were filled with evergreen bushes with red berries, coloured heather plants and deep pink pernettya plants. The planters around the edges had an eruption of coloured cyclamen and white heathers. It was beautiful.

Cassidy looked out over the horizon. Everything about this spelled Christmas to her. She wondered what plants they had in Australia at this time of year. Would there be anything as nice as this? How could anyone feel festive in a baking-hot climate?

She'd thought about that often over the last few days, the thoughts just drifting into her mind when she least expected them. She'd had numerous friends who'd emigrated and they all raved about it, saying it had been the best move of their lives. They sent her pictures of spending Christmas Day on the beach, cooking on the barbeque or having dinner in the sunshine next to the pool.

But Christmas always meant cold weather, frost and snow to Cassidy. She just couldn't imagine it any other way. Could she really feel festive in a bikini?

'Hello, dear. Who are you?'

Cassidy flinched and pushed the thoughts from her mind as her gran spoke to her, her eyes suddenly bright with life.

'I'm Cassidy, your granddaughter. I've come for a visit, Gran.'

'How lovely. Do you have any tea?'

Cassidy smiled. Her gran was a true tea genie and could drink twenty cups a day. She slid her hand into her gran's. 'I've come to tell you that I've met a nice man, Gran. One who's making me think about a lot of things.'

Tillie nodded but didn't say anything. Cassidy took

a deep breath. 'When I found your coat, I also found a parcel of letters.' She hesitated for a second. 'I hope you don't mind, but I read them, Gran. The ones from Peter Johnson, your US Air Force friend.'

She paused, waiting to see if would get any reaction. She knew some people would think she was strange, trying to have a normal conversation with a confused old lady, but to Cassidy she couldn't communicate any other way. She loved and respected her gran, and she hoped beyond hope that some of what she said might get through. 'He looked lovely, Gran.'

She pulled out the black-and-white photograph. 'I found a picture of you—you look so happy.' She couldn't help the forlorn sound to her voice as she handed the photo to her gran.

Tillie took it in her frail fingers and touched the surface of the photograph. 'So pretty,' she murmured, before handing it back.

Cassidy sat backwards in her chair. 'He wrote you some lovely letters. You never told me about him—I wish you had.' She stared out the windows, lost in thought.

She'd read the letters the night before, tears rolling down her face. Peter Johnson had met her gran while he'd been stationed in Prestwick with the US Army Air Force. His letters were full of young love and hope for the future. Filled with promises of a life in the US. Most had come from Prestwick, with a few from Indiana at a later date.

Had he been her gran's first love? What had happened to him? Had he gone back to the US and forgotten about her? Her gran could have had the chance of another life, on another continent. Had she wanted to go to the US? What had stopped her? Had she suffered from any of the doubts and confusion that she herself was feeling right now?

She looked back at her gran, who was running her fingers over the sleeve of her coat. 'I wish you could tell me, Gran.' Tears were threatening to spill down her cheeks. 'I really need some advice. I need you to tell me what I should do.'

'What a lovely colour,' her gran said suddenly, before sitting back in her chair. 'Did you bring tea?' she asked.

Cassidy gave Tillie's hand a squeeze. 'I'll go and get you some tea, Gran,' she said, standing up and heading over to the kitchen. She'd been here often enough to know where everything was kept.

The girl in the kitchen gave her a nod and handed over a teapot and two cups. She glanced at her watch. 'I thought it was about that time for your gran. I was just about to bring this over.' She smiled as Cassidy lifted up the tray, before reaching over and touching the shoulder of her coat. 'What a beautiful coat, Cassidy. It's a really nice style. It suits you.'

Cassidy blushed. 'Thank you. I found it the other day.' She nodded over her shoulder. 'It was Gran's.'

'Really? I'm surprised. It looks brand new.' She raised her eyebrows. 'I bet she cut up a storm in that coat a few years ago.'

Cassidy's felt her shoulders sag. 'I don't know, Karen. Truth is, I never saw my gran wear this coat. But I found a picture of her in it and she looked amazing.'

'I bet she did.' Karen gave her a smile. 'You know, Cassidy, I know it's hard seeing your gran like this, but you've got to remember that she's happy here. Although she's frail, her physical health is good for someone her age and most days she seems really content.'

Cassidy nodded gratefully. 'I know, Karen.' She looked over to where her gran was sitting, staring out the window again. 'I just wish I could have the old her back sometimes—even for just a few minutes.'

Karen gave her arm a squeeze. 'I know, honey.'

Cassidy carried the tea tray over and waited a few minutes before pouring a cup for her gran. She was fussy about her tea—not too weak, not too strong, with just the right amount of milk.

Cassidy kept chatting as she sat next to her. It didn't matter to her that her gran didn't understand or acknowledge what she was saying. It felt better just telling her things. In the last year she'd found that just knowing she'd told her gran something could make her feel a million times better—sometimes even help her work things out in her head.

'I've met a nice Australian man. He's a doctor who's working with me right now.' Her gran nodded and smiled. Often it seemed as if she liked to hear the music and tone of Cassidy's voice. 'The only thing is, he has a little girl who is missing right now. He really wants to find her. And when he does...' she took a deep breath '...he'll go.'

The words sounded so painful when she said them out loud.

And for a second they stopped her in her tracks.

What would she do if Brad just upped and disappeared? How would she feel if she could never see him again?

It didn't take long for the little part of her she didn't like to creep into her brain again. Chances were Melody might never be found. Brad might decide to stay in Scotland for a while longer.

She felt a wave of heat wash over her like a comfort blanket. That would be perfect. Maybe she could consider a trip to Australia? That wouldn't be so hard. It was a beautiful country and it might even be interesting to see the differences in nursing in another country.

She looked outside at the frosty weather. Her gran had started singing under her breath. A sweet lullaby that she used to sing to Cassidy as a child. Memories came flooding back, of dark nights in front of the fire cuddled up on Gran's couch.

Part of the issue for Cassidy was that she loved the Scottish winters and cold weather. As a pale-skinned Scot, she'd never been a fan of the blazing-hot sunshine. And even when she'd gone on holiday, she hadn't lain beside the pool for a fortnight; she'd needed to be up and about doing things.

Most people she knew would love the opportunity to live in a warmer climate but Cassidy had never even considered it. Not for a second.

Could she really start to consider something like that now?

Everything was making her head spin. Her relationship with Brad was becoming serious. She really needed to sit down and talk to him again.

She looked at her gran, who was sipping her tea delicately, trying to hear the words she thought her gran might say in her head.

She could imagine the elderly lady telling her not to be so pathetic. To make up her mind about what she wanted and to go get it. She could also sense the old-fashioned disapproval her gran might have about the fact Brad had a child with someone else. A child he wasn't being allowed to fulfil his parental duties towards. Her gran would certainly have had something to say about that.

But would she have been suspicious like some of Brad's colleagues in Australia? Or would she have been sympathetic towards him?

Cassidy just wasn't sure. And finding the letters and photographs made her even less sure. She'd thought she'd known everything about her gran. Turned out she hadn't. And now she'd no way of picking up those lost strands of her life.

She heaved a sigh and looked out over the garden again. She was going to have to sort this out for herself.

30 November

Brad came rushing into the restaurant ten minutes late, with his tie skewed to one side and his top button still undone. 'I'm so sorry,' he gasped as he sat down opposite her. 'There was a last-minute admission just before I left, and Luca was at a cardiac arrest so I couldn't leave.'

Cassidy gave him a smile and lifted her glass of wine towards him. 'No worries, Brad, I started without you.'

He reached over and pulled the bottle of wine from the cooler at the side of the table and filled his glass. She leaned across the table. 'Here, let me,' she said as her deft fingers did up his top button and straightened his tie.

She didn't care that he'd been late. His conscientiousness at work was one of the reasons she liked him so much.

He raised his glass to her. 'Cheers.' The glasses clinked together and Cassidy relaxed back into her chair.

Brad ducked under the table. 'Here, I bought you something.' He handed a plastic bag over to Cassidy.

She raised her eyebrows. 'Did you wrap it yourself?' she quipped.

'Ha, ha. Just look and see what it is.'

Cassidy peeked inside the plastic bag and gingerly put her hand inside—all she could see was a mixture of red and green felt. She pulled out her present and felt a mixture of surprise and a tiny bit of disappointment. It was an advent calendar, the fabric kind with pockets for each of the twenty-four days. The kind she'd told Brad she didn't like.

She looked over at him and he gave her a beaming smile. 'I thought in the spirit of making some nice Christmas memories I would try and convert you.'

She wrinkled her nose. 'Convert me? Why?'

He shrugged. 'You like the paper-type advent calendar. I always had one of these in Australia that my mum made for me. She used to put something in the pockets for only a few days at a time because she knew I would have looked ahead otherwise.' He touched the first few pockets and she heard a rustling sound. 'And they're *not* all chocolates.'

She nodded and gave him a smile. 'So, you're trying to convert me, are you? Well, I'm willing to give it a go. But how do you plan on filling up the other pockets?'

There it was. That little twinkle in his eye as he took a sip of his wine. 'That's the thing. If you want your calendar filled, you'll have to keep letting me into your flat. In fact, I'll need unlimited access.'

She loved the way his smile stretched from ear to

ear. The restaurant was dim, with subdued lighting and flickering candlelight. His eyes seemed even bluer than normal, their colour amplified as they reflected off his pale blue shirt.

'Did you plan this just so you could get into my flat?'

He shook his head, his face becoming a little more serious. 'I just think you've been a little quiet these past few days. As if something was on your mind.' His fingers reached across the table and intertwined with hers. 'I'm just trying to find a way to stay in your life.'

She felt shocked by the openness and honesty of his words. She kept her gaze stuck on the advent calendar as she tried to think of what to say. Things had been a little unsettled between them.

'I'm just a little unsure of what's happening between us,' she started slowly. She lifted her eyes. 'I like you, Brad.'

'And I like you, too, Cassidy. You know that.'

He wasn't making this any easier. It was hard enough, trying to get the words out. His fingers were tracing little circles on the palm of her hand. Just like he did after they'd made love together.

'I'm just worried that I'm getting in too deep and before we know it you'll be gone.'

His brow creased. 'Why would you think that?'

She pulled her hand away from his. It was too distracting. 'I don't know. I just think that I'm from Scotland, you're from Australia…' She threw her hands up in frustration, then levelled her gaze at him. 'I know you don't want to stay here and I don't want to move away. So where does that leave us?'

She could feel tears nestling behind her eyes. That

was the last thing she wanted to happen. She didn't want to cry.

Her mind was flooded with thoughts of her gran. Truth was, she would never find out what happened between her gran and Peter Johnson. Maybe it had only been a wartime fling, with no substance behind it. Or maybe her gran had given up the chance of a lifetime to go and live abroad with the man who'd made her face sparkle.

What Cassidy would never know was whether her gran regretted her decisions. If she could go back, would she do something different?

Was *she* about to make the same mistake?

Brad reached back over and took her hand again. 'Cassidy, I have no idea what's going to happen. All I know is I love spending time with you and I don't want it to end. I've no idea what will happen in the next few years—I've been offered an extension to my job here for another six months, and I've decided to take it. You know I'm not going to stop looking for my daughter. Is that what this is all about? Melody?'

Cassidy shook her head. 'No, it's not about Melody.' Then she hesitated. 'But I don't know what to think about all that. At the end of the day, Brad, we could continue to have a relationship for the next few months and then you could get a call one day about Melody and just disappear. I don't think I could handle that.'

And there it was, staring him in the face. All the while he was practically telling her she was bullheaded and stubborn, her biggest vulnerability lay on the table between them. Abandonment.

He'd sensed it in her for a while. When she'd mentioned her ex-fiancé, her parents or her ill grandmother. That fear of being alone.

He shook his head, the expression on his face pained. 'Remember, Cassidy, I've been on the other side of this fence. I've had someone disappear out of my life with no warning. And I know how much it hurts. I would never do that to another human being.'

She could tell her words had stung, and she hadn't meant them to. It was just so difficult to describe the mishmash of emotions in her head. Even she couldn't understand them, so how could she expect Brad to?

The waiter appeared at their side with some menus, and Cassidy pulled her hand from Brad's to take one. Her eyes ran up and down the menu quickly before Brad lifted it from her hands.

'Don't tell me, you'll have the mushrooms and the chicken.'

Cassidy groaned. 'Don't tell me I'm that predictable.' She grabbed the menu back and ran her eyes along the text again with a sinking realisation that Brad was right. She *did* always have the mushrooms and the chicken. The only time she ever deviated was if neither was on the menu.

He leaned forward, giving her that smile again. 'Why don't you surprise us both and pick something totally different? In fact, close your eyes and just point at something and order that.'

Cassidy shivered. 'Yuck.' Even the thought of doing that was too much for her. Imagine if she ended up with something she didn't like—or never ate? That would be hideous. 'I can't do that, Brad, I might get seaweed or fillet steak.'

His eyes gleamed as he did a pretend shudder.

'Mmm, and that would be awful, wouldn't it? Take this as a test, Cassidy.'

'A test for what?'

He folded his napkin in his lap, as if he was choosing his words carefully. 'For a thoroughly modern woman, you can be pretty closed-minded about some things.'

An uncomfortable feeling crept down her spine. 'What do you mean?'

'You can have some pretty fixed ideas.'

Cassidy shook her head. 'I just know my own mind. There's nothing wrong with that.'

He paused. 'I didn't say there was. But sometimes you make your mind up about things without looking at the whole picture.'

Cassidy was feeling rattled now and a little irritated. So much for a romantic dinner. 'What do you mean exactly?'

He licked his lips and she saw him take a deep breath. There was something different in his eyes. The normal laid-back look was gone. 'What I mean, Cassidy, is that you've written me—and others—off with no thought or regard for our feelings, just because we live in a different country. Now, if you'd been abroad and stayed there for a while and didn't enjoy it, it might seem a reasonable conclusion to have come to. But you haven't. You've never done it. You've never even tried. And what's more—you won't even consider it.'

He looked frustrated by her, angry even, and she felt a tight feeling spread across her chest. Not even Bobby, her Spanish fiancé, had called her like this. She'd just refused to go with him and that had been that. He hadn't questioned her reasoning behind her decision. He hadn't made *her* question her reasoning behind the decision.

But Brad hadn't finished. He was on a roll. 'It's the same with your menu choices and your Christmas traditions.' He leaned over and picked up the advent calendar. 'You say you only like the picture calendars but you've never even tried one of these, have you?' She saw his shoulders sag, tension easing out of them, and the tone of his voice altered.

'All I'm trying to do is get you to look outside your box. To look at the world that surrounds you and open your mind to other ideas, other experiences, other...' he paused before ending '...possibilities.'

He was holding his breath, waiting to see what she would say. She should stop, she should think and ponder what he was saying to her and why. But Cassidy went with her first instinct. She was mad.

She flung her napkin on the table. 'So why are you bothering with me, Brad? You don't date someone with the idea of changing them. You date someone because you like them the way they are, not the way *you* want them to be.' She spat the words at him.

'I'm not trying to change you. I like you, everything about you. But if we have any hope of a future together, you're going to have to learn to bend a little.'

'Meaning what?'

'Meaning that I would love to promise to stay with you in Scotland for the next thirty years, but what if I do get that call about my daughter? What if I do need to go to the States? That's it for us? Just like that—because you won't even consider any other possibility?'

He made it all sound so unreasonable. So closed-minded. But inside she didn't feel like that.

'Or what if I get a great opportunity to work in another country? You won't even consider coming with me? Because you can't leave Scotland?'

'But my gran, I can't leave my gran.' It was the first thing that sprang to mind. The first brick in her feeble wall of defence.

Brad shook his head. 'I'm not asking you to leave your gran, Cassidy. Even though you know she's somewhere she's been taken care of. I'm just trying to see if you'll at least *consider* the possibility.'

Silence hung in the air between them. Her temper had dissipated as quickly as it had arisen.

He was making sense. Inside she knew he was making sense. But to admit it made her seem so petty.

The waiter appeared at their side again. 'Are you ready to order?'

Cassidy didn't even glance at the menu, she just thrust it back at the waiter. 'I'll have the chilli prawns and the Cajun salmon,' she said as she looked Brad square in the eye.

She could see the pulse at the side of his neck flickering furiously. How long had he been holding all this in? Chances were he'd been waiting to say this to her for the last few weeks. And he was right.

Although there was no way she was going to admit it right now.

Tiny little thoughts of Australia had started to penetrate her brain. Little sparks, curiosity and wonder had been creeping in over the last few weeks. Would she like it there? What would it be like to be in a different country for more than a two-week holiday?

It wasn't as if she'd never left the sunny shores of Scotland. She'd been all over the world—Spain, Italy, the US, even the Bahamas. But only for two weeks at a time. And by the time the plane had hit the tarmac back at Glasgow Airport, she'd always been glad to get back home.

But she had lots of friends who'd gone to other countries to work. The most popular place lately had been Dubai. Five of the nurses she'd worked with in Glasgow City Hospital had all upped sticks and gone to work there. All of them loved it and most had no intention of coming back to Glasgow. Two other members of staff had gone to work for aid organisations—one to Africa and one to Médecins Sans Frontières.

Why was she so different? Why had she never wanted to go and work somewhere else? Why did she feel as if her roots were firmly planted in Scottish soil?

Brad lifted the wine bottle and topped up her glass. She hadn't even heard what he'd ordered. She only hoped it was chicken so she could swap her salmon for it.

He lifted his glass to her. 'So, what do you say, Cassidy? Can we raise a toast to trying new things?'

She swallowed hard, her fingers brushing the tiny pockets of the advent calendar on the table in front of her. This couldn't be too hard. She could try this, couldn't she?

He was staring across the table at her, with those big blue eyes, tanned skin and perfect smile. Everything about him made her stomach still lurch. She'd never felt like this before. Could she honestly just walk away?

This had to be worth fighting for.

CHAPTER EIGHT

4 December

CASSIDY woke up with a smile on her face. She glanced at the calendar hanging on her wall. Maybe embracing new change wasn't such a bad thing.

Brad's gifts had proved personal and thoughtful. She'd found an orange Belgian chocolate in the first pocket—one that she'd remarked on that night at the George Square market. For once she hadn't been instantly offended by the thought of a chocolate-filled calendar.

Next had been a tiny green sequin Christmas tree complete with red string, and in the third pocket she'd found a sprig of mistletoe.

It only took her seconds to push her feet into her red slippers and wrap her dressing gown around her shoulders. Brad had been on call again last night, so she hadn't seen him.

Her brow wrinkled. Pocket number four looked distinctly flat—maybe he hadn't had time to put something in there yet? She flicked the switch on the kettle and pulled a cup from the cupboard, before finally touching the pocket. There was a faint rustling noise. She pulled a piece of paper from the pocket and unfolded it.

It said, *'Look under the tree—not everything can fit in these tiny pockets!'*

She left the kettle boiling and walked through to her living room. There, under the tree he'd helped her decorate a few days before, was a red, glistening parcel. She couldn't wipe the smile from her face as she unwrapped the paper. It was a book. But not just any book. It was the latest thriller from her favourite Glasgow author— one she'd been meaning to buy herself.

Cassidy sagged back against the cushions on her sofa. Yet another thoughtful gift. One that meant something to her. Picked up from a chance conversation they'd had in the middle of the night on one shift.

She looked out at the overcast sky. It was going to be another miserable day. Time to wrap up warmly and head up the frosty hill to the hospital. She heard a noise at her door—a key turning in the lock and a whoosh of cold air blasting across the room.

'Brad, what are you doing here?'

Brad was barely recognisable among the layers of clothing he was wearing. All she could really see clearly were his blue eyes peering out from the balaclava-type headwear he'd started wearing to protect himself from the cold. He was brandishing some cups. 'A skinny caramel latte for my favourite woman.'

She smiled. 'I'd hug you, but you're too cold.'

He sat down next to her, hands clenched around his cup. 'I'd take off my jacket but let me heat up first. It's Baltic out there.'

She laughed. 'So, you're finally connecting with our

language. That's something I would normally say—not you.'

He nudged her. 'You must be rubbing off on me.' He bent over, his cold nose brushing against her, and she let out a squeal.

'Get away, ice man!' He wrapped his arms around her, trapping her on the sofa.

'This is an emergency. I need some body heat. I can't take these cold winters!'

She pretended to squirm as he held her tight. 'Drink your coffee. That will heat you up.'

'I can think of a better way to heat up,' he whispered as he grabbed her hand and led her back through to her warm bed.

10 December

Today she had a magic wand. Pocket ten had held another little note that had led her to find it wrapped in silver paper, balanced on the branches of the tree.

He'd asked her favourite film character the other night and she'd declared she'd always wanted to be Glinda, the good witch of the north, from *The Wizard of Oz*. So he'd bought her a magic wand. And right now she really wanted to wave it above her medical receiving unit.

In the last twenty-four hours every single one of the thirty beds in the unit had been emptied and refilled. Patients were never supposed to stay in the medical receiving unit. Patients were supposed to be assessed and transferred to one of the other wards, but the current rate of transfer was ridiculous, for both the staff and the patients.

She replaced the phone receiver. Her staff was run ragged. The bed manager was getting snarky—she had patients in A and E waiting to be admitted. The normally pristine ward looked chaotic. There were a few random patient belonging bags sitting at the nurses' station, obviously misplaced or forgotten in the preceding few hours. And as for the ward clerk—she'd disappeared in tears five minutes ago.

Cassidy took a deep breath. This was the story of Scottish hospitals in the middle of an icy winter. It was only eight o'clock in the morning. She had to take control of this situation. Something was going to give. And she didn't want it to be her—or her staff.

She lifted her hands above her head. 'Everyone, stop!'

For a second there was silence. Cassidy never raised her voice on the ward and her staff looked startled. A few heads stuck out from doors down the corridor.

'Everyone…' she gestured her hands towards the desk '…come here. This will take five minutes.'

Her bewildered staff walked towards the nursing station. Some were carrying electronic nursing notes, some bed linen and towels.

Cassidy waited until they'd all assembled. One of the phlebotomists and ECG technicians appeared, too. She took another deep breath.

'Everyone, let's calm down. I want you all to take a deep breath and tell me calmly what help you need.' She laid one hand on the desk. 'I can tell you that right now, no matter what the bed manager says, we will not move another patient until after lunchtime today. We need time to assess these patients properly.'

She gestured to the bags on the floor. 'We need to

make sure that patients' belongings don't go astray.' She lowered her voice. 'More importantly, I need my team to know that they do a good job.'

She could see the visible calm descending on the ward as the rumble of the meal trolley could be heard approaching. 'What about the patients in A and E?' asked one of the younger staff nurses.

Cassidy shook her head. 'A and E is full of competent nursing staff. They are more than capable of starting the assessments for their patients. I'm going to phone them now and tell them to arrange breakfast and lunch for those patients. They won't be moving any more up here until after lunchtime.'

A number of shoulders relaxed around her.

'What about the bed manager?'

Cassidy smiled. 'Let me deal with her. Now…' she looked over at the staff surrounding her '…Fiona and Claire, go for your tea break. Michael…' she nodded to the tall, dark-haired nurse beside her '…you start the drug round. Linda and Ann, you help Joanne, the domestic, with the breakfasts.' The two auxiliaries scurried off, glad to have a simple task to perform.

Cassidy noticed Janice, the ward clerk, sniffing at her side. 'What's wrong, Janice?'

'It's the off-duty. It was supposed to be in for yesterday. But there's still a few shifts that need to be covered.'

Cassidy's eyes swept over the blank spaces in the book. Her brain shifted into gear. One of her senior staff nurses had asked if she could start taking over the off-duty rota. And she'd made an absolute mess of it, something Cassidy would have to deal with at a later date.

Just what she would have expected. One short for

the night shift on Christmas Eve. The same thing happened every year without fail.

Her mind drifted back to the night at smelly-cat-woman's house. She almost cringed as she remembered she'd offered to do the night shift if she was a Christmas bride.

She could almost laugh out loud. Although the thought didn't seem anything like as ridiculous as it had before.

Things between her and Brad were good—better than good. Her brain had started to rationalise things for her. Australia was one day away. All twenty-four hours of one day, but still only one day away from Scotland.

The more stories he told her about his life there, the more curious she became. But something else was becoming clearer to her. Just like it had when Brad had naturally came home to her flat the other day after his shift had finished.

She wanted to see him all the time. She wanted to be with him all the time. If he was on call and she didn't see him one day, she missed him. Something that had hit her like a bolt out of the blue.

Cassidy had spent the last two years living life on her own. Her gran's memory had deteriorated to the point she didn't recognise Cassidy, and it had left her feeling even more alone than before. She rarely heard from her parents. But all of sudden it felt as if she had family again.

And having Brad around just felt so *right*.

She didn't expect to be a Christmas bride, but she did expect to have Brad in her future.

She pointed. 'Swap these two around. Lorna prefers

her night shifts together. And I'll cover the night shift on Christmas Eve. Okay?'

'Are you sure?' The clerk was looking at her through red-rimmed eyes.

She gave her shoulder a squeeze. 'Yes, I'm sure. Now, just send it in and go make yourself a cup of tea.'

She went through to her office and made an uncomfortable call to the bed manager then walked quickly through the ward, helping the auxiliaries sit some patients up in bed for breakfast and helping another few patients into chairs. Luca appeared at her side and started reviewing some of the patients who had been admitted overnight. He gave her a smile. 'I hear you're leading a revolt up here this morning.'

She nodded. 'Happy to join in?'

'Absolutely. I feel as if I hardly got to see some of these patients in A and E.'

'It was the same for my staff. We weren't getting the chance to assess the patients properly before we sent them on.' She looked up and down the length of the ward, which seemed much calmer. 'I'm not allowing that to happen. We have a duty of care to these patients and I won't compromise.'

'Tell that to the bed manager.'

'I just did.' She shrugged her shoulders. 'Although she hates me right now, first and foremost she is a nurse, so she does understand the issues.'

The phone started ringing again, and since she'd sent the ward clerk off for tea, Cassidy leaned forward and picked it up. 'Medical receiving unit, Sister Rae speaking. Can I help you?'

The words she heard chilled her to the bone, and she

gestured frantically to Luca for a piece of paper and then started scribbling furiously.

'What's wrong?' he asked as she replaced the phone.

'It's my grandmother. She's had a fall at the nursing home—they think she might have broken her hip.' She started to look around about her, searching for her bag. 'I need to go. They've taken her to another hospital at the other side of the city.'

Luca stood up. 'What can I do?'

Cassidy started pulling on the cardigan that was draped over her chair. She couldn't think straight. She couldn't think at all. The rational parts of her brain had stopped working. Gran was in her eighties and had chest problems. How often did an elderly person have problems with the anaesthetic? What if this was the last time she'd ever see her gran again?

She started to pace up the corridor. 'Michael, are you there?'

His head ducked out from behind a set of curtains.

'I'm really sorry but I need to go. It's an emergency— my gran. They think she might have broken her hip.'

'Of course, Cassidy. No problem.'

'You've got the keys to the drug trolley, haven't you? Here's the controlled-drug key.' She unpinned it from inside her uniform pocket. 'Can you let Lucy, Sister Burns from next door, know that I've had to leave?' She was babbling and she knew it.

'Cassidy, we'll be fine. I'll get some help from next door if we need it. And I won't start transferring any patients until after lunch.' He gave her a quick hug, then placed a hand firmly at her back. 'Now, go.'

* * *

His pager sounded again, and Brad growled and rolled over. 'I'm sleeping. I'm not on call any more. Leave me alone,' he groaned.

But the pager wasn't listening. It sounded again. And again. And again.

Brad was mad. Last night had been ridiculous. He hadn't stopped—not even for a minute. And on the way to work last night his Mini had made the strangest sound then phutted to a stop at the side of the road. And all he wanted to do this morning was lie in his bed and vegetate.

He flung back the covers, squinting at the light coming through the blinds, and lifted the pager to his scrunched-up eyes.

'Call Joe immediately.'

All of a sudden he was wide awake, his heart thumping in his chest. Joe Scott was his very expensive, US private investigator. He emailed Brad every few weeks, telling him any leads he was following and how he was getting on.

They had an understanding. Joe knew that Brad was a doctor, frequently on call, and had agreed that Joe would only contact Brad via his pager if something significant turned up. It had seemed the easiest solution as messages to a busy hospital could be lost, and depending on his rota sometimes Brad could be away from his house and normal emails for a few days at a time.

He reached for his phone, pushing in the number that was ingrained there.

'Joe, it's Brad Donovan. What have you found?'

'Haven't you read the email I sent you? I sent you some photographs.'

It took a few seconds for Brad's ears to adjust to the

American accent. Email. He hadn't looked at his emails for two days.

He moved automatically to his laptop, his bare feet padding across the floor. It took for ever to boot up.

'I'm just opening the email now, Joe,' he said. 'Give me a few minutes.' He wasn't sure what was waking him up more quickly—the shock phone call or the cold air.

The email took for ever to open. He could sense Joe waiting impatiently at the other end of the phone. He didn't even read the content, just clicked on one of the attached photographs.

There she was. Blonde ringlets framing her face, dressed in a green puffy coat, throwing back her head and laughing. It was a beautiful sight.

'Is it her?' The US voice cut into his thoughts.

For a moment he couldn't speak. She'd grown so much. She looked like a proper little girl now—a little lady even, rather than a toddler. His eyes swept the surrounding area. Alison was standing in the background, holding a baby. She was laughing, too. Melody was positioned on the pebbled shoreline of a lake and was clutching stones in her hands.

He tried not to let the rage overwhelm him. He couldn't let that get in the way right now. This was the first time he'd laid eyes on his little girl in nearly two years.

'Brad? Are you there?' The voice was strained now, obviously worried by his lack of response.

'Yes,' he croaked. 'It's Melody.' There was an unfamiliar sensation overwhelming him right now. It was a mixture of relief, joy, bitterness and excitement.

'Great. I was sure I'd found them, but needed you to confirm it.'

Brad's mind started to race. His eyes couldn't move from the photograph. They looked to be out in the middle of nowhere.

'Where are they?'

'North Woods, Wisconsin. Lots of hills and dense woods, terrible phone and internet reception. Took the photo two days ago. You were right about Alison, she got married. Her name is now Alison Johnson. Married to Blane Johnson—a paediatrician in Wisconsin—and they have a baby daughter, Temperance.'

Brad could tell he was reading from the notes in front of him. But he didn't care. He still couldn't believe it. And the picture was crystal clear. Not some blurry snap, which he might have expected. He could almost reach out and touch her. Did she remember him? Did she remember she had a dad who loved her very much?

His fingers brushed the screen. She looked happy. She looked healthy. Part of him gave a little sigh of relief. His daughter was alive, happy and healthy. For any parent, that should be the most important thing.

He was trying so hard to keep a lid on his feelings. He'd spent the last two years thinking about what he'd do when he found her. Thoughts of taking his time and trying to contact Alison separately, engaging a lawyer, getting advice on his legal rights in another country, finding out about extradition from that particular state in the US. And now all those rational, sensible thoughts were flying out the window.

Something registered in his brain—geography had never been his strong point. 'Where is it? Where's North Woods, Wisconsin?'

He heard Joe let out a guffaw. 'I thought you might ask that. Not the most straightforward place to get to. For you, the nearest international airports are Minnesota or Chicago. I don't think you can get a flight from Glasgow to either of them direct. Probably best to fly from Glasgow via Amsterdam and then Chicago. I'll make arrangements for you from there. Just let me know if you're coming into O'Hare or Midway International.'

Brad nodded. Chicago—some place that he'd heard of. He'd be able to find a flight there. 'I'll get online now. I'll get the quickest flight out that I can. Give me a couple of hours and I'll email you back the details.'

'No problem, son. See you soon.'

Brad put down the phone. His hands were shaking. He clicked into the rest of the email. There were four photographs. Two pictures of Alison with her baby and two of Melody. She was still his little girl. She had his blond hair and blue eyes. She even had his smile. And if he played his cards right, he would get to see her again.

He quickly dialled another number he had in his phone. A US attorney he'd been put in touch with who specialised in family law. Best to get some advice before he set foot on US soil. The last thing he wanted to do was cause a scene and get deported.

His brain whirring, he opened a travel website to search for flights. Only one from Glasgow. Leaving in six hours. He didn't hesitate. A few clicks and he was booked. He'd already been to the US in the last two years and knew his machine-readable passport meant he didn't need a visa.

This was it—he was finally going to see his daughter again.

Then something else hit him. Cassidy. He had to tell Cassidy.

He looked at the clock. It wouldn't take him long to pack. He groaned as he remembered his Mini still abandoned at the side of the road. He could get a taxi to the airport. But he couldn't leave without speaking to Cassidy first. It took a few minutes to wrap up his call to the lawyer then he pulled on his jogging trousers and trainers. He could run up the hill to the hospital. Cassidy would be on the ward. He could speak to her there.

He remembered that look on her face in the restaurant. She'd worried about this moment. And to be honest, he'd reached the stage that he'd wondered if this would ever happen.

And now it had.

And he had to go.

But he wouldn't go without speaking to Cassidy. Without reassuring her that he would come back for her. He loved his daughter with his whole heart. But he loved Cassidy, too, and he wanted her to be a part of his life. He looked over to the table where he had an array of little gifts organised for her—all to be placed in the pockets of the calendar. He would do that once he got back from the hospital.

First he had to reassure her. First, he had to tell her that he loved her.

'Where is she?'

'Where's who?' Michael was in the middle of drawing up some heparin. 'Who are you looking for?'

'Cassidy, of course!' Who did that big oaf think he would be looking for? He was out of breath, panting.

He wasn't really dressed for the cold, with just a T-shirt and tracksuit top in place, and the run up the hill in the biting cold hadn't helped.

Michael's face paled a little. 'Oh, I take it you haven't heard?'

'Haven't heard what?' Brad's frustration was growing by the second.

'Cassidy had to leave. Her gran had a fall in the nursing home and they thought she might have broken her hip. They are taking her to the Wallace Hospital—on the other side of the city. Cassidy left about an hour ago.'

Brad felt the air whoosh out from him. He pulled out his phone and started dialling her number. But it connected directly to her voice mail.

'Not supposed to use that in here,' muttered Michael.

Brad grabbed his arm. 'How far away is the Wallace? How would I get there at this time of day?' This was the worst possible time for his car to die.

Michael frowned. 'You in a hurry?'

Brad nodded. 'I need to see Cassidy, speak to the boss and arrange a few days off, then get to the airport.'

'You are joking, aren't you?' Michael's eyebrows were raised.

'No. No, I'm not. Give me some directions.'

Michael shook his head. 'At this time of day it will be a bit of a nightmare. You'd need to take the clockwork orange...'

'The what?'

'The underground. That's what we call it around here. You'd need to take the clockwork orange to Cessnock and then get the bus to the hospital. It'll take you about an hour.' He looked at the clock on the wall opposite. 'What time do you need to get to the airport?

Because you'll need to get a train to Paisley for that. Then a bus to the airport.'

Brad's head was currently mush. There was no way he was going to get across the city—find Cassidy in a strange hospital, get back, pack and get to the airport in time.

He threw up his hands in frustration and left the hospital, walking back down the hill towards his flat.

He tried her phone again three times and sent her two text messages—but it was obvious she had her phone switched off. What could he do?

He got back home and pulled the biggest suitcase he had from the wardrobe and started throwing things inside. Jeans, jumpers, boots, T-shirts—anything he could think of.

He sat down and tried her phone again. Straight to voice mail. 'Cassidy—it's Brad. I heard about your gran. I'm really sorry and I hope she's okay. I really, really need to speak to you and I don't want to do it over the phone. Please phone me back as soon as you get this message. Please…' He hesitated for a second. 'I love you, Cass.'

He put the phone down. A wave of regret was washing over him. The first time he told her he loved her should have been when he was staring into her big brown eyes—not leaving a message on a phone. But he needed to let her know how he felt. She had to know how much she meant to him.

He looked at the rest of the items on the table. Her flat was only five minutes away—he could go around now and put them in the calendar for her. He could also take some time to write her a letter and explain what had happened. That way, if he didn't get to speak to her, she'd know he'd never meant to leave like this.

He looked at the clock again. Did he really not have the time to get to the other side of the city and back? His heart fell. He knew he didn't. Latest check-in time at the airport was two hours before his flight left. He would never make it. This was the only flight to Chicago that left in the next three days. He had to be on it. The chance to see his daughter again was just too important. He'd waited too long for this moment. He couldn't put this off, no matter how much he wanted to see Cassidy.

He picked up the items from the table and grabbed his keys. He had to try and make this right.

Cassidy leaned back against the wall. The cool hospital concrete was freezing, cutting straight through her thin top, but she welcomed it as she felt completely frazzled. Six hours after she'd got here, her gran was finally being wheeled to Theatre. Her hip was definitely fractured and she was in pain. The orthopaedic surgeon had tried to put her off until the next day, but he hadn't met Cassidy Rae before.

She'd waited until she was sure her gran had disappeared along the corridor to Theatre before she started rummaging around her bag. She badly needed a coffee. Her mobile clattered to the floor as she tried to find her purse.

She picked it up and switched it back on. It had sounded earlier in the A and E department and one of the staff had told her to switch it off. The phone buzzed back into life and started to beep constantly.

Text message from Brad. *'Phone me.'*

Another text message from Brad. *'Phone me as soon as you get this.'*

Text message. *Two voice-mail messages.*

Cassidy felt her heart start to flutter in her chest. She hadn't managed to phone Brad since her gran's accident. Was he worried about her? Or was it something else?

She walked along the corridor and out of the main door, standing to one side and pressing the phone to her ear. She listened to the first message. What on earth was wrong? What didn't he want to say on the phone? Her brain started to panic so much she almost missed the end of the message. *'I love you.'*

Brad had just told her he loved her. On the phone. And while she wanted the warm feeling to spread throughout her body, she couldn't help feeling something was wrong. His voice—the tone of it.

Had something happened to him? She pressed for the next message.

'Cassidy, honey, I'm so sorry. I really wanted to speak to you. I've left you a letter at home—it explains everything. I will be back, I promise. And I'll phone you as soon as I get there. And I'll email you as soon as I get near a computer. I love you, Cassidy.'

Get back from where? Her fingers scrolled for his name and pressed 'dial'. It rang and then diverted to voice mail. His phone must be switched off.

Where was he?

Her agitation was rising. She didn't need this right now. Her gran was in Theatre. She should be concentrating on that. And he should be here with her, helping her through this. Where was he?

She sent him a quick text. *'Still at hospital with Gran. What's going on? Won't be home for a few hours.'*

Maybe he'd been called into work again? Maybe that was it. But something inside her didn't agree.

She walked back inside. There was nothing she could do right now. She had to stay here and be with her gran. There was no telling how she'd be when she woke from her anaesthetic. Cassidy wanted to be close.

And no matter how much she wanted to know what was going on with Brad, he'd just have to wait.

CHAPTER NINE

20 December

THE alarm sounded and Cassidy groaned and thumped the reset button with her hand. Even stretching out from under the warm duvet for a second was too cold. She heard a little muffled sound and seconds later felt a little draught at the bottom of the duvet.

Bert. The alarm had woken him and he was cold, too, so he'd sneaked into the bottom of her bed just as he'd done for the last ten days.

Ten days. Two hundred and forty hours—no, it had actually been forty-seven hours since she'd last spoken to Brad.

Sometimes when she woke in the morning—just for a millisecond—she thought everything was all right again. But then she remembered he was gone, searching for his daughter in North-blooming-Woods, Wisconsin. She'd had to look the place up on the internet—she didn't even know where it was.

By the time she'd got back from the hospital that night, Brad's flight had been in the air for four hours. He was long gone.

And although it helped just a little that he'd tried to

contact her and that he'd left her a letter, it didn't take away from the fact that he'd gone. Just like that. At the drop of a hat.

She knew she was being unreasonable. He'd waited nearly two years to find his daughter—of course he should go. But her heart wasn't as rational as her head tried to be.

Her heart was broken in two.

What if he never came back? What if the only way he could have contact with his daughter was to stay in Wisconsin? What if he fell back in love with Melody's mother?

Every irrational thought in the world had circulated in her mind constantly for the last ten days and nights. Even Bert wasn't helping.

He kept looking at the door and sniffing around Brad's shoes in the hope he would reappear again.

She had to be the unluckiest woman in the world. Twice Brad had phoned her mobile—and both times she had missed his call. Both times she'd been working and both times she'd been with a patient.

He'd phoned the ward one day but she hadn't been on duty. And when he'd phoned the flat she'd been visiting her gran, who was still in hospital.

Every time she tried to call him back she'd received an 'unobtainable' signal.

He'd warned her. He'd warned her that North Woods was aptly named, surrounded by thick woods and hills with poor reception for mobiles and internet connections.

He'd sent two emails letting her know that he'd contacted a family lawyer and made contact with Alison. After some fraught negotiations he'd been allowed supervised access to see Melody twice. They were currently stuck in the land of legal mumbo-jumbo, trying to figure out the parental rights of two Australians in the US. Alison was covered—she'd married an American. But Brad's position was more difficult, particularly when he was officially only on 'holiday'.

It didn't help that his lawyer was advising him to look at extradition since Melody had been removed from Australia without permission.

She really, really wanted to talk to him.

She wanted to hear his voice, feel his arms around her, feel his body pressed next to hers. Particularly now. A warm dog around her feet might be nice, but it just didn't cut it.

She didn't even feel festive any more. Her favourite time of year had been blighted by the fact the man she loved was on the other side of the Atlantic. The flight had taken fourteen hours to reach Chicago, and then another few for the air transfer to North Woods. It wasn't exactly the easiest place to get to. And it wouldn't be the easiest place to get home from either.

But as soon as he did, she knew what she was going to do. She knew what she was going to say. This forced separation had clarified everything for her. She'd made up her mind.

Now all she could do was wait.

Brad's heart was in his mouth. His little girl seemed completely unfazed by him. Alison was another matter entirely.

Ten days of trying to keep his temper in check. Ten days of biting back all the things he really, really wanted to say.

Once she'd got over the initial shock, Alison had been shamed into a visit at his lawyer's office. She'd brought her husband along, who seemed equally outraged that Brad had dared to appear into their lives in North Woods, Wisconsin.

It hadn't taken long for his lawyer to go through the legal aspects of removing a child from another country without parental consent. Alison's lawyer had been surprisingly quiet and encouraged his client to agree in principle to some short supervised access spells.

He'd been here ten days and had spent three hours with his daughter.

He'd also spent innumerable hours trying to contact Cassidy back home.

Home? Scotland?

In Brad's mind right now, home was wherever Cassidy was. Wherever they could be together. He wanted to spend hours on the phone to her, talking through things with her and telling her how he felt.

But North Woods didn't seem to be a place with normal communication methods in mind—and to be fair, Joe, his private detective, had warned him about this. In theory, he would have managed to co-ordinate time differences, shift patterns and visiting schedules. But reality was much harder. Right now it seemed as if an old-fashioned carrier pigeon would be more effective than modern-day technology.

He glanced at his watch. Time for another visit. Time to see his gorgeous blonde, curly-headed daughter, who could skim stones across the lake like a professional. Time to get the wheels in motion to learn about more permanent types of access. Time to set up an agreed method of communication between them all. One that meant he could talk to his beautiful daughter without having to face the minefield that was her mother.

Time to get his life in order.

22 December

A Christmas bride. That's what smelly-cat woman had told her. Was there any chance she could go and demand her twenty quid back?

Right now it felt as if she'd been conned. False pretences. That's what they called it. But she'd never heard of a fortune-teller being sued. Just as well she'd never believed any of it.

Cassidy tugged her thick black boots on, trying to ignore the trickle of water inside that instantly soaked through her sock. There was about three feet of snow outside. It had been the same last night when she'd come home from work.

If she'd been organised—or cared enough—she would have stuffed her already soaked boots with newspaper and stuck them under the radiator. Instead, she'd flung them across the room and fallen into bed instantly.

She couldn't even be bothered to prepare something to eat. Her cupboards were a disgrace. Oh, if she wanted chocolate or crisps or bakery items like chocolate éclairs or cupcakes, she was fine. If she wanted anything substantial to eat, she was well and truly snookered.

Cassidy pulled on a cardigan, her gran's red wool coat and a black furry hat. It shouldn't take too long to get up the hill to the hospital. Her only problem would be if the pavement hadn't been gritted. Yesterday she'd picked up three people who'd slipped, trying to climb the hill, and caught another as he'd almost slid past her.

Maybe a coffee would help? A skinny caramel latte would be perfect.

She gave Bert a pat on the way out—even he was too intelligent to want to go out in this weather.

The cold air instantly stung her cheeks. Snow was starting to fall again already. Within a few hours there could easily be another few feet on the ground. Getting home again would be a nightmare.

The aroma caught her. The smell of a freshly prepared caramel latte. She closed her eyes. Heaven on earth.

'Cassidy?'

The voice stopped her in her tracks. It was quiet. Like a question. Unsure, uncertain.

'Brad!'

She didn't hesitate. She didn't care who was in the street around them. She didn't worry about the slippery pavement covered in snow beneath her feet. She launched herself at him.

'Oof...'

He fell backwards and the latte he'd been carrying toppled, leaving a trail of pale brown on the white snow.

'Why didn't you tell me you were coming home? When did you arrive? Do you know how many times I tried to phone you? What on earth is wrong with that place? Why can't you get a decent signal there? And how dare you tell me you love me in a message?' She finished by slapping her gloved hand on his chest. Her knees pinned him to the ground beneath her.

All he could see was her face. Her curls were escaping from the sides of the black furry hat and her cheeks were tinged with red. A face that he'd longed to see for the last twelve days. It looked perfect.

He lifted his head from the snow. 'Is this a happy-to-see-me greeting or a mad-as-hell greeting?'

She furrowed her brow for a second then she broke into a smile and bent towards him, kissing the tip of his nose. 'What do you think?'

His head sagged back against the snow. 'Thank goodness.' He moved underneath her. 'Can I get up now?'

Her grin spread from ear to ear as she turned her head sideways and noticed people staring at them lying on the pavement. 'I suppose so.'

He stood up and brushed the snow from his back. 'I've missed you,' he said as he wrapped his arm around her shoulders.

'Me, too.'

'Can we go inside?'

'Yes, I mean no. I want to do something first. I promised myself I would do something the next time I saw you. Come with me.' She grabbed his hand, waiting until he'd grabbed the handle of his wheeled suitcase and pulled him across the road.

'Sounds ominous. Where are we going?'

'You'll see.'

She walked quickly along the road, in her excitement almost forgetting he was pulling a heavy suitcase through snow. But in a few moments she stopped and smiled. 'In here,' she said.

He looked around him, puzzled by the surroundings. They'd moved away from the busy street to a small church with an even smaller cemetery, virtually hidden from the road. Its tiny spire was the only thing that made it noticeable among the surrounding buildings.

'I didn't even know this was here.'

'Lots of people don't. But two hundred years ago this was one of the main roads into Glasgow.'

He waited while she pushed open an iron gate and walked behind the railings. He followed her in, totally bemused.

'What on earth are we doing here? Is this the church you normally go to? You've never mentioned it.' He looked around at the old worn gravestones. Some of the writing was barely visible now, washed away through time, wind, rain and grime. 'Looks like no one's been buried here in a very long time.'

Cassidy nodded and pulled him under one of the trees. All of a sudden her rose-tinged cheeks looked pale. He could feel the tremors in her skin under her coat. The snow was starting to coat the fur on her hat in a white haze.

Her voice was shaking as she started to speak. 'You told me you loved me.'

He clasped his hands around her. 'And I do, Cassidy. I didn't want to tell you like that, but things happened so quickly and I didn't want you to think I'd just walked away. I wanted you to know how I felt about you. I wanted you to know that I was definitely coming back.' His voice tailed off.

'I didn't want you to think I was abandoning you.' It was so important to him. To tell her that he wasn't like Bobby or her parents. To tell her that he would never abandon her. That he wanted to be with her for ever.

Her eyes were glazed with hidden tears, but she didn't look unhappy. Just very determined.

'What is it, Cassidy? What's wrong?'

'I was wrong. When I spoke to you about Christmas

and its traditions and not leaving Scotland—I was wrong.'

The cold air was making her breath come out in a steam. Short blasts.

'You were right when you said it was about the people—or person—you spend it with.' Her eyes swept around them, taking in the ancient church and graveyard. 'I love Scotland. You know I love Scotland. But I love you more and I want to be wherever you are.'

Brad blinked, snowflakes getting in his eyes. A two-hour flight, followed by another fourteen-hour flight, all worrying about Cassidy. How she would be, whether she would forgive him for leaving without saying goodbye, whether she would be angry with him. 'You love me,' he said slowly, his sense of relief sending a flood of warm blood through his chilled skin.

She nodded, the smile on her face reaching right up into her brown eyes.

'You love me,' he said again.

'Yes, yes, I love you. Do you want me to shout it out loud?' Her voice rose, sending some birds fluttering from the tree above.

He bent his head and kissed her. Taking her sweet lips against his own, pulling her close to him, keeping out all the cold that surrounded them. He'd wanted to do nothing else for the last twelve days. Twelve days and twelve long nights without Cassidy in his arms had driven him crazy.

'How do you feel about fourteen-hour flights?' he whispered.

She pulled backwards a little, nodding slowly. 'To North Woods, Wisconsin?' She reached up, pulling her hand from her red leather glove and running her finger down the side of his cheek. 'I think that's something we can do together.'

He sucked in a breath. She was prepared to go with him to see his daughter. She was prepared to meet the challenge of their life together. She'd come full circle. Just like he had. Eighteen months ago he couldn't have been lower. Cassidy had lit up his world in every way possible. He couldn't imagine life without her.

A shiver stole down his spine. He nuzzled into her neck. 'You've still not told me, what are we doing here, Cass?'

He watched her take a deep breath. She looked at him steadily. 'I've decided I'm a modern woman and want to embrace life—in every way possible. I've always loved this place—especially in the winter.' She swept her arm across the scene. 'How do you feel about this as a wedding setting?'

Brad froze. She hadn't. She hadn't just said that, had she?

She looked terrified. Now that the words were out, she looked as if she could faint on the spot.

'Did you just propose?' He lifted his eyebrow at her in disbelief.

'I think so.' She trembled.

He picked her up and spun her around. 'Isn't this supposed to be my job? Aren't I supposed to go down on one knee and propose to you with a single red rose and a diamond ring?' He pressed his face next to hers, his lips connecting with hers again.

'You were taking too long,' she mumbled. 'It took you a full month to kiss me. What chance did I have?' She hesitated. 'So what do you think?' There was fear in her voice, still that little piece of uncertainty.

'I think you should look in pocket twenty-four of your calendar.'

'What?' She looked momentarily stunned. Not the answer she was expecting.

Cassidy's brain was desperately trying to click into gear. She'd just asked the biggest question in her life. What kind of an answer was that? She hadn't looked at the calendar since the night Brad had left—she'd just assumed he wouldn't have had a chance to fill it before he'd gone.

He set her feet down on the ground. The grin on his face spread from ear to ear, his head, shoulders and eyelashes covered in snowflakes. 'Well, I'm not entirely a modern man. This is my job.' He dropped to one knee on the snow-covered grass. 'So much for taking too long—let's just cut right to the chase. Cassidy Rae, will you do me the honour of being my wife? Will you promise to love, honour and keep me, in sickness and in health, for as long as we both shall live?'

She dropped to her knees beside him. 'That's not a proposal.' She looked stunned. 'That's a wedding vow.'

'That's okay,' he whispered, pulling her even closer. 'I've already got the wedding ring.'

Her eyes widened. 'Pocket twenty-four?'

He nodded. 'Pocket twenty-four. I didn't know there was a church around here. I was hoping that we could say our own vows.'

She giggled. 'Looks like I'm going to be a Christmas bride after all.'

He looked completely confused. 'What on earth are you talking about?'

She smiled. 'Well, one day I might tell you a little story...'

EPILOGUE

One year later

'YOU'VE got to pick the best stones, Cassidy. They need to be flat on both sides.' The blue eyes regarded her seriously before the little face broke into a broad smile. 'That's why I always win,' she whispered, giving a conspiratorial glance over her shoulder towards Brad, who was standing at the lakeside waiting for them both.

'What's going on with my girls?' he shouted.

Melody held her gloved hand out towards Cassidy as they walked back over to Brad.

Cassidy looked down at the blonde curls spilling out from the green woolly hat. She gave Brad a smile. This was their third visit to North Woods, Wisconsin, and Brad had finally been allowed some unsupervised access to his child. Melody was a loving, easy child who, luckily enough, seemed totally oblivious to the tensions between her natural parents.

She spoke to Brad online every week and had been happy to meet Cassidy, loving the fact that her dad had a Scottish wife. She'd even painted Cassidy a picture of them all living in a Scottish castle.

Cassidy winked at Brad. 'Melody and I needed some time to make our plan. We think we've found a sixer.'

'A sixer? What on earth is that?' He shook his head in amusement at them both.

Melody's voice piped up. 'You should know what a sixer is, Daddy.' The stone-skimming champion looked at him seriously, holding up the flat grey stone in her hand like an winning prize. 'This stone will skim across the water *six* times before it goes under.'

'Aha.' He knelt down beside her, touching the stone with his finger, 'A sixer? Really?' He shook his head and folded him arm across his chest. 'No way. Not that stone.'

'It really is, Daddy.'

Brad's face broke into a big smile as he straightened up and slung his arm around Cassidy's shoulder. 'Prove it.'

They watched as Melody took her position at the lakeside edge, narrowing her gaze and pulling her hand back to her shoulder. She let out a yell as she released the stone, sending it skimming over the flat water, bouncing across the lake.

Cassidy leaned against Brad's shoulder. 'One, two, three, four, five, six. Your daughter was absolutely right. It was a sixer. Now, where does she get that skill from, I wonder?'

He laughed. 'Her dad, definitely her dad. I could throw a mean ball as a kid.'

He picked up Melody, who was shrieking over her success. 'What a star!' he shouted as he threw her into the air, catching her in his arms and spinning her round.

Cassidy pulled her red wool coat further around her,

trying to ward off the biting cold. North Woods was nearly as cold as Glasgow at this time of year.

Brad came over and whispered in her ear. 'Happy anniversary, Mrs Donovan.' His cold nose was pressed against her cheek as he wrapped his arms around her waist.

Cassidy felt herself relax against him. After all her worries, all her stresses, things had worked out just fine. They'd married two weeks after his proposal in the churchyard—as quickly as they legally could.

Her gran had recovered quickly from her broken hip and recuperated back in the nursing home with some expert care. She was on a new drug trial, and although her Alzheimer's hadn't improved, it certainly hadn't got any worse. The relief for Cassidy was that the episodes of aggression seemed to have abated. She still visited her gran as often as possible but she was confident in the care the nursing home provided.

That had given her the freedom she'd needed to join Brad on a two-month visit to Australia and on three trips to the States to see Melody.

After a few tense months, Alison's lawyer had finally talked some sense into his client and visiting rights had been sorted out. It meant that every few months they could have Melody for a week at a time to stay with them.

Brad had looked at a few jobs nearby and been interviewed for a position at the local hospital. Cassidy had just seen an ad for a specialist nurse to help set up an anticoagulant clinic and knew it was just what she was looking for. There was only one more thing that could make this perfect.

She turned round and put her arms around his neck.

'Happy anniversary, Dr Donovan.' She kissed him on his cold lips.

'So how do you feel about North Woods, Wisconsin?' he asked, his smile reaching from one ear to the other.

Cassidy looked over her shoulder at the lake with ice around the edges and thick trees surrounding it. 'I think it has potential.' She smiled.

He raised his eyebrows. 'Potential? Potential for what?'

He was waiting. Waiting to see what she would say. He didn't know she'd just found an ad for her dream job. He didn't know that there had been a message from the hospital after he'd left to collect Melody, offering him the job he'd just been interviewed for. But all of that could wait. Right now she wanted the chance to still surprise her new husband.

She rose up on the tips of her toes and whispered in his ear, 'I think North Woods, Wisconsin might be a nice place to make a baby.'

His jaw dropped and his eyes twinkled as he picked her up and spun her round. 'You know, Mrs Donovan, I think you could be right.'

* * * * *

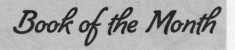

MILLS & BOON® *Book Club*

2 Free Books!

Get your free books now at
www.millsandboon.co.uk/freebookoffer

Or fill in the form below and post it back to us

THE MILLS & BOON® BOOK CLUB™—HERE'S HOW IT WORKS: Accepting your free books places you under no obligation to buy anything. You may keep the books and return the despatch note marked 'Cancel'. If we do not hear from you, about a month later we'll send you 5 brand-new stories from the Medical™ series, including two 2-in-1 books priced at £5.49 each and a single book priced at £3.49*. There is no extra charge for post and packaging. You may cancel at any time, otherwise we will send you 5 stories a month which you may purchase or return to us—the choice is yours. *Terms and prices subject to change without notice. Offer valid in UK only. Applicants must be 18 or over. Offer expires 31st January 2013. **For full terms and conditions, please go to www.millsandboon.co.uk/freebookoffer**

Mrs/Miss/Ms/Mr (please circle)

First Name

Surname

Address

Postcode

E-mail

Send this completed page to: Mills & Boon Book Club, Free Book Offer, FREEPOST NAT 10298, Richmond, Surrey, TW9 1BR

Find out more at
www.millsandboon.co.uk/freebookoffer

Visit us Online

0712/M2YEA

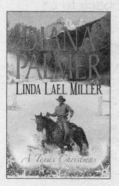

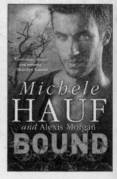